*

BEST NEW
ZΘMBIE
TALES

Volume Three

*

*

- BOOKS of the DEAD -

BEST NEW ZOMBIE TALES Volume Three

BOOKS of the DEAD

Cover Design by Cynthia Gould
Cover Art by Danielle Tunstall
Model Danielle Tunstall
Interior Design by James Roy Daley
Edited by James Roy Daley

FIRST EDITION

10 9 8 7 6 5 4 3 2 1

For more information subscribe to: booksofthedead.blogspot.com

For direct sales and inquiries contact:
besthorror@gmail.com

This book is dedicated to zombie master,
George A. Romero.

COPYRIGHT ACKNOWLEDGEMENTS

*

EDITED BY

JAMES ROY DALEY

*

*

Sleepwalk
Undying Love

by Robert Elrod

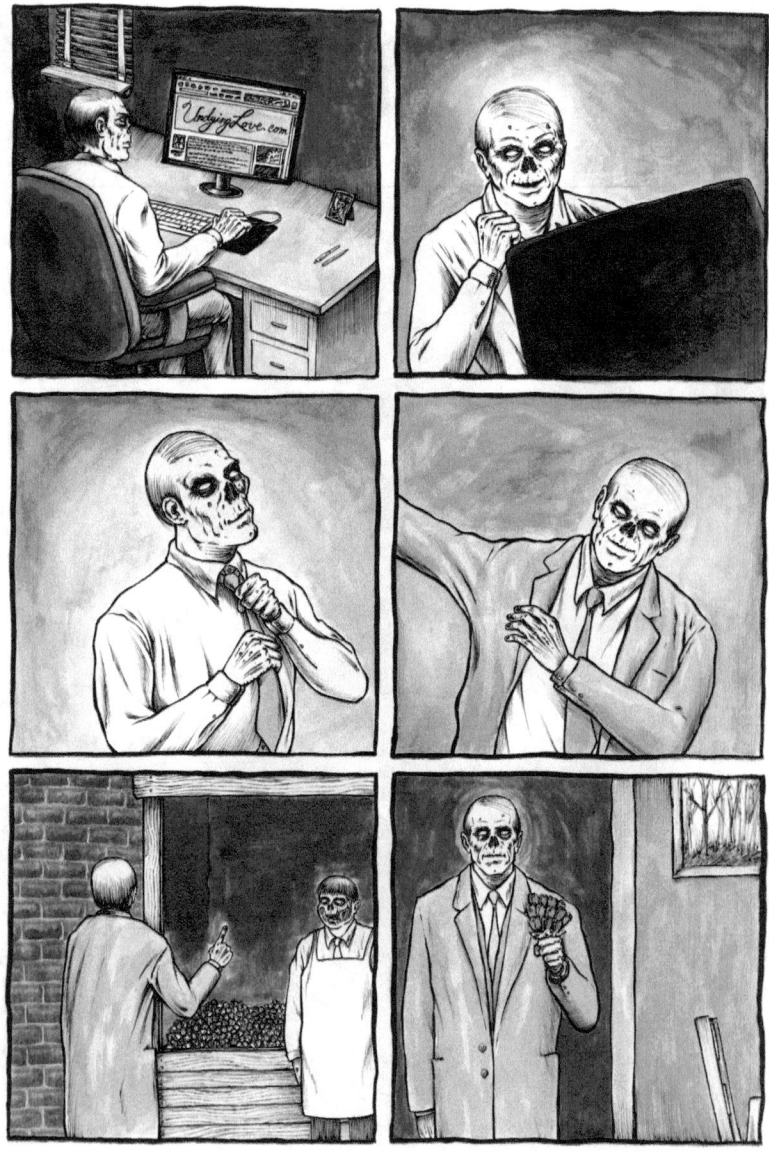

VIII

- BOOKS OF THE DEAD -

ZOMBIE #3

½ OZ OVER-PROOF RUM

0.5 OZ PINEAPPLE JUICE

1.5 OZ ORANGE JUICE

½ OZ APRICOT BRANDY

½ TABLESPOON CRUSHED EYEBALL

½ TABLESPOON SUGAR

1.5 OZ DARK RUM

1.5 OZ LIGHT RUM

~

1. SHAKE LIGHT RUM, DARK RUM, APRICOT BRANDY, PINEAPPLE JUICE, ORANGE JUICE, LIMEJUICE, AND POWDERED SUGAR WITH ICE.

2. STRAIN INTO A COLLINS GLASS.

3. SPRINKLE EYEBALL INTO OVER-PROOF RUM AND FLOAT ON TOP

4. GARNISH WITH A FRUIT SLICE, SPRING OF MINT AND A CHERRY.

5. SERVE.

Great titles from:

<u>BOOKS OF THE DEAD</u>

Best New Zombie Tales

CONTENTS

BOOKS of the DEAD

Introduction 3
JAMES ROY DALEY

THE RELEASE DATE for Best New Zombie Tales Volume Three has been delayed as long as possible. I've had a folder full of excuses tucked away inside my mental Rolodex for a while now, probably since the day Zombie Tales Two was made available to the general public. I've told people all kinds of things, crazy things: the book wasn't ready, the stories weren't quite right; I'm waiting for my book sales to improve; I'm worried about flooding the market.

Lies.

All lies.

Every word that fumbled over my lips. Lies.

In truth, there's only one reason volume three was put on hold. Only one.

H. P. Lovecraft.

The moment Zombie Tales Three was ready for print I knew he would come to see me, seeking vengeance, seeking retribution. Zombie-Lovecraft chewed the hand from my arm the first time I released a zombie book (see Zombie Tales One), and he sawed the foot from my leg the next (see Zombie Tales Two). Neither incident was enjoyable in any possible way. Both experiences were painful, leaving me scarred mentally, physically, and emotionally.

So why put out a third volume? Why not keep rolling out the excuses until the day I die?

Honestly, I'm not sure that I have an answer for that one. Maybe it's because I grew up with a punk rock attitude, or maybe I'm just too damn stupid to do the intelligent thing. Or maybe, just maybe, I figured I could fight the son-of-a-bitch, and give him a piece of what's comin'.

In the months following the release of Zombie Tales Two I spent a lot of time in the hospital. My leg, which was in terrible shape, endured three separate operations. The first was an emergency operation performed hours after my attack. During the second surgery, which was completed a few weeks later, I had part of my leg amputated in preparation for the third operation—a procedure known as osseointegration.

Osseointegration is a new way of attaching an artificial limb to a body. Up until recently the 'stump and socket' method was used, causing significant pain to the amputee. This new 'direct attachment' method works by inserting a titanium bolt into the bone at the end of the stump. Several months after the operation is complete the bone will bond with the titanium. Once the bone and the titanium are connected an abutment is fastened to the bolt, which extends from the stump. The artificial limb can then be fastened securely. Some of the benefits of this method include better control of the prosthetic, the ability to wear the prosthetic for an extended period of time, and the ability to do things like drive a car, or in some instances, play a musical instrument.

I had this new procedure done twice: once for my arm and once for my leg.

Afterwards, I healed.

I watched a thousand movies while I was being restored back to health, nothing too dramatic. Comedies mostly.

Comedies, Disney, musicals... *Evil Dead 2*...

In the movie Evil Dead 2 the main character—a klutz named 'Ash'—attaches a chainsaw to his severed arm.

I decided to do the same thing.

And get my revenge on Lovecraft.

My tool of choice was a Poulan Pro, 42cc, 18-inch, gas-powered chainsaw. The Poulan Pro is a pull-start model with a Duralife engine that comes with a tool-less chain tensioning system, an anti-vibration handle, an air-filter system, an automatic chain-oiler, a carrying case, and a two-year warrantee... all for the low, low price of $239.99. The only problem with the saw is its weight. The Poulan Pro weighs in at 11.8 pounds before gassing-up, and 13.1 pounds after.

The saw wasn't my only expense.

The cost of my two prostheses was just shy of $80,000, but thanks to health care and my insurance company I paid a little less than a thousand bucks. However, with my third prosthetic, an arm that was immediately disassembled and used for parts—and deemed unnecessary by both the government and my insurance company—my cost skyrocketed to nearly $25,000.

For weeks I avoided buying that extra arm; I thought for sure I'd be able to find a way around it. After all, Evil Dead Ash seemed to have no problem sticking a chainsaw onto his arm with nothing more than a roll of duct tape and a screwdriver; he made it look easy. Things were different for me, though. In the end, after weeks of trying, I couldn't get the chainsaw fastened to my limb. After countless hours in my workshop, trying to make the impossible possible, I did what I had to do: I dug deep into my pocket and ordered the extra prosthetic arm from a company called CR Equipments. I then waited eleven days for the equipment to be shipped, and dismantled it a few hours later.

Around 7pm the next day everything was set. The chainsaw was modified and fastened to my abutment, which was connected to the titanium bolt, which had been directly fused with my bone.

Everything was perfect.

I wore the chainsaw day and night. Not wanting to be seen in public with this new modification, I had all my food delivered, I never invited company over for a visit, and I never left my home. I wore the tool to bed too, even though it was a bitch to sleep with and it leaked gasoline all over my sheets. In a perfect world I would have worn the saw every last minute, but the world isn't a perfect place, and occasionally, I was forced to take it off.

You see... I couldn't wear it in the shower.

And I was in the shower when Lovecraft came to visit me.

He was pissed.

∞☉∞

I heard the loud BANG as the bathroom door was kicked open. The shower curtain was ripped from the rod before I knew it would happen. I stood there, naked, confused, and cursing up a storm with a glorified plastic bag wrapped around my prosthetic leg—a bag that I purchased from CR Equipment for a measly $345.95—and a second glorified bag wrapped around the stump of my arm, which, for the record, cost a few dollars less.

Hiding my manhood with my only hand, I was about to say, "What the hell is going on here?"

But then I saw him.

H. P. Lovecraft.

My chainsaw was sitting on the toilet seat.

And I was in deep trouble.

I looked left. I looked right. I looked at the chainsaw, which suddenly seemed to be very far away and completely useless to me. I thought about pushing my attacker away, I thought about screaming, I thought about begging for my life, but begging didn't do much the last couple of times that I saw the man, so why would it be any different this time?

Lovecraft said, "Another zombie book? You have *got* to be kidding me! You've got balls... kid. I'll give you that."

"Wait!" I shouted. "Please... God, just wait!"

"No. There will be no *waiting* this time, you injudicious, ill-advised, imprudent, accretion of Homo habilis defecation... you inconsequential, negligible, trifling, paltry, stump of—"

My mouth opened and closed. Arguing with a man that memorized the dictionary is a skill I have not yet mastered.

I said, "But—"

"But nothing!" Lovecraft barked. Then he raised his hand and I saw it:

The axe.

The fucker had an axe with him.

I stepped back, away from the maniac, and slipped on my prosthetic limb bag. My back slammed against the wall and I fell, landing in the tub. At the same time Lovecraft brought the axe down hard.

And missed.

I found myself beneath him, looking up. My arms and legs—or what was left of them—were thrashing about like I had been electrocuted. Panicking, an image came to mind: an overturned turtle, lying on its shell, feet moving uselessly in the air.

Lovecraft raised the axe again.

"Stop it!" I shrieked, still thrashing about. "What's wrong with the second zombie book? There was nothing wrong with it! Zombie Tales Two is good! IT'S *GOOOOOOD!*"

Holding the axe high, Lovecraft unleashed, "I don't care if it's good! That's not the point! *No more zombies!* Do something original! Do something better!"

"But I am! I've done a Best New Vampire Tales book and I'm about to release a Best New Werewolf Tales book! Do you know about those?"

Oh my God. I thought he was mad before, but the anger that consumed his pale and oddly shaped face doubled, becoming a 9.9 on the wrath scale. I had never seen anything like it.

"Werewolves?" he mumbled, offended by my words. "Vampires?"

"Yes," I whispered, trembling, knowing I was in worse trouble than before.

"You've missed the point, you despondent and miserably dejected wad of cephalopod tentacle! Do you really think that werewolves and vampires are original?"

"Uh…"

"Do you?"

What could I say? He created Yog-Sothoth and Cthulhu and I created… no, not created… rehashed—he created Cthulhu and I rehashed werewolves, vampires, and zombies… again. I was up shit creek with the words 'yes - I think werewolves and vampires are original' written across one paddle, while my other paddle announced: 'no - I don't think werewolves and vampires are original, but I'm releasing them anyway.'

I rolled the dice. *"Yes?"*

"Yes?! *YES?!* You think werewolves and vampires are *original?"*

"Well… *maybe…?"*

"No! Not maybe. Oh… you're **DEAD**!"

Lovecraft brought the axe down hard and caught me in the foot. Not the prosthetic one, the real one.

I screamed.

Blood splashed.

And Lovecraft lifted the axe again.

The second time he hit me the blade landed on my shin.

Something cracked. The lights seemed to dim.

As I started to black out I heard him say, "You going to release a fourth volume, zombie boy?"

The word "no" escaped my mouth in a squeak, but the truth of the matter was this: the fourth volume was almost complete.

∞Θ∞

Ahem.

Let me clear my throat.

Dear literate zombie fans; my name is James Roy Daley. What you're looking at is a little idea of mine, brought to life by the power of hard work. If you've read the first two volumes you know what I'm doing here. I'm putting together the best zombie tales I can get my hands on. If you haven't read the first two volumes I figure you're missing out. The first two volumes are loaded with great stories by some of the best writers in the biz, writers like: Gary McMahon, Jeff Strand, Kim Paffenroth, Jonathan Mayberry, Rio Youers, Mort Castle, Tim Waggoner, Matt Hults, Ray Garton, Gord Rollo, John Everson, Nate Kenyon... the list goes on and on. What I'm trying to build here, inside this little series of mine, is the definitive collection of zombie stories. I'm hoping that in the years to come— when the next generation of zombie enthusiasts start looking for zombie fiction—people will point them towards the Best New Zombie Tales Series. After all, the first two anthologies were excellent and volume three, which you're reading now, might just be the best of the bunch.

So get comfy.

Get ready.

Get reading.

First up, a novella by an award winning master, Paul Kane...

The Lazarus Condition
PAUL KANE

PROLOGUE

> '*And he that was dead came forth, bound hand and foot with graveclothes; and his face was bound about with a napkin. Jesus saith unto them. Loose him, and let him go...* '
> *John 11.44*

No one paid any attention as the dead man walked down the street.

A familiar street to him, with children playing football on the grass verge, wives gossiping on the corner next to the shop. He took in all the streetlamps, never having noticed them, *really* noticed them before. Now he was scrutinizing everything, from the pebble-dashing of the council houses to the rickety nature of the peeling fences—which could so easily have been resurrected with a lick of paint.

Given new life.

He paused to look up at the sky, seeing the birds there catching the mild breeze, returned from their winter migration now that spring was here. They'd been drawn to sunnier climes, just as he was being drawn to this place, pulled as surely as if he was made of metal and someone was holding a gigantic magnet. He continued up the street, passing more people as he went: a man walking with a stick, newspaper jammed under his arm; a young woman pushing a buggy with a screaming kid in the seat; a postman making deliveries to each of the houses. None of them looked closely enough to *truly* see him. None of them ever looked too closely at anything, they just went about the business of their mundane lives, worrying about bills—the same ones the postman was shoving through letterboxes that very morning—about the weather, about their families.

He was almost there. The house he was looking for was just across the road. He stared at the overgrown hedge and front garden: once neat and trim with a pond in the middle and gnomes fishing with tiny rods. What had happened to those? He couldn't remember. In the great scheme of things did it really matter? Things came, things went. It was how it was.

He made to cross over the road, almost stepping into the path of an oncoming car. He pulled back just as the driver blared his horn, shouting through the open window: "What the hell's wrong with you? You tryin' to get yourself killed?"

The dead man watched him drive to the end of the road and follow the curve around. Those words went around and around in his mind: "Get yourself killed... Get yourself killed..." He closed his eyes, images flashing across his field of vision below the lids:

A flash of red, of light. Hands clutching at something, tight, white knuckles and a ring on the third finger of the left hand. A pair of eyes, dulled but open in shock. A—

He snapped *his* eyes open, flinching when he felt the hand on his arm. "Are... are you all right?" asked an Indian woman standing beside him. He searched her features but found nothing recognizable. Again he just stared, not saying a thing. In the end the woman let him be, not knowing what else to do. As she walked on up the street, she looked over her shoulder just once.

Turning, he checked for traffic this time, and crossed the road to the house.

He studied the small semi, the windows gaping back at him in disbelief. He put a hand out for the gate, which was hanging off by the hinges. It creaked heavily as he moved it aside, the latch long-since vanished. The path was overgrown too, each carefully laid slab now raised slightly at the side by the sheer amount of weeds pushing up from beneath, like a healthy tooth dislodged by its crooked neighbor. He trod the path slowly, dead flowers on either side, leading him to the front door, its mottled glass set inside a faded varnished frame.

Raising a hand he prepared to knock on the door. He hesitated. Why, he had no idea. This was what he was meant to do, he felt sure of it. And yet…

He shook his head and rapped twice on the wood. The wait was excruciating. He gave it a few minutes, then knocked again, cocking his ear at the same time. He heard movement from within, a voice calling, "All right, all right. I'm coming."

The door opened a crack and someone peered out. It was difficult to see clearly as it was dark inside the hall, but then the door opened more fully. It wasn't because the gray haired woman standing there was willingly allowing him entrance; it was more that she was in a state of severe shock.

She put a quivering hand to her mouth, eyes wide and filling with moisture. "Matt… Matthew?" The old woman made to take a step towards him, but her already unstable legs gave out. "No… no it can't be." He covered the distance between them in an instant, hands there to catch her as she fell back into the house. Her eyes rolled up into her head and she began gasping for air.

"It's okay, I've got you," he said, experimentally talking again. He half-carried her into the house, then closed the door on the outside world. He tapped her face gently with his fingers. "It's me, Mum," he told her. "It's really me."

But she fainted again—the result of seeing her dead son standing on the doorstep after seven long years.

Chapter One

Mrs. Irene Daley woke from her nightmare to find herself on the couch.

She'd had the most awful dream. In it she'd been watching the television, *The Breakfast Show* had just finished and she was about to turn off a report on the troubles abroad—the commentator stating that they were on the verge of yet another 'conflict.' Then there had been a knock at the door. She hadn't heard it at first due to the explosions on the TV, but when the knock came again she'd switched off the set with the remote then got up to answer it, her back aching as she lifted herself out of the high seat chair.

Whoever it was they were persistent. *Might be the postman?* she'd mused as she turned into the hallway. But why would he knock? No one ever sent her any packages, not even her own family. She was lucky if she got any mail at all that wasn't simply junk. She'd called out that she was coming, and she could see the shadowy shape through the misted glass at the door. Irene even considered putting on the chain, but it was the middle of the morning not ten o'clock at night. Nobody would be trying to break into her home this early on in the day, surely. She decided to meet the potential threat half way, only open the door a tiny bit. That way she could shut it again quickly if need be, but she could also see who was so eager to get her attention.

When she opened the door she thought her eyes were playing tricks. Through the gap she looked out at a face she hadn't seen in over half a decade. A face she'd adored more than anything in this world, last seen under a very different set of circumstances. Her boy; *her* Matthew…

But that couldn't be. It only happened in dreams, in nightmares. So when she'd collapsed in the hall and everything had gone black, it only lent more weight to the argument that it was all in her head. That she'd made it all up because yes, even after this length of time, she still missed him so, so much.

She'd heard him say something, but by that time darkness already had her. And now that she was rising from that deep pit of despair and pain she was even more convinced the events that put her there were a product of her imagination.

Irene resolved to open her eyes, get up, and pop the kettle on—to try and put this whole episode out of her mind. But that was going to be incredibly difficult, because as she turned her head and looked at the chair facing the couch, she saw him again. He was sitting there with his hands clasped, staring at her. No, that wasn't strictly true; his eyes weren't so much staring as burrowing into her. She turned away again, quickly, not able to meet his gaze, nor accept what must be the truth. That Matthew was in the room with her, right now. Unless she was still dreaming? Could that be it? Irene pinched the loose skin on the back of her hand, nipping it tightly and hoping the pain would deliver her back to the world she knew. Back to sanity.

She didn't fully turn, but caught him still sitting there in the periphery of her vision.

Seconds passed like hours, until finally she knew she had to speak. "Who... who are you?" Irene asked. "What do you want?"

"I..." he began, and she felt compelled to look at him now as he shook his head. "I'm your son." The man said it so certainly that for a moment she almost believed him. For one thing he was saying the words in her son's voice.

"No... no you're not. You can't be."

He nodded. "But I am."

Irene sat up against the cushions, where he'd placed her, and brought her legs around with a slight crack of the bones. "You look like him—"

"I *am* him," he interrupted.

"You have his face, but..."

Oh sweet Lord did he have her son's face. It was exactly the same, every line, the dimple in his chin, the crowsfeet that were beginning at the corners of his eyes even though he was barely into his thirties. Those hazel eyes were the same too, and the way his hair made him look like he'd just got out of bed in spite of trying to brush it flat. All the same, all the same. And those clothes… were the shirt and trousers part of the suit they'd buried him in, or just very, very similar?

"Why won't you believe me?" It was a simple enough question and yet staggeringly complex. "You know, deep down, that I'm telling the truth."

Irene could feel tears starting to form in her eyes. "You're…" she managed before she began to cry. The tiny beads of water crawled down her cheeks, running into the rivulets created by her wrinkles and breaking up. "You're… you're…" She couldn't get the word out, and when it did eventually slip free it came only as a whisper. "Dead."

He frowned, saying nothing. What could he say? If he was her son, as he so vehemently claimed, how could he deny that? Yet here he was, in the 'flesh,' in her living room—that was a good one, *living* room—sitting in the armchair he always used to occupy when he visited. "I can't explain it," he finally offered. "But I know who I am, and I know that I love you, Mu—"

Irene held up her hand. "Don't. Please don't."

He got up, putting his hands in his pockets. Walking over to the window, he pulled aside the net curtains and peered out. Then he looked down at the photo in the frame on the windowsill. He lifted it up.

"Put that down," said Irene.

He held it out instead to illustrate his point. It was a photo taken at least ten years ago, of Matthew with his arm around his mother. "Look," he said. "This is me… this is me here with you."

"No," said Irene again. She was crying freely now.

There was a noise at the back door and they both turned. A shadow appeared in the hallway, small and dark, followed by another: this one very much alive. The jet-black cat froze when it reached the doorway, the swinging and creaking of the cat-flap still carrying into the living room.

Irene was half standing, looking from the cat to the man holding the picture.

"Tolly?" he said.

The cat had something in its mouth. It looked like a toy at first, but when the animal dropped it onto the hall carpet they could both see it was a sparrow the cat had stalked and caught, just like it always loved to do. The feline—named after Tolstoy, because of its long tail—was now locked in a battle of gazes with him. He took a step towards the creature and its fur stood on end, hackles rising. On some level it could sense there was something wrong. Was this really the man it used to curl up to, making itself comfortable in his lap while pressing its feet into his thighs as if making a nest?

One more step and the cat hissed, spinning around and shooting off in the direction it had come, leaving its prey behind. The man stood and looked across at Irene. She knew exactly how the cat felt—didn't want him coming anywhere near her.

"Mum," he said.

"Don't call me that!"

"It's who you are," he insisted. "You're my mother."

"I was Matthew's mother. I... I don't even know *what* you are."

He looked wounded.

Perhaps she was losing her mind. Was that it? Were these the first signs of Alzheimer's? Or a brain aneurysm? Was she conjuring up this whole scene because she wanted to see Matthew so badly, at this time of year especially? Was this all her doing? Irene shook her head. No, this was real; the man in front of her was real. And she had to figure out some way of dealing with it before she really did go insane.

"I'm Matthew. I'm not an hallucination," he told her, seemingly reading her mind.

"I don't believe in ghosts," Irene said.

"I'm not a ghost either," was his reply. "I'm solid, as solid as I was in this photograph. See?" He reached over and grabbed her arm and she nearly fell back onto the couch in an effort to escape him. But there was no force in that grip; it was merely to illustrate his point. "I carried you back in here, remember?"

Her eyes were wide and white as dinner plates. He let go of her, slowly, and Irene was profoundly aware that she was trembling.

"I'm sorry. I didn't mean to scare you. It's just, well, I don't know how else to convince you."

"T-Tea," said Irene, her mouth a straight line. "A cup of tea…"

The man smiled. "Of course, tea. The cup that cures." He said it like he knew that was her mantra. Like he knew that all the problems there had ever been in this house had been solved over a cup of hot, steaming tea. "I'll go and put the kettle on."

Irene almost laughed then, a nervous laugh. Her dead son, or at least someone who purported to be so, was now offering to go and brew up. She nodded and watched as he put the picture down on the coffee table and left the room. From the kitchen she heard cupboards being opened, the tinkling of china—he knew exactly where to look. Then the sound of the kettle being filled with water.

Irene snapped out of her daze. She picked up the cordless telephone she always kept down the side of the couch when it wasn't charging. And, with one last glance at the photo, she stabbed the buttons with her finger.

Chapter Two

"I remember there used to be a poster here when I was growing up, some band," the person claiming to be Matthew Daley said, examining the wall of what had once been 'his' bedroom.

The request had come after he'd brought back the tea on a tray, along with a plate of biscuits, taken from the jar Irene always kept on the counter next to the bread bin. He wanted to see his old room, asked her politely and with that same lilt Matthew once had in his voice. Irene simply agreed, not knowing what else to say. She led the way up the rickety stairs, checking behind her all the time to see if he was still there. He was, and he followed her to the room where her son had spent much of the first twenty-two years of his life.

"The TV was there, the stereo over… there." He pointed to a sideboard. "I bought it with my first month's wages from the plant. You used to keep telling me to turn down the racket, you remember?"

Another nod.

"It's not there anymore, is it?"

For a second she thought he was still talking about the stereo, but then she realized he meant the place where he'd worked since he was in his late teens. "They… they shut it down a few years ago," she managed.

He nodded and walked over to the wardrobe, a cheap flat-pack one that was still—remarkably—standing, after many years of service. He opened the door nearest to him, taking out a jumper on a hangar. It was navy with pink zigzag lines running across the middle. "I can't believe this is still here. You gave me this one Christmas when I was about fifteen. I didn't like it, but I wore it anyway because I knew you did."

Irene thought she had the tears under control, but now they came again. "How do you know all these things?" she asked him.

"I thought we'd been through that. I'm your son."

At the risk of repeating herself, she said it again; this time the last word was more emphatic. "My son is *dead*."

He thought for a second or two. "Then who am I?"

"I... I don't know."

He put the jumper back inside the wardrobe and his eye caught something on the floor inside. Stooping, he picked it up; it was a small red racing car. Irene stood in silence as he brought the toy up to his face, turning it over.

There was a knock on the door downstairs, much the same as the one she'd answered earlier that morning. The 'stranger' in her home didn't appear to notice; he was too transfixed by the car her son had once played with and which had been left, forgotten, in the bottom of the wardrobe. The knock came again and Irene made for the door of the bedroom. She thought at any moment he would try to stop her from answering it, but he didn't. There was no hand on her arm this time, no sharp words. He—whoever he was— seemed to be in a world of his own.

She ventured down the stairs, more quickly than she had ascended them. Another shadow was visible through the frosted glass, but this time she knew exactly who it was. And for a moment, when she opened the door, it was like déjà vu. Irene was back in time, seven years ago, the two policemen standing at the door waiting to tell her the news. Except this time it was the uniformed officers waiting for her to speak, not the other way around. She'd known instinctively that Matthew had passed on even before she saw the Police Constables, just as she still knew he was dead—*should* be dead. Now it was a case of how to explain it to the policemen without sounding like she was on some kind of medication.

"Mrs. Irene Daley? We've had a report of a disturbance," said the first copper, a young black man.

A disturbance? That was one way of putting it.

"That someone was in your house," chipped in the other officer, a much older man with a graying beard.

"Y-Yes," she said, not really knowing where to begin. "He's... upstairs."

"Right," said the younger man, entering the house. The older man put a hand on his shoulder and gestured up towards the top of the stairs. Irene followed their gaze and saw 'Matthew' standing there. It sent a shiver up her spine.

"Sir, would you mind coming down here?" said the bearded officer. "Hands where I can see them."

He started to descend, a disappointed but resigned expression on his face. He held his hands palm outwards, and there was nothing in them.

"Now," continued the older man, "perhaps you'd mind explaining to me what you're doing in Mrs. Daley's home."

The man said nothing.

"Mrs. Daley... have you been hurt at all?"

"No signs of forced entry at the doorway," the younger PC confirmed.

"I... I opened the door and..." Irene was still crying and they took this as a sign to proceed.

The young black officer turned the man around and handcuffed him, just to be on the safe side. Their prisoner stared at Irene, half in disbelief, half resentment.

"So, perhaps we can get a few things sorted out now," said the bearded PC. "Who exactly are you and what are you doing in Mrs. Daley's home?"

"I'm her son," he said at last.

"Her son, eh? Mrs. Daley, is this true?"

She hesitated for a second, then shook her head.

"My name is Matthew Daley," stated the handcuffed man as he was patted down. The young PC found nothing, no ID, no weapons—nothing, save for a small toy car in the man's pocket, which he handed to his colleague.

"So he's not your son?" pressed the bearded policeman.

"He... he looks like him, but..."

The police officers exchanged glances.

"I am him," insisted the man.

"You *can't* be!" screamed Irene, finally reaching the end of her tether. "My Matthew has been dead for seven years!"

The bearded man sighed. "There's obviously been some kind of misunderstanding here. I think the best thing we can probably do is take you down to the station for a little chat. Valentine, stay here and get a statement from Mrs. Daley." He tugged on the intruder's arm and tried to lead him out of the house. For a fraction of a second he held fast, refusing to move, and it looked like they were going to have a struggle on their hands to shift him.

Then he spoke again before allowing the bearded PC to take him. "Dad would have believed me."

Irene leapt forward, all her trepidation forgotten, her hands turning to claws ready to rake this intruder's flesh. Luckily the black officer saw this coming and was able to hold her back before she could do any injury. "Let PC Wilson take it from here," Valentine said.

"You'll see me again," 'Matthew' told her.

"All right, that's enough," said Wilson. The bearded copper led the man out the door and down the path. Irene watched with the other policeman standing alongside. A small crowd of people had gathered now, attracted by the police car at the front of the house. A man with ginger hair and a pot-belly was leaning against his open doorway, scratching himself and eating a sandwich. The kids who'd been playing on the road had picked their football up; one held it under his arm like a headless ghost.

All paid attention now, all noticed. The handcuffed man was bundled into the back, PC Wilson slamming the door after him. Then the policeman climbed into the front and started the engine again.

The car drove off, away from the scene, and Valentine started to close the door. Something flew past them and out through the gap.

It was a small brown bird, a sparrow.

They watched it climb up into the air and join the others overhead, circling the house. Neither of them said anything. But as Valentine finally shut the door and took out his note-pad, Irene couldn't help noticing the hallway was empty.

"So then, Mrs. Daley," Valentine said hopefully, breaking into her daze, "perhaps you could explain to me what all this is about."

Chapter Three

"Tell me again just why we're holding him?"

Detective Chief Inspector Robbins, a long thin streak of a man with cropped hair and a chin that was so lantern shaped people expected to see a flame flickering in his mouth whenever he talked, was leafing through PC Wilson's notes on their new arrival. He'd been woken early that morning by a phone call from his third ex-wife asking him if he'd taken the hedge trimmer with him when he left the previous summer, and if so, could she please have it back as her new boyfriend would quite like to make a start in the garden that weekend. There were several cases waiting for him on his desk when he arrived, which looked in no rush to solve themselves. And his acid indigestion was playing up again, making it feel like someone was stirring his guts around with a red-hot poker. So he was not in the best of moods, and definitely not in the mood for his time being wasted.

"We're not exactly holding him as such, sir," replied the bearded man, "I just thought it best to place him in an interview room before coming to you with it... while we figured out exactly what had happened."

"So?"

"Looked like a simple case of forced entry, except he claims he was let in, and even made Mrs. Daley a cup of tea."

The DCI's eyebrows shot up. "Your average hardened criminal then. Why are you bothering me with this?"

"Also claims to be her long lost son."

"Long lost, as in Australian soap opera plot?" said Robbins with a sarcastic smirk.

"No. As in deceased, sir."

Robbin's smile faded. "All right, you've got my attention. Maybe we should bring up a few records on our…" He read from the notes. "…Mr. Matthew Daley. Where's the mother now?"

"Valentine's with her, going over what exactly happened." Wilson opened his mouth, then shut it again.

"Go on, you looked like you were about to say something."

Wilson nodded. "It's just that there's something funny about this whole thing, that's why I came to you with it. There's something about him that gives me the creeps."

"How do you mean?"

"I can't put my finger on it," Wilson scratched his beard. "He just doesn't seem right to me." The veteran policeman had come across many people in his time, from all walks of life, and Robbins knew this. You got a sense about them, whether they were lying, whether they were about to punch you. When he said something wasn't right about this business, Robbins would be a fool to just dismiss it.

"You think he might have a screw loose, that it?"

"I don't know."

Robbins shrugged. "All right, what the hell. Let's see what we can find out about him. Then we'll have a nice little talk with our deceased friend."

∞☾∞

The chair was uncomfortable, nothing like those in the house earlier. In fact this one was *designed* to make people uncomfortable, ill at ease. But if *he* felt any discomfort at all he didn't show it.

Police Constable Frank Wilson stood by the wall as Robbins took a seat opposite the man. Wilson thought about the drive over to the station, how he'd kept looking in the rear view mirror, how the man had seemed to stare right back at him in the reflective surface. He hadn't said a word until they were halfway there, and then it was only to reiterate that he was Mrs. Daley's son, that he had made her a drink to calm her nerves, and he couldn't understand why he had been taken away. It was a thread that was picked up again when Robbins sat down, placing a manila file of papers on the table between them, and turning on the tape recorder to the left of him.

"Why have you brought me here? Am I being charged with something?" His words were even and considered.

Robbins turned it back on him. "Why do *you* think you're here?"

The man sighed. "My mother rang you."

"And why do you think she did that?"

"She couldn't accept—"

"Accept who you are," Robbins finished for him.

There was no reply.

Robbins took off his jacket and hung it on the back of his chair. "And who exactly are you?"

"Her son."

Robbins shook his head. "According to her, and…" He tapped the files in front of him. "…according to this, Matthew Daley died seven years ago. With the best will in the world, you can't be him… trust me."

"How do you know?"

"It was before my time here, but I've read the medical reports, seen the photos," Robbins said, narrowing his eyes.

"Photos?" asked the man.

"From when they brought him in. You don't know, do you?" Robbins looked back over at Wilson.

"Know what?" asked the man, leaning forward.

"That's interesting." The DCI faced him again. "You don't know how Matthew Daley died. Why is that?"

The man said nothing for a moment, then, "I can remember some things, but... others are a bit hazy."

"Well, there is no way on Earth that you can be him, I assure you. There's a resemblance, I'll give you that, but Mr. Daley..." Robbins stopped himself, unable to continue. "You can't be him; simple as that. Which begs the question, who are you? Who are you *really*? And what did you want with Mrs. Daley? Money, was that it?"

"Money?" The man seemed confused by the accusation.

"Yes, were you hoping to get money from her?"

"Why would I want her money?"

"You're telling me her money wouldn't interest you?"

"Course not."

"Were you hoping she'd be so confused and upset that she'd just hand over whatever savings she had to you?"

The man shook his head violently, slamming his fist on the table. "I didn't want her money," he insisted. "I... I just needed to see her. She's my mother."

"I don't think we're getting through to him, Wilson," said Robbins. "As I said before, Mr. Daley is dead. He's been in Westmoor Cemetery, in the ground, for seven years. You, sir, on the other hand, appear to be remarkably spry." Robbins folded his arms and sat back in his marginally more comfortable chair. "Surely you can see how we—and Mrs. Daley— would have a problem with that?"

"I can't explain it, I just know that—"

"Listen to me!" shouted Robbins, "I don't know what your game is, but in this station we don't take very kindly to men who scare little old ladies out of their wits for kicks."

"I never meant to frighten her. I just—"

"You just needed to see her, yeah you said."

The man was wriggling about now, agitated. "Isn't there some kind of test you can do? You said you had medical reports there—"

"The reports from the *autopsy*," clarified Robbins.

"Isn't there something you can—"

Robbins laughed. "Why should we, when we already know the answer? You're not Matthew Daley, sunshine. Live with it." He realized the significance of what he'd just said and a mocking grin creased his face again.

"But—"

The DCI took something out of his pocket and placed it on the desk. "Care to tell me why you had this about your person when you were picked up?"

The man went rigid. His eyes were glued to the little red car now on the table.

"Thought it might be worth something?"

"It's… It's mine. Or at least it was."

The man reached out to take it from the table and Robbins grabbed his wrist. "You'd better start giving us some answers, whoever you are or…" He let the threat tail off, letting go of the man's hand as he did so. Ignoring him, the man carried on reaching out for the car and picked it up.

"PC Wilson, would you escort our 'guest' to a cell. Maybe some time alone will help loosen his tongue."

Wilson walked over to the man, hesitating slightly before taking him by the arm as he'd done when he led him out of Irene Daley's house. The man didn't look at Robbins as he left.

When they'd departed and the door closed; Robbins let out a long, slow breath. He rubbed his chin and opened up the file again, flipping through the reports and statements, notes from his predecessor DCI Croft. The same bloody Croft whose shoes he'd had to fill when he moved to this district. Hadn't been able to solve this one last murder, though, had he? Robbins was drawn again to the pictures, the photographs of Matthew Daley. He screwed up his face at the sights before him: the blood, the deep gashes, the plump bruising of the skin that had turned the flesh a dull violet color.

He slammed the file shut again and leaned back in the chair once more, arms behind his head this time. "No way," he said to himself in a whisper. "No way in the world."

∞☉∞

PC Wilson placed the man in cell number thirteen, the only one free. It could have been worse, he thought, could've been a Friday.

"Here you go," he told him. "Now I suggest you think about what DCI Robbins said and drop the act, mate."

The man ignored him. His shoes and socks had already been taken off him, and now Wilson thought about asking for the toy as well. Prisoners weren't meant to have any personal effects in the cells. But something stopped him from doing so, and he left the man be.

"If you come to your senses, shout," said Wilson.

Then he shut the 'dead man' away, all alone in the small, dark, confined space. And as Wilson locked up and walked down the corridor he had the strangest feeling.

The feeling that this wasn't the first time the guy been shut away. That the last time it had been an even smaller, and even darker space.

Chapter Four

It was dark.

A blackness so overpowering, so unbearable it was like being drowned in pure liquid night. It was hard to gather his thoughts, but he felt sure he was walking, placing one foot in front of the other, just trudging on towards something. And he was granted a sense of where he might be—the walls of this place closing in on him, but they were round rather than flat, a roundness that stretched out into the distance. A tiny speck of light appeared at the far end of this tunnel. He felt compelled to look in its direction, an urgency to head towards it for some reason.

The light was growing stronger; it changed from a tiny speck to a bright glaring ball, meaning he was getting nearer to the end, although he didn't feel like he was walking at all anymore. Yet the light was still growing nearer. Perhaps he was floating; he had no idea, but it was a strange sensation. The light was getting bigger and bigger. Soon it would all be over, soon he would find out what was at the end of this conduit, what the light meant.

He put up his hands to stop it from blinding him, but it shone right through—such was its intensity. Then, suddenly, the light was upon him. He was a part of the light and it was a part of him.

All the answers, the things out of reach would soon be revealed.

Just a few more seconds, just a few more—

∞⊖∞

The hand shook him awake and gave him a start.

"Dead to the world." Inspector Robbins' face hovered above him in the cell. The man sat bolt upright on the bunk. "Time to wake yourself Rip van Winkle," he said in a snide voice.

The man swung his bare feet onto the cold tiled floor.

"We have a visitor for you."

"Mum?"

Robbins shook his head, grinning. "Afraid not. No, I thought about what you said—about checking you over. You're right; we have to make sure you're not whacked out on something that might be making you delusional. Wilson?"

The PC stepped into his field of vision, bringing someone with him—a woman in her late thirties, early forties. Her hair was a light shade of bronze, with the merest hints of grey beginning at the temples. She wore a beige trouser suit with an off-white blouse beneath the jacket. And she was carrying with her a black leather case.

"This is Doctor Preston," Robbins informed him. "She's going to examine you. Now, PC Wilson is going to be just outside, so don't give her a hard time, okay?"

Dr. Preston came further into the chamber, looking around her as she did so. Then their eyes met, only severing contact when Robbins said something to her.

"I'm sorry?"

"I said: twenty minutes all right?"

"Fine," she told him.

Robbins gave a satisfied nod. "All right then, we'll leave you to it."

The DCI exited the cell, with Wilson hanging back a few moments longer before leaving the door open a crack and waiting outside.

"So," said Dr Preston to break the silence that had descended, "what's your story?"

The man stared at her blankly.

"Not one for idle chit chat, I understand. Okay, well if you wouldn't mind getting undressed, we'll make a start."

He did as he was told, unbuttoning the shirt and shrugging it down over his shoulders. Then he took off his trousers; there was no underwear beneath. Preston opened her bag and took out the tools of her trade, listening to his heartbeat—steady and strong—looking in his ears, taking his temperature, testing his reflexes. It was there that she caught a glimpse of the birthmark on the top of his leg. It was dark red and shaped like a map of some unknown land. But she got on with her job, not giving it another thought. Everything seemed in working order. "Now this won't hurt much," she told him, taking out a needle, "I just need to draw some blood."

He nodded vaguely, looking down as she shoved the needle into his upper arm, pulling back on one end and filling it with redness.

"There, all done. You're in pretty good nick, if you'll pardon the expression," she said.

"I'm alive," he said as he got dressed again, and the sound of his voice startled her. She wasn't quite sure whether it was a question or a statement.

"Er... yes, in my professional opinion. Why, don't you feel very well?"

He laughed softly and caught her eyes again. "They haven't told you yet, have they?"

Preston's eyebrows creased. "About?"

"It doesn't matter, you'll find out soon enough."

"I don't like mysteries Mister—?" She waited for him to give her his name. When he didn't she said, "My first name's Bethany, by the way. Beth for short."

"Matthew," he told her. "My name's Matthew."

"There now, see—that wasn't so difficult. Right, well, I think we're all done here Matth—"

He shot out his hand so fast she didn't have time to move away, and his fingers were around her wrist seconds later—not tight, just enough to draw her face in closer. "What're you..." She was just about to call for Wilson when he said:

"Don't blame yourself. You did everything you could." His hazel eyes were intense, piercing, and she felt a shudder go through her entire body. "*She* doesn't blame you."

"What?"

"You have to let it go, all of it. All the guilt."

She wrestled her hand free, moving back sharply as if stung. Beth grabbed her bag and raced for the door.

"Sarah's happy," said the man plainly.

She closed her eyes and opened them again, looking back at him. "What... what did you just say?"

"You heard me."

The doctor was gazing at him in disbelief. "You... you can't..."

He turned away from her. "I'll see you again."

Beth yanked open the door and virtually walked into the PC who was standing guard there. She motioned for him to lock the cell again.

"Are you all right, Dr Preston?" he asked her.

But she didn't hear him. She was looking through the slit in the door, watching the man in there as he held up a toy car and stared at it.

"Dr Preston?" His fingertips brushed her arm and she jumped back. "I'm sorry."

"Take me to Robbins," she said. "Take me to your DCI right now."

∞☉∞

For the third time that day there was a knock on the door.

This time it was PC Valentine who answered it, welcoming in the visitor Mrs. Daley had called at his suggestion.

"Is there anybody who could sit with you? Anybody you could ring?" said the black policeman once he'd finished taking her statement—a statement that made about as much sense as the rest of that morning's events.

Mrs. Daley had nodded, and he'd handed her the cordless phone.

Now he was here, standing at her door. And just as the dark uniform that Valentine wore betrayed his profession, so too did the dark shirt and suit that this man had on. But the most significant piece of attire was the dog collar at his neck.

"Father Lilley?" asked Valentine of the priest who was only marginally younger than Mrs. Daley herself.

He bowed his head in greeting. "Where's Irene... Mrs. Daley?"

"Through here." Valentine took him to the dining room; he hadn't been able to get her back into the living room at all. She was sitting at a small round table with her hands clasped together, bible to the right of them.

"Thank you, my son," said Lilley to the PC, noticing the woman flinch at those last two words. Then she got up and fell into the priest's arms.

"Oh father, I'm so pleased to see you."

"There, there," said Lilley, patting her back. "Whatever's the matter, Irene? I couldn't make head nor tail of your call." He looked to Valentine for an answer, but he was asking the wrong person.

"Some… something terrible. Matthew…"

The priest's expression changed and he cut short the embrace. "Matthew? I don't understand. I thought you'd had an intruder?"

"She did," Valentine reported, "of a kind."

"He… he looked just like Matthew, Father," Irene added.

It seemed like Lilley didn't know what to say, then he talked slowly as if to a child. "Irene, haven't we talked about this before? Matthew's gone. He is with Our Savior the Lord where he has found his peace. 'His kingdom *is* an everlasting kingdom, and his dominion *is* from generation to generation.' The Book of Daniel, Chapter Four, Verse Three. Matthew wouldn't want you upsetting yourself like this, now, would he?"

"He said he *was* Matthew."

"The man in your house?"

She nodded.

"Said Arnold would have listened, would have believed him."

"Irene, Matthew's no longer with us. I buried him myself."

He saw that she remembered all too well that day: the angry clouds had gathered as if in sympathy, looking down at the patch of grass behind the church. A group of mourners, dressed in black, standing around the hole in the ground as the perfectly polished coffin with the brass handles was lowered into it.

Ashes to ashes. Dust to dust.

Irene had broken down on that day too. At one point he thought she might even stagger forward and follow the coffin into the ground. But instead she had held back, tears pouring from her eyes for a son who had been taken prematurely.

"Officer, who was this man?" Lilley asked Valentine.

"That's what we're trying to find out, Father. But he's insistent that he's Matthew Daley."

"That's impossible."

"I know," said the PC, a little offended that he had to explain that to the priest.

"I'd like to see him," said Lilley.

"Perhaps, in time," Valentine told him. "But for now..." He nodded towards Irene. "I think Mrs. Daley needs you here."

The priest's eyes flashed momentarily, as if he didn't like being told his job. Then the kindness returned to them and he said, "Of course." He led his charge back to her seat, pulling out the chair nearest to her for himself. "Don't worry, Irene. I'm sure this will all be sorted out soon. Everything that happens is according to God's design and purpose, even if we can't see it at the time. 'Trust in the Lord with all your heart, and lean not on your own understanding; in all your ways acknowledge Him, and He shall direct your paths.' Proverbs Chapter Three, Verses Five to Six." He held her hand in his and patted it. "Trust in the Lord, Irene, and He will show you the way."

∞☉∞

"I don't like being hung out to dry, Steve."

Dr. Bethany Preston paced up and down in DCI Robbins' office, arms folded. He was sitting back behind his desk, watching her, like a member of the audience at Wimbledon.

"I wasn't hanging anyone anywhere," he said, after telling her repeatedly to calm down. He'd never seen her so agitated.

"You deliberately withheld information from me about that prisoner, didn't you?" As she said this last bit she jabbed her finger in his direction.

"I didn't want you walking into there with any preconceptions. Besides, you never asked."

Becky threw her hands up in the air. "And what exactly was I supposed to ask... oh and excuse me, but by any chance was this guy picked up for impersonating a dead man?"

"I told you everything you needed to know at the time."

"Bullshit. You told me he was a weird one, that he might be on something, and to try and get him talking if I could."

"You've done it before. You have a good... bedside manner."

"People tell me things, Steve. They trust me. I don't abuse that trust. Unlike some." Now she was standing with her hands on her hips.

"Let's not make this personal again, Beth."

"If I recall rightly, it was you who made things... 'personal' the last time."

He winced at that remark. "No need to dig up the past. What exactly did he say to you in there? What's really got you like this?" Robbins rose from his chair and leant against his desk.

She avoided his eyes. "Nothing."

"I don't believe you."

Beth raised her head, but her eyes were far from warm. "Your prerogative. But you're right about one thing."

"What's that?"

"He is a weird one. In fact, in all my years as a Doctor, and the last few years working for you lot, I don't think I've ever come across anyone quite like him."

Robbins folded his arms now. "No, me either. But he isn't Matthew Daley."

"You sound very sure of that."

"Oh come on, Beth. You've seen the photos and the report now, what that fucker did to him. It's just not possible. He was dead by the time they loaded him into the ambulance. The paramedics called it on the way to Accident and Emergency. They buried him for Christ's sake."

Beth rubbed her forehead. "I should be going," she said.

"Wait."

"Look, you want me to test the blood, Steve, I'll test it." She picked up her bag and left, shutting the door behind her.

Leaving Robbins to stare at the space she'd occupied only moments before.

Chapter Five

He saw things as he waited in his cell. More quick flashes he wished he could slow down, more images—this time accompanied by smells and sounds too. A burning, acrid aroma, a scream that turned rapidly into a yelp. The stink of faeces, a thudding. And there was music, a rock band belting out their latest hit for all they were worth. All of this mish-mashed into a nonsense as he sat there.

He'd been given his meals by Wilson, but the man couldn't bear to be in his presence for more than a few minutes. Not that it really mattered, not that any of this really mattered. The important work was still yet to be done; he felt that, knew it somehow. He knew what some of it should be, too, while other parts were still hidden. Just like his ragged and torn memory, some bits perfect, others barely more than fuzzy blurs.

As day passed to night and dawn broke again, he explored the confines of his cell more fully, discovering a spider's web in the bottom corner. There was no sign of the spider itself, but there was the carcass of one of its victims caught there on the fine gossamer strands. He felt exactly like that fly, stranded here. Trapped with no means of escape.

When Wilson next came in to bring him breakfast, he asked if there was any word yet from Dr. Preston. He also asked when he would be released and whether they were intent on charging him with anything.

Wilson could answer neither.

So he had to be patient. Wait until it all started to fall into place.

∞Θ∞

"It still doesn't prove anything," Robbins said as he gripped the phone tighter, bringing his other hand up and almost wringing the plastic.

"No it doesn't. But the man in your cells and Matthew Daley definitely had the same blood type," Beth told him down the line.

"Along with how many other millions?"

"Granted. But here's the thing: I noticed yesterday that the man you're holding has a birthmark on the top of his left leg."

"So? The autopsy reports don't mention anything about a birthmark," Robbins snapped.

"That's because the thigh was a bloody mess, Steve. But according to Matthew Daley's local practice, he *did* have a birthmark on the upper part of his leg."

"All right, so they've both got birthmarks."

"Same blood type, same birthmarks, same height, hair color, eye color..." Beth continued.

"All right, all right," Robbins said. "But they can't be the same person. What're we talking here, twins?"

"I think Mr. and Mrs. Daley would have noticed if there was a baby missing at the birth," said Beth.

"A fluke, a look-alike?"

"I don't know what to tell you, Steve. None of this makes any sense to me. Not really."

Again he wondered just what had spooked her in the cell yesterday.

"But there were certain... anomalies in the blood itself," she said after a pause.

"How do you mean? Drugs?"

"No, he was clean, like I said. It's just that his white blood cell count is incredibly high... and his humor immunity is quite outstanding."

He swapped the phone to his other ear. "In English, Beth."

"There are an inordinate amount of antibodies in his system. Triggered by what, I don't know. Some exogenous antigen I can't identify."

"I do believe I said English."

"Simply put, it means he's extremely resistant to infection."

"Okay," Robbins said slowly.

"And there's something else."

Robbins sighed. "Do I have to ask, or were you planning on telling me eventually?"

"Matthew Daley had type two diabetes, but there's no sign of that now in this blood."

"Then it *can't* be him."

"You'd think so, and yet... Steve, we really need to do some more tests."

"Look, Beth, I'm not really interested if he's the scientific discovery of the century. The bottom line is, I have someone in custody and I don't know what to charge him with... if anything. Trespass, possibly. But there aren't any laws against looking like someone who's died. Give me something to go on."

He could almost hear her mind ticking over. "The case is still open, right?"

"Technically yes. They never caught who did this to Matthew Daley."

"Then get a decent DNA sample. The people who were handling all this back then weren't exactly CSI material. Exhume the body, Steven."

Robbins asked her to repeat what she'd just said in case he'd misheard it. He hadn't.

"Jesus… we can't do that, Beth. The mother would go ballistic, and as for the church… Valentine says that the local priest hasn't left Mrs. Daley's side since this happened."

"Get a court order."

"By tomorrow? You know how many strings I'd have to pull?"

Becky tutted. "You're telling me you can't? From what I hear Croft would've been able to manage it."

He ground his teeth. "It'd be professional suicide."

"And the career always comes first, doesn't it?" said Beth.

Robbins exhaled another deep breath. "The shit's really going to hit the fan."

"It's the only way to be sure."

"About what?"

She didn't answer that one, but he knew the answer anyway. He placed the 'phone in the crook of his neck, took a packet of indigestion tablets out of his pocket, and tapped a couple into his palm.

"I'll see what I can do," he said, tipping the tablets into his mouth.

"One more thing," said Beth before she hung up.

"Yeah?"

"I want to be there."

"What?"

"I want to be there when they open the coffin up."

"You?"

"Don't sound so shocked. You're the one that brought me into this, Steve."

"Okay," Robbins promised her. Then he looked up at the ceiling, wondering just what he was about to set in motion.

Chapter Six

The morning was an overcast one.

As the group waited around the grave they resembled the mourners from the funeral that had been held there seven years ago. Except these people had only come to know about Matthew Daley's life in the last forty-eight hours or so. They hadn't watched him grow up, hadn't loved him or grieved over his passing. They were here for one reason only: the truth.

Bethany Preston had arrived early, as soon as she'd been given the call. Robbins told her that it hadn't been easy, but they'd been granted express permission to exhume—in spite of Father Lilley's protests. Lilley had been particularly vocal when the teams of police and forensics experts arrived at Westmoor. Said it would be a sacrilege in the eyes of the Lord. Valentine had to hold him back from the scene, while Robbins tried to explain their position.

"I'm really sorry, Father, but this has to be done."

"Heathens, all of you. 'Depart from me, all ye workers of iniquity; for the Lord hath heard the voice of my weeping!' Psalm Six, Verse Eight," shouted Lilley, shaking his fist. When that didn't work, he tried another tack. "My father was a Captain in the army. He died in the war. Died so that our freedoms should be upheld."

"We need to give Mrs. Daley peace of mind. There might be evidence in that grave which could help in the investigation—"

"Investigation!" Lilley spat. "You couldn't find the person who killed him the first time, what makes you think you will now? Leave the poor boy in peace, I'm begging you."

"And what about Mrs. Daley's peace of mind?" asked Robbins.

Lilley squinted with one eye. "This is about the man who came to her house, isn't it?"

"It might help to settle things," replied Robbins, deflecting the question.

"In the name of the Lord our God, man, she doesn't need things 'settling.' She knows already, knows that man *cannot* be her son. The peace of mind you're talking about will only be shattered by this."

"The case was never closed though, Father," said Robbins. "This is important."

"This is unheard of! You'll burn for it," Lilley warned them. "All of you. 'Upon the wicked he shall rain snares, fire and brimstone, and a horrible tempest; this shall be the portion of their cup.' Psalm One Verse Six."

Beth had heard the commotion but was crouching by the gravestone itself, reading the inscription there.

MATTHEW KEVIN DALEY
DEVOTED SON, HUSBAND, AND FATHER
TAKEN FROM US EARLY
SLEEP WELL, ANGEL

There were a couple of stems from long dead flowers that had been left there possibly weeks or even months ago. When Robbins returned from his encounter with Lilley, chewing more of his tablets, he gave the order for the exhumation to begin. Beth stepped back to allow the police to start digging. It took them the best part of two hours to reach the coffin, though even then it was only because of their numbers.

She watched as the men in white suits fed straps under the coffin, signaling for it to be lifted out slowly and carefully. Like a huge wooden baby, it was cradled back down again to the earth.

"Are you sure about this, about being here?" said Robbins, now at the side of her. "It's not going to be pleasant."

"Steve, I'm a Doctor for Christ's sake. And I'm a big girl."

Robbins gave the order for the coffin to be opened, which the men did, again with the utmost professionalism, care, and respect. Beth and Robbins drew closer as the final nail was removed and the lid heaved off.

∞Ө∞

Irene Daley lay in bed, unable to move.

She knew what they were doing that morning. Father Lilley had broken the news to her as gently as he could. They'd obtained an order to exhume Matthew, earthly laws obviously carrying more weight than religious ones. She'd run the gamut of emotions then: surprise, fear, anger, resentment. But hadn't there been something else at the back of her mind, a little voice telling her that at least they'd know for sure when it was done? At least she'd be able to get the picture of that person out of her head, the man who'd sat in Matthew's chair, who'd looked around his old bedroom and found the forgotten toy car in the wardrobe. The man who'd told her that his father—no, Matthew's father—would have believed him.

Irene's eyes were dry that morning. There were no more tears left. In the past two days she'd cried so much she thought her eyeballs would simply float out of her head. But now, on the morning they were digging up her son's coffin, and opening it, she found she couldn't cry at all. She felt numb; she might as well have been in that coffin herself.

Yet as the hands on the clock next to her bed reached midday, Irene did feel something. At that precise moment she knew the lid was being taken off... and she knew what they would find inside.

She knew more positively than she had ever known anything in her life.

That was when she started crying again.

∞Ө∞

"So what happens now?"

"I honestly wish I knew," Robbins, still clearly stunned, told Beth.

"We need to talk to him again."

"We?"

"We," she repeated.

Robbins rubbed the back of his neck. "Heavens knows what I'm going to tell my bosses. This is growing way beyond a simple cold case now."

"I think it was before." She tentatively placed a hand on his shoulder. "You did the right thing, Steve."

"I doubt the priest back there sees it that way. Did you know we're all going to burn in Hell for this, Beth?"

"Been there, bought the t-shirt."

"None of this makes any sense."

"No it doesn't."

They began walking away from the grave again, back towards the church. Robbins marched past Valentine and Lilley without meeting their gaze. Neither Robbins nor Beth spoke again until they reached the police cars parked on the road. Then one of the women police officers there—Adams, Beth had heard him call her—took Robbins to one side. Beth shifted her weight from one foot to the other and waited as the WPC whispered something to him.

"What?" she heard Robbins say, raising his voice. "He can't be... Well how did...?" Robbins listened some more, then shook his head violently.

Beth rushed over, but waited until Robbins had dismissed the junior officer before asking what had happened.

"He's gone," the detective told her bluntly.

"What do you mean?"

"What do you think I mean, Beth, *he's fucking gone!*"

She recoiled as if slapped.

"'I'm sorry," he said, but his voice was still hard.

"I don't understand... how can he just be gone?"

"One of the duty officers found Wilson in there, sitting in the corner of the cell. They can't get much sense out of him, he's talking nonsense."

"Didn't anyone see anything?"

"Apparently not. And there's nothing on the bloody CCTV cameras either." Robbins broke away from her and started towards his car.

"Wait a minute, where are you going?"

"Where do you think? Back to the station, I'm going to try and work out where our boy is... before anything else happens."

Chapter Seven

Jason loved dinner hour.

All morning long he'd been stuck in a fusty classroom working first on math problems, then looking at a book where the principal character traveled back in time to visit some of the most famous historical events, like the Roman era and the middle ages when knights battled it out with big swords. Jason didn't want to *read* about such things. He wanted to be in the sunshine, acting them out, just like he would be in the holidays.

So, after a dinner of what was supposed to be some sort of stew, followed by a dessert that was part sponge, part custard, and part something else he hadn't been able to distinguish, Jason had raced out onto the playground attached to the small school, swinging his imaginary sword and chopping away at an imaginary black knight. A surge of boys and girls came behind him, breaking off into smaller fragments: some going into corners to trade cards from the latest Japanese cartoon series; some kicking around a small tennis ball on the floor; some playing chase; others simply racing around and around, screaming at the top of their voices, as if trying to release all the energy that had been building for the last few hours.

Jason had now dispatched his evil opponent and was looking for any dragons to tackle—although, as his teacher Miss

Bellamy had tried to drive home to them all that morning, dragons didn't strictly exist during that era. Didn't exist at all, in actual fact.

"What about St. George?" asked one little girl near the front, Mary Hodgkins.

"Ah, well, the tale of St. George and the dragon is what we call a fable, children. Like Sleeping Beauty. In this case the dragon just represents a form of evil."

"Did they have talking lions in the middle ages, Miss?" asked Leon Keogh.

She'd sighed wearily. "No Leon, it wasn't Narnia. This was real."

But Jason, like Leon, wasn't too fond of the real. Real was boring, and dragons breathed fire and had scales and were, when all was said and done, pretty damned cool. In his imagination, he found the dragon he'd been looking for: a bright red one that flapped its wings on approach and was guarding a cave full of treasure. He ran at the beast, swinging his sword left and right, dodging the fire that came his way. And running straight into the path of one of the school helpers, Mrs. Shaw, a woman who could, in her own way, also lay claim to the title of dragon.

She towered over Jason, holding the youngster by the arm. "Why don't you look where you're going?" said Mrs. Shaw in that rasping voice of hers. She was one of the old crowd, one of the small handful of helpers and teachers who still thought it had been a bad idea to get rid of corporal punishment, because a smack or several hadn't done them any harm when they were little—apart from giving them the impression it was okay to do that to others later on. Mrs. Shaw would never openly strike any of the kids there, but every now and again she liked to put the fear of God into one, just to keep the rest in line.

Jason hoped today wasn't his turn to be on the receiving end.

"I'm... I'm sorry," he said. He wondered about telling her what he'd been doing, but thought better of it. Mrs. Shaw wasn't the kind of person you told about your imaginary fights with fantasy creatures. Mrs. Shaw wasn't the kind of person you told anything to really.

"Come here," she said, pulling Jason into a small corner of the playground, away from the windows of the school. Away from prying eyes.

"Please, I didn't mean to—"

"Don't give me any of that sniveling," she rasped again. "I get enough of it from my husband."

Mrs. Shaw bent, bringing Jason closer as she did so. "If I ever catch you running about like that, swinging your arms again, I'll—"

"You'll let him go," said a voice from behind them. It was even and soft, but had a harder edge to it underneath.

Mrs. Shaw rose slowly. Jason had never seen this look on her face before, a look you get only when you've been caught doing something you shouldn't be. She immediately let go of Jason's arm, turning round to see who had spoken.

Jason saw the man a few seconds after her, as she moved aside, allowing him a clearer view. He was about average height, with dark tousled hair, and he was wearing a shirt and trousers. As Jason looked down, though, he saw the man was barefoot.

When Mrs. Shaw realized he wasn't a member of staff, nor did he look like anyone in any kind of authority—more like a tramp who'd wandered in through the gate—she shouted, "And who the hell are you?"

"That doesn't matter," he told her.

"Some kind of pervert, eh? Come to spy on the kids at playtime?"

"No."

"Well, we'll just see what the headmaster has to say about that one, shall we? You do realize that you're trespassing?"

He said nothing, merely stared at her.

Mrs. Shaw took a step towards him. "What's the matter with you anyway? You on drugs or something? And where are your shoes?" She took two more steps, then paused, and took another.

The man saved her the trouble of coming any closer and covered the remaining distance himself. He grabbed her arm, just as she had done with Jason in the playground. She didn't have time to get away. Mrs. Shaw was about to scream when he said, "Do you ever think about him anymore, Jean? Do you ever think about Oliver?"

"What… what are you talking about?"

"You can tell yourself that what happened to him was an accident, that you had nothing to do with it, but you made his life a misery. And for what? All because he was a bit over-weight?"

"Who are you? How… how could you know…?"

"How did you feel when you heard the news, Jean? When you heard how he'd died? You can keep moving, but it follows you wherever you go, doesn't it?"

Mrs. Shaw wrestled herself out of his grip and backed away, pointing at him. "You… you stay away from me!" She gave him one last look, then turned tail and ran away in the opposite direction.

Which left Jason alone with the man.

"Hello, Jason," said the older of the two.

Jason didn't reply. He'd been told often enough not to speak to strangers. But wasn't there something about this man, something he recognized, however vaguely? And hadn't he just helped Jason escape from Mrs. Shaw's clutches?

"You've grown so much since the last time I saw you."

Jason wanted to run—should be running away, just like Mrs. Shaw had done. But something was keeping him here.

"You're not afraid of me, are you?" asked the man, coming nearer.

The nod Jason gave was barely a tremble of the head.

"Don't be, I've come such a long way to see you. Probably can't remember me, can you?"

Jason half shook his head, half nodded.

"I'm not surprised. It's been a while. You were still a toddler when I... when I left."

"W-Who are you?" asked Jason.

This time the man gave an answer. "I'm your Dad, Jason. I'm your Dad."

∞☉∞

When a very shaken Mrs. Shaw returned, with the headmaster in tow (he'd already had some harsh words to say to her about abandoning one of their pupils to an intruder) the man had vanished.

Jason was standing in the same spot he had been when she'd run off, but now he had his back to them and was looking down at something.

"Jason?" said, the headmaster, reaching out a hand and pulling it back again.

Jason didn't look; he was concentrating on whatever he had in his hands.

"Jason, are you all right? Did... did that man do anything to you?"

Jason shook his head.

"What's that you've got there?" asked the headmaster, walking around to the front of the boy.

Jason finally looked up, then showed him the object that was in the palm of his hand. "It's a present."

The headmaster picked up the tiny red car and examined it.

"He gave it to me," Jason said. "Said to keep it safe. And he said he would see me again very soon..."

Chapter Eight

Constable Bernard Wilson was lying down on the cot in the cell when they arrived back. A policewoman was trying, unsuccessfully, to get him to take a sip of water. His face was the color of spilt milk.

Robbins indicated with a wrench of the neck that she should leave them alone, which she promptly did.

"Wilson?" asked the DCI. "Care to tell me what happened here?"

Beth pushed past him to check on the PC, feeling his pulse first, then his brow. "His heart's racing, and he's quite hot."

"My heart's racing as well," snapped the detective. "There's a man out there on the loose who's..." He let the sentence evaporate.

"What happened?" asked Beth this time. "Where did your... prisoner go?" She hated using that word, but couldn't think of anything else to call the man. They'd been keeping him here against his will, after all.

Wilson looked at her, his eyes large. "He... he told me things," was all he would say.

"I don't suppose he told you where he was going by any chance? *After* you let him out." Robbins' voice had lost none of its harshness.

Beth scowled at him. "Steve, can't you see he's still in a state of shock?"

"Aren't we all? But we need to find this man and we need to find him right now!"

"You think I don't know that? But this isn't help—"

"He... he told me my aunty and uncle were safe and well. Told me he'd seen them," Wilson interrupted.

"And you let him go because of that? Because he told you he knows your family? Jesus Christ!"

"My aunty died in 1985 of cancer, my uncle ten years later. T-They brought me up." Now it was Wilson's turn to snap.

He sat up and his voice had a chilling edge. "T-Told me things only they could know."

Both Beth and Robbins were silent.

"What did you find in the coffin?" asked Wilson. "He wasn't there, was he?"

Robbins ignored the question, and repeated his own. "Where is he now, Wilson? Do you have any idea?"

"I'm right, aren't I?" said the policeman, but Robbins still didn't answer him. Wilson turned again to Beth. "Who is he, doctor? *What* is he?"

"Right now, he's missing," she replied. "And we need to find him if we're to answer any of those questions."

"Sir?" came a voice from behind. It was the WPC again. "You're wanted on the phone."

"Can't it wait? I'm busy here." Robbins flapped at a fly that was buzzing around his head, making its bid for freedom through the open door.

"It's about the man from this cell," she told him. "There's been a sighting."

∞⊖∞

"I should have seen this coming. Why didn't I send a uniform to keep an eye on the place as soon as I knew he was free?" Robbins banged the steering wheel with the palm of his hand.

Beth, in the passenger seat, stared out the window at the small school they were approaching. The red brick of the building, and gray-slated roof, looked remarkably like her old primary school. "No wonder your stomach is always playing up. Which, by the way, I've told you to get looked at... Listen, you weren't to know this would happen."

"You read the gravestone same as I did: 'Devoted son, husband and *father*'. He'd already visited Mrs. Daley. There was a huge probability he'd try to get in touch with his... with *the* son again. Shit!"

Robbins was still reluctant to recognize the man as Matthew Daley, even after what he'd seen. She recalled the conversation they'd had on the way to the station when he'd asked her for theories. "How about this: Matthew Daley dies, is pronounced, then buried. But he's not really dead."

Robbins grimaced. "What do you mean, not really dead? How can he not be dead when he's had a fucking autopsy?"

"Happens more often than you think," she replied. "Patients even wake up in the middle of autopsies sometimes. Or when they've been buried prematurely. The medical term for it is Catalepsy, where the patient suffers from a form of temporary paralysis and appears dead." *Sleep well*, it had said on the gravestone—and perhaps that's all he had been doing, just sleeping. "The latest thing now is to put a web-cam in the coffin so you can keep checking on the deceased."

Robbins pulled a face. "Beth…"

"Ask Poe, it scared the crap out of him."

"I suppose you'll be saying next that *he's* alive and well and still churning out stories," Robbins said snidely.

"Now you're just being a dickhead."

"Can we just cut to the chase?"

"Okay, so say he does wake up for some reason. Starts banging on the coffin—"

"Nobody would hear him."

"Say that they did," Beth argued. "Say someone dug him up then just put everything back the way it was."

"Why? Why would they do that? And why would he wait until now to come back?"

"I've no idea. You're the detective."

"But the state of him, Beth… How could anyone recover?"

"I don't know. A freak of nature, recuperative powers, something to do with the blood…"

"None of which was picked up in the autopsy."

"Perhaps it was where he worked."

"What's that got to do with anything?"

"Steve, that place was closed down because of all the leaks. God knows what working there for so long might have done."

He waved his hand dismissively.

"At least we have some samples from the coffin. We can work on a DNA match now." And they'd left it at that, not getting any further at all. Now here they were, looking for a man who should have been inside that coffin but wasn't. A man who had come to see his little boy.

They pulled up, the white and orange car following them doing the same. Valentine and Adams waited inside their car while Robbins and Beth got out and went through the school gates, pressing the buzzer at the main door. A secretary opened it and Robbins flashed his ID. They were taken through to an office where the headmaster of the school greeted them with a worried frown. "We've never had an incident like this before," he assured them, "we pride ourselves on keeping the pupils safe."

"I understand," said Robbins. It was difficult to tell from his voice whether he was being sarcastic or not.

"Mrs. Shaw, one of our helpers who drew this to our attention, was very distressed by the whole thing and had to be taken home."

"I'll bet. We'll need to talk to her later, get a statement. Now, if you wouldn't mind…"

The headmaster gave a nod of understanding, taking them through the school where lessons were carrying on as normal that afternoon. "We've put him in the quiet room," the headmaster told them. When Beth and Robbins looked puzzled, he explained, "Oh, it's where the children go if they want to read alone or have some time to themselves."

Inside this quiet room, which was much smaller than the other classrooms they'd seen, a little boy with tousled hair was sitting at a desk. He had a toy car in his hands, turning it over and over. The scene was like Robbins' first encounter with the man back at the station, only in miniature. The boy seemed to have the same mannerisms, even had a look of the man they were pursuing. Robbins crouched down beside him. "Hello…" He looked back over his shoulder at the headmaster.

"Jason," prompted the man.

"Hello there, Jason. I'm Chief Inspector Robbins."

The boy looked at him, then continued to study the toy car.

"Do you think you could answer a couple of questions?"

The boy shrugged.

"That's a nice car, who gave it to you?"

Jason shrugged again. Robbins looked over to Beth for help.

The doctor walked to the desk and pulled out a little chair, sitting down opposite. "Hi Jason, my name's Beth. It's very important that we talk to the man who gave you this. Do you know where he went?"

Jason shook his head. "He didn't say, but I'm going to see him again. He told me that."

Robbins gave Beth a worried look.

"Let me through. Where's my son!" A commotion at the door to the 'quiet' room drew their attention and they turned to see a woman with short black hair pushing her way in, past the headmaster.

"Mrs. Hill, you got the call—" he began, but she ran to Jason and hugged him tightly, checking every inch of him over with her eyes. It was only then that she seemed aware of the other people there. "Who are you two? What were you doing with my son?"

"Please calm down, madam," said Robbins.

"No, *you* calm down. I'll calm down when I find out just what in God's name is going on."

"That might take a bit of explaining," said Beth. "We're not really sure we understand it ourselves."

"I saw Dad today," said Jason before anyone else could speak.

This took the woman aback. "Your Dad? Sweetheart, your Dad's at work. You know that."

"No, he said he was my real dad. What did he mean?"

All the color drained from the woman's face. She brushed a hair out of her son's eyes. "Sweetheart, that's... that's just not possible. Remember, we talked about this before. Your real father... he's not with us anymore."

"But I saw him," Jason insisted.

The woman looked up at Robbins and then Beth, confusion in her eyes.

"I think we need to have a little chat," said Robbins. "Alone."

∞⊙∞

The dead man had watched from a distance. Watched as Robbins and the doctor arrived, accompanied by two uniforms—one of them the black man who'd come for him at the house.

Then he'd seen her arrive on foot. Caroline. Her hair was much shorter than he remembered, but still that raven black, still framing the pretty face he could recall cupping in his hands—so vividly they *had* to be his memories. He couldn't stop the recollections then; they came with a vengeance and he closed his eyes to savor them. The first time they'd met at that café one Saturday afternoon, and he'd looked up from his drink to see her walk in with one of her old girlfriends. They'd exchanged quick glances the whole way through their coffees——he'd actually made his last much longer than usual—until eventually the friend, Sally, noticed and came over to him because it looked like neither of them were going to do a thing about it.

"So, you single?" she'd said getting to the point right away.

"Er... yes."

"So is she. What are you waiting for? She's free tonight."

The inevitable first date complete with nerves, the 'getting to know you' conversations, the first time he'd walked her to her flat, and kissed her lips.

The first time they'd shared a bed, after a party when they'd drunk more than they should have, but not so much they couldn't do anything about it when they got back to her place.

He could feel the movement of her beneath him even now, her hips arching, legs hooking around him as she often did, urging him on with her moans.

Their wedding day, her standing there in that white dress, looking almost... almost like an angel. And when he'd danced with her and looked into those deep blue eyes, he'd known he would love her forever.

Then suddenly he saw the other images again, felt the pain this time—heard the scream, cracking of bone, the blood... saw the light, saw the tunnel...

Snapping his eyes open he noticed Caroline emerge from the school, holding Jason's hand. He almost went to her then, just as he'd been compelled to do before. But for one thing she was crying, and for another she was getting into the back of the squad car, the police about to escort her home.

It wasn't the right time yet. He knew that.

But soon, as he'd told Jason, he'd see them again.

∞Θ∞

"So where do we go from here?" asked Beth as they stood by the car and watched Valentine drive off.

"My superiors will want to try and contain this," Robbins said, not really answering her question.

"That's going to be a bit difficult." Beth leaned on the top of the car. "For starters, we don't know where he is. We don't really know *what* he is."

"He's a problem," said Robbins. "They'll bring in... outsiders. I've seen it happen before."

Beth raised an eyebrow. "You've seen *this* happen before?"

"Not this exactly, but other situations just as serious. I once saw a whole crime squad get muscled out when there was all that terrorism stuff."

"With the best will in the world, Steve, this is not a terrorist threat situation."

"You're right. It's much, much worse. There isn't a handbook about what to do when a dead man comes back and wants to talk to his family."

"So you're accepting the possibility that this could be Matthew Daley now?"

Robbins rubbed his face with his hands. "Oh, I don't know what to think anymore. But I do know we need to find him." He thought for a few moments, then said. "When we get back to the station, I think the best thing you can do is head to the hospital. Do those DNA tests before they bring in a bunch of government scientists I don't know. Get me some answers."

"And what are you going to do?"

"My job," he told her. "I'm the detective, remember?"

Chapter Nine

Caroline Hills poured herself a brandy.

Jason was upstairs in his bedroom, TV blaring. Today hadn't really fazed him at all, but that was kids for you. He spent half his time in a fantasyland anyway. She, however, was still trying to get her head around what she'd been told. It wasn't everyday you found out someone was impersonating your dead husband. Although, hadn't there been something in the Chief Inspector's voice, something in the looks that doctor kept giving him? Like they were holding things back from her. Then she'd pushed for it; pushed for answers which they'd given, eventually. Told her what they knew, told her what had happened over the last couple of days. And it was then that she wished they'd simply kept lying to her. It was then that she felt as if she was losing her mind.

It was like that scene from *Dallas* when Bobby Ewing had turned up in the shower and the previous season had been a dream. Had her life for the last seven years been a dream too? Had the tears she'd cried for months been just a nightmare, had facing life as a single parent just been a hallucination? Had finding someone else, when she thought she'd never love again, been just—

Jesus, what was she going to say to Rob? What could she say when she didn't even understand herself? The words they'd spoken, she'd thought they were a joke at first—kept expecting them all to start laughing at any moment, for a presenter to come out and tell her where the hidden cameras were. In poor taste, but a joke all the same. Yet when she put it together with what Jason had said, that's when it really hit home.

"Why wasn't I told about this before?" she screamed through the tears (though would she have believed it—did she even now?). "I'm still his widow, aren't I?"

But was she? Was she still his widow now that he might be out there somewhere, back from the grave? Caroline gulped the brandy, the fiery liquid scorching her throat, and poured herself another.

She carried it to the window and looked out through the net curtains. The police car was still out front, down the street, in case the man should try to make contact with Jason again. Caroline's hand shook at the very thought of it. If he should come here, if she was to see him...

Forget the fact that he was meant to be at rest—how *would* she feel seeing someone she never thought she'd see again... at least not here on Earth? But even that, what faith she'd boasted had gone, along with her husband, while his mother had been exactly the opposite: her belief was strengthened by the loss of her boy. While Irene had taken comfort in the fact that Matthew would be with God now, Caroline had railed against a deity that would snatch away the man she loved (still loved?) so casually, so cruelly. She would have rung the woman, save for the fact that they'd parted on such bad terms. And as for the fact that Caroline had remarried…

Now, somehow, there was a chance that the man they'd both loved so much was back. (How? How was that possible?) She dropped into a chair and drank more of the alcohol.

And waited for her husband to return from work.

∞☉∞

Robbins spread out the files on his desk, running his hands through his short hair.

He looked at the notes DCI Croft had left behind him, all leading to dead ends. There had been an investigation into Matthew's death, of course there had—the media had demanded it—but it had turned up precisely nothing. In fact, reading this, Robbins couldn't help wondering if it was the pressure he'd been under that had led to Croft's retirement and his eventual heart attack, paving the way for Robbins' transfer and promotion.

But there had to be something here. Some clue, some pattern, some explanation as to what this was all about. As to why Matthew Daley was back.

He shook his head, and not for the first time. No, it couldn't be Daley—*how could* it be Daley?

He let out a tuneless whistle, picking up the photos again. Something Croft had missed and which he must find. Something that would be the key to this whole thing.

Something… something…

Robbins leaned back in his chair and tried not to think about how badly he needed a drink. He reached down and opened the drawer on his right, then took a bottle out.

∞☉∞

It was growing dark by the time Beth returned to the hospital. There were a few messages waiting for her when she got back, some about the shifts she'd traded to take the day off, some about patients she was keeping tabs on, and one from an anesthetist she'd been out for a drink with the previous week and wouldn't leave her alone. Why she'd done it was beyond her now, the guy was a total sleazebag. But he'd asked, and she'd agreed, then spent the whole damned evening wishing she was somewhere else.

As she made her way down the corridor to her office, she said hello to the doctors and nurses she knew—and the porter, Gary. He was wheeling a patient back to his ward after going for a scan.

The lights were off in her office, so when she opened the door she reached around for the switch inside. Beth flicked it, but nothing happened.

"Blast," she said, considering going back out to look for Gary. Then she felt it. There was someone in the room with her. Beth scanned the dark office, the shapes of her filing cabinet, the desk, even the fish tank she kept on the side—the fish helped her to relax—but she could see nothing out of the ordinary. Yet...

She heard breathing, slow and shallow.

"Hello?" she ventured.

The lights came on suddenly and she jumped.

"Dr. Preston... Beth, you have to help me," said the man she'd examined yesterday. He was standing only inches away.

This wasn't like the first time. Now she knew what he was—or thought she did. Not just some oddball prisoner in a cell, but someone whose grave she'd been standing by that very morning. She tried to speak but couldn't get the words out.

"Please," he said. It was the one word she couldn't resist, and somehow he knew it.

"Matthew."

He clapped his hands together and smiled, albeit briefly. "Thank you, thank you."

"For what?"

"For calling me by my name," he said.

She slid sideways along the wall. "It's who you said you were."

"I *still* am," he replied. "That's what I keep trying to tell you people. You know, don't you? You've known from the start."

Beth found herself almost in the corner of her room, and remembered how Wilson had been found. She stopped. "How did you get away this morning, what did you say to PC Wilson?"

"Nothing he wasn't meant to hear." His voice poured ice water over her. "Same as you. Sarah *is* happy, you know. She doesn't blame you."

"Stop it," said Beth, shaking her head. "I don't—"

"It wasn't your fault."

She rounded on him now. "I've heard that from the best counselors around, I don't need to hear it from you!"

"Hear it from someone, hear it from her maybe?"

Beth remembered what Wilson had said about his aunty and uncle. She'd heard enough. "Stop it, stop talking about this right now!"

"I'm sorry," he said.

"How dare you!" Beth's eyes were starting to well up. "How bloody well dare you? You come back here and expect people to just take it in their stride—your mother, you son, your widow—to deal with it like it's something that happens every day of the week. And now we're meant to think you're in touch with…" She couldn't finish her sentence. "I hate to break it to you, but that's not normal. None of this is normal."

"You're upset, I—"

"What do you expect?" She was having trouble staying on her feet now, and he made to help her. "Stay back where you are."

"I should go," he said, half turning.

"No, wait," she replied instinctively. "Let me call Robbins."

"And be locked away again?" He stared at her. "Or worse? I just thought you could help, that's all. I was wrong."

Was it her imagination or was there genuine hurt in his voice? She blinked away another tear, tasting the salt water as it trickled into her mouth. "What is it that you want?"

He hesitated before speaking, then examined a spot on the floor. "I'm seeing things. Things from when I died, I think. But it's all so muddled. I can feel the pain. I can remember bits and pieces and a tunnel of bright light."

She couldn't help laughing at that. "Pretty standard for NDE."

"For what?"

"Near death experience."

He nodded his understanding.

"White light, figures beckoning, then something stops the person from going any further and they come back. Not exactly what happened to you..."

"No," he agreed.

"If you're really who you say you are, then you've been where nobody has before."

"I don't know what to tell you. All of that, all the important stuff is a blank."

"But the fact is you've come back, Matthew. You've come back. The question remains why? And how exactly do we all deal with it?"

"Will you help me to remember?" he asked her.

She chewed on her lip a moment before answering him. "On one condition. You let me take you to Robbins, so he can call off the search."

"I'm not going back to that cell."

"He's not as bad as he seems, you know. And he might be able to help you get to the bottom of this too."

"All right, I believe you," he said finally. "So, where do we begin?"

"Tell me everything you can remember about the night you died," said Beth.

Chapter Ten

The dead man talked for the better part of an hour.

He told Beth what he could remember of the images, the sights, smells and sounds. She listened intently as she'd learned to do in her particular trade, pushing all thoughts about who or what he was to the back of her mind. For a little while at least he was simply another patient, one she wanted to find out more about. One she wanted to help if she possibly could. The talking was as much for her benefit as his, really. But it would take time for him to remember fully, she told him. Things would come back to him in small chunks, when they were good and ready. It was hardly surprising he'd blotted out so much of what was possibly the most traumatic thing that could ever happen to a person. Visual stimuli might help too, perhaps visiting familiar surroundings from that night. But for right now she wanted to get him back to the station, back to Robbins.

Beth led him out of the office and down the corridor. Past the doctors and nurses she'd seen on the way in—his bare feet drawing odd looks and whispers—past the wards of people in bed. The man she called Matthew glanced at them, with a certain amount of sadness. Especially at the ones with eyes closed, heads back on the pillow as if they had already given up the fight.

"You see it every day here, don't you?" he said.

"I'm sorry?"

"Death. People die all the time here."

Beth nodded. "Unfortunately, yes."

They took the stairs rather than the lift, bringing them out onto the floor of the Accident and Emergency department. There was a smattering of people waiting, seated on plastic chairs and looking up at a digital display that repeatedly informed them they would be there for some time.

Beth's charge held back as they entered. "I... something about this place. I remember something," he told her. Then he pointed. "I was here, but not here. I-I was sort of looking down on this."

"Like you were hovering over the scene?"

He nodded sharply. "I was here. This is where they brought me, isn't it?"

Before she could answer, the set of double doors at the far end of A&E burst open and two figures in green wheeled in a stretcher. All eyes turned in this direction, the most excitement they'd had all evening.

"Motorcyclist, got hit by someone pulling out of a junction," they heard the first paramedic state. "He's in a really bad way."

A doctor in a set of blue scrubs came to attend to the patient, then the gurney was wheeled out of sight, away from the people in the waiting room. The man who claimed he was the late Matthew Daley followed, breaking into a run.

"Matthew, no!" Beth wasn't far behind him, reaching out to grab his arm but missing by a mile. The crash team were working on the motorcyclist in a side room and hadn't had time to close the door—they were too preoccupied with trying to save his life. The nurses had cut away the leather of his jacket, and there was blood everywhere. The man's eyes were rolling over white into his head. Matthew was at the doorway looking inside when Beth caught up with him. She tugged at his arm to pull him away, but he didn't see her at all. He was in a trance.

"We're losing him," said the doctor, now holding the paddles of a defibrillator in his hands. The whining sound of the patient flatlining cut through the air. He told everyone to stand back and shocked the motorcyclist. His body jerked, and there was a weak pulse, then he crashed again. The doctor repeated this process three times but it was the same result. "I'm calling it at seven fifty. All in agreement? He'd suffered massive trauma; there was nothing any of us could have done. Have his family been contacted?"

"Come on, we shouldn't be back here," Beth told Matthew.

He shook his head. "No."

Pushing her to one side, he walked into the room. The doctor was so shocked he stood back. One of the male nurses came around the bed, in an effort to stop Matthew's approach, but it was too late. He was next to the motorcyclist and his hands were on the man's chest.

"Someone call security," shouted a female nurse.

The male nurse tried to pull Matthew away, but he shrugged him off. "No, I won't let this happen." He closed his eyes.

"Matthew!" shouted Beth, and the doctor recognized her.

"Dr. Preston? Who is that? What's the meaning of all this?"

There was confusion in the room, lots of voices and shouting. Then a sudden beep sent everyone quiet. It was followed by another... then another. The nurses all looked at each other, then the doctor looked at Beth. "Dr. Preston?"

The noise had drawn a crowd of people from the other rooms and cubicles in A&E, mostly relatives who were sitting with their sick loved ones, but a handful of patients too—their gowns flapping as they tried to get a better look.

"Did you see that?" said one person behind Beth. "He just brought that man back to life."

"You what?" said a late arrival.

"I swear to God. Just laid his hands on him. Doctors had given up."

"Bloody hell."

The beep of the heart monitor was strong and sure. The doctor who'd pronounced the motorcyclist walked slack-jawed towards Matthew and the bed. "What… what did you just do?" The nurse who'd called for security was crossing herself.

"Vitals are stable," said the male nurse, blinking at the monitor.

Matthew stepped back from the bed, retreating to the door. Someone out in the corridor held up a mobile phone and snapped a blurry picture with a mechanical *whir*. Matthew pushed past them all, pushed past a speechless Beth, and began to stagger back off up the corridor. There was a second's lapse, then she followed him again, back out of the department. He was running at a trot, but this time she did catch up with him, grabbing his arm and twisting him around.

"You can't just walk away like that. Hey!"

He faced her. "I-I think I know what happened to me," he told her. "I think I remember."

"Look, we can't stay here now. You're attracting too much attention." Beth looked over her shoulder at the group of people following them: relatives, doctors, patients.

"You're right. I have to go." He pulled away from her and ran out through the double doors into the ambulance bay. The doors flapped back on her as she tried to follow. Beth Preston pushed on them and stumbled out into the night air.

She looked left and right.

But Matthew was gone.

Chapter Eleven

Detective Chief Inspector Steven Robbins yawned.

It had been a long day, a long week, and he hadn't seen much of his bed. The statements, reports and notes on his desk were all merging into one. The photographs, though still disturbing, had now lost much of their power to shock since the first time he'd seen them. The Matthew Daley case would never really be solved until they found the man who claimed to *be* him. Robbins couldn't help smirking at that one; it wasn't every day that the deceased ended up helping the police to solve the mystery of their own murder.

He closed his aching eyes, then rubbed them.

The door to his office opened, the hinges squeaking just like they always did. "Never hear of knocking?" he said, attempting to open his eyes again. The figure before him was out of focus, like the letters on an optician's board when they put in the wrong lens. He screwed up his eyes, and the figure started to take shape. The man was older than Robbins, older than Wilson even. He took a seat opposite and smiled, the lines on his face stretching to accommodate it.

"Make yourself at home," said Robbins.

"Thanks," said the man, "don't mind if I do." He looked around the office, nodding contentedly. "It's changed a bit in here."

Robbins let out a tired breath. "Look, I don't know how you got in, but I'm a bit pushed right—"

The man reached out and picked up one of the reports from the desk. He flipped through it casually. "You're looking for connections where there aren't any," he said. "Frustrating, isn't it?"

"If I wanted the advice of a total stranger then I'd ring one of my ex-wives."

The older man laughed. "But I'm not a *total* stranger, Robbins. You know me."

Robbins studied his face, but couldn't place him. "If we've met before then I can't remember it."

"Ah, well, we haven't exactly met as such. But you know me all the same."

"It's getting late, and I haven't got time for riddles tonight," Robbins said impatiently.

"I've come to give you that one piece of information you're looking for."

A look of enlightenment suddenly dawned on Robbins' face. "You're here to take over, is that it? I'm being replaced? I wondered how long it would be. You're welcome to it, the whole fucking thing. I'm in over my head anyway."

The man chuckled again. "I've done my share and it was enough for me."

"I... I don't understand."

"I'm here to tell you how to solve the case. And to tell you where Matthew Daley is."

"Who are you?" asked Robbins.

The man stretched. "Nice to be able to do that again without the pains in my chest."

"Without the..." Robbins sat up straight in his chair. He shouldn't have been too shocked, though. It wasn't the first dead man he'd encountered this week. "Croft?"

"Bingo. How are you finding my old job? It's a killer, isn't it?" This last line was said in all seriousness.

"You... you're not really here."

"Then where am I? Feels like I'm here." He put his feet up on the desk, pulled a cigarette case out of his pocket, removed one and tapped it on the silver metal. "You got a light?"

"I don't smoke."

"Wise man," said Croft. He held up the cigarette between thumb and forefinger. "I smoked forty of these a day from being a kid. And I used to keep a bottle of scotch in that bottom drawer just there." Croft gestured towards Robbins' side of the desk. "Told myself it was for medicinal purposes. What a load of crap. You were just thinking you could use a belt yourself though, weren't you? Don't suppose there's any still in there?" He flapped his hand. "Naw, what am I thinking. I've been gone too long for that."

Robbins didn't know how to answer him, so he didn't bother; he just reached down and opened the drawer. Robbins produced the bottle of Milk of Magnesia he kept hidden away. Croft let out another long laugh as Robbins took a swig.

"Wasn't quite what I had in mind," said the erstwhile DCI finally. "You know, you should get that stomach sorted out. I left things till the last minute and look what happened."

"It's fine," stated Robbins.

"Ignorance is bliss, eh? We're not that dissimilar, you and I. You're a man after my own heart."

"With the greatest respect," Robbins told him, "I certainly hope not."

Croft took a drag on his cigarette. "I'd imagine it was quite a thing when you realized about Matthew."

"That's one way of putting it. Now, you said you had some information about the case."

Croft smiled again. "Getting straight to it, I like that in a DCI. Very good. Life's too short, if you'll pardon the expression."

"The information," Robbins pressed.

"It doesn't become clear you see... until *afterwards*. Then you know everything. There are no secrets."

"I'm not following you."

"Not yet, no. Matthew's returned to find his peace, Robbins. His was such a sudden passing."

"I know. I saw the pictures."

"I saw the *body*," Croft reminded him.

"You're telling me he's after revenge on the person who did this?" Robbins pointed to the files.

"He's being tested."

"And you know who that person is."

Croft smiled one last time and blew out a stream of smoke. "Things aren't always clear cut, you know. Good and evil are rarely as easy to spot as we think. It's all a matter of judgment."

"Get on with it," snapped Robbins.

"Something's coming, Steven. The world's not going to be the same soon."

"It isn't now," said Robbins. "Tell me."

The phone rang loudly in his ear. Robbins woke with a start on the desk. He looked over at the empty chair opposite.

The ringing persisted and he picked up the receiver. "Robbins."

"Steve, I need to talk to you. I've seen Matthew."

"What?"

"He gave me the slip again, but listen… I think I know where we can find him. I think he's going to return to the place where this all began. The place where he died."

"No, Beth," said Robbins, his nose twitching at the smell of smoke which lingered in the air. "He's going after the person who killed him."

Chapter Twelve

They sat in silence.

Robert Hills was tracing the pattern on the carpet with his eyes. Caroline was nursing her third brandy of the evening. She'd done her best to explain, but it was so difficult.

"There's a police car outside," he'd said as he returned from the bank, then he'd seen her red and puffy eyes. "What's happened? Are you all right?"

Are you all right? It was a good question. Would she ever be all right again after today? "Something happened at school."

"Jason?"

"He's in his room."

Rob began towards the stairs, but she stopped him. "What's happened?" he asked again, his voice cracking. So she took him into the living room and she told him. Just like that. As if she was telling him they'd had a burst water pipe or the microwave was on the fritz. He'd looked at her that same way she'd looked at the detective and the doctor, like she was mad.

"Caroline, Matthew is dead."

"Tell that to Jason," she'd replied, a little too harshly. "Tell that to my son."

"*Our* son," he corrected.

Caroline didn't miss a beat. "He saw him."

"Saw someone who said he was Matthew, you mean."

"He saw... The police have... Rob, they dug up his grave."

"What?" He walked over to the fireplace and leaned a hand on the mantle. "This is ridiculous."

"I know... I know."

"How many of those have you had?" he asked, pointing to the drink.

"What, you think I'm making this up? You think I'm drunk?"

Rob rubbed his eyes. "No, it's just... How can it possibly be your dead husband? It can't be him. People don't just—"

"Come back from the dead?" she finished for him. "No, they don't, do they."

He couldn't say anything to that; they both knew it was impossible. Only here was his wife, the woman he trusted more than anyone in the world, telling him these things. "There has to be some kind of terrible mistake."

"I don't know. I just don't know."

"What did they tell you exactly?"

So she went through what the policeman and doctor had said. How they'd exhumed the body gaining authority because the case was still open on Matthew. How they'd been called to the school after he'd made contact with Jason. Everything. She'd laid it all out for him, and as she spoke it felt like she was explaining the wild plot of some sci-fi film. Caroline wasn't sure how much of it Robert had taken in, or how much she had herself, but when she'd finished he said: "So why are the police still here?"

"In case he comes back," she explained.

"To see Jason, or to see you?"

Caroline's eyes dropped to the floor. He'd slumped down in the chair then, and not said a word since. Now someone needed to speak. If they didn't do it soon Caroline feared they might never speak again. That they might just go about their normal (and what was normal anymore anyway?) lives in total silence from that moment on. "Say something, Rob," she pleaded.

He looked up at her. "What do you want me to say?" His tone was hollow and weird.

She felt the tears welling again and couldn't stop them coming this time. "Say that you love me, and that everything's going to be okay."

Robert said nothing at first, and then her whole body began to shake with sobs. He got up and went to her. She dropped the brandy on the floor as she got up and fell into his embrace. He held her tightly and she continued to cry, both of them with wasted expressions on their faces.

Then he told her that he loved her. That everything was going to be okay.

He meant the first part. Robert Hills had never loved another person the way he loved his wife. But as for the second... he knew that this couldn't have a happy ending, that things would be far from okay from this moment on.

∞⊖∞

He watched them from the shadows on the stairway.

A frozen image for so long, neither of them speaking, neither of them talking. He knew he must have caused it, however indirectly. Beth's words haunted him, just as surely as he was haunting this family: *"You come back here and you expect people to just take it in their stride—your mother, your son, your widow—to deal with it like it's something that happens every day of the week. I hate to break it to you, but that's not normal. None of this is normal."*

Then Caroline, *his* Caroline—but at the same time not—begged the man to say something, to tell her he loved her.

And when she began crying all he wanted to do was burst in and take her in his arms, tell her what she needed to hear, that *he* still loved her—had never stopped loving her in all the time he'd been... away. He even rose slightly. But then the man—Rob, her new husband—had got up and he'd gone to her, taking her in his arms and holding her so close.

That was when the realization finally hit him: although time had barely moved on for him, it had been seven long years for her. She'd had to struggle on without him, had to bring up their child alone. And she'd finally met someone else that she could love. Not the same, never the same, but it was blatantly obvious that she did. He could never turn back the clock and have what he had then.

So he cried too. Cried because this never should have happened, cried because all this had been taken away from him. Cried because none of this had been his fault.

It had been someone else's. Someone who he now felt compelled to visit.

But first, he had something to do.

∞☉∞

The TV was still blaring away from its position on the side unit, even though the light was off and Jason was fast asleep on the bed, covers half over him, half kicked off.

The black and white images on the screen projected themselves into the room—a man and a woman in a graveyard—and he heard tinny voices coming from the speakers. "They're coming to get you Barbara. They're coming..."

He flicked off the set and walked across to the sleeping boy. For precious moments he looked down on the lad, taking in the features. He had his mother's eyes but definitely his father's nose. He bent down to kiss him on the forehead. "Sleep well, son," he said.

Then as he rose he saw the toy car on the bedside table. He stood stock still, staring at it.

Jason rolled over in the bed, and said something, his dream broken. The man withdrew from beside him, just as the boy opened one eye a crack.

Jason thought he saw movement in the corner of the room, thought he'd heard someone talking to him. Not his mum or his 'dad' (his other dad, not his real one). But must have been mistaken; there was nobody here now. Except... except hadn't the TV been on when he'd dropped to sleep?

With tired eyes, he rolled over to the bedside table and reached out for the car that had been given him that afternoon. It was gone. His hand searched the table, fingers like spider's legs on the surface. Jason turned on the bedside light, squinting at its brightness.

His room was empty. Nobody in sight.

With a puzzled frown he sat back against his pillow. And although he wondered where his new toy had gone, it wasn't too long before his eyelids felt heavy again.

Then he settled back down in the bed where he fell back into a long, deep sleep.

Chapter Thirteen

Douglas Knowles was nowhere near drunk enough yet.

But he'd run out of money some time ago, nursing his last short for at least twenty minutes. And the more kindly patrons of *The Bull's Head* would only stand you so many rounds without seeing any bought back in return. Sometimes Phyllis the barmaid would let him finish off the last dregs of drinks that had been left by punters, but not tonight. Tonight she was being watched very closely by the landlord after he'd found a fiver missing out of the till.

(It had actually dropped down the side when she'd been putting it in the register, but neither of them would find it until the following morning when the cleaner came in. That didn't help Phyllis right now. And it didn't help Douglas either.)

So he had no choice but to return home, or the dingy little one bedroom flat he called home. He kidded himself that maybe he'd find a bottle or two of unopened spirits in there somewhere, but he knew he'd finished off whatever he'd had in the flat when his benefits had first gone in.

He hadn't resorted to drinking that bottle of meths yet. The one he'd bought originally to clean his brushes when he'd thought about redecorating. That had been after the last time he'd gone to AA, turned over a new leaf—yet again—in an effort to encourage Jane to let him see his two daughters. It hadn't worked, neither coming off the booze, nor convincing his estranged spouse. Tonight might just be the night he tried that meths. It depended on how desperate he was when he got back in. He looked at his watch, a cheap digital one with fading numbers.

Christ, it was only just turned ten. He'd be home by ten thirty, and then what? A night of not being able to sleep ahead of him, a night of remembrance when all he wanted to do was get completely smashed and forget everything. Not have to deal with reality.

It hadn't always been like this. He could remember the better days, the great days—when he had a good job working for an insurance firm, when Jane had looked up to him and the kids weren't ashamed to be seen with Daddy. He'd had a career with flexible hours, a nice car—

But then the problem had slowly crept up on him. At first it was only social drinking when he met up with clients. It was okay, he told himself, he'd gone out and got hammered most nights when he was younger, before Jane had come along, so he could handle a few every so often now. The only thing was that 'every so often' became more and more frequent. Slowly but surely the drinking started to take over his life. He began to crave that fix, the warm tingling you got whenever you were getting nicely merry. Some of his friends in the trade even slipped him soft drugs now and again; nothing hard, he insisted on that, just some coke or cannabis. What could it hurt? What harm could it do?

Plenty.

Especially that one night, the night he'd been at a late dinner with a couple of colleagues. Jane was at her folks with the kids that week for the holidays so he was in no rush to get back, not that it would have bothered him anyway. So it ended up being gone twelve when he'd climbed into the car, more than a little the worse for wear after two bottles of wine between them, some cocktails, and a few trips to the bathroom. One of the men had suggested taxis, but the other insisted that taxis were for suckers and why should he pay twenty quid to get back home when he had a perfectly good Audi sitting in the all night multi-storey across the road.

Sadly, Douglas had sided with him.

They'd said goodnight and gone their separate ways, Douglas climbing into the front seat of his souped-up maroon Sierra. Once out of the city, he'd taken the dark and lonely back roads to avoid any police traps that might be waiting for him—he wasn't that stupid! He'd enjoyed the drive, slipping in one of his favorite CDs and just cruising along the country roads that would skirt the town where he lived and take him into the suburbs. Take him home. He'd opened her up a little then, singing along to the rock tracks and pretending he was in one of those adverts where he had the whole road to himself.

Then it had happened. He'd just about negotiated a hard bend and skidded inside, skidding almost into the wall of the tunnel he'd entered. Douglas fought hard to control the steering, but his reactions were terrible. And then…

Douglas shook his head as he'd done so often in the intervening years. It never did any good; the memories always came back to him. He remembered making it back home, putting the car away in his garage. He locked up and staggered around the side of the house, then just about made it inside to the bathroom to throw up, before carrying a bottle of vodka to bed with him for comfort. It had taken most of the bottle to put him out and when he woke the next morning, he'd thrown up again on the floor. Not all of it down to the drink. It was as he'd been straining that the events of the previous night came back to him. Afterwards he realized he had a decision to make; there wasn't the luxury of time on his side. Now he was sober Douglas considered doing the right thing, but then he'd lose everything he'd spent so long building up over the years. The fact that he was on the verge of losing it anyway didn't really register. Then he thought about the people he knew in the trade, some less law-abiding than others. People he'd done favors for, fixed claim forms for. They owed him, and if ever he needed to cash in those favors it was now.

He'd picked up the phone and made a few calls.

By the time everything was splashed over the papers he was in the clear. The car was put to rights quickly and sold on through some disreputable dealer using fake documents. It wasn't unusual for him to swap his car as often as his underpants, not in his line of work, so no one blinked twice when he acquired a new one.

But when Jane returned with the kids nothing was the same. She'd started nagging him even more about the booze, the restless nights.

"What's got into you these days?" she shouted at him that final evening when the girls were in bed.

"Leave me alone," he said as he turned his attention back to the drinks cabinet. "Just leave me alone."

"Not until you answer my question," she'd persisted, grabbing his arm.

He'd only meant to shrug her off, but she'd tumbled backwards and almost banged her head on the coffee table.

Douglas made a move towards her, to help her up. "Jane, I'm—"

She slapped his hand away, eyes filled with hatred. Jane rose and stormed off to the bedroom, calling back, "I'll leave you alone all right!" Then he heard the door slam and knew that she'd locked it from the inside.

The next day she left and took the kids with her. Her solicitor demanded that the house be sold and that she get most of the profits. He hadn't argued. Most—if not all—of the fight had gone out of him. Problem was, that meant he'd lost his edge at work as well. Within nine months he went from virtually running the place to losing his job completely.

The government forced him to look for jobs, but he always screwed something up and was sacked. In the end they stopped hassling him, realizing that he was, over time, building up a resumé that made him virtually unemployable. Now he just went down, signed on, did the courses they sent him to— the last one was something about spreadsheets—and he drew his money, most of which went to Jane and the kids, the rest on the essentials of life. Or *his* life at any rate.

Which was how he came to be there, climbing the steps of the block of flats because the lift wasn't working (and someone had taken a shit inside it anyway). How he came to open the door and find someone waiting for him. Someone he recognized, but his brain told him that the man couldn't— *shouldn't*—be sitting in his torn second-hand chair with the wooden arms, so when Douglas turned on the light the man almost frightened him senseless.

"You... you..." said Douglas, his hand outstretched and quivering.

"Yes," said the man. "Me."

"I-I'm imagining this. It's the drink."

"Always the drink," said the man in the chair.

Douglas rubbed his eyes, scrubbed at them, in fact. The apparition was still there. He looked slightly different, that was true—hair a bit longer and more unkempt—but there was no mistaking that face. It was the one Douglas saw every night when he woke up in a cold sweat; the face his mind had recorded that night as he'd swerved to avoid hitting the wall of the tunnel, only to hit something, some*one* instead.

It was the face of the man he'd killed seven years ago.

∞ʘ∞

"I still don't understand. How do you know where to go?" Beth asked again. Robbins had answered the first time with a "You wouldn't believe me if I told you."

"I got a tip-off," said the DCI at last, letting the wheel slip through his fingers as he turned into a side road.

"From who?"

"That's not important, but... I believe what he said." Robbins had considered telling her about the conversation he'd had with his dead predecessor, but decided against it. If he began to go through it, he might just start to believe it wasn't just some bizarre dream. You could sleepwalk, why not sleep-smoke? The fact that he hadn't had any cigarettes on his person didn't come into it. "Just go through it again, what happened back at the hospital," he urged her.

She patiently explained about how 'Matthew' had been waiting for her when she got back, how they'd talked about the night of his accident and his hazy recollections. Then she related the incident in the Casualty Department. "I think something about the biker must have jolted his memory. They were in similar states."

"But you say he brought the man back to life?"

"That's what it looked like, at least. Davison, the doctor in charge, had called it. They'd given up the ghost."

Robbins pressed his foot down on the accelerator and they shot forward over a roundabout. "They might just have made a mistake."

"It's possible," Beth admitted. "But you had to have been there."

"I would have been if you'd called me."

"I was bringing him *to* you. He would have bolted if I'd rung you first."

"As opposed to what he did anyway?"

Beth hugged herself. "I did what I thought was right, Steve."

He looked over at her briefly, then returned his eyes to the road.

Beth waited for the apology she knew would never come. Instead he said, "So what's the conclusion about him then? Any more theories?"

"Plenty, but all crazy. Right now I'm thinking, what if Matthew's got some kind of virus."

"What, you mean he's sick? I thought you said he had a high immunity."

"What if that's part of the disease? Something that makes you well. Better than well, in fact. What if it can bring you back from the dead?" Robbins gave a half laugh and before he could dismiss what she was saying, she continued: "It would explain the weird results from his blood test. Think about it, a disease that can regenerate dead tissue. That can restart a dead person's heart, make the blood flow again in their veins."

Robbins' eyes narrowed. "That's just—"

"Ludicrous? More ludicrous than a man who's been dead for seven years turning up on his own mother's doorstep? More ludicrous than opening his coffin and—"

"All right, all right. I get the picture," said Robbins. "If what you're saying turns out to be true—"

"And we won't know that until more tests are done," she broke in.

"Right, but if it is… it really will be the discovery of the century, the millennium."

"Ah, so now you *do* care." She smirked. "Steve, it'll be the discovery of the last two millennia," said Beth, looking over at him. "Not that I'm going to get into the whole science versus religion thing, but you do realize what time of year it is, don't you?" He caught her eye for a moment, then they broke it off. They drove the rest of the way in silence, the inference hanging heavy in the air. And with the question still unanswered:

who had passed this condition on to Matthew in the first place?

∞Θ∞

"Why don't you come inside and shut the door?" said the dead man. "We have things to talk about, you and me."

Douglas Knowles was freeze-framed in the entranceway. The words broke whatever spell was holding him there and for a second he found himself doing as he was bid, walking slowly inside. Then he stopped again.

Douglas was still staring at the man, unable to properly take in what was happening—or to grasp that it might be real. The last time he'd seen that face it had been through his wind-screen, cracking the glass, panicked and bloody. (A scene his mind had recorded especially for him to play back the high-lights.) Then as a dark lump in his rearview mirror after he'd finally screeched to a halt. Douglas had been breathing heavily, eyes flicking up to his mirror, then back down at the white knuckles clenching the wheel, his wedding ring digging into the third finger on his left hand. Rock music was belting out from the speakers, the soundtrack of this particular night-mare... and many more to come. Part of him had wanted to get out of the car and go back to see if the man was all right, but a larger part told him he didn't need to see that—if he drove away he might just get away with it. So before he knew what he was doing, he'd put the engine, still idling, into gear. He was bringing his foot off the clutch, finding the biting point; moving off, away from the scene.

There were no other cars around, no houses, just a road that led up to the chemical plant where the man must have been walking from, facing oncoming traffic just like you were supposed to do. But Jesus, how was Douglas supposed to see him in a pitch black tunnel like that? Even if he hadn't been trying to swerve to avoid the wall he might still have hit him. It had been an accident, that's all. An—

"Accident?" said the man, now rising. "An accident!"

"Y-Y-Yes," said Douglas, although there was hardly any conviction in his voice.

"You didn't even bother to report your 'accident.'" His tone was unforgiving. "I had to wait to be found. There might have been a chance if—"

"Get out of my head," said Douglas, closing his eyes and backing away.

"You still don't understand, do you?"

When Douglas opened his eyes again the dead man was standing inches away, grabbing him by the wrists.

"I'm real, Doug. This isn't one of your guilt dreams. I'm not the Ghost of Christmas Past. I'm here, in the flesh."

Douglas shook his head. "No, no!"

"I lost everything that night. Missed seeing my son grow up. And now my wife, she's…" He let the sentence tail off. "All because of you and your *accident*."

Douglas tried to wrestle out of his grip but couldn't manage it. "I-I didn't mean to—"

"You had a choice that night; I had none," said the dead man. "See… *feel* what I felt!" The dead man shoved something into Douglas's hand, a toy. A small child's car.

Suddenly Douglas experienced that night in a way he never had before. He was the one who'd set out to walk home after his shift, who'd been in that tunnel when he'd seen the light. Who'd felt the force of the car, doing almost 50 miles an hour on that bend, ploughing into him. His legs no match for the metal of the bonnet. He felt the agonizing pain as the bones broke in several places, as his hip cracked and he went tumbling over that same bonnet. Heard the music coming from inside, the loud thumping of the stereo. Saw the knuckles on the steering wheel, looking up to gaze into his own shocked face behind the wheel—the pair of them becoming intertwined in that moment. Then the rest of the 'accident' was filled in for him, spinning over the roof, his shoulder coming out of its socket, then back down onto the boot and finally colliding with the rough concrete of the road, raking his skin, shredding his thighs, blood pouring from him freely, nose breaking and splintering with the fall. He blinked once, his vision blurred, then again. Everything was black but he couldn't tell whether it was the darkness of the tunnel or that he was losing consciousness. And it hurt so much. He couldn't move a muscle. It hurt so much he actually prayed for death to come because then it would end. But he still managed to mutter one thing: "You'll... you'll see me again."

"Do you understand?" shouted the dead man, pressing him up against the balcony wall.

Douglas was crying now, and spit ran from his mouth. "Please... please... stop."

"You took my life away from me. Now—"

"Now," he blurted through the tears. "Now what? Now you're here to do the same, to take it away from me?" Douglas found hidden reserves from somewhere, his voice becoming stronger. "So do it. What do I have to live for now anyway?"

The dead man looked him squarely in the eyes, those tired eyes desperate for sleep. A sleep denied him by the drink. He looked back over his shoulder at the place where Douglas now lived. Was it enough, this punishment? How could he weigh it against what he had been through?

It was a decision, a choice only he could make.

And so he made it.

Chapter Fourteen

On approach it looked like a bird.

Robbins pulled up outside the block of flats just as the body fell. It seemed to drop forever, coat flailing behind like a pair of wings. Then right at the last minute it speeded up, like one of those slick shots in a TV show. It hit the ground with all the grace of a safe landing on a cartoon character's head.

That is to say, it would have hit the ground had there not been something there to break its fall.

The body slammed into the roof of the middle car of three, parked just opposite and further down from them. The battered old Metro—nobody had decent wheels around there——crumpled up as if it had been placed in a decompression chamber, metal and glass folding itself around the shape that had fallen from the balcony above. They gaped at the wreckage, not one of them knowing quite what to do next. Then Robbins said, "Shit! We're too late."

They got out of the car, but still stood staring at the crushed roof of the vehicle. It was Beth who moved first, her instinct being to try and save whoever this was who'd plummeted the seven floors from above. Except as she got there, Robbins radioing for an ambulance as she did, she realized what a waste of time that would be. The man's face, white apart from the occasional dash of red, was pretty much intact: it was only his eyes that gave away his state, rolling back into his head like two boiled eggs. As for the rest of him, it was difficult to tell where the flesh stopped and the metal began. Both were twisted and intertwined, his limbs—for she could see it was a man now—were bent into the most awkward of positions. His legs were shooting out at bizarre angles, the bottom halves, below the knee, bending back like a contortionist's. His arm had split wide open at the elbow joint and there was bone protruding through, while his left hand, having been severed by the glass of the Metro's window, was dangling—almost off—by the tendons. Something dropped out of that hand onto the ground: a red toy car.

Beth reached into the hulk, scratching her hand on a piece of sharp metal as she did so. Robbins' face soured when she pressed her fingers to the man's neck. She turned to him and shook her head. The DCI followed the diver's descent again, looking up to see another figure on the balcony where he'd fallen. Beth saw it too. This time Robbins called for backup.

"Matthew," she said out loud, "what have you done?"

They wasted valuable moments trying the lift in the block of flats, then were forced to race up the stairs.

Turning on to the floor that contained the flat they were looking for, they fully expected the figure to be gone by now. But he wasn't; he stood there looking down on the scene below, both hands on the balcony rail. The door to the flat was open behind him.

They approached him slowly, cautiously. Robbins spoke first, telling him to keep his hands where he could see them.

"You think I did this," said the man. It wasn't a question.

"I don't see anyone else around here," said Robbins.

"Matthew," said Becky, "why?"

He turned then to answer her. "It wasn't up to me to judge him, he knew that."

"What the hell's that supposed to mean?" asked Robbins.

The man didn't say any more, and he offered no resistance when Robbins took him by the arm, cuffed him, and started to lead him away. "We'll take him back to the station," he said to Beth, "but I've no idea what will happen after that."

Beth leaned over the balcony and looked down at the fall. She shut her eyes when she thought what that man had just been through. Then she followed Robbins and Matthew back down the stairs again. By the time they reached the street an ambulance had arrived, and the police. Robbins pushed his prisoner's head down as he deposited him in the back of a squad car. The residents of the flats, all used to minding their own business, came out through their doors to look when they heard the sirens. The owner of the car was screaming about insurance and asking who was to blame. (Ironically, in his heyday Douglas Knowles would have been able to point her in the right direction.)

More white and orange vehicles were arriving now and Robbins knew that this could go on well into the early hours of the morning. Statements would need to be taken, the body disentangled and taken away.

Beth joined him again. "What about Matthew? What about who, *what* he is?"

"Tomorrow," the DCI said softly, chewing on an antacid tablet. "We'll talk about all that tomorrow."

Chapter Fifteen

He'd sat with Irene Daley that night until she'd finally dropped to sleep.

They'd prayed and read from the Bible together, but Father Lilley was extremely concerned about her. It wasn't so much the stress of the last few days, although it was clear that had taken its toll. She was a shadow of herself, having barely eaten in all that time. But no, it was more the way her mind was working now. She was having dangerous thoughts about the person who had shown up at her doorstep and couldn't possibly be Matthew.

"But father, what if—"

"Irene, he is not your son. He *can't* be. You said yourself."

"And the grave?"

He shook his head. "I don't know, I can't explain it. But I do know that Matthew is with Our Savior right now, not walking this earth."

He firmly believed it. That *thing* might look and sound like Matthew, but it certainly wasn't the boy he confirmed, the man he'd listened to as he confessed. The man he'd put in the ground while his family stood around the graveside: a grave now thoughtlessly desecrated because of the *creature* pretending to be him. The more Lilley himself pondered on it, the more convinced he became that this person—if indeed he was a person at all—was here for the most wicked of purposes.

Already it was infecting Irene Daley's mind, and was in the process of convincing others that it *was* Matthew. He looked to the good book—as always—for help and guidance, references to the Devil, how he might send his minions back to wreak havoc.

'And as ye have heard that the antichrist shall come, even now are there many antichrists' John 2:18.

Had Matthew's body been invaded by a demon or ungodly spirit? Lilley hadn't ever performed an exorcism and wasn't about to start now.

As he sat downstairs in Irene's house, the dawn about to break on this another day, he looked at the photograph of mother and son together. Lilley wondered how his own father, the staunch Catholic who had instilled in him all that was right and good, might have dealt with such a challenge of faith. He thought he could almost hear the man's voice telling him what to do then. Lilley nodded. It was time for him to become a soldier of God himself, to become the Lord's right hand.

He *had* to stop this evil from spreading. And there was only one way he could think of to do it.

∞Θ∞

The phone in Robbins' office hadn't stopped ringing all morning, and by midday he had his orders. The case was being taken out of his hands and the man they were holding with relation to the death of one Douglas Knowles was to be transferred to a secure facility for questioning. The further tests Beth had wanted to perform would also be handled by 'more experienced' government doctors, Robbins was told. Arrangements would also be made at some point to move Knowles' body from the local hospital.

"See," he told her when he finally emerged. "Just as I thought."

"They can't do that. What's going to happen to him?"

He looked her in the eye and said seriously, "I don't know, but you can't charge a dead man with murder, Beth."

Wilson, now back at work but refusing to go anywhere near the cells, drew their attention to the television in the corner. Several officers were gathered around it, listening to the report. Becky recognized a pixilated picture of Matthew from the hospital, the newscaster telling the world about the miracle recovery of motorcyclist Phil Barnes. There was also some confusion as to who exactly the man in the photo was, although the likeness to a 'hit and run' accident victim from seven years ago was definitely uncanny.

"It'll only be a matter of time before they link it with the exhumation and what happened last night," Robbins said.

By two o'clock that afternoon the police station was besieged with reporters and TV crews, and the internet was awash with rumors about Matthew.

Becky observed the crowds gathering outside. "It's going to be hard for anyone to keep all this quiet now."

An unmarked van arrived for their guest at four. Robbins was to give it an escort of squad cars until it reached the motorway, then the whole thing would be out of their hands. When Robbins and Beth went down to the cells, where he was under constant surveillance by three police officers, the man was still not speaking. He hadn't said a thing since the balcony.

"Time to go," Robbins told him.

As Valentine and WPC Adams led the man out of the cell, he paused when he caught Beth's eye. "Don't worry, you'll see her again," he told her.

Robbins watched him go. "What did he say? See who?"

Beth fought back a tear. "Doesn't matter."

They walked with him to the back door of the station, opening it up to see the van there in the car park, waiting. But even before they'd reached the second step at the entranceway a deluge of people started piling in behind the van. Someone had tipped them off and the news people weren't about to miss the biggest scoop of the year, if not the decade.

They all took notice of him now: the dead man. The people there saw him walking. Soon the whole world would see it too.

Robbins barked at the uniforms on either side of him, telling them to get more men out for crowd control. The plain-clothes officers driving the van backed up when they saw what was rapidly turning into a mob. There was total and utter confusion. Cameras flashed, Dictaphones were pushed through.

And there, at the back, Robbins saw her—short dark hair, craning her neck along with the other people to see who had gathered here today: Caroline Hills. He turned to see that the man they had in cuffs had noticed her, too. A look passed between Caroline and the person who so resembled the husband she had lost, and Robbins almost felt sorry for him. But then the DCI was being jostled to one side and more policemen were emerging from the station to deal with the numbers.

"Can we just ask—"

"Where are you taking—"

"What connection he has to—"

"What you found at Westmoor Cemetery—"

The gaggle of voices was terrific, so much so that they wove themselves into one loud hum.

Then it happened.

Beth spotted it first and grabbed Robbins' shoulder. There, in the crowd, was a hand clutching a gun. It was an old-fashioned type of pistol, nothing that might be used on the streets today—more like a relic from a museum. Robbins doubted whether it would even fire.

But it did. Three loud bangs.

He saw the man in cuffs go down, two bullets hitting him hard. Then Robbins felt a pain in his own arm, as he dove across to try and shield Beth. If there was confusion before, then there was mass panic now that the shots had rung out. Robbins tried to shout out to his men: apprehend the shooter; secure the area. But the plainclothes officers from the van had already pulled their own guns, which caused even more hysteria.

Robbins clutched at his arm and his hand came away red. Then Beth was there, examining the wound.

She told him to keep the hand on it and apply pressure. "You silly sod," Beth whispered, and kissed his forehead, before checking on the other injured party. She scrambled along the floor to where he'd fell.

But when she got there she found nothing. No body, no Matthew.

Nothing except a patch of blood where he'd lay, spreading out like wings on the concrete floor.

Chapter Sixteen

The next few days were just as confused as that afternoon.

For a while the news had concentrated fully on what had happened: about Matthew, about who he might be, about where he might have gone after the assassination attempt, about his revenge on the man who had 'killed' him. It was discussed on every message board and talk show, theologians offered their opinions and scientists expounded on what Beth had already suggested. But there was no proof, no concrete evidence of anything. So rationality soon began to reign. If nothing else it was a diversion, a curiosity along the lines of raining fish and the Yeti. Certainly nowhere near as exciting as reading about which politician was having an affair or which celebrity had suddenly been diagnosed with bulimia.

Then, just as Croft had predicted, the world began to change.

The first thing that happened was that Phil Barnes, the motorcyclist Matthew had apparently brought back from the brink of death, got up from his hospital bed and went for a walk himself. The nurses thought he was going to the toilet, a good sign that he was recovering even more. But he wasn't. Phil was going down into the morgue.

He walked past the attendant in charge, who was listening to *Nessun Dorma* on his ipod at the time, as if he hadn't even seen him. The man asked him exactly what he thought he was doing and Phil simply replied:

"They're asleep, that's all. Just asleep."

Then he pulled open the freezer drawers and woke them up, one by one: men, women and children. In no time at all, the morgue was filled with reanimated corpses and the attendant had collapsed on the floor in a dead faint. He was used to cadavers making noises—groaning and farting as he moved them—but not used to them climbing out of their drawers. The last person to be woken was in quite a bad condition. His limbs were broken and he was still scarred, bruised and cut from the fall.

However, when he looked down on himself, Douglas Knowles found that he was entirely healed, that his body was as good as… no, *better* than new. Life surged through him, the blood pumping in his veins full of vitality. The last thing he could remember was being on that balcony. When the man he'd killed refused to put him out of his own misery, he'd suddenly been overcome with a sense that there was no point in going on. And he owed the person standing there some kind of justice. That was when he decided to throw himself off.

He smiled. It was a miracle.

"Come on," said Phil, showing the others a way out of their resting place, up into the light.

In his hospital bed, recovering from being shot and being treated for the 'full house' of ulcers they'd now found in his gut, DCI Robbins saw the strange procession go past. And saw Knowles tagging on at the end. But he put it down the strong medication he was on, just as he had the return visit from Croft.

"I can't stand these places," he'd told him, eating Robbins' grapes, "they remind me of the time I had my heart attack."

He'd mention it to Beth the next time he saw her.

But Beth would have other things on her mind entirely by then.

∞Θ∞

That night, Dr. Beth Preston was down in the lab—going through blood samples she'd squirreled away while she was still able to—when she was interrupted in her work by a child calling out her name.

She rose from the microscope slowly, then nearly lost her balance, clutching onto the desk for support and knocking over the vials.

"Hiya Bethany," said the little girl in front of her. She was the only one who'd ever called her by her full name.

"S-Sarah?" She shook her head, not trusting the evidence of her own eyes. "Sarah, is it really you?"

The girl with long golden locks ran over and hugged her. "Course it is, silly. Who else?"

Beth's hand wavered, then it found the child's back and she hugged her tight. The girl felt as real as anyone she'd ever met, as solid as... well, as solid as Matthew had been. Tears were tracking down the doctor's cheeks, and she could taste saltwater on her lips.

"It's... it's so good to see you," Beth told her.

"It's good to see you, too. I was getting bored of waiting."

In spite of herself, Beth laughed. She held Sarah by the shoulders and bent down. "I don't understand any of this."

"You're not meant to," Sarah said. "Not yet. But you will." She took Beth's hand and began to tug it.

"Where are we going?"

"You'll see."

Beth hung back. "Hold on, Sarah. I have to say something."

Sarah looked puzzled. "Can't it wait?"

"No," said Beth, shaking her head. "Not really."

Sarah looked up and nodded.

"I'm sorry," said the doctor.

"What for?"

"You know, for what happened."

The penny dropped and Sarah suddenly grinned. "Oh *that*. It's okay, it wasn't your fault."

"But if I'd picked it up earlier then maybe—"

"It was *meant* to happen, Bethany," Sarah told her. "There was no way you could have known about the clot." She tittered. "Sounds like cream, doesn't it?" When Becky didn't join in, Sarah said, "Could've happened anytime."

"But I'm a doctor, I should've seen the signs—"

Sarah put a finger to her lips. "It made you a better one. Think about all the good you've done. Now," she said seriously, "we've really got to go, there are things to do."

It was Beth's turn to be puzzled. "What things?"

"You'll see."

"Wait." Beth pulled her back again. "I need to tell you one last thing."

Sarah sighed. "Kay."

"I love you."

Sarah beamed. "I love you too, sis. Now let's go." She pulled on Beth's hand and led her out of the lab.

∞Θ∞

These weren't the only occurrences.

All around the country, all over the globe, people were seeing the dead. Not ghosts, but living, breathing human beings—of a kind. Mrs. Shaw, the school helper, woke up from yet another troubled sleep only to see the figure of young Oliver at the foot of her bed, burn marks from the rope still around his neck. Terrified, and thinking she'd brought the images from her nightmare into the real world, she tried to wake her husband. But he just kept on snoring beside her.

Oliver held out his hand for her to take it, and she felt compelled to do so...

Across town Thomas Valentine was shocked to see that his best friend from college, Martin Raines, who had drowned during the Tsunami disaster in Sri Lanka, was playing computer games on the X-Box in his living room. Meanwhile WPC Trisha Adams' discovered that her Granddad, who'd passed away from a stroke when she was only a little girl, had come to visit offering her a bag of those sticky toffees he always used to bring.

And as PC Frank Wilson was sitting down to eat breakfast, he found that his Uncle Ted and Auntie Rita, the couple who had taken him in as a child and brought him up as their own, were suddenly in the room with him. Ted was making himself a cup of coffee and Auntie Rita was asking him if there was any toast left. He was scared and happy at the same time, but he wasn't really surprised. After all, the dead man in the cell had told him he would see them again soon.

∞⊖∞

In the cold, damp cellar he waited.

It wasn't comfortable: he was hungry and he couldn't feel his hands now, but he had to wait it out. What he'd done had been right, of that he had no doubt. But the authorities wouldn't see it that way. They'd probably been to search for him already, though he doubted whether they'd find this hiding place—used to protect the faithful during the blitz when the bombing had been fierce. Why, they'd even held services down here.

Smiling, he patted the instrument he'd used to rid the earth of that monstrous creation. His father's trusty old service revolver, given to his mother after the great man's death. It had been used back then in the name of good, fighting the forces of evil, and he'd put it to use in much the same way.

Father Lilley struck a match and lit the altar candle he'd brought down with him. He wished to consult the good book once again. But in the half-light he saw something stirring there. A shadow at the back of the cellar.

"Who's there?" he asked, snatching up the revolver.

The shadow drifted closer and, in spite of himself, Lilley let off another bullet.

"Put that thing down, right now," said the voice, stern but with genuine feeling. "Put it down before you hurt anyone else."

Lilley recognized the voice, but it couldn't be who he thought it was. "Father?"

The Captain, still in uniform, walked over towards him shaking his head. "Gerald, what did you think you were doing?"

"This isn't real," gibbered Lilley. "It's a trick, the Devil's work."

"He has been at work, yes, but not here. Not today. It was not me who told you to shoot that man." His father, the moustache he sported twitching, reached forward and took the gun from him.

"Our father who art in Heaven—" began Lilley.

"Not anymore," said his own father, seriously.

"Begone demon. I smite thee from the Earth!"

The army man picked up the bible and leafed through it. "You're so fond of quoting these passages, Gerald. Here's one for you: 'And I saw the dead, small and great, stand before God; and the books were opened: and another book was opened, which is the book of life, and the dead were judged out of those things which were written in the books, according to their works. And the sea gave up the dead which were in it, and death and hell delivered up the dead which were in them: and they were judged, every man according to his works.'"

Lilley's face froze. "The Book of Revelation."

His father nodded. "The immortal body is real, Gerald. And yet that same body can pass through an object, or pick up the object." He looked down at his old gun. "They also have none of the defects they had in life."

Lilley was shaking. His father grabbed him by the hand and started to drag him up the stairs to the hidden door beneath the altar itself. "No!" screamed Lilley. "It can't be."

The soldier dragged Lilley out into the church and forced him to look through the window. There, in the graveyard, were the dead. Each one standing next to the grave they had risen from, the soil on top untouched (in fact the only hole there was at Matthew Daley's plot). Their clothes ranged from the quite recent, to centuries old. All were looking at him, all were pointing.

"Now do you understand, Gerald? Around the world, those who have died in conflicts like mine—those who are *still* dying—they are coming back, too."

Lilley grabbed the gun off his father and placed it against his head. Before the Captain could do anything, the trigger had been pulled and the last bullet punched a hole in Lilley's skull. To the priest's own amazement, though, he didn't fall down. He dropped the weapon and touched the wound in the side of his head, looking at the disgusting mess on his fingers.

His father went to the font and dipped a cup into the water, bowing his head at the stained glass image of Christ above him. The he returned to his son and washed away the blood on his scalp. The hole was gone.

"'And immediately there fell from his eyes as it had been scales: and he received sight forthwith, and arose, and was baptized.' That's Acts Nine, Eighteen, Gerald," said the man.

Lilley started to cry. "I'm so sorry. I didn't know."

The Captain held him for a moment, then pulled away. "It's time to go, boy."

He placed a hand on his son's back and led him out of the church. Lilley turned and looked up at his much younger father. "Will I be spared for my foolish actions?" he asked.

The Captain didn't reply. He just carried on walking, the dead from the graveyard following them both on their way up the road.

Epilogue

Irene Daley woke from the deepest sleep she'd had in years. She could remember the priest being here, them praying and discussing Matthew. And then she must have fallen asleep, except she had the vaguest recollection of trying to wake up and not being able to. She looked at the clock by the side of her; it was just gone nine. But the date must have been wrong on it, because according to that she'd been in bed the past few days.

There was a knocking at the door downstairs. It was probably Father Lilley back again to tell her what was happening. She got up, feeling none of the usual aches and pains that came with age. No cracks of the knees, no arthritis, which was always wicked first thing in the morning. In fact she felt better than she ever had in her life.

Pulling on her dressing gown she went downstairs. There was a shadow waiting there and she hesitated, flashing back to that morning almost a week ago. But something told her not to be afraid this time, something told her to open the door.

So she did.

And it was like a replay of before: There was the man who'd looked so much like Matthew, who she now knew *was* Matthew, only he'd been changed, just like she herself had been changed. And it was time to go somewhere, she knew that as well, although she had no idea how.

"Hello Mum," said Matthew.

Instead of passing out this time, instead of being afraid, lashing out, she put her arms around him and kissed him on the cheek. "Welcome home, son," she whispered, her eyes watering. "I'm sorry. I'm really sorry."

"It's okay," he assured her. "None of that matters now anyway."

"We have to go, don't we?"

He nodded. "I was allowed to come and get you. But yes, they're waiting."

"*Right,*" *she said. Irene shut the door behind them and was about to lock up when she realised how daft that would be. She took her son's arm and he walked her down the path. Birds were flying overhead—huge birds, almost humanlike—and it was a beautiful day. The flowers were blooming on her front lawn. He opened the freshly painted gate and the new hinges didn't make a sound.*

The streets beyond were full of people. Some she recognized from round and about, like the pot-bellied man from across the road, others she'd never seen before. Relatives: long lost sons, daughters, mothers, fathers, grandfathers, grandmothers, and back further still. It would be the same the world over; she knew that as well.

"Will he be there, too? Arnold?" she asked Matthew as they went through the gate.

"Dad?" he said. "Of course. He's waiting for us."

Irene smiled at that and patted her son's hand. "You're a good boy."

They joined the throng, fitting into place alongside them. The living, the dead—all were here. All were heading off over the horizon. As finally, it had come: a time to be judged rather than to judge.

The day that lasted a thousand years had finally begun.

> *'Marvel not at this: for the hour is coming,*
> *in the which all that are in the graves shall hear his voice,*
> *and shall come forth; they that have done good,*
> *unto the resurrection of life; and they that have done evil,*
> *unto the resurrection of damnation.'*
>
> *John 5:28-29*

Of Cabbages and Kings
NATE SOUTHARD

Holly stumbled down the winding country road, her feet sore and her legs tired. She tried to remember how long she'd been walking, but she couldn't. It felt as though she'd been shuffling along forever. Her eyes drooped closed, and she forced them open again.

Jesus, she wanted to sleep.

But she knew that was a bad idea. She hadn't seen any dead since she'd escaped the bus, but that didn't mean anything. They were quick, and if one caught her off guard, she wouldn't stand a chance.

Just like those poor bastards in the bus.

Twenty-two souls, all that was left of Millwood. They'd barely made it five miles before the dead had swarmed them. She could still hear their shrieks of terror, smell the rot-reek of the dead as they surged over the moving bus or crunched beneath its wheels. She felt the twist of her stomach as the vehicle lurched, spun, and finally rolled, sending the people inside this way and that.

And then the dead had come through the windows.

And Holly had run.

It was luck, dumb fucking luck. The wreck had knocked her off her feet, and she'd rolled down the aisle until she rested against the emergency exit. An instant after the bus had finally stopped her wits had returned in full, and she'd thrown the exit open, setting off the bus's alarm. The sound had confused the dead for the briefest of moments, and in that time she'd leapt from the bus and bolted to the edge of the forest.

She'd been too scared to drag anyone else along with her

Even now, more than a day later, or maybe it was closer to two, she felt a great weight of shame on her shoulders. There had been children on the bus, and elderly. They had been her responsibility because the escape plan had been hers.

Well, hadn't she escaped?

She almost cracked a weak smile at the thought, but another crushing wave of guilt fell on her and she felt a fresh round of tears well up in her eyes. She blinked and they spilled down her cheeks, cutting furrows in the grime that had built up there. She wanted to squeeze her eyes shut until the tears stopped, but every time she tried she heard the screams emanating from the bus, the cries to God and others, pleas for help or mercy that had gone unanswered as the dead tore everyone inside to pieces. She remembered how she had felt so powerless and scared standing just beyond the edge of the forest, knowing a braver person would try to help, would think of a way. She had only stood there, however, afraid to move and make any sound that might give her hiding spot away. She had watched for more than an hour, terrified and sickened, as the dead ate the people she cared about, not stopping until they had finished every last morsel. And then they had charged back up the road toward Millwood, no doubt hoping to find others who might not have made it out.

Holly turned to look behind her. In the distance, filtering the morning sunlight, rose a column of black smoke. She assumed it was from Millwood, but she couldn't tell with any certainty. She wasn't very good with direction or distance, never had been. Even now, she could only guess that she was somewhere between Versailles and Madison. She had probably walked more than twenty miles in the last day, but she couldn't be sure. She wasn't even positive she was heading toward Madison. She had to stay away from the main roads and towns. That's where the dead gathered. Then again, the bus had been on a country road yesterday and it had still been attacked. Maybe the dead had been on their way to Millwood, coming from Milan or Dillsboro, and had just lucked into a meal.

She growled to herself, trying to push the thought out of her brain. She didn't want to think about the bus anymore, about the wreck or the screams or the dead surging through the windows and doors or how she could only—

STOP IT!

Shrieking with rage, she fell to her knees and pounded both fists into the gravel. She hissed as the rocks bit into the flesh of her hands. She punished the ground again, crying out, and felt the warmth of her own blood as it trickled down her wrists. She cursed herself. The dead could smell blood, or at least she was pretty sure they could. She'd have to move faster now. If any were in the area they'd have no trouble locating her.

She pushed herself to her feet and continued along the gravel road. Her hair fell in her eyes and she brushed it back with her fingertips. It was getting long again. She'd kept it so short over the last twenty months, ever since Blake had failed to return from Rundberg and she'd decided to take a more active roll in Millwood's welfare. The shorter hair had helped keep the others off balance, see her as something other than John Manton's daughter, who used to work the counter at the Dairy Barn. The short hair had helped them see her as a leader, somebody to listen to. She had kept it short right up until things started to get bad, until the pressure began to weigh on her as she had to think first of the town's defense and then of escape. Now it was long enough to cling to her face and chin. Had it been months? Had it really been so long?

She wondered if it was really June. Had her people paid close attention to the days? The weather had been rainy recently, and that made her think she was in the ballpark, that she was deep in the middle of June, but she could only guess at the actual date. Eighteenth? Nineteenth? She didn't know.

She pushed herself to her feet and began to walk again.

A breeze fluttered down the road, cooling her dirt-smeared and sweat-soaked skin. She began to breathe deep, a reflex, but caught herself. She didn't like to breathe too deeply anymore, not since the dead had returned. Now, the air always carried a stench along with it, a smell like roadkill or a pig farm, just underneath the natural scents of the world. Holly could only imagine what the larger cities might smell like. She'd met a few people who'd made it out of Cincinnati, and they'd said the odor of rot had been unbearable, even in those early days.

She looked to the sun as it rose to her left, determining which direction was east. She figured she was east of Highway 421. Soon, she could turn right and head into the forest. If she was correct, and that was a big *if*, she would reach 421 where it ran alongside the Jefferson Proving Ground. The military base, a former testing area for bombs and other weapons, would be fortified. It had been their original destination when they'd made their escape from Millwood. The proving ground was huge, surrounded on all sides with a razor wire-topped fence and armed to the teeth. If any place had withstood the rise of the dead, it was Jefferson. And even if it had fallen, maybe she could find a weapon, something she could defend herself with until she found a more permanent shelter.

Or maybe she'd just lower her arms and walk into the dead, give herself up and end the whole stupid thing.

Maybe that would be better.

Holly wiped the blood from her hands onto her jeans, and listened to the shuffle and crunch of her boots over the gravel. The rhythm, slow and rumbling, did little to comfort her, but it took her mind off of other things. She listened to her own footsteps so closely, so intently, that she didn't hear the piano until the trees fell away to her right and she saw the church.

The structure was old, but then again, most of the buildings in this part of the state were. The white paint of its clapboard sides had faded to a dull gray, the wood beneath was peeking through in more than one place. Its shingles still held on, but there was a sense of desperation to their grip, as if the next puff of breeze might strip the entire roof bare.

A single sign, built of sturdy wood, stood by the roadside. Holly could still make out the words *Fellowship Baptist Church*, but they had been painted over with a single coat of white. On top of this, the words—

NEW WORLD MINISTRY

—had been written in uneven letters with blue spray-paint. Holly came to a halt, considering the words for a moment, and an uneasy fluttering passed through her belly. She couldn't quite understand it, but something about the words frightened her the slightest bit.

"How ya doin'?"

She jumped at the masculine voice, her breath catching in her chest and her hands drawing up defensively. She hadn't heard human speech in well over twenty-four hours, so the words, despite their friendly tone, startled her. Her eyes darted to the church, standing alone in the middle of the field with only an empty blacktop lot to keep it company. An upright piano sat on a small porch that surrounded the church's main entrance. A man in a white dress shirt and a green ballcap sat behind the keys, banging out hymns. He looked back at her as he played, and Holly could only assume this was the man who had greeted her.

As if to answer her suspicions, the man called out, "You okay?"

Holly nodded. It never occurred to her that the man might not be able to make out her weak movements.

"You gonna stand there all day?" the man asked. "Once that sun gets all the way up, it's gonna get pretty hot. Muggy, too. The rain we been getting lately's wreaking havoc on the weather, but I guess I don't need to tell you that. Come on over and rest your bones a second!"

Holly smiled at the invitation. She could use a rest, no doubt about that. Her legs and feet practically begged for one. A sudden wave of exhaustion, more powerful than she was prepared for, rolled over her, and she knew she needed to sit down for a while.

She let out a long sigh and left the road, shuffling across the grass toward the old, gray structure. The man continued his recital, the hymns taking on a more regal, buoyant quality, and Holly almost smiled as she realized he was giving her some marching music, announcing her arrival. Her trek across the field seemed to take forever, the grass cushioning her stride but slowing her pace. She glanced at the church and wondered if it was really getting closer, almost afraid to believe so until she finally placed her hand on the banister that ran alongside the four steps that led up to the porch and entrance.

"Good morning!" the man behind the piano called. His voice seemed to bounce alongside the chords he played.

"Hi," Holly managed. Her voice seemed little more than a croak compared to the piano player's.

"Come to rest your weary bones? Come to make peace with the Lord in these times of never-ending trouble? You have come to the right place, my friend. You have come to the right place."

He changed chords and began to sing, his voice deep and resonating.

"Then sings my soul, my Savior, God, to thee. How great thou art. How great thou art!"

Holly eyed the man as he rocked back on the piano bench, his fingers shuddering over the keys and his eyes drawing closed even as his jaw dropped open to deliver his voice. His face was rugged but handsome, the skin tanned and rough, his jaw freshly shaven. His dress shirt shined in the early morning light, the cleanest thing she'd seen in well over a year. His hat displayed the John Deer logo with pride, though it was a bit more weathered than the shirt. A pair of light blue corduroys and some old loafers completed the out- fit, conveying an image of trustworthiness despite its simple origins.

He hunched over the keys again, making the chords shiver, and Holly lowered her face into her hands, thankful for the opportunity to rest.

"Oh Lord my God, when I in awesome wonder..."

Though she could probably do without the singing. She wasn't so sure she believed in God anymore, not after what he had let happen to the world. Still, she couldn't deny that some people, in times of crisis, felt better with a little religion in their lives. If it helped them, where was the harm? Why should she give a damn?

Besides, the guy at the piano had a pretty good voice. He was no Elvis, but he wasn't half-bad.

She looked up at him, but he was bent low over the keys, his eyes squeezed shut and his face drawn in a long expres- sion of emotion—something between joy and sorrow—as he sang. She decided to let him finish. There were worse ways to spend the time.

The man's voice rolled through the hymn, swelling with each chorus and falling to a reverent hush with each verse. He finished with a prolonged note, his vibrato perfect, and the piano fell still, ringing out one final note before leaving the church and the clearing in silence.

Holly opened her eyes at the sudden absence of sound, realizing for the first time just how loud the man and his song had been. Wasn't he afraid of the dead hearing him? That kind of racket could probably draw the walkers from more than a mile in any direction.

Maybe the dead had left the area, decided to head toward someplace more urban.

Or maybe this asshole didn't have a single goddamn lick

of sense.

The man spun around on his bench, swinging his legs behind him. He stuck out his hand, his lips spreading into a wide, jubilant smile.

"Hi there! Name's Toby. Brother Toby, I guess. It's a great pleasure to see somebody come along this Sunday."

Holly reached up, took the man's hand. She was amazed at how soft the skin of his palm and fingers felt. It didn't seem to match his rough appearance.

"Is it Sunday?" she asked. She really didn't know.

"To the best of my knowledge. It's not like the TV Guide shows up every Monday anymore. I just marked the days off on an old calendar. Once we reached a year, I started marking 'em again. This isn't a leap year, is it? That would've thrown me off."

Holly shook her head, a little dumbfounded by the man's rapid speech.

"That's great! I've been worried about that for months. Don't want to go calling to worship on a Saturday, right? It's not like we're Catholics here."

She shook her head again. Her mouth tried to form words, but only a light *click* escaped her lips.

Brother Toby dropped her hand, and it fell back into her lap. She hadn't even realized they were still shaking. Something about Toby confused her, seemed to sap her intelligence and will. Maybe it was his rapid and boisterous method of speech. Maybe it was that smile that seemed to grow wider and wider with each passing moment.

Maybe she had just grown paranoid over the past year. Billy Hudson's assassination attempt would have had that effect on anybody. It was possible that there still good people in the world. Hell, until a few minutes ago, she hadn't been sure there were people of any kind left.

She took a deep breath and decided to give Toby the benefit of the doubt. At least he was still alive.

"So, sister. What should I call you?"

She blinked, hoping she hadn't been silent so long it was noticeable. Time had been slipping away for her so much over the past few months, and she'd spent the last day or so wondering if she'd ever have a conversation with anyone other than herself again.

"Holly," she said, and she gave him something she hoped looked like a smile.

"Sister Holly! It is a real pleasure."

"Please, Holly is fine. I was never anybody's sister."

Toby shrugged. "We're all brothers and sister to one degree or another. The Lord says so."

"He does?"

"Sure, he does. It's right there in the bible."

Holly wasn't about to argue with him. She was a lot of things, but a bible scholar had never been one of them. If Toby said it was in there she was willing to take his word for it. It sounded biblical, at least.

She decided to change the subject.

"How long have you been here, Toby?"

A shadow crossed his face. "Since shortly after... well, I'm sure you know. I came from near Friendship."

"Really? I'm from Millwood."

"Millwood? That's marvelous! I've been through Millwood a time or two. Nice little place. What brings you my way?"

"Long story. We tried to get out. We didn't make it. I guess that's the short version."

One of Toby's eyebrows arched upward.

"We?"

"There were others. A busload, as a matter of fact. There was a wreck, though, and the dead got everybody else. I managed to escape and hide in the woods. Later on, I started walking."

He nodded. His face was a map of concern.

"I'm so sorry to hear that."

"It's okay." It was a lie, but she didn't feel like being the brunt of his condolences right now. She just didn't have the strength.

"So where were you headed? Were you just wandering, like Moses in the desert, or did you have a destination in mind?"

Moses? she thought. The guy was a little over the top. She'd thought the evangelicals and such stayed farther south. Was she going to hear about a plague of frogs next, or did he plan to jump right to the Second Coming?

"I'm headed toward the Jefferson Proving Ground," she said. "Thought it might be safe there."

He nodded, then shrugged. "Maybe. Then again, maybe not. Jefferson's a ways off, and I'm afraid I just can't tell you one way or the other."

She'd figured as much. The lines of communication had unraveled since the dead had risen. Even Millwood had only received news whenever a fresh crop of refugees arrived, and that hadn't happened in more than four months.

"Am I headed in the right direction at least?" she asked.

"I think so. You'll have to cut east eventually, but that shouldn't be so bad. You'll hit Route 62 if you keep along this road, and that'll take you to 421. It might not be the easiest path, though. I'd recommend you stay away."

"Really?"

"Sure. What place is safer than a house of the Lord?"

Holly fought the urge to roll her eyes.

"I'm sorry, Toby. I'm just not sure I believe that anyplace is safe nowadays."

"Belief is usually the problem."

She looked up. Toby's face had grown solemn, the lines in his dark skin deep and shadowed. He didn't look angry, though, just sad.

He shook it off.

"Look, I'm sorry," he said. "I'm not trying to freak you out or preach to you, okay? I'm just trying to offer some kind of... I don't know... stability in this big clusterfuck we've got going on now.

"I found this church about a year ago. The preacher and his wife were dead, so I got rid of them and set up shop. I'm not really a holy man or anything. I'm just feeling my way as I go. I pulled the piano out here, and I play every Sunday. Every now and then somebody hears it and wanders along. Most of the time they don't. I'm just trying to make a difference Sis—Holly, give a little comfort to anybody who might happen by. I don't mean to creep anybody out."

Holly stared at the worn wooden steps for a moment, then nodded. "I'm sorry. Really. I didn't mean to come off like that. It's just, well, you know what's happened to the world. We all do, right? We've all got to be careful, and I guess I'm trying to be a little more cautious than most. Like I said, I'm sorry."

Toby dismissed her with a wave. "It's not a problem. I won't have you pretend that it is, okay? You stay if you want, or you go along your way when you feel you're ready. In the meantime, let me know if there's anything I can do to help."

The offer made Holly's throat burn, and she realized she had been without water for at least a day. She tried to swallow, but a scratchy dryness prevented it, and she almost coughed out a few rough notes before she managed to recover.

"You got any water?" she asked, and her voice sounded raspy, like old newspaper tumbling across hot concrete. She rubbed her throat with one hand, wincing at the pain the sentence had caused.

Toby's fingers leapt from the keyboard. He stood almost as quickly. "Water? Sure! I always keep a few jugs handy. It's not cold, of course, but it should help your thirst a little bit, regardless."

"Thanks."

He stepped to the church's double door and motioned for Holly to stand. "C'mon in, Holly. It'll do you good to get out of the hot sun, anyway."

She couldn't argue with that. Even this early in the morning the heat and humidity seemed to press down on her from all sides. A few minutes inside, where she would at least be in the shade, would probably do wonders.

She grunted and pushed herself to her feet. She dusted her jeans off with her hands. "Sounds good, Toby. Lead the way."

Toby opened one of the doors wide. He gestured with a flourish. "After you."

She gave him a playful curtsy. His smiled turned into a chuckle. She laughed, as well, and then she stepped through the door and into the small church.

The smell hit her at once.

The dark church reeked of death. The rotting, clinging smell squeezed the air from every direction, forcing its way past Holly's nostrils and down her throat. She gagged, bending in half as her stomach fought to expel its meager contents. She bit the urge back, but her body convulsed once, twice, and then she fell to her knees, vomiting all over the church's carpet.

"Yeah," Toby said behind her, "I never really got used to the smell either."

She looked back over her shoulder, straining to see Toby through the darkness and her own tears. She saw his fist cock back and she tried to move, but he was too fast. The hand struck her just behind the ear and she collapsed into unconsciousness.

∞☽∞

"Wake up, Sister Holly. Time to rise and shine!"

Something wet and cool splashed against her face, and Holly sputtered. She tried to blink the liquid—she hoped it was only water—from her eyes. She tried to wipe her face off, but her arms wouldn't budge. An instant later, she awoke enough to feel the ropes cutting into her wrists.

Toby had tricked her. She'd let down her guard for a single moment and the bastard had gotten the drop on her. Now she was trapped in an isolated church in a world where nobody would hear her scream for help.

Helluva a mind you got there, Holly. You're a step ahead of everybody, a real thinker.

She let the thought die and concentrated on her current problem. She was tied to a chair, and Toby stood over her. He grinned down at her, his face smug and frightening at the same time. A gleam that could only be considered malevolent blazed in his eyes.

She couldn't see much of the church. It was too dark, and Toby stood too close. She guessed she was at the front, near the altar, or whatever you called it. She could catch a glimpse of sunlight filtering through the stained glass windows, bursting through in solid rays where the glass was broken. That clinging aroma of death and rot filled the room, and she could make out the rattling of chains somewhere beneath the ringing in her ears.

She glared up at Toby, wishing she could burn him with her hate.

"What the fuck is this, you piece of shit?"

"This?" he asked, spreading his arms wide and looking around. "This is my church." He pointed toward the door.

"Back there is the steeple."

He crouched in front of her, his face filling her vision.

"I brought you inside…"

He whirled away.

"…so you could see all the people!"

Molly screamed.

The pews were full of the dead, their rotting bodies writhing and shaking. There were men and women, adults and children. They wore clothes of every type: suits and sundresses and t-shirts and shorts. Some had been dead longer than others—their flesh hung from bones in dried strands and clumps—while others were fresh, their skin moist while it decayed.

A leather collar wrapped around the neck of each, a chain securing them to the pew. Their arms had been removed, the stumps raw and black and running. They hissed through their teeth, snapped their jaws, straining against their binds. The pews were heavy, though, made of sturdy wood, and they never even budged as the dead fought their trappings.

Holly stared in wonder, her mouth open and her voice dying to a rasp. The dead leaned toward her, their remaining teeth clacking uselessly as they ached for a meal. Holly shook her head violently, then looked to Toby with frantic eyes.

She could see now how insane he was. It was so obvious.

He patted her head.

"Okay. Maybe I wanted to freak you out a little."

She looked back out at the living corpses that filled the pews. There were at least two-dozen, maybe three. How long had they been here? How long had Toby been keeping them, and why?

As if in answer, Toby slipped an arm around her shoulders.

"I know. It's hard to understand. I get that; believe me. I wasn't lying to you before, Sister Holly. I did live in Friendship. Lived there my whole life, as a matter of fact. Hell, I was there, sitting in my living room, when the first reports came over the tube.

"Like just about everybody, I guess, I watched the first week or so on television, wondering what to make of the whole thing. I mean, c'mon! Dead people were returning to life, eating the living people, and turning them into walking dead folk. That's not something you see everyday!

"So, I sat there, and I watched, and I searched my mind for an answer. There had to be one out there, some way to make sense of all of it. I just had to sit and ruminate on it long enough. Sooner or later, it was going to dawn on me.

"And it did."

Holly watched him, holding her breath.

He leaned in close and whispered to her. "Angels."

He took a step toward the first row of pews, swinging a single arm wide.

"Angels, Sister Holly! What else is going to make the dead rise from the grave? What else could possibly stop death in its very tracks and transform it into life? The angels have come down from heaven and taken root in the only form available to them, that of the dead and rotting.

"I realized they're trying to tell us something, Sister Holly, something important. All we have to do as a species is prove ourselves worthy of God's love. Once we've done that, the angels will deliver their message, and a new era of peace will greet the Earth!"

Holly let his words settle for a minute, then she replied, her eyes never leaving Toby's. "You're fucking crazy."

His fist struck hard and fast, jolting her head back like a speedbag. She let out a single groan and tried to shake the cobwebs loose.

"You think I'm crazy? Who the fuck are you, Sister? Miserable little shit, got her whole town massacred and ran away from it! You aren't holy, bitch; you're a Goddamned heathen! You just want to feed off the Earth, suck it dry! I want to learn, Sister Holly! I want God to bestow his blessings onto me so that I can heal this sick world!"

"By killing these people? You killed them, didn't you?"

He shook his head. "I did no such thing. I made vessels ready for the coming angels, and if I take good enough care of them—if I can prove myself worthy and ready—they'll deliver God's lesson."

"Take care of them? Is that what lobbing their fucking arms off is for?"

He frowned. "I'm not a fucking retard.

"Truth of the matter is, The Lord works in mysterious ways. These angels, they're one of those ways." He walked down the center aisle, and the dead on either side snapped at him, their chains keeping them at bay.

He patted one on the shoulder, snatching his hand away when the zombie tried to bite him. "See? They kill us, but they want to save us. It's all very Old Testament; I don't expect you to understand."

"So what do you expect me to do, Toby? You going to kill me, make me another member of your little flock?"

A hurt expression flashed across his face. He placed a hand to his heart, leaning back. "What? Why, no, Sister Holly! I have enough angels. Now, I just need to take care of them, bestow blessing unto them until they feel the desire to bestow their blessing unto me."

A chill raced down Holly's spine. She closed her eyes for a moment, opened them. She had an idea what was coming next.

When Toby drew the knife out of his waistband, she realized she was right.

He approached her slowly, letting her get a good look at the blade. When he drew close enough, her grabbed a fistful of her hair.

"It appears it's communion day!"

The knife sawed through her hair, yanking the roots from her scalp. She screamed, then bit down and rode out the pain.

The pressure suddenly eased, and Toby stepped away with a handful of her hair, the hair that she hadn't even realized had been growing so long.

He stepped toward a zombie seated directly across from her in the first pew. It wore a filth-smeared suit that might have once been a lighter shade of blue.

"This used to be the preacher here," Toby said. "I believe he told me his name was Michael, but I can't be too sure. It was a pretty long time ago."

He pulled a few strands of hair from the fistful he carried with him, dangled them over the dead man's head. The former preacher leaned back, his jaw opening and closing, black tongue flopping out like a dying fish.

"That's right, Padre. Little appetizer for ya." Toby lowered the hair into the corpse's mouth, and the preacher sucked it in like pasta, chewed it for a long moment.

Holly had to turn away when the creature swallowed.

She heard a crescendo of groans, heard Toby cheer the dead on as he fed them morsels of her hair. She tried to think. There had to be a way out of this, someway to break free. She pulled against her binds, but they held fast. The son of a bitch had tied her to a chair. She was his to play with until he felt differently.

She guessed that would be a long time coming.

She tried again, leaning forward as far as she could, opening her eyes to watch her captor as he fed his congregation. She eyed him so carefully that she almost didn't notice the chair's rear leg's lift from the ground.

Her eyes widened. She could move! She watched Toby, making sure he wasn't watching, and she checked her balance. She leaned forward, curling in half until the chair lifted completely off of the ground. She lowered it to the floor again, but continued to struggle. She had an idea, but she knew she would only have one chance, and that depended on catching the lunatic off guard.

She glanced at the dead folk in the pew in front of her, watching as the former preacher and three others chewed on her hair, an expression like ecstasy filling their faces. They looked so anxious, so hungry. She knew the next thing Toby carved off of her wouldn't be hair, and she also knew she couldn't let that happen.

He'd have to kill her first.

"All gone!" he said, his voice almost child-like.

You can do this, Holly, she told herself. *You ran a town for almost a year. You can handle one religious psychopath.*

"What happens now?" she asked, putting an extra hint of terror in her voice.

He smiled. "Oh, I think you know, Sister Holly." He pointed the knife at her, twisting it in the air as he stepped closer. "I think you have a really good idea what I'm gonna do next."

He stepped past the first pew, stood directly in front of her.

"Do you have a good idea?"

"Yeah," she said. "I've got a fuckin' great one."

She screamed at the top of her lungs as she surged forward, lifting the chair behind her. She slammed her shoulder into Toby's gut, and she almost smiled when she felt him double over, the air whooshing from his lungs. She kept pushing, pumping her legs across the carpet, until she hit something solid.

Toby flew off of her, landing on the preacher and the rest. He tried to scramble away, but it was too late. Their teeth had already clamped down on him. The dead holy man had him by the throat, and with a great wrenching movement, ripped the flesh and tendons and veins away, spraying the area with blood.

Toby's scream died before it could even get started.

Holly staggered backward, then leapt into the air, leaning back. She landed with her full weight, and the chair cracked and splintered around her. She kept her eyes on Toby, watching the light drain from his eyes, as she struggled to her feet and managed to wrench her hands free of the rope coiled around her wrists.

"Is that the message you wanted?" she asked, but the only reply was the sound of teeth chewing meat.

Slowly, Holly walked down the center aisle, ignoring the dead as they leaned out, trying desperately to reach her with their jaws. She didn't bother to stop and look for water. She would find a creek in the forest. Instead, she stepped across the church's deserted lot and onto the country road beyond. She would walk until she found Route 62, and from there she'd make her way to the proving ground.

Maybe there she would find something worth believing in.

Those Below
JEREMY C. SHIPP

SAY YOU'RE LOST in the hustle-bustle of the local farmer's market in search of some shiny bibelot for your girlfriend, and you find your mother mouth-to-mouth with a man who isn't your father. In fact, he's nothing like your father. He's skinny and shaggy and short. You tell yourself that if he at least looked like your father, you could stomach the scene. Deep down you know that's not true.

And maybe that's not how it happens. Maybe you track her down. Maybe you climb the fruitless mulberry in front of their house and that's how you cut your leg. Maybe you bought yourself some night-vision goggles off of e-bay. Maybe you're watching and waiting, and when you finally do see them together, in their bedroom, naked, you drop a bomb of vomit onto an unsuspecting yard gnome below.

You think, "Get your fucking hands off my mother."

But she's not your mother, is she? She used to be. Before she moved in. Before she changed her name. Before the funeral. Say this was your mother, and this is your life. You'd be here too, like me. You'd hear about Porter from a friend of a friend, and you'd show up at his doorstep with a hundred bucks and a wrenching knot in your gut.

Porter opens the door. "Yeah?"

I open my mouth, but nothing comes out.

"You're Hadley?" he says.

"Yeah."

"Alright. Come in.

I follow him inside. My mind spins, but I still notice that

his home is a shitty place. Every step and my feet crunch down on trash and squish on soggy carpet. Lines of duct tape patch a few holes in the wall, but most are left gaping. I stop breathing through my nose before I have time to identity the sour stench assaulting the air.

He takes me to an empty room. At this point, the walls are more hole than wall. Under more relaxed circumstances I would crack up over such irony as the tarp on the floor, but I'm more in the mood for weeping.

"You brought the money?" he says.

I nod and hand him the bill.

He gives it back. "Not until after."

"Oh."

He takes another look at the money. "That's a hundred dollar bill, huh?"

"Yeah."

"I don't think I've seen one before. In person, I mean."

"Oh." I stuff the thing in my pocket, almost violently.

"Should I get undressed?" he says, and starts for his belt.

"I'm not here for… that."

"I know, man." He grins. "Just some people like me naked when they're doing it. I don't mind either way."

I consider this. "Keep your clothes." Part of me, though, wants to give the other answer. The thought makes me shudder.

"Whatever floats your boat." He kneels. "Whenever you're ready."

I take a step forward, and then pause. "Is this going to hurt you?"

"Fuck, man, what do you care?"

"I care."

"You say that now. Let's see if you ask me again in five minutes."

"Maybe I'm not your normal clientele."

He sighs. "No, we don't feel much pain, so clear your fucking conscience."

"Are you just telling me that or do you mean it?"

He runs his hand down his face. "Look, man. You can either do this or go home. But no one ever goes home, so just face the fucking music and get on with it."

So I do. I start off by slapping him hard across the face, and go from there. Five minutes later, I'm not asking, "Is this hurting you?"

Five minutes later, I'm straddling his chest, smashing his mangled face in with my bloody fists, over and over and over. He's shouting, "Stop it!" and I'm loving every second of it.

Hafwen's nickname is Zippy. She likes to skip and sing about the dishes as she's washing them, and write poetry with waterproof paper in the rain. She'll call me up just to tell me that she's discovered the name for those imprints left in the skin when you press it against a textured surface too long. A frittle.

So when I see her sitting cross-legged on my bed, motionless, not frowning, but not smiling, I know something's wrong.

I sit beside her and kiss her. "What's up, Haf?"

She doesn't look at me. "I have to tell you something."

My insides erupt. I'm afraid.

I'm afraid her feelings for me were just a frittle in her heart and now she wants to end what we have before I even have the chance to tell her I love her.

"Tell me," I say. I try to sound brave, but I fail.

"My mom," she says. "She's a Remade-American."

"Oh," I say. "I didn't know Cambree wasn't your real mom."

"No, Hadley. Cambree is my real mom. She's a Remade-American."

"Oh god… I'm so sorry. When did this happen? I saw her last week."

"No, Hadley. She was a Remade since before she married my dad."

"Oh."

"I'm a Remade, Hadley."

"But…" I can't think of anything else to say except, "You don't look like one of them."

"One of them?"

"I'm sorry. I…"

She looks at me now. "I should've told you before we started going out, but I liked you so much. I wanted you to get to know me first before you… you know… decided."

"Oh."

"I told myself that I wasn't lying to you, because I never said that I was alive, but keeping this from you was deceitful and I'm sorry. I understand if you're angry at me. I'm angry at me too."

"I'm not angry," I say, and that's true. I'd have to be feeling anything to feel angry."

"I don't know if that's a good sign or a bad one," she says.

"Me neither."

She puts her face in the bowl of her hands and makes crying sounds. No tears come out, obviously.

I almost put my arm around her, but I don't.

"I can't keep living this way, Hadley," she says. "I'm a Remade. I'm tired of hiding it."

I want to tell her, "Don't worry."

I want to tell her, "I'll love you no matter what."

But I fail.

I thought Hafwen was happy before. But she tells me she wasn't. She says she was smiling on the outside and crying on the inside.

Now, she cries a lot.

Now she's pale, because she's stopped wearing makeup. She's cold, because she's stopped wearing heated clothing. Her hair is white, because she's stopped dyeing it. She looks dead, and says she's the happiest she's ever been.

I should be happy for her. Instead, I keep thinking about how someone else used to inhabit her body. I can't look at her the same way anymore.

She's used.

Second-hand.

Impure.

She says a lot of Remade girls try to pass for living, because they're ashamed of who they are. They buy into the whole natural is ugly paradigm. But natural isn't ugly, she says. Death isn't ugly.

Whether she's right or not, I don't know.

If there is a beauty in death, I don't want to see it.

I hate death. I hate that my mom died of thirst in a ditch on the side of the road. People drove by, but they didn't see her. They didn't hear her. Now when Hafwen stands right in front of me, I try to look through her. When she talks to me, I try to tune out her voice. Deep down, I know she doesn't deserve this kind of treatment. I also know that Porter doesn't deserve the beatings I give him every Tuesday morning.

I just don't care.

"Animal brains have to be illegal," I say. I say it with conviction, but I don't really know what I'm talking about. I defend the living and the systems controlled by the living only because doing otherwise would feel like a betrayal. "They're a gateway to human brains."

Hafwen laughs. "You really think there are hordes of Remades out there feasting on the brains of the living?"

"I don't know," I say. "It could happen."

"Hadley, animal brains are illegal because Remades eat them. They make us feel good."

"Have you ever eaten any?"

"No, but that's not the point. The point is, prisons are filled with Remades, and most of them are there just because they've eaten animal brains. The government sells these prisoners to corporations to use for manual labor, and every living person involved makes a lot of money. Doesn't this seem wrong to you?"

"I guess," I say. "But you have to admit, violent Remade crime is a big problem."

"If you read the statistics, you'd know that violent living crime is an even bigger problem. It only seems like a Remade problem because the media publicizes Remade crime a lot more often. A lot."

"I don't want to talk about this anymore."

"But we are talking about it, Hadley. It's important to me."

A few days ago, Hafwen told me the story of her parent's divorce. I expected her to say that her mother lied about being a Remade, and when her father found out the truth he left her.

But that's not how it happened.

Her father, Barry, knew her mother was a Remade from the very beginning. He was an activist for Remade rights and that's how they met in the first place. He loved Cambree and he wanted to start a family with her. So they had a baby. Her name was Bronwyn. Since she was born from a Remade mother, Barry and Cambree knew that at any time she could pass away and be Remade with a new personality. This happened when Bronwyn was 19 years old. Barry loved Bronwyn, and refused to connect with Hafwen in any meaningful way, and all the while he blamed Cambree for his daughter's death. One day he left for work and never came home again.

Now, this story buzzes in my head. I know that Hafwen's just looking for some living person to listen to her. To understand her. To say, "You're right. These things are very unfair."

But instead I say, "I'm going to bed."

This is our coffee-shop, Hafwen's and mine. Neither of us drink coffee but we enjoy the comity and the photographs of dancing mannequins on the walls.

Today, I don't invite her. I've never seen a Remade in here before, though I tell myself the reason I don't call her is because I need some alone time.

A man and a woman at the next table converse in loud whispers.

I stare at my book like I'm reading.

"I'm no racist," the woman says. "But they have no legal right to be here."

"I say send them back to where they came from," the man says. "Start paving all the cemeteries and let that be the end of it."

At least I'm not them. I don't want to get rid of the Remades. I'm all for equal rights. Hell, I'm even dating one of them.

I'm not a terrible person. So why do I feel like such a monster?

Minutes later I'm in my car making a call.

"Porter?" I say.

"Yeah," he says. "Hey, man."

"Do you want to hang out?"

"Hang out?"

"Yeah. We could go bowling or something."

"I hate bowling."

"Whatever you want."

"I don't know, man. I don't usually hang out with clients."

"Come on."

"Alright."

Fifteen minutes later, and I'm in a Remade bar. My mind spins, but I still notice that this is a shitty place. Like it hasn't been cleaned since it opened. Maybe that's true.

The waitress, who's either a living person or one of those Remades who buy into the natural is ugly paradigm, hands me my chai, and gives Porter a wad of tin foil.

"Thanks, man," he says to the girl.

She smiles and walks away.

Porter unwraps the foil.

"What is that?" I say.

"Brains," he says.

"I know that. I mean, what kind?"

"Human."

"Oh." I swallow.

"I'm just fucking with you, man. They're pig. Want to try some?"

"No!" I'm louder than I expect.

"Calm down, man."

I try.

Porter nibbles at the brains. He trembles.

After a few sips of my tea, I say, "Is it really so bad being dead?"

"What do you mean?" he says, gazing at his hands.

"I mean, why do so many Remades eat brains? Is it such a horrible existence?"

"No, man. Being dead is cool."

"Then why do you eat brains?"

His expression changes to one that I've never seen on him before. It's one of the looks my mother used to give me, when she was disappointed in me, but showed sympathy at the same time. "Figure it out yourself, man," he says, very quietly.

"Fuck you!" I say, standing.

"Let go of me."

I realize my hand is squeezing his arm. My other hand, it's in a fist.

"I think you should go, man," he says.

Part of me wants to stay and beat the non-living shit out of him. I want to blame him. Not just for how I'm feeling right now, but for everything. My mother's death. The state of the world.

Everything.

Instead, I release him and say, "Yeah."

Say you're lost in the orange groves behind your apartment complex because you're not ready to go home again, and you find three guys dragging a tied-up young woman toward a hole in the ground, with three shovels nearby. They're alive and she's not. You tell yourself that if they were dead and she wasn't, the scene wouldn't be so disturbing, because it's supposed to be the dead who do things like this. Deep down you know that's not true.

You think, "Get your fucking hands off her."

Say all of this happens. You'd be here too, like me. You'd crouch down behind the nearest trunk you can find, waiting and watching, with a wrenching knot in your gut.

For a moment I consider racing out into the clearing, bellowing and swinging my fists. But these guys, they're not like Porter. They'd fight back. They'd kill me.

So I watch them bury the poor girl. I listen to her muffled screams.

They dump her in the hole and start shoveling.

They say things like, "You like that dirt in your face, don't you, bitch?" and "Fucking zombie whore."

I try to study their faces, so that I can identify them later, but it's so dark. And I'm crying too much.

When they finish with the dirt, they pound the backs of their shovels against the grave, over and over and over. They laugh, and high-five.

Finally, they leave.

I dive onto the ground and start digging with my bare hands.

What I'm uncovering isn't just a young dead girl.

From deep within myself, I pull out a truth that I've always known but never wanted to admit. Remades don't eat brains because of the pain of being dead. The real pain comes from how the living treat them. How I treat them.

I pull her out of the hole. I remove the gag.

She looks at me with fear in her eyes.

I'm afraid she's going to scream.

I'm afraid she thinks I'm one of them.

But her face changes. It's one of the looks my mother used to give me, after I did something bad and then made things right. "Thank you," she says, very quietly.

I put my arm around her, and in my heart I'm embracing Hafwen at the same time.

I see her when I close my eyes. She's beautiful.

I'm ready to go home.

The Traumatized Generation
MURRAY J.D. LEEDER

LAND SNIFFED AT THE AIR. He felt a kind of peace out here, so different from the city thick with industrial fumes and soldiers. The prairies sprawled in every direction, wilder and more overgrown than they had been in more than a century, and the Rockies were lost in a pink haze to the west. All of it sent Land back to a childhood spent traipsing around the countryside, when he didn't need to be worried about what might be hiding in the wheat.

He rapped on the front door. Eventually a woman answered in her nightgown, slightly older than him, and glowering. She knew what was happening, and Land's heart sank when he realized what he was about to do.

"Mrs. March? I'm Michael Land, Paul's homeroom teacher. I'm here to pick him for today's..." He hesitated. "Today's field trip."

"I didn't give permission for any field trip," she snorted, and Land put his hand against the door to stop her from closing it.

"I'm afraid the school board doesn't require parental permission when the field trip has been made mandatory by the government of Canada."

"The government," she said. "You mean the military, don't you? Either way, I'm not about to send my son away to be traumatized by your bloodshow."

"Mrs. March," he told her. "In that car is the sergeant they sent to escort me up here. If Paul doesn't come out of this house in ten minutes, she'll have to come and talk to you herself. Nobody wants that."

There was desperation in her voice. "Mr. Land, you and I remember a time before the military controlled our lives. You're an educator... how can you stand idly by and—"

"Just get your son, Mrs. March. Please. Just get Paul."

Mrs. March breathed in deeply. "Wait here," she said. "I can't believe I'm doing this."

She returned a few minutes later with the round-faced, serious little boy, dressed in unfashionable garments that made him a target for jeers too often.

"It's good to see you, Paul," Land said, and the boy half-smiled up at him. Land knew the boy all too well—smart, shy, sensitive, and far too vulnerable for this world. Just like the young Michael Land, back when CNN reported that the dead were rising from their graves.

The car door opened and Sgt. Hazelwood walked over to the door just as Paul was slipping on his coat. She was blond and beautiful but Land disliked her intensely. She was just the kind of rhetoric-spouting career army type that Land had encountered too often during his own tour of duty in Alaska. "All ready to go?" she asked, wearing a false smile that Mrs. March did not return. Ignoring the sergeant's presence, Mrs. March dropped to her knees and embraced her son.

"Remember not to be too scared," she said, and Paul nodded uncertainly.

"Do something for me," Mrs. March said to Land. "Promise me you'll sit by him. Try to keep him from being too scared. He has a weak heart."

Land nodded; before he could speak Hazelwood interrupted. "Then we'll just have to strengthen up that heart a bit," she said, ushering the trembling boy toward the car.

As Land looked back at Mrs. March he wanted to gaze into her eyes and assure her that everything would go all right, whether it was true or not, but found that he couldn't do it.

∞Θ∞

The huge chain-link fence encircling Calgary was intended to keep the zombies out, which it did, but it also served to keep the people in. The rule of law didn't need to enforce this, for few wanted to leave. Officers waived Sgt. Hazelwood's transport through the military checkpoint at the city's north gate. They continued down the vacant Deerfoot Trail, bound for the Saddledome. In the distance Calgary's downtown was silhouetted against the morning sky, postcard pristine, like a snapshot from Land's childhood.

Paul was quiet the entire time. His parents certainly taught him to avoid talking to anyone in a uniform. Land felt like he was ferrying a prisoner to an execution. He always hated this day, the worst of any school year. Nothing he'd seen up in Alaska bothered him half as much as the sight of ten thousand schoolchildren screaming for gore.

Yellow school buses dotted the Saddledome's parking lot, and Hazelwood weaved through the crowds of kids before they found Mr. Land's grade-seven class. Land hoped they'd arrive first, to spare Paul the humiliation of arriving under military escort, but no such luck. Built for the 1988 Olympics, the Saddledome had served for years as sports arena and concert venue. Now the military had appropriated it and remade it into their modern-day Coliseum.

"You get out here," Hazelwood said. "I'll go park in the barracks and join you inside."

"What?" Land said. "Isn't your duty here finished?"

"No." The sergeant flashed him an unreadable smile. "I'm with you for the whole day."

Land coughed in disgust. She probably thought he'd let Paul slip away from the show at the first occasion. She was probably right.

The rest of the class caught sight of them as they stepped out of the military vehicle. Land saw Bruce Tomasino say something to Jason Barrows, and they sent their whispers all along the line.

"Don't worry about them, Paul," Land said softly. "Just take your place in the line."

His student dutifully shuffled over to the uneven row of students. Land addressed them: "I don't want to see any shoving or shouting. When we get the signal, I want us to go in a straight line inside and take our seats. Any questions?"

"I got a question," asked chubby Jimmy Schwab. "Is it true... I mean, we heard a rumor that Zombie Bob will be here."

Please, no, Land thought. That would make it even worse; the presence of a TV celebrity would change this field trip from a military demonstration to a rock concert. Robert Smith Harding went with a camera crew behind the lines in lost cities and in infested countryside, found zombies and inevitably killed them in daredevil ways. His weapons of choice ranged from a jackhammer to a katana. The kids loved him, wore his picture, talked about him constantly. Land watched Paul's face grow grimmer still at this news.

A whistle blew somewhere across the parking lot, and the rows of students started proceeding up the concrete stairs and into the Saddledome itself. A uniformed officer waved Land's class ahead, and he took up the end of the line to watch them keep their course. Amid all the noise of kids gabbing away, he could barely hear Bruce and Jason talking about Paul. He made out one sentence: "That corpse-hugger's going to wet his pants when he sees this."

Land was always impressed by how little the Saddledome had changed since his childhood. This wasn't a real surprise; though the military owned it now, it was still a sports arena of sorts. The floors were still sticky and the plastic seats still painful. The Jumbotron was still there too, leftover from hockey games. Now it flashed messages like "ENJOY THE SHOW" and "THIS IS FOR YOU KIDS."

The most visible changes were the sideboards. The protective glass now went up much higher than in the old days, and they needed to be cleaned of splattered blood and brain meat nightly. As usual, the arena was covered with a layer of freshly tilled dirt. At one end there was a raised platform with a few microphones, and at the other there was a black velvet drape, which hid the zombie cage. A trained crew with cattle prods were ready to send the zombies into the arena on cue.

When the students took their seats, Land called for Paul to come sit with him by the aisle. He'd wished he could have done this more subtly—Paul didn't need to be a teacher's pet on top of a zombie-lover—however, he did agree to sit with the boy. As the other students chatted away, he asked Paul: "What do you think of all this?"

"I don't know," the boy said. "I've never been anywhere like this before."

"Your parents didn't want you to come here," Land said. "You know that."

"But they made you get me."

Land nodded. "The military thinks it's important that you be here."

"Why?"

The question caught Land by surprise. It was a good question—why? Why did one child deserve all this special attention? He stammered, searching for an answer, before one was provided.

"Because someday you'll be called to the service, and we think it's best you know what it's all about." Sgt. Hazelwood stood in the aisle, grinning down on them both. She had changed from her green field outfit into a brown dress uniform that accentuated her curves.

That's not a real answer, Land though, but he couldn't say anything here.

"Got room for one more?" Hazelwood asked.

Land looked at the empty seat next to him and tried to think of an excuse to keep her from sitting there, but could not. "Sure," he said. "Have a seat."

"No." She shook her head. "You sit there, and I'll sit on

the other side of Paul."

Land wanted to protest but thought better of it. He stood, and as she slipped past he felt her body against his, her holstered pistol rubbing against his thigh.

She took her place next to the boy and smiled at him. "Your parents don't let you have a TV, do they?" she asked.

Paul shook his head.

"Then you don't know who Zombie Bob is?"

"Well, I know who he is because the other kids..."

"Oh good," she said. "It just so happens that I'm a friend of Bob's, and after the show I could take you to meet him backstage."

"Well," said Paul, "I don't really know if..."

"Just you, out of all these kids." She gestured at the thousands of schoolchildren around them. "That could really help you could make friends, Paul. They'll want to know you for sure after that."

Land shot her a disapproving look, but she only grinned. Fortunately, the lights began to dim. He heard Hazelwood whisper "We'll talk about this later" as a hush settled over the Saddledome.

A spotlight sprang into life, illuminating a lone figure on the platform. It was a silver-haired man in a brown dress uniform, metals dangling at his pocket. His image appeared a thousand times larger on the Jumbotron above.

"Howdy, kids," he said. "I'm Colonel Patrick Simonds. I recently got back from directing the troops on the coast, and the top brass said to me, 'Pat, you've done such a great job in Vancouver. When you get back, just you name it and it's yours.' And I said, 'I want to be the one who talks to the kids at the Saddledome.'"

Simonds wore a politician's smile he was never seen without. Affable and grandfatherly, he was just the kind of public face the military needed as it pressed its endless, costly war against an enemy that neither thought nor planned.

"Yup," Simonds, went on, "that's my favorite duty, because it's so important for the future. Once we recapture Vancouver and Toronto the real challenges will be open to us. New York, *Lost* Angeles…" he paused briefly as some of the audience chuckled at the popular pun, "maybe even London, Tokyo. That's where you kids will be fighting the zombies. You should think of this day like a 'thank you' in advance. I think the very least we can do is show you how to do it."

Another spotlight suddenly cut through the darkness, lighting the black drape at the opposite side of the arena. Out stumbled a putrescent walking corpse, flailing its arms and awkwardly making its way forward. Its jaw was slack, its tongue lolling out in anticipation of its next meal. A collective sigh filled the arena.

"Look at it," Simonds said. "I bet this is the first zombie most of you kids have ever seen. That says something about how far we've come. It's hard to imagine, but there was a time when zombies even walked the streets of Calgary. But thanks to the vaccine, developed right here in Canada, none of us will ever be zombies. Remember that: kill a zombie, and that's one closer to killing them all.

"That disgusting creature you're looking at was somebody's brother, father or son once. I'm not going to lie to you about that. But he isn't no more; in fact, he's not a *he* at all, but an *it!*"

The colonel pulled his service pistol from its holster and carefully aimed at the brightly lit target, before firing. It sounded little more potent than a cap gun, but Paul twitched in his seat anyway. The bullet struck the zombie's shoulder, and it barely even noticed as it kept shambling forward.

"Ah, I didn't quite get him, did I?" Simonds said. "I've seen zombies lose all their limbs and keep on going. Their brain and their hunger drives them forward. They want to eat our flesh. That's all they want. And they never hesitate before they strike."

The zombie lurched steadily forward, having made it almost halfway to the podium. Many children clenched their teeth with the tension, but Land knew it would take a minor miracle for that zombie to actually reach the colonel.

"Now," said Simonds, "some people say, because these things were once our loved ones we shouldn't kill them. We all know people like this. These zombie-lovers think zombies are trainable—maybe we can toss them the odd steak to keep them happy, and teach them to fetch our slippers. But I challenge anyone to look in the eyes of the dead and see anything worth saving. Fellas, can we focus in on that?"

The Jumbotron zoomed in until the zombie's twisted, drooling face filled the screen.

"No life. No intelligence. In humans we see some kind of spark of life; I don't know what it is, but it's always there. You don't see that in zombies. That's what zombies are: humans minus a certain spark, and that's what makes them a perversion in the face of God. There's only one thing to do to them!"

Simonds fired again. This time it struck the zombie square in the head, a perfect killshot. There was a splash of bright red blood, and the creature fell. The Saddledome erupted with cheers and shrill whistles.

The house lights came up. "Pretty cool, eh?" Sgt. Hazelwood whispered to Paul.

"Now before I bring out a very special friend of mine," Simonds said, "we should all rise for the singing of our national anthem." An organ started up with *O Canada*; as they stood Land extended his arm behind Paul's back and nudged Hazelwood.

"Sergeant," he whispered. "We need to share a word outside."

"But Mr. Land, it's disrespectful..."

"*Now*," he said, just a little too loud, and he started away from the arena. She placed her drink at her feet and stomped after him. He led her outside, right onto the Saddledome's front steps, and there she began to snap at him.

"Who do you think you are that you can—"

"Who do you think you are to mess with my student like that?" Land shouted back at her. "God, a military pick-up, you hanging over his shoulder... Do you think this isn't hard enough for him anyway? The other kids will never let him hear the end of this."

"Good," Hazelwood said. "I don't want him to forget today. I want him to be traumatized as hell. He'll thank us for it later."

"When? When will he thank us?"

"When he's been dropped in some hellhole and told to kill." There was an absolute conviction in her voice.

"He'll be a man then, and better equipped to handle it than these kids are," Land argued. "Listen to them: they're whistling and cheering! It's just a show for them. That's just how you want them. They don't consider things. They don't think about things. The military doesn't want them to. I don't know who's more brain-dead, zombies or soldiers."

"How dare you!" Hazelwood cried, her throat hoarsening. "This isn't our world any more! It's theirs! We let our guard down, and they tear our throats out! Society *must* be prepared, prepared in every way, for war! It is the only way!"

Land shrunk back at the force of her argument. "Do you remember," he said, his voice cracking, "when they used to say that watching violent movies was desensitizing, and that was a bad thing?"

For a long time there was silence, and then Hazelwood said, "You've been wondering why there's so much special treatment for this one kid? What makes him so important?"

Land nodded.

"That was my idea. When I heard about Paul from your school's liaison office, I thought about the way *I* was before the zombies: a quiet, rural life. No TV. I'd never even witnessed violence. Then I watched a zombie tear my father's head off while he was working the fields. You know what I did? I didn't run, I didn't scream—I just shut off. The shock almost killed me. But that made me who I am."

Hazelwood was trembling slightly. She clenched her fists where she stood to steady herself. "Maybe you're a zombie-lover too, but you earned that right by fighting for your country up in Alaska. Mr. and Mrs. March never served, but their son will have to. Maybe it was noble once to be a conscientious objector, but now it's lunacy. The more they shelter Paul, the more they try to protect him, the more harm they do.

"I know you have stories like mine. We all do. We are the traumatized generation. A bit older and maybe we could have been better prepared for what was happening. A bit younger and we'd never have known a world without the zombies. If we are to spare the new generation what we went through, they must grow up impervious to trauma. Understand me. I value innocence. That's what Paul is. But in this world of ours, innocence kills." There were tears in her eyes. "It seems wrong, I know. Sometimes I spend whole nights crying into my pillow. But it's the only way. Let them cheer when zombies die. Better they cheer than scream."

Land turned away from Hazelwood and gazed at the skyscrapers of downtown Calgary, built so many decades ago, standing there like silent memorials to a dead world. "I wasn't made for these times," he said.

"None of us were," she answered.

Land wiped his eyes and turned back to face her. "They've probably brought out Zombie Bob by now. We should get back to Paul."

"Yes," Hazelwood agreed. "He needs our support."

Inside, the Saddledome pulsed with rock music. Land recognized the Doors' "Peace Frog," which, thanks to the tastes of a certain general, became something of a military anthem. To its steady beat Zombie Bob, dressed in full western garb with a white Stetson, wove his way between ten or so zombies, a roaring chainsaw in his hand.

It was part of Zombie Bob's appeal that it seemed like he

could die at any moment.

Colonel Simonds was still on the platform, now protected by a half-dozen guards with submachine guns, offering commentary as Bob played the clown, always making it look like the zombies were just about to get him, before getting them instead.

"Careful Bob, there's another deadhead behind you," said Simonds. Bob did a cartoon-like double-take and slid the saw around to his back. Then he slid backwards on the dirt, driving the saw through the hapless zombie's midsection. Bob did a pirouette, slicing the zombie mostly in two before slamming his weapon right through its neck. A thick plume of blood shot out.

Land winced at the display. No one he had known in Alaska would attempt anything remotely like Zombie Bob's antics. He and Hazelwood slid back into their seats on either side of Paul, and Land asked the boy, "How are you doing?"

Paul March sat there in wide-eyed, stunned silence. "I uh…" was the best answer he could manage.

"Remember," Hazelwood whispered, "there's glass between you and the zombies. They can't get you."

Zombie Bob's opponents seemed selected for maximum diversity: an old granny, a slender college girl, a middle-aged Chinese man, and so on. All that was missing was a child zombie. The media always shied clear of those.

"Wow, look at that, kids," Simonds said. "Remember, you can see Zombie Bob's adventures every Wednesday at 3 p.m. on CBC."

"Peace Frog" ended and the music switched gears to a whimsical country waltz. Bob took a while to forget the zombies and offer a few dance steps, tipping the white hat now splattered with blood. Bob pulled away from zombies for a moment to wave to the crowd, eliciting laughter as the zombies lurched up on him from behind. Then he sprang into motion, running circles around the zombies, causing them to bump into each other, trip over each other, fall down. The crowd roared with laughter.

Paul made fists of his hands, squeezing until his knuckles were white. He was trembling hard, unstoppably. Land put a hand on his shoulder, trying to steady him, and he felt the reverberations through to his bones.

In this confusion Bob rushed forward with his chainsaw swinging at chest level. He caught two zombies right next to each other and forced the saw through bone and flesh, slicing both of them. Their legs collapsed, useless, but their upper torsos were not dead and pulled across the dirt with their strong arms. Bob moved away, ignoring them for the time.

"Two at once, Bob!" Simonds declared. "You've outclassed yourself this time. I don't see how you can top that."

The crowd went mad, screaming, whistling, stomping their feet, and the sounds echoed through the Saddledome's steel rafters. For a moment Land felt like he was a kid again, listening to a crowd cheering for a wrestling match, or a fight in a hockey game. Paul started making noises like little yelps. Land and Hazelwood looked at each other.

"Are you all right, Paul?" Land asked, looking into the boy's eyes. They were beginning to look glossy. Paul grasped hard onto his forearm and squeezed. Land cried out.

Zombie Bob slipped among his remaining foes, so that they lurched at him from every side. Most weeks on his show, he performed some variant of this, positioning himself directly in the densest collection of zombies and fighting his way out. It was a crowd-pleaser with any weapon, and the chainsaw was best of all. He swung it at the zombie in front of him, smoothly slitting it through the middle. On the Jumbotron they could see smoke billowing out of the chainsaw. As he retrieved, it seemed to sputter and die.

The camera caught the expression on Bob's face. It was real panic. This was not that unusual; the TV cameras often found Zombie Bob running for his life.

"Uh-oh," said Colonel Simonds. "Looks like ol' Bob's got himself in trouble again."

Somebody cut out the music just in time for everyone to hear Bob release a stream of profanity. He threw the dead chainsaw in the face of the closest zombie and dove past it, his Stetson tumbling off his bald head in the process. He kicked up dust as he raced away from the remaining zombies, but had the misfortune of tripped over something, landing face-first in the dirt. Before he could run, a strong zombie hand clamped down on one of his legs. He looked back to see a half-zombie, one of those he'd sliced in two earlier, its entrails dragging through the dirt behind it. It squeezed tighter on his leg, shattering bone and pulling away a handful of flesh. Bob's scream hit the steel roof and resonated through the Saddledome's every corner.

"Fuck!" shouted Simonds into his microphone. There was no doubt now—this was not part of the show.

The smell of fresh blood spurred the other zombies on to greater speed. Zombie Bob tried to pull himself to his feet, but they were on him in no time, ripping, tearing at his clothes and his flesh. The entire Saddledome could hear his screams. Piece by piece they devoured him, stuffing human meat by the handful into their mouths. So here it was at last, the death of Robert Smith Harding. Everyone knew he'd die violently, himself most of all. But nobody expected that it would be witnessed by ten thousand schoolchildren.

This would be remembered as the great trauma of a generation. They weren't screaming in excitement now. They were screaming in terror.

Land felt Paul's hand go limp on his arm.

"Fire! Fire! Fire! Fire!" Colonel Simonds shouted the command like a mantra, and his bodyguards loosed a hail of bullets into the mass of zombies. Many of the bullets struck their targets, but those that didn't impacted the bulletproof glass, ricocheting through the arena and off into the crowd. One of these stray bullets caught Simonds in the chest and he collapsed on stage, barely noticed amid all the pandemonium.

Children and adults alike crawled over each other, fueled

by the most primal surge of adrenalin, frantically seeking to escape the danger. Bodies swamped the exits and fell from balconies. Land grabbed Paul, ready to carry him out of the Saddledome, but found him limp and cold. He reached for Paul's jugular but felt no pulse.

He has a weak heart, Mrs. March had told him. She must have meant it. This shock must been too much for poor sensitive Paul, and his little heart gave out. Hazelwood looked at him open-jawed, and amid all this chaos noise and chaos everything suddenly seemed so still and calm.

Then Paul's eyes jumped open.

Thank God I was wrong, Land thought first, but then he saw his eyes. He could never explain this to anyone who hadn't seen it for themselves, but the eyes of the dead were different. Simonds was right; they lacked spark, life. This was true even of the freshest zombies.

Paul sank his teeth into Sgt. Hazelwood's forearm, biting down hard. Her legs kicked involuntarily, knocking against the seat in front of her. Her mouth opened to scream, but no noise came out as her eyes glossed over and she sank back into her chair, growing increasingly inert as Paul gnawed through to raw bone. Land grabbed Paul by the hair and yanked back, but even a child zombie possessed inhuman strength, and Paul wouldn't release his grasp on his prize.

The Marches, Land thought. *They live outside of the city. The inoculation drives must have missed them somehow.*

Damned zombie-lovers—they didn't even inoculate their own kid against becoming one of them! How irresponsible can they be?

Land slid his hand down Hazelwood's thigh to her holster. He pulled out her service pistol, drove it into Paul's chin, and squeezed the trigger.

The Cyclist
SIMON WOOD

BEFORE YOU CONDEMN ME, know this: I'm a product of society. You made the monster you see before you, the monster who will ultimately take your life. Just remember, you brought this upon yourself. You are responsible. I'm not. And what has changed me from someone like you into someone like me? If I had to put a label on it, I would have to say your selfishness. People like you stopped me from doing what I love: cycling.

Ignoring health and environmental benefits, cycling is one of the last bastions of modern life where the individual defines the limits. I could ride as fast as I liked. I could ride where I liked. It was freedom. But it's freedom I don't possess anymore. I'm cursed; damned by all motorists to trawl the streets searching for vengeance. But, don't worry; I only kill those who deserve it. And you deserve it.

You ran the light. You didn't think about me. The shriek of tires matched the panic in your eyes when you realized it was all too late and you wouldn't stop in time. I bet you shit bricks when you hit me and thought you'd killed me.

I wonder, did you see me smile? No? Pity. You should. It's a sight to behold. Scar tissue isn't as resilient as skin and splits easily. My face bleeds when I smile too hard. Are you sure you wouldn't like to see me smile?

Don't turn your head away. Look at me. You should see this, the damage you've done, your contribution to my tapestry of wounds. Yes, the scars are nasty and the malformations are disfiguring. When you've shattered every bone in your body and have had every square inch of flesh flayed from you, from repeated collisions—like I have—what do you expect? I'm a patchwork of past agonies.

But don't worry; it doesn't hurt. It used to, but I'm incapable of hurt now. I'm calcified bone and scar tissue. My bones can't break and my nerve endings can't bond to my scars. I'm indestructible, like a superhero.

Two months after the doctors had set my last bone and grafted my last scrap of virgin flesh, a UPS truck struck me. I should have been killed, but I didn't have a scratch. I realized I had a gift and shouldn't waste it. That's when I knew what I was meant to do.

Lying there, watching the driver panic, euphoria and hatred mixed in my veins creating a volatile cocktail. I got up and snapped that UPS driver's neck. I can't remember ever being happier. I was striking back for the cyclist, giving back what we'd been taking all these years.

I don't kill drivers indiscriminately. I'm not a psychopath. I kill those who would have killed me. The universe has to remain in balance. Someone has to pay the ferryman, right? If it's not me, then it has to be you.

Actually, I'm performing a public service, ridding the world of the irresponsible, the reckless, the drunk and the fun seekers who hurt cyclists for kicks. You wouldn't believe the number of people who've run me down because they think it's funny. People have thrown bottles at me, squeezed me into walls and flung doors open as they've passed me. But the fun ends when I tear the smile from their faces.

Yes, I know, you didn't mean it, but what has that got to do with anything? Just because you got lucky hitting someone like me today doesn't mean that it couldn't have been someone less resilient. You've done what you've done and you have to pay.

You have no idea how much I despise you drivers, and how much pleasure I get from watching you squirm. I'm so driven by hate that my bile is corrosive. My spit cuts through blacktop like it's wet Kleenex, so you can imagine what it can do to flesh. Shall I spit on you to demonstrate?

I wish you wouldn't plead. Look, being a parent is no qualification for having your death sentence commuted. I was a parent once. You wouldn't think it to look at me, I know. My wife and child left me when I refused to give up my bike. They were seeing a transformation from husband and father to… this. I couldn't give up cycling, you see. I'd done nothing wrong. Outlaws surrounded me and I was the last innocent man… and innocent men don't surrender. I learned that from western movies.

No, I won't look into my heart. I already saw it when an eighteen-wheeler ripped my chest open. My heart did nothing but twitch and squirt my blood out of holes that shouldn't have been there. Give me one good reason why I should let you live. Think long and hard now. Impress me and I might just reconsider, but if you don't, well, you know what will happen.

Hmm, an interesting point. No, I don't have anyone to tell my story. Everyone who knows me is dead, like me. Do you think you can make me a legend?

Are you just saying that so I'll let you go?

No? Good. But I can't let you off that easy. A spook story never convinced anyone by itself. People like to have something tangible to believe in. They'll believe you if I leave my mark. You can tell my story, but you'll never drive again. I'll let you go, but I'm taking your eyes.

You had to know there would be a price. Now don't wriggle. You're not going anywhere. If you thought my spit could burn, you'll be amazed by the heat of my uric acid.

Ah, your screams flatter me.

Don't worry; the pain won't last. When it's over, tell everyone I'm riding the roads. They won't know which cyclist is me and they shouldn't try to guess. They should just know to beware the Cyclist. I'm here and I'm waiting for them to break the rules.

Family First
JG FAHERTY

INTENSE PAIN filled the man's head. He couldn't think clearly. He tried to focus but a burning hunger filled him, obliterating all other thoughts.

Where am I? Woods, trees. Daylight. This is all wrong. I was in my car. Driving... those people, on the road...

Teeth, biting... blood.

The rest disappeared into a hazy, black cloud. When it cleared, new thoughts came to him.

Wait... my name is John. I have a family. A wife. Sheila. She's blonde. The children...

The ground slanted in front of him, causing him to lose his balance.

Must climb, go home. Find my family. One hand on the ground, then the other. Move my feet.

I can do this.

He reached the top of the hill. A car sat there, the door open, the windows broken.

My car? Was there an accident?

Why didn't anyone find me?

Walk, must walk. Someone will see me. Find me.

He took one step and then another. It was hard to move his feet, as if they didn't want to obey.

So hungry. It hurts, hurts inside. Need a hospital.

Need food.

The sound of an approaching truck broke the stillness. The tractor-trailer came to a stop in a squeal of airbrakes.

He tried to speak to the man climbing out of the cab.

"I… I… help…"

The sudden smell of food overwhelmed him, pushed away all other thoughts.

Food. Must eat. Must…

Oh, God, no! I…

Must eat.

∞☉∞

"Mom, why can't we leave? Everyone else is gone." Bobby Grainger set down his binoculars and turned his piercing blue eyes, so much like his father's, towards his mother.

"You know why, sweetie. It's too dangerous. Those things are out there. There's no place for us to go." Sheila ran a hand through her hair, smoothing it back from her face. Her hand came away greasy. It'd been four days since the dead rose up. Since then, the closest she'd come to bathing had been washing her hands and face in the kitchen sink.

There was no way she was leaving Bobby and Stacie alone, not even for ten minutes. And at ages nine and eleven, they refused to stay in the bathroom with her, or bathe together.

She knew the severity of the situation hadn't sunk into their MTV-trained attention spans. To them this was something new, something exciting, not a life-threatening catastrophe.

Not yet.

It would take them a while to realize television, school, their friends, the mall, all those things might be gone for a long time to come.

Maybe forever.

"There're zombies here, too, Mom," Bobby said, using the one word she hated to hear. "Maybe we could drive into the city, find the police. Or go deep into the woods, to a cabin or something."

Sheila shook her head. "No. All the cities, from Princeton

to Manhattan, are full of them. Don't you remember the news before the TV went out? And we don't know what's in the woods. They could be there, too."

"Besides, dorkwad, you don't know the first thing about camping. You couldn't start a fire with matches and gasoline." Stacie, her dark blonde hair still streaked with pale yellow from their vacation at Seaside last month, gave her younger brother the kind of smug look pre-teens seem to develop from nowhere.

"Oh, yeah? Well you…"

"Enough, both of you." Sheila used what her kids called 'the tone.' Four days stuck in the house with her two children and they were already on each other's nerves.

For the thousandth time she wished John was here with them. He had a way of saying just the right thing, a funny, off-the-cuff comment or a calming word, to diffuse almost any situation.

He'd gone missing the same day the dead began rising from their graves. He'd been working late—she hadn't expected him back 'til after midnight—so it wasn't until morning that she'd realized he'd never made it home.

By then, the police had their hands full and weren't even answering the phones, let alone looking into missing persons cases.

Every time she thought about him, a reluctant acceptance of his death struggled with the hope that he'd gotten off the turnpike and found a place to hide, a motel or office building, and that he was alive.

And if he was alive, she knew he'd find a way back to them. That was the real reason they weren't leaving. But she couldn't broach that subject with Stacie and Bobby.

It wouldn't be fair to get their hopes up.

Not when the chances were so small.

∞☉∞

John Grainger looked down at himself.

God help me, I did it.

The memories had returned, his thought process almost normal. As if…

As if the flesh and blood restored them.

He wiped his hands on his torn and filthy shirt, leaving red smears, strings of skin and tissue, and pink gobs of brain.

He'd devoured the man from the truck. Torn his throat out. Clawed into him until he reached the softest parts, the juiciest tidbits.

His mind had screamed in horrified disgust but something else had control.

The craving.

The human meat had tasted better, more satisfying, than any meal he'd ever eaten in his life.

And it had restored him.

I'm a monster.

But was he? Maybe it was only this one time; maybe the human flesh had returned his sanity, his 'self.'

I need to get back to Sheila and the kids. They'll be worried. Have to make sure they're safe, then they can get me to a hospital, a research lab. Someplace where they can study me, find a cure.

Return me to normal.

John stepped over the remains of the driver and looked inside. The oversized gear lever and confusing array of buttons and gauges convinced him he'd be better off walking.

Home. Have to get home.

John headed north on the Turnpike towards Fort Lee.

Towards home.

∞⊖∞

"Mom, I see something."

Sheila hurried over to the front window, alarmed by the quiver in her daughter's voice. It had been three days since the last creature approached their cul-de-sac, let alone came near their house. One of the neighbors had shot that one, just before he'd packed his whole family into their Denali and taken off for God knows where.

The body still lay on the sidewalk, a bloated sack of putrefying flesh after seventy-two hours in the hot, muggy July weather.

It's like a giant version of a dead woodchuck, she thought, barely able to contain a sudden insane giggle.

Now isn't the time to lose it. Get a grip.

She moved Stacie aside and peeked out the window. Sure enough, something was moving at the far end of the street where it branched off from Culver Avenue, right by the Henderson's house.

"Bobby, give me the binoculars." The sudden magnification made it seem as if she'd leaped down the street.

The person was dead, no doubt about that—the herky-jerky movements, the shuffling feet, the dirty, torn clothes covered in blood.

Sheila's stomach did a flip-flop, threatening to release the tomato soup she'd had for lunch. She closed her eyes and concentrated on keeping the food down.

They didn't have enough to spare to waste it on being squeamish.

When she had herself under control, she opened her eyes. The thing—*zombie, dammit. Call it what it is*—had turned away and was now walking towards the Henderson's front door.

She realized the Henderson's car was still in the driveway. Were they still home, hiding out the same way she had her family hidden here?

The zombie stopped and tilted its head, turning first one way and then the other. She couldn't see its face but it looked as if the creature was sniffing at something.

Smelling for food? Can they do that?

"Bobby, Stacie. Shut all the windows in the house. Hurry."

"But Mom, it's hot out. If we shut the windows…"

"Goddammit, Bobby, shut up and do what I say!" She kept her voice low, not shouting. If the things could smell people they sure as hell could hear them.

Footsteps behind her let her know the kids had gone off to do what she'd told them. She'd explain later. She pulled down the windows nearest to her, the ones on either side of the front door, and closed the gauzy, blue curtains as well.

She pushed aside the material just enough to aim the binoculars out.

The undead man had moved again. She managed to catch a glimpse of his leg as he went around the side of the house, heading for the Henderson's back yard.

She watched him open the gate, realized they couldn't be as mindless as the news said. *Theirs is funny. It sticks. You have to jiggle the latch and pull up on the gate at the same time. Unless you knew that you could stand there forever trying to open it.*

The kids came back down the stairs, Bobby's sneakers thump-thumping on the wood. The way his feet grew, he'd soon need another pair.

Doesn't look like we'll be shopping anytime in the near future. By now the Paramus Park and Garden State malls look like something from Dawn of the Dead.

Hell, we might all *be barefoot by winter.*

If we're still alive.

That last thought was a black crow that circled endlessly through the landscape of her thoughts. She'd catch sight of it during the day, sometimes far away, sometimes close by. At night it roosted right over her as she lay on the bed, Bobby and Stacie sleeping on either side of her.

"Mom, can I have something to drink? I'm thirsty."

You think you're thirsty now? Wait until the water's shut off and we're living on what falls from the sky, she wanted to shout at him, but John's face appeared, telling her to stay calm.

They're just kids, he would have said. *You're the adult. Act like it.*

As long as the water's working let them drink all they need.

"Go ahead. In fact, let's all go get one."

∞☉∞

I'm a monster.

John couldn't deny it any longer. He stood in the Henderson's living room, which resembled a charnel house more than the relaxed, classically-decorated space it had been before he'd arrived. The last thing he remembered was opening the gate, the one that stuck all the time.

When his awareness returned he'd been standing over Tom Henderson's corpse, his mouth full of blood and tissue and loops of intestines around his hands, their other end still attached to Tom's body.

Puddles of blood soaked into the Persian rug; more splattered across the walls and furniture.

And the taste—oh Lord, the exquisite, wonderful flavor!

A gaping hole in Tom's abdomen revealed where the delicious bounty had originated. Chunks of brownish-red liver lay strewn around the floor.

From where he stood John could see into the kitchen. Enid Henderson lay on the linoleum, her gray-haired skull shattered and empty. A brick lay beside her, which he must have used to crack open her head like a walnut.

All to satisfy his unholy lust, his craving for human flesh.

"Jesus Christ." It came out as garbled moan.

The past three days had been spent alternating between cloudy awareness and bestial savagery. Walking the Turnpike. Scavenging among the corpses in their cars.

But now his head was clear.

He remembered why he was here.

Bobby. Stacie.

Sheila.

He had to get them somewhere safe, away from the monsters.

Monsters like him.

John closed his eyes, tried to block out the explosion of gore surrounding him. There had to be a way to be around his family without losing control.

A shadow moved past one of the front windows.

He walked to the front door, peered outside. Three men staggered down the center of the street, heading towards the far end of the cul-de-sac.

Towards his house.

Quietly, slowly, he eased the door open. From the small front porch he could see to the end of the road. There was movement in one of the windows of his house, a twitch as a curtain fell back in place.

Sheila and the kids. They're still alive. And those things—things like me—are heading towards them.

But how can I save them? I can't even trust myself around them. What if I get hungry again? Images of his wife and children torn apart to feed his unnatural appetite filled his head.

No!

He turned away and was immediately confronted with the abattoir he'd created. Even now, with his stomach filled to bursting, the sight and scent of the bloody organs sparked a hunger in him.

Wait. That's it!

He knelt down by Tom Henderson's corpse and started stuffing pieces of intestine and other organs into the pockets of his gore-crusted pants. From a closet he took one of Tom's jackets and put it on, filled those pockets as well.

The only way to keep from becoming a dangerous, crazed monster like those things outside was to keep his stomach filled. And if that's what it took to save his family, by God he'd do it.

He chewed and swallowed two big pieces of Enid's liver and then ran out the back door. This time he didn't bother with the gate. Instead, he crashed through the hedges separating the Henderson's property from the Thompson's. From one backyard to the next, dodging lawn furniture and swimming pools, he made his way towards his family.

I'll show them I'm not a monster.

∞☉∞

Sheila watched the three zombies shambling down the street and knew her family was in trouble. They hadn't looked at any of the other houses; in fact, from the moment they'd appeared they'd been staring in their blank, malevolent way at only one home.

Hers.

Damn John. Why couldn't he have owned a gun?

Why couldn't he be here now to protect them?

"Bobby. Go get your sister's baseball bat."

The fact that he didn't ask any questions, just took off at a run for his room, let her know the seriousness of the situation must have finally sunk in.

"Mom?" Stacie stood by the other window. "There's more coming."

Sheila looked past the three approaching in their lumbering but steady fashion and saw that her daughter was right. More of the creatures were visible at the end of the road, their heads and shoulders cresting the top of the hill where Turtle Dove and Culver split. Six of them, maybe more.

Bobby returned with the bat.

"Go down to the basement and hide," she told them in her best no-nonsense voice, the one she only used when they were in the worst of trouble.

"What about—?"

"Just go! I'll be fine."

She grabbed each of them and gave them a hard kiss, then pushed them towards the kitchen. As she turned back to the window, a flash of movement behind the Pasternack's house caught her eye, but when she looked nothing was there.

Too fast to be one of them. Must have been a cat or

something.

The first three zombies—the word came so much easier now that she'd accepted her fate—were only two houses away. Close enough to see their green-brown rotting skin and the way their sunken eyes and open mouths gave them a death's head appearance. One of them wore the remains of a white lab coat with Pascack Valley Hospital stitched on the breast pocket; the other two were naked, with giant 'Y'-shaped autopsy incisions on their chests.

The squeal of tires from of the Pasternack's driveway startled her so badly she dropped the aluminum bat and felt a sharp pain in her chest as her heart gave an extra kick. The lime-green Cadillac roared down the driveway and into the three reanimated corpses, sending them into the air like human bowling pins. The car skidded to a stop and then backed up, crushing the skull of one naked zombie and sending grayish matter flying across the blacktop.

The driver leaned out the window and time seemed to freeze for Sheila.

John!

Then he ducked back into the car, turned it around, and gunned the engine, aiming the heavy vehicle right at the large group of walking dead further up the street.

He's alive!

Then, on the heels of that thought, the image of his face came back to her. The pale flesh, the dark hollows under his eyes.

No. It's impossible. He can't be one of them.

She watched the car drive over the dozen or so zombies at the beginning of the circle. John piloted the car back and forth, a neon-green shark feasting on trapped seals. None of the zombies attempted to avoid being struck, further evidence in Sheila's mind that none of them had enough brainpower to start a car, let alone drive one.

That meant John had to be alive. Hurt, maybe. Tired, exhausted, even sick.

But alive.

With the final zombie dealt with, the car turned and came back down the road at a more sedate pace. Without warning it swerved and struck a mailbox, coming to rest halfway across a front lawn. The driver's door opened and John staggered out, his movements uncoordinated and slow. Even from three houses away she could see blood covering his clothes.

Oh, God, he's hurt. She grabbed the binoculars and hurriedly focused on her husband.

Just in time to see him pull something that looked like a giant pink sponge from his pocket and shove it into his mouth. Gobs of the strange material fell onto his shirt as he chewed and gulped like a starving man who'd just found a steak.

Her stomach did a slow somersault as the hammer of truth struck her.

John, *her John*, was gone. Replaced by something that shouldn't even be possible.

As she watched, the man who had once been her husband shoved the remains of the unidentifiable organ into one pocket, straightened up, wiped his arm across his mouth, and began walking in a normal fashion towards the house.

What the hell's going on?

A crash from the kitchen interrupted her thoughts. Turning around, she found a fat woman with one arm climbing through the broken glass of the patio door. Two more of the undead waited behind her.

"John!" The unintentional scream burst from her. Without looking to see if he'd heard, she picked up the aluminum bat and prepared to defend her home.

∞Θ∞

John Grainger knew Sheila had seen him. He was too far away to tell what her expression had been, but there was no mistaking the flash of blonde hair as she turned away from the window. Hopefully she'd noticed how he'd taken care of the monsters, that he wasn't like the others.

"John!"

Sheila's voice. Something was wrong. He sprinted for the house, slammed his shoulder into the front door. There was no pain, just a loud crash as the door pulled from its hinges and fell to the floor. He looked around the living room but she wasn't there.

Glass broke in another room. *The kitchen.*

He hurried across the room.

∞⊖∞

The bat hit the dead woman's head with the same sound as when Stacie connected with a softball. The corpse's face caved in on one side and her jaw hung at an angle, but the single hand still reached forward. Behind the woman the other two zombies entered through the shattered door.

She tried to swing again but the bat struck the wall, throwing her aim off.

"Mom?" Bobby shouted from the top of the stairs.

She leaned against the door. "Stay there! Don't come out!" With one hand she pushed the button to lock the door.

Something heavy hit her, knocking her to the floor. At the same time, a sharp pain exploded between her neck and shoulder. She shoved the end of the bat under the dead woman's head and pushed. The creature fell back, blood and green slime running from its mouth. Sheila looked at her shoulder; a piece of skin the size of her fist was missing.

The zombie swallowed and leaned in for another bite. Sheila brought the bat up again but the woman was too heavy; despite only having one arm, her extra strength forced the bat down towards Sheila's neck.

Then the weight was gone.

Shelia sat up and saw her attacker struggling with someone in an ugly brown jacket.

John!

Her husband grabbed the woman's misshapen head with both hands and pulled. The entire thing came free, tearing from the neck in a staccato series of snapping bones. Without pausing, John put his shoulder into the next zombie, an old man in blue pajamas, and knocked him into the teenage zombie. All three of them went down but John rose almost immediately, moving just as fast as she'd seen him do on the racquetball courts for so many years. He grabbed a carving knife from the butcher block and stabbed each of the monsters in the eye. The damaged orbs collapsed inward and stinking yellow fluids gushed out.

The zombies collapsed. Neither rose.

Dropping the knife, John turned to her. "Are you all right?"

She started to answer, but then the room seemed to swim.

Everything went black.

∞⊝∞

John carried his wife into the living room. He heard the children shouting and pounding at the door, but for now Sheila occupied his thoughts.

He laid her on the couch and tore her blouse away, exposing the damage done by the zombie's teeth. Blood still oozed from the wound. Staring at it, he found himself wanting to put his mouth to it, to taste the blood, feel the flesh against his teeth, tear her open with—

No!

Backing away, he dug pieces of intestine from his pockets and gulped them down. In a moment, the feeling passed and he was able to touch his wife without thinking of her as food.

Her eyes opened.

"John?"

"It's me, honey. I'm here."

"But you're…"

He nodded. "I don't remember how it happened. But I'm okay, as long as I…" He stopped, unable to tell her that the only way he could remain human was with a constant supply of human flesh.

"One of them bit me." Tears welled in her eyes as she said it.

He held her hand. They both knew what it meant; the only question was how long before she turned.

"Will I be like them or you?"

He smiled. "No, I'll make sure you're like me. We'll do what we have to. I won't lose you."

She started to reply but her eyes closed and her head fell back onto the pillow. He touched her neck. No pulse.

She'll be hungry when she wakes up. Have to keep the kids safe from her.

Only one way. Now, before his own hunger came back.

The monsters don't eat their own kind.

He went to the cellar door. "Bobby? Stacie? It's me, Dad."

"Dad?" Their voices, so eager, so innocent.

It's for the best. After, I'll bring them food.

Hopefully they'll understand why I had to do it.

"I'm opening the door. Everything's going to be fine."

The Way of Things in Fly-Over Country
AARON POLSON

THE SEARCH BEAMS CROSSED in front of the gate when my buddy Dan—broad and strong like a spit of granite—hunched over on all fours, making a little scaffold out of his back for me to climb. I scrambled over his shoulders, flopped over the gate, and dropped to the ground on the other side. The first over, Davin, was waiting for me with his shotgun poking out into the kill zone. Once I dusted off a bit and straightened my glasses, we waited for the lights to swing by again before tossing Dan the rope; I held the outside end steady while he climbed. Davin kept me covered. I was scared, shaking like chimes in the wind, but Davin held steady.

Once Dan dropped to the ground I reeled in the rope, and the three of us hunched in the shadow of the big gate while the lights swung by once more. Davin looked at Dan and me, smiled crookedly, and nodded. The lights rotated away and we sprinted for the shadows at the edge of Old Town. I figured the guards probably saw dumb kids like us half the time, but no one ever fired a shot.

So there we were: seventeen, full of piss and stupidity, creeping through ruined streets on a Friday night with a couple of jars of Uncle Jeb's homemade booze, our guns, and an ache to celebrate Dan's eighteenth birthday. One week later, hopping the fence would land Dan in the stockade—a crime believed to endanger the whole village, but this was coming of age, our ritual. Plenty of other dumb bastards snuck out of the compound before they officially became men; Dad even admitted to sneaking out just before his brother's eighteenth.

I glanced over my shoulder at the wall: randomly fused sections of steel, brick, concrete, and stone. Originally a desperate measure against the walking dead, that wall had stood for something like eighty years. For boys raised in captivity the world outside the wall reeked with mystery, and we devoured grand lies that became our motivation to hop the wall—a man's right to be free, all that crap. The older men in the compound filled us with stories, baiting us like a lantern to a moth, knowing we'd bite, go over, and look for danger. The stifling closeness behind the wall pushed us, too—personally caught me in the throat. "What'll it be, boys?" Davin asked once we found the shadows. The moon shone pretty bright that night, drawing the silver out of the world. Davin shimmered like a bit of fresh aluminum.

"Hell, I'm itching to splat a couple tonight." Dan walked ahead a few steps with long, loping strides, the pinnacle of our small triangle.

"Old man Jantz says we have to check out the church. Says it's beautiful, sacred ground. Inside the building, with a moon like this, the whole place lights up like a rainbow." Davin stopped and cocked his head to once side, pointing toward the hill that led to the little building. We all knew about the church, the center of so many stories. Supposedly, that building remained mostly intact after all these years; a vestige of old superstitions lurking in our new ones kept folks from smashing it up.

"Fine, but I want to show you guys something first. Something my brother told me about." Dan pointed the barrel of his shotgun into a thick patch of inky shadow and strode forward.

Most of the big trees in Old Town were gone, knocked down for safety, but saplings, crooked grass, and snaking weeds groped toward the sky all around. I was surprised at how well I could see with just the moon. With the bright searchlights back at the wall, the rest of the night world look as black as spent oil, but the hunched backs of old houses, broken business, and other buildings rubbed against the blue night and field of stars in plain detail as we walked through Old Town.

I'd heard some stories, mostly from Grandpa, that the bigger cities had drained the plains of their population long before the end. In the meantime, the big corporate farms finished off the aquifers and sucked the land dry. Without water, there wasn't much reason to live in the flat land. Without too many people out here, there couldn't be too many of *them*, the zombies. Hell, I'd only seen maybe a dozen in my life, but they left the taint of decay smeared across everything. You could see it all over Old Town.

As we stumbled down the split asphalt of an ancient street, Dan reached into his pack, rummaged around, and produced a jar of booze. It was nothing but rot-gut moonshine, but it was all we had because most drivers wouldn't risk a run through the wastelands just to drop off some beer for a bunch of hold-out hicks. That's the way Grandpa painted it, anyway. The scavengers in the wastelands seemed worse than a whole stockyard of zombies. Dan screwed off the lid, tossed back a swig, and shook his head. "Not bad, boys." He slowed, passed the jar to Davin.

"No," Davin said, waving Dan off with the barrel of his gun. "Not until I'm kicked back in the church."

"Nate?"

"Sure," I said, cupping the jar in one hand while clutching my shotgun in the other. The gun had been my great-grandfather's. Grandpa said he used it on birds—quail and pheasant, mostly—as a boy. I'd only fired the thing a few times myself, typically at wooden targets that wouldn't bite. The guns did make me nervous; we were warned against using them as the report would rouse any undead in the area. I tossed back a swig from the jar. Damn, that shit tasted awful, but the warm humming feeling that grew out to my fingertips after a few swigs kept me going.

"Did hear about Stacy's cousin over in New Colby?" Dan asked, reaching for the jar.

"Yeah," Davin muttered.

"Gawd, I never want to see another burning in my life." Dan spat on the street. Davin's eyes narrowed. "I don't want those superstitious old bastards to set me on fire when I kick off."

I shook my head and fingered Dad's old lighter in my pocket, fighting a shiver born of too many burnings. Mom, for one, after Melina was born. Too much blood, not enough medical knowledge, a bad mix of both. Dad tried to explain the need for a burning, the whole ritual, but I wanted none of it. I know you can't just bury the dead anymore—paranoia, hysteria, and the real likelihood that the undead will sniff out a fresh corpse. When I was five, watching my mother burn to black ash, none of that rationalization amounted to a hill of shit. Grandpa whispered something about Viking warriors in my ear that day, trying to cheer me. "Great big pyres, big as a house," he said, "it was *pride*, not fear and shame made 'em build those pyres."

Dan clicked on the lantern he'd taped to the barrel of his gun. "Here we are fellas. Used to serve food here. C'mon." The light reached out, starting to grope the heavy shadow inside a mashed up brick building. I'd never heard anything about that particular spot, and I couldn't figure what he wanted us to see.

Rows of benches stretched down a tiled hallway; some broken with bits tossed askew to the grid. Across a counter to our right sat the old kitchen, a steel grill and some broken cash machines. A few coins littered the floor, shining on the floor like dead minnows. The whole place rested under a thick dust like frost on a January morning.

"Ssssh." Dan, walking just ahead of us, waved back with one hand. My heart started pumping against my ribcage until I thought it would spring free and skitter across the floor. I heard why Dan shushed us then, I could smell the thing, too–

—a rotten, fishy stench mixed with mud.

Davin pushed forward, raising his gun, "Dan, give me a little," he whispered, and Dan obliged, poking his flashlight around the corner."

Use a baton," I whispered, fearing gun's report and its siren song to other zombies. I reached down to my side and fingered the black rod hanging on my belt.

Davin glanced back at me and uttered a low, "Naw."

Then I saw it, a little thing, bobbing its matted blonde head up and down as it munched on something—most likely a rat or stray cat. Davin clicked his tongue to get its attention, and the thing rotated to face us. It was a girl, six or seven maybe, although she could've been six or seven for years now. The undead didn't age like us. Her little mouth, blotted with blood, opened and a little moaning sound trickled out. I closed my eyes for a moment and saw my sister's face.

Davin raised the gun, butted the stock against his shoulder, and said, "bye, bye sissy." The building shook with his report, frozen for an instant in a muzzle flash, and settled under Dan's dim yellow beam. Its body slumped over on the ground, headless.

"Nice shootin', Tex." Dan thumped Davin on the back. Davin nodded, fished in his pocket for a folding knife, and carved a notch in the stock. I staggered to bench and held my head.

"You alright, ya pansy?" Dan kicked my boots.

"Yeah. Fine. Hand me the jar, okay?" After Dan and I swallowed a few more swigs, he led us out back, to the barrels. In my mind's eye, every shadow grew arms and reached for us. All the warnings about the guns materialized in my imagination.

"This is what I wanted to show you boys." He leaned his shotgun against the grey boards of an old fence, a little shelter that hid two black-steel drums. "My brother told me about this shit. Says they used to cook food in it, but even the rotbags won't touch it." His hands worked one of the lids free, and it dropped to the ground with a dull *THUNK*. The barrel looked to be half full of thick oil, black as midnight blood. The smell—heavy and sweet—knocked me back.

"Can you believe people used to eat this?"

∞ꙩ∞

The world started spinning while we humped over to the church. Not the whole world, just my piece of it—my brains sloshing around inside my skull, knocking against my ears. I thought maybe it was the booze; loads of stories circulated about bad home-brew. Dan seemed fine, striding ahead like usual, and Davin hadn't touched the drink.

"Gawd, you're a pansy." Dan called after I stumbled and called for a break. I didn't wallow on his insult, but the shadows started poking their fingers at me. I kept seeing that little girl's face, smeared and dead, hissing at us as Davin sprayed her brain matter across the dusty tile. We slipped from the relative safety of the compound, only to find our freedom rotten and decayed.

I staggered to my feet after a few minutes. We made the church while the moon was still high, floating overhead like a glowing bobber in a still, blue-black pond. I huffed and puffed up the hill a little more than I'd like to admit. My stomach and head still danced, but I knew once inside we'd loiter a bit and I could lounge, letting my guts come to a rest. Davin spotted something ahead and sprinted out in front of Dan.

"Mother fuckers," he hollered.

"What?" Dan jogged to his side. I stumbled behind, nearly slipping to the ground on a patch of fresh mud.

"They chained the god-damn door." A heavy chain was wrapped in repeated loops around the handles, and Davin tapped it with the stock of his gun. "Somebody cries about a few 'bags and they lock down the fucking church." He was a small guy, but swelled when angry, his skin burning through a few shades of red. The compound militia had done it; they must have locked up the place.

Davin and Dan took a few steps back. Davin raised his gun like he was going to take a shot at the chain, but lowered the barrel a moment later. This was a thick, coiled bit of steel; a blast from his shotgun wouldn't scratch it, and we weren't prepared with anything that could get at the lock. If it was anything but the church, we'd quickly smash up the windows and hop in. All the stories were about the beauty of those windows, and I doubt any of us wanted to smash those stories.

"Give me the jar," he called to Dan.

I stood apart from the other two and glanced into the night behind us, half expecting a few lumbering undead to stumble from the paper-thin shadows. The waiting, the not knowing, grabbed and twisted at my stomach. I turned back to the church, admiring the long windows decorated with faint images. Grandpa called them stained glass. Almost every other hunk of glass in Old Town had been shattered many times over by guys like us, but something in the artistry of those high panes kept them from harm. I thought how odd and almost blank they looked from the outside, when inside they supposedly burned color across everything.

I looked around at Davin as he tossed an empty jar to the ground, having polished off the last bit. He reached down, palmed a hunk of rock, and stared at the building. "Nobody tells me what to do," he muttered, taking a few steps closer to the big windows.

The next moment leaked into my eyes slowly, like the whole planet groped through molasses. Davin's arm sprang forward like a little catapult; the rock tumbled end over through the air, and struck a window dead on. The glass cried out, split, and crumbled in a tinkling heap. It had been the picture of a lady in blue with a little kid on her lap—Mary and Jesus, I think. The frame held, but most of the glass fell, just leaving this odd grey outline of a woman suspended across the opening.

Davin went pale; I think he was struck by how easy the whole thing crumbled. The low buzz of night bugs and bull-frogs slowly swelled to fill the silence. I scanned the slope behind us. Nothing.

"Damn, Davin. Nice toss. Well, might as well head back. Fun's over, I suppose." His voice fell flat, like he couldn't really disguise his disappointment. We'd all expected something else out there, maybe legions of undead that would make us happy we stuffed our pockets with shells. Dan trudged downhill, back toward the road leading to the gate. I followed, still queasy and a little unsteady. Davin's boots crunched against the gravel behind me, and then stopped. I turned and looked at him, this flat emptiness across his face.

"No."

"No?" My palms started to sweat. The little guy had a temper. I remember one time he knocked Dan flat, bloodied his nose, just because Dan gave him shit about being so short. I'd seen Davin drop a handful of other guys the same way.

He looked at the moon for a moment, and I caught the shine shimmer off the whites around his eyes. "No, I'm not done yet. The whole world has gone to hell." He flashed around, hurried up the hill to the side of the building, and tumbled inside the rectangular entrance left by the broken window.

I cupped one hand against my mouth and called down the hill. "Dan!" He stopped about thirty yards away, turned, and moved toward me.

"What? Where the hell is Davin?"

I pointed to the church.

"That little bastard," Dan said, and strode uphill.

Shotgun blasts rocked from inside the church. Dan passed me and paused at the side of the building. All I had was the moonlight, but some of the glass glistened a bit, wet with what I confused for oil or some of that grease in the old barrel. Dan and I kicked in the rest of the window, hopped inside, and found our buddy reloading his shotgun, his face covered in a mix of sweat and blood.

"Fucking bullshit, all of it." He raised the shotgun again, pointing at the large windows opposite us. Five more shots in rapid succession rocked the inside of the chapel, shattered the windows, and brought years of dust and debris raining from above. Sheets of bright glass cascaded to the floor.

Dan placed his hand on Davin's shoulder. "C'mon, man. Let's get out of here." I backed away, ready to flee, afraid of being trapped inside. Surely the noise would bring the dead. My ears still rang with the recent display of firepower, but my eyes jerked to a noise—a snarling, moaning wail from outside the window. I glanced outside and saw a small group of meat bags shambling towards us. Five of them—fifty yards away.

"Guys…"

Davin shrugged away from Dan and rushed to the window. "It's about time," he muttered. He knocked out the remnants of the window with the butt of his gun and sprang outside. "Bring it, you bastards," he hollered, charging down the slope. The dead responded, lurching toward him, moths to a fire. He hadn't reloaded his shotgun, but hurried toward the ghouls with it raised like a club.

Dan pushed me aside and started out of the window. As I followed, my pounding heart choked the breath from my chest.

Shadows danced in front of us. Davin howled—not pain, but pleasure. He screamed like a berserker, a mad warrior in his final fight. The stock of his gun smashed through a few skulls; one head came completely off. Dan raised his gun, trying for a clear shot, but cursed under his breath. It was over before we were close enough to help.

Davin knelt, panting, in the midst of five ruined bodies. He managed to bludgeon each into submission, a pile of grey flesh like rotten logs. His clothing, arms, and face were caked with zombie sludge, blood, mud—all except two streaks trailing from his eyes down either cheek.

"That... was... fun," he breathed. His eyes met mine, sparkling in the moonlight. He held up his left arm, leaning on the shotgun like a crutch with his right. A red gash cut across the forearm where one of the things bit into his skin. "That last little bastard got me..." I looked at Dan. His face flushed white. "No..."

"You gotta do it, fellas. I'm toast." Davin shook his head. "What a way to go, huh?" He grinned, white teeth flashing from a mask of blood and offal.

"No." Dan dropped his gun. "I can't."

Davin looked at me. My hands trembled around the gun. I pushed the stock into my shoulder. The trigger was cold against my finger.

"Do it." Davin's body toppled backward with the thunder.

I looked away as I pulled the trigger, ashamed to fear the blood and worried more rot-bags smelled the fresh kill, or heard the shot and would swarm the place.

Dan didn't move for a few minutes; he just hunched on grass and stared at Davin's body. The moonlight filtered through a few drifting clouds, casting a somber pall of blue over the scene while the wind whispered across the jagged tops of nearby trees. After a minute I heard this sob, starting low like a moan. I clutched my shotgun with white knuckles and turned to Dan. He was crying.

"Stupid bastard. Stupid, fucking bastard." He drew one foot back as if to kick Davin's body but stopped, rubbing a sleeve across his face. "We gotta get him outta here," he said, almost choking on the words.

I looked back at the corpse. His face was ruined, but in my mind's eye I saw Davin as he was alive. I saw his cock-eyed smile and confident flicker in his eye. I knew what would happen if we carried him back to the compound.

"We can't take him back."

"What?"

I thought of Mom; the last time I saw her they doused her with fuel, dropped their torches, and her skin cracked and blackened, sending an angry plume of black snaking into the sky. Maybe the booze did it, worked on my stomach and my brain, but I knew we couldn't bury him out here—the zombies would make a meal of his remains before the day was out. We couldn't take him back with us either. "I'm not letting those paranoid bastards make a little bonfire of his body. He didn't want that."

"Are you nuts?" Dan slumped into a pew. "Those rotbags will chew him up if we don't." Silence filled the little church before he spoke again. "What the hell do you want to do, stuff him in one of those damn grease barrels?"

I reached for Davin's gun. The stock was battered now, blotted with dried blood and mud, but I could make out the groove Davin had carved with his knife. I counted thirteen older marks from his father and grandfather. Five more tallies for the dead at our feet would make nineteen. That gun had been his grandfather's, passed down for generations.

"No, we send him out right."

∞⊖∞

Dan helped me drag a few pews into a pile, and then I turned over a little table at the center of our kindling. Dan was stronger than me, so he hoisted Davin's body over his shoulders, lugged him to the front of the church, and laid him out on the table. I pried open our remaining jar of booze and doused his body with it. It tasted like shit, so I knew it was strong enough to burn well. Poking my hand in my jeans, I fished around for the lighter, Dad's old thing with the initials engraved on the side.

I snapped the lighter open against my leg. With a quick flick of my thumb a small flame lurched toward the dark ceiling of the church, and I touched the fire to the edge of the table, watching it explode as a magnificent pyre fit for our friend. We stood outside the building for a while, chased back by the heat. I wanted to wait until every beam in the church blackened, devoured by the orange fire, and collapsed on itself. Dan and I were silent. The world was silent. As the fire melted into an ash pile we turned and stumbled down the hill. On our way back to the wall I glanced off into the sunrise. We spotted a zombie, a lanky thing stumbling away from us down a quiet street—he hadn't come with the others, and how many more shambled about in the darkness I would never know. It faced the other way and didn't see us. Dan raised his gun but hesitated. "Aw hell," he muttered as he dropped the gun.

Behind the zombie, the eastern sky started to balloon with pinks and oranges, and I took it in, trying to memorize the look of the morning sun cresting a hill. You couldn't see a sunrise like that in the compound. I realized that the rest of my life would be spent behind the wall, and understood why Davin had charged headlong into the arms of the dead. At that moment, I feared the stifling closeness inside more than the few pathetic, undead bastards that littered fly-over country.

The Beach
TIM LEBBON

"SUNDAY," Ray said.

I nodded. "Sunday. Day of rest." From behind us, the regular crack of rifles.

He sighed. "I'm dead beat. Stiff as a bugger. Do you think there's any hope?"

Without looking at him, I uttered something between a giggle and a sob. I'd been feeling pretty weird lately. "There's always hope. So long as we have bullets, there's always hope." I drew a shape in the dew-speckled grass, but did not know what it was meant to be.

"Cliché King strikes again."

We faced the house because it implied normality, a façade from the past. It stood alone on the plain, a supposed retreat from all that was happening. We had come here because we thought it would be safe. We thought nobody else would know about it. Our complacency had marked us out.

Behind us, another cascade of rifle shots. Ammunition was running low. The snipers were using their rounds sparingly, trying to line up two or more to make the most of the shot. Each miss was another two steps closer to the end; each hit was merely one.

"I never thought it would end like this," Ray said. "When we came here, I mean. I thought it would be safe. We can see for miles around. I thought it'd be safe." He often used the word *safe,* as if repetition could imbue it with power over unrelenting reality.

I glanced at my watch, but did not know the time. The

smashed face recorded forever the instant of my fleeing the city, where I had abandoned Gemma to her fate. She had been dead already, but I could have done so much more for her. I hated myself for that. I hoped she did not hate me too.

Sometimes I thought I saw her on the distant hillside, shuffling towards the house with interminable, relentless steps. I prayed every night that it would not be my shift when she arrived.

"Our shift," I said. Ray and I stood, turned from the house—the mental placebo for our sickness—and faced the real world.

I took a rifle from Dawn. I smiled encouragingly, but she had been at the barricade for two hours, and her face was molded grim.

The gun was still hot. The rack of magazines was sadly depleted. I'd have to make every shot count.

There must have been a million of them. They seemed to be coming here from all over the world. Dead but walking, all their stagnant attention was focused on our house. We were the centre of the world, and it was hopeless. I wished they would all turn around and walk back the way they had come, but eventually, I knew, they would simply travel around the globe and reach us from the opposite direction.

I took aim and fired. A head exploded into dry brains and shattered skull.

We were an island in a sea of moving dead. They walked over the pathetic corpses of those we had already shot. They came slowly, like a glacier of doom, guaranteed to sweep us away eventually but content in the knowledge that they need not rush things.

I took aim and fired. One went down with half a head, the bullet ricocheting and punching through the spine of another. A bullet well spent.

In the distance, flaming red hair. A smile borne of decomposition, not love. Gemma.

It would be another hour or so before she was near

enough to be worth shooting. It was an hour I spent reliving our time together, like an extended flashback experienced by a drowning man. And I was drowning. Choking on the inevitability of things. Putting off the end, as mankind had for decades, the difference being that I had no faith in redemption. I was not waiting for God to intervene; I simply wanted a few more hours of life.

At the end of the hour, when she was close enough for me to see the empty sockets where once resided the eyes I loved, I took aim and pulled the trigger. But there were no more bullets left.

Fast Eddie's Big Night Out
JOHN L. FRENCH

SAFE, THAT'S WHAT HE FELT *like when he finally became aware of himself. Safe and warm. He hadn't felt like this since, since— he didn't know. It didn't matter. Wherever he was, he was at peace.*

∞☉∞

He called himself "Fast Eddie." It wasn't his real name. That was Wallace—Wallace Cromwell. He'd hated that name. Hated being called Wallace. Hated "Wally" more. Hated being asked how the Beaver was. Then one night he saw a movie on late night TV about some guys shooting pool, Paul Newman and a fat guy. Newman's name was Fast Eddie. He liked that and started using it as his own.

By then he was typically alone. He still lived in his mother's house, but his bedroom was in the basement. He came and went as he pleased. Mostly he went home to eat, sleep and get clean laundry. Some days he didn't go home at all. There was too much happening on the street—people to see, stuff to do.

Some of the stuff involved drinking—beer, wine, whatever he could get. And some of it involved girls—those who gave it away, those who traded it. And some of it involved drugs—reefer, crack, whatever made him feel good and forget the boredom that was at the bottom of his life. And all of it involved money. Money he usually didn't have and always needed. Money his mother had stopped giving him. Money he had to get from somewhere no matter what.

He tried street jobs, but that was low percentage. The guy you robbed might not have any more than you. Or he might be armed, and your payoff would be a knife in the side or a nine in the head. It was better to B&E. Less chance of getting caught, and VCRs, DVDs and computers always brought him enough to get by.

He went home less and less. One night he went back and didn't have his key. Hadn't had it for a long time. How long, he didn't know. He pounded on the front door. No answer. He went around and pounded on the back. Still nothing. He broke the pane of the basement door, reached it and unlocked it.

Things were changed. None of his stuff was there. He didn't know the man standing in the basement. He did know the man had a gun. And he knew that the sirens in the distance were coming for him.

Nobody believed that he thought it was still his house. His mother hadn't lived there for months. What had happened to her he never found out. Without money for bail he sat in the Baltimore Detention Center for six months, awaiting trial. In that time his prints came back on six other burglaries. He got three on top of the half he'd served. Overcrowding forced him back on the street inside the year.

When Eddie came out he went back to the B&E, back to yoking tourists who went down the wrong street, back to jacking cars from the fools who came down from PA looking to buy drugs. He had to. Inside he had picked up the habit, and now it needed to be fed every day.

He went inside the second time because he got stung. The guy in the Honda looking to buy turned out to be a cop. When Eddie pulled his piece the cop pulled a bigger one. Without turning around, Eddie knew that there were two more big guns pointing at the back of his head.

Two years this time. Eddie's cellmate was a no-parole lifer who had found Jesus. Or was it Allah? Whoever It was, the lifer always talked to Eddie about a better way. With nothing else to do, Eddie listened.

It didn't make sense until three months after Eddie was out. Out in the cold and rain, huddling in a doorway, the better way that the con had talked about seemed very good to Eddie. He'd change, Eddie told himself. He'd find a program and get clean, give up this half a life and start living again.

Getting clean was harder than scoring without cash. All the programs were full. The drug treatment centers had waiting lists. Despite his wanting it, no one was offering any help. Desperate, and willing to do anything to escape the Limbo he was in, Eddie did the one thing he never expected to do. He called a cop.

∞☉∞

"Yeah, I'm interested... Thought there might be, how much?... Oh! That might take some doing... No, didn't say it couldn't be done, have to pull in a few that's all... Give me your cell... Thought everybody did... Pager then... Well then, call be back in two days... Yeah, this number. I'll work something out, get you clean." Detective Dante Amberson hung up the phone.

"Who was that?" Andy Russell asked his partner.

"Some stoner called Fast Eddie," Amberson replied, turning to his computer. He logged on to the Citynet and searched "drug treatment centers—open beds." There weren't that many.

"I remember Eddie, we almost shot him, what, two years back?"

"That's why he called us, because we didn't shoot him when we could have. Thinks he can trust us." Amberson started copying names, numbers and email addresses into a document, highlighting the ones he'd try first.

"What's he want?"

"To give us Santos."

Russell's eyes widened. Antoine Santos wasn't a major

drug dealer, but he was big enough that once arrested, he could be squeezed until he gave up a few people who were. "How's Eddie know Santos?"

"Used to work for him, still does some running." Amberson hit print. Two lists came out of the printer.

"And for Santos he gets——?"

"Placement in a drug treatment center. He wants out of the life."

"That's it, no money?" Russell was amazed; everybody wanted money.

"He wouldn't turn it down, but without treatment, no Santos."

"We better make some calls."

Amberson handed Russell one of the lists. "Tell me about it. Start calling, partner."

Two days later Eddie called back.

"All arranged, my man," Amberson told him. "Got a room at the McCulloh Treatment Facility with your name on it… That's right, where Church Home Hospital used to be… You're getting the works—detoxification, blood cleaning, counseling, job placement, everything. You be there tomorrow morning, eleven sharp. We'll get you settled, then you give us what we need on Santos… What's that?"

But Eddie hadn't been talking to Amberson. The detective heard him say something to somebody, his voice low as if turned away from the phone. There was a muffled reply, then three loud pops.

"Oh shit! Eddie! Eddie!" Amberson yelled into the receiver. To his partner, "Andy, call 2284. Get this line traced. Get an ambo started. Eddie!" he yelled again. No answer.

"Got it," Russell said calmly. "Units and medics are rolling. Anything on your end?" Amberson shook his head. "Damn. Well, let's get out there." Amberson looked at the admissions folder they'd gotten from McCulloh. "Damn," he said again, "and after all our hard work."

When the two detectives rolled up on the scene they saw

the ambulance pulling away.

"Follow that," Amberson told his partner. "Let the district guys and the Lab worry about witnesses and spent casings. If Eddie's still alive we'll get his statement."

Russell followed the ambulance down Wolfe Street. He groaned when it turned right, bypassing Johns Hopkins.

"Taking him right to Shock Trauma," he said. "Must be bad."

Madison to Central. Central to Fayette. From Fayette straight to Shock Trauma and the best emergency care available. Russell knew the way—every detective did—and he stayed close to the wagon. He wanted to be there when Eddie was pulled out, to hear him say who shot him, hoping the name was "Santos."

Lights flashing and siren screaming, the ambulance raced down Central. But when it turned on Fayette, it went silent and dark as its emergency system shut down. It slowed, now keeping pace with traffic rather than weaving in and out.

There could only be one reason for the sudden lack of urgency. "Damn," Amberson's fist hit the dash. "They lost him."

Still, Russell followed. From Fayette Street the wagon turned on to Penn Street and from there, down the ramp that led to the Medical Examiner's Office.

Russell parked along side the ambulance. The detectives caught up to the paramedics just as they were wheeling Eddie into the receiving area.

"He say anything?" Amberson shouted as soon as he got into the room.

"Like?" asked the medic. He was on the twelfth hour of a sixteen-hour day. He'd had two "breaks." Once he stopped for a coffee and doughnut at a convenience store, both of which he gulped down rushing to yet another overdose call. An hour later at Hopkins he stopped briefly to call his wife and use the bathroom. Somehow he couldn't bring himself to get as excited about this dead junkie as the detective was.

"Like did he say who shot him?"

The medic shrugged. "Maybe. I wasn't listening." In fact, the medic had stopped listening a year ago. He'd heard a dying declaration from a gunshot victim, reported it to the police. That lead to his going to court several times, spending hours waiting in a cold, dark hallway only to be told the case was once again postponed. When he finally did get to testify, he was on the stand three hours, as a team of defense attorneys challenged his competency, questioned his hearing and subtly suggested that he'd let the victim die so that declaration could be used in court. When a "not guilty" verdict came back the medic decided that from then on, he'd be deaf to anything not directly related to treating his patient.

∞Ө∞

Like a baby, Eddie felt himself being cradled in someone's arms. There was a gentle, rocking motion. Gradually, the arms became a hand, with Eddie cupped in its palm as if being weighed. He became aware of all the decisions, good or bad, he'd ever made in his life. He saw too all the decisions he'd failed to make. Every path his life could have taken was revealed to him. Some were worse than the one he had lived. Most were better.

From somewhere there was a voice. "A life mostly wasted. An effort at redemption towards the end." A light appeared—a golden light. Eddie was drawn toward it. But he knew without the voice telling him that despite his yearning, he'd get no closer to the light than where he was now.

∞Ө∞

"Can you make the ID?" the attending examiner asked Amberson and Russell.

The detectives looked down at the body. There wasn't much to see: a body ravaged by drugs, thin and dirty from too many months on the street.

"Yeah," Russell answered. "For your records, I identify this body as one Wallace Cromwell, a.k.a. Fast Eddie."

"And do you agree, sir?" the examiner asked Amberson. There was a slight lilt of the Caribbean in his voice.

Amberson nodded. "Well, Eddie," he said to the corpse, "I guess you won't be needing that treatment now. I just wish you'd held on long enough to give us Santos."

Now would be a good time, the examiner thought. In his six months in this country, five months doing this job, he'd seen too much of this tragedy, too many wasted lives. It was time to do something about it, if these men were willing.

"He still could."

Both detectives looked at the examiner, who had finished weighing the body and was now filling out a toe tag.

"Excuse me, Mr.—?" Amberson asked.

"Jones, Dominic Jones. I said that maybe he still could."

"And how, Mr. Amberson, could he do that?"

"I am from the Dominican Republic. My country, as you may or may not know, shares its island with Haiti. When I was in medical school, it was close enough to Haiti that, occasionally, myself and other students would slip across the border to study, shall we say, comparative medicine and religion."

"Voodoo," Amberson said softly.

"Vodou," Jones corrected, giving the word a slightly different pronunciation.

"Wait a minute," Russell said, almost shouting, "you're saying you can bring this guy back from the dead?"

Jones smiled. "Not exactly. Rather, it may be possible to awaken a soul, as if from sleep, before it passes on. If so, one can ask what questions one needs to, before the soul is called away forever."

Russell gave a derisive laugh. Amberson, on the other hand, asked, "And you can do this?"

"I have seen it done. An old man, called back to tell where he had hidden his wealth. A woman, dead after childbirth, summoned from the dark to say which man in the village fathered her child. In each case, the priest performed the ritual. In each case, an answer came from the corpse."

Russell interrupted. "And there are guys in Vegas who stick their hands up dummies's butts who can do the same thing."

"Ventriloquism, Detective? Maybe. But the money was found where the old man's ghost said it would be. And the child grew up in the image of his announced father."

"Do you know the ceremony?" Amberson asked suddenly.

"This is crazy!"

At his partner's exclamation Amberson said, "And we haven't seen crazy before? Besides, it's not like we got anything to lose. Unless you've got a better idea?"

"I can do it, Detective. I have watched the priests and studied with them. One thing about this place: it's got everything I need, except... do you know where we can get a live chicken?"

∞☉∞

Eddie drifted. Try as he might, he couldn't move closer to the glow. Then he felt himself being pulled away. He thought he heard someone call his name. And then—something else. There was something else he had to do. The golden light got fainter, smaller. Like the dot on an old TV, it faded away.

∞☉∞

"Eddie, Eddie, can you hear me?" Amberson shouted, shaking the corpse. "Come back, Eddie! Give us Santos!"

"It's no good, partner." Russell drew Amberson away. "It was dumb idea to begin with."

"It should have worked," a despondent Jones said. He looked at the bodies of the dead pigeons in the biohazard waste bin. "We should have used chickens."

"Yeah," Russell turned on him, "and I should maybe run us all up to Mercy for an emergency commitment. Me searching the parking garage for those birds, catching them yet. I have to be crazy."

"The only other choice was regular or extra crispy," Amberson said. "Come on, we've already wasted two hours. Let's get some papers signed and get back to work. Mr. Jones, thanks for your effort, but let's not mention this to anyone."

"Agreed, detective. Now if you two will step into my office, we can get the paperwork out of the way."

It took Jones about ten minutes to find and fill out the forms. Amberson signed them and gave them back. Jones was just putting them into a folder when an alarm sounded.

"What's that?" Russell asked.

"The door to our vehicle bay," Jones explained. "Someone's coming in."

They went out into the receiving area to see who it was. Russell was the first to notice the empty gurney where Eddie's body had lain. "Or someone left."

Beside him, Amberson swore quietly.

"You know," Jones said, staring at the empty place where Fast Eddie had been, "when you use a chicken they don't get up and leave."

∞Θ∞

Eddie woke up, sort of. Light and sound rushed back in. His chest hurt. He felt the cold steel of the gurney beneath him. Not knowing where he was or how he got there, Eddie got up and walked toward the door. It opened automatically, as did the gate of the vehicle bay when Eddie crossed the electric eye. Driven by a need he didn't understand, Fast Eddie walked out into the night.

He was confused. Memories of a warm, safe place where he was loved conflicted with other thoughts. He was talking to someone, someone who was helping him. He heard a noise. He turned. Talking, then more noise, louder this time. Pain. Eddie looked down at his chest. His shirt was open. He could see the holes the loud noise had put there. A clear liquid was seeping from them.

Eddie was still looking at the bullet wounds when he wandered into the street. There was a screeching of wheels, then Eddie was struck by steel, glass and steel again as he went up and over the car that hit him. Eddie stood up and, ignoring the curses of the driver, slowly walked away.

∞☉∞

"Now what do we do?" Amberson asked no one in particular.

"I don't know about you two, but if he's not back by six a.m., I'm shredding everything and he was never here."

"We'll find him, Jones,"

"We will?" asked Russell.

"Of course," Amberson assured him. "How far can a dead guy go?"

The detectives left the ME's and walked out on to an accident scene: a late-model sedan with pedestrian damage to the hood, windshield and roof; two patrol cars blocking the street; a uniformed officer taking a statement from a distraught driver. No victim, no ambo.

"What happened?" Russell asked one of the officers standing by.

"Damnest thing," came the reply. "Driver here says some junkie walked out in front of him. He couldn't stop in time and the guy went up and over. Says he came down hard, then got up and walked away."

"Driver didn't try to stop him?" Amberson asked.

"Would you?" The officer shook his head. "You'd think the guy would be dead, wouldn't you?"

Amberson looked at Russell. Russell looked back. Neither

said a word.

∞☉∞

Eddie wandered, his thoughts a jumble. He sensed a need, but for what? Dimly he recalled the taste of food, of strong drink. He vaguely remembered the touch of a woman and how that made him felt. Then there was the needle, the high that had made him float and forget. It had taken the place of the others, but it was still not enough, not now, not tonight.

Brightness blinded him. His wanderings had taken him out of the dark streets and alleys and now he found himself on Greene Street.

Streetlights, stoplights, neon and the glow of the not so distant Oriole Park all hit his too sensitive eyes at once. It came back—he needed the light, the golden light he'd been denied earlier. But no, that light was gone, taken from him when he was called back. Its absence left a yearning, a hole to be filled. Instinct turned Eddie to the east, towards the one man who had always given him what he needed.

∞☉∞

"We've been driving in circles for hours," Russell complained. "It's time to give it up."

"It's only been an hour, and we're not giving up," Amberson said in a flat, determined tone.

"Can't we at least put out a description?"

"And say what? Eastern CID looking for a walkaway from the Medical Examiner's; suspect's a light-skinned black male, about five-nine and believed to be dead?"

"That would do it," Russell said after some thought. "Look, Danny, we're never going to find him this way. We turn right, he goes left and we miss him. We drive straight, he turns down an alley, he's gone."

"So we quit?"

"No, we start thinking like cops looking for a suspect. Eddie never was that bright, and I'm betting that whatever smarts he had died when he did and didn't come back. He's down to memory and habit. Let's hit the Eastside, check out his haunts. See if anybody saw a zombie tonight."

Nobody had. Russell and Amberson hit all the corners where Eddie hung out. They questioned some of the girls he saw when he had the stuff to trade for their favors. They braced the low-level dealers Eddie knew. Everywhere was the same story.

"Nope, ain't seen him."

"Guess you ain't heard, Eddie bought one tonight."

"Hasn't been around."

"Eddie gone, some fool done kilt him over a phone call."

"Eddie got wasted."

"I want a lawyer. This is police harassment."

"Fast Eddie who?"

"You guys don't talk to each other, do you?"

"Eddie wouldn't get off the phone. Junkie wouldn't wait. Blew him away."

"You 5-0, I don't talk to 5-0."

"Thought I saw him. But he be dead, so it wasn't him."

The two detectives questioned this last one more thoroughly. "Where'd you see him? Which way was he going? How long ago?" For answers they got "Around, down there, don't know."

"The good news is," Russell said, as Amberson turned down yet another side street, "is that he's here somewhere."

"So says one lowlife out of ten. And what's the bad news? Other than we haven't found him yet."

"Who says there's bad news?"

"There's good news, gotta be bad news."

Russell thought for a moment. "I guess the bad news is that Santos didn't kill him. Just some crackhead who thought Eddie was taking too long on 'his' phone."

Amberson gave a rueful smile. "Yeah, it would have been nice to pin this one on Santos. Murder one, killing a witness––you get the needle for that."

"Damn shame," agreed Russell. "Santos would have sung just to do twenty to life. Actually would have worked out better than if Eddie have stayed alive to give him up."

Amberson stopped the car, looked at his partner, an idea forming in his mind.

∞Θ∞

I got a good life, Antoine Santos told himself. Not great, but good. A decent house, plenty of food, a nice ride, women when I want them. It's not a mansion in Guilford, steak every night, a Mercedes and Playmates, but it's better than the slobs I deal with have.

Unlike his clients, the ones who bought and resold his product, Santos lived outside the drug area. His house was on the east end of Federal, close enough to the Eastern District police station that it was in a safer neighborhood than most. That's why he bought it, for the security. He also liked the idea of the police helping to keep him safe, that the same cops trying to put him away were, by their very presence, protecting him. Irony, he thought, remembering an old English lesson. It was what Miss Helens back in high school would have called irony.

And was irony, he wondered, about how it ended with that Fast Eddie guy? Word from the street was that Eddie was shopping him to the cops; that he'd worked some kind of deal to trade what he knew about the organization for cash and a ticket out. Santos was going to have the boy hit then he'd found out tonight that he wouldn't have to. Poor Eddie, guess he forgot that you didn't use the holy phone anytime St. Kevin was around. Hell, everybody knew that. Kevin thought that that phone was his direct line to God, that one day the savior would call him up and invite him to Heaven. He got very upset if anyone used it. God might call, and what if He got a busy signal? And who would have thought Kevin had a gun?

As Santos contemplated his life, he heard a pounding on his front door. Who the Hell is that, he wondered. Wasn't cops, they'd have broken down the door. Can't be clients, they knew he didn't sell direct. And his boys had the word not to come to the house. Always some fool didn't get the message. Well, he'd get the message tonight, Santos decided. Find out who that fool is, then fire him or cut him off. He'll be flipping burgers for his cash and going to the Westside for his stuff.

Santos moved to go downstairs. The banging got louder. Then the crashing of glass. Santos paused, got his nine from under the bed, made sure the clip was good and the chamber was hot. He tucked it in his dip, just in case.

More banging, more glass breaking. Santos got to his door just as the invader came through. "What the…" he started as he saw who it was.

Fast Eddie stood in his doorway, his shirt bloody, clear fluid leaking from the wounds on his chest. His face and arms had a death pallor and he moved with the stiffness of the rigor that had come over him.

"Saanntoooosss," Eddie's voice creaked as he raised his pale hands towards the drug dealer. "I neeeedddd…"

Santos reached into his dip, pulled out his nine. "You're dead," he cried, recognizing the absurdity of his statement while realizing at the same time that it was true.

Eddie ignored the gun, kept coming one step at a time. Santos fired—once, twice, a third time. Eddie's body jerked with each impact, but he kept coming. Backing up, Santos emptied the clip. Eddie slowed, stopped, fell.

Relief washed through Santos; he had stopped the Eddie-thing. He wondered what to do next, Eddie's left hand twitched, then clawed the carpet. His right hand moved, fingers clutched the carpet and pulled his body forward. Slowly,

Eddie crawled toward Santos.

Russell and Amberson were just pulling on to Federal Street when they heard the shots. They looked at each other. "I got the back," Russell said as they both bailed out of the unmarked car. Amberson gave his partner time to get around back before going through the open front door.

Russell got to the rear of the house just in time to see Santos run out the kitchen door. Both men had their guns out. Santos saw Russell, made him for a cop and dropped his piece. A good thing. A second later, Russell would have done Santos like the dealer had tried to do Eddie.

"You okay?" Russell heard his partner call form inside the house.

"Okay," Russell confirmed, snapping the cuffs on Santos. "You secure?"

"Under control. Come on in."

"Let's go," Russell urged Santos forward. The dealer balked.

"Not going back in there. Don't take me back," Santos pleaded.

Russell shoved the dealer into the doorframe—hard. "Walk or get dragged. Either way you're going in."

Amberson looked up as Russell came in from the back, pushing Santos ahead of him. "Found him," he said, indicating the mostly lifeless body on the floor.

Eddie was still trying to get to Santos, hands and knees weakly moving him along. Hearing the detective's voice, a distant memory came back. He turned towards Amberson, raised an arm and pointed it towards the dealer. "Saanntoooosss," he croaked out. Then, his appointed task done, and with what could have been a smile, or maybe just the effects of rigor, Fast Eddie collapsed and was finally still.

The detectives were quick to seize the situation.

"Doesn't look good, Antoine. Dead man in your house, your bullets in him," Amberson told Santos.

"Why'd you steal him from the morgue? Going to dig the

bullets out?" continued Russell.

"No, no," Santos protested. "He was dead when he came in and…"

"And nobody's going to believe that, Antoine." Amberson interrupted. "Except maybe me and my partner." The sound of sirens in the distant, getting closer. "You gonna deal, deal now, else you get you a manslaughter charge."

Men in blue uniforms rushing the house from front and back, Amberson and Russell, weapons holstered, holding up their hands and badges to stem the charge. "I'm yours," Santos shouting over the initial confusion of men and voices. District detectives then homicide men arriving. Amberson and Russell holding tight to their charge.

By the time morning came Santos had given up his entire network, from suppliers down to runners. In exchange, he was charged as an accessory after the fact in the death of Wallace Cromwell, a.k.a. "Fast Eddie," with minimum sentencing guaranteed.

As for how the theft of Eddie's body was explained, Amberson and Cromwell referred anyone who asked to Dominic Jones. Jones, in turn, told the questioner to ask Santos. Santos, whose reputation was only enhanced by the belief that he had committed such an audacious crime, always denied it, but in such a way as to assure his listener that he had beyond doubt done the deed. The Medical Examiner's Office did get a new state-of-the art security system to keep whatever had happened from happening again.

With no one to claim it, Fast Eddie's body was turned over to the Anatomy Board. Unusually well preserved for an unembalmed corpse, it was used for three weeks before it was cremated and the ashes disposed of.

∞Θ∞

Safe and warm, Eddie again felt the warm embrace of loving arms. He floated, bathing in the warmth of the golden light. It was not for him, not this time. He'd been judged and he acknowledged that the judgment was fair and just. He felt a tug, somewhere a new life was being created. Consciousness faded as the soul that had once been Fast Eddie Cromwell sped off towards another chance at doing things right.

Night of the Living Dead Bingo Women
SIMON MCCAFFERY

EVEN ON HER BAD DAYS, Edna Mae Brewer was invincible.

She'd won five straight games since arriving at noon, excitedly calling out "Bingo!" after marking the last winning square on her playing sheets. The third time she fairly shrieked it in excitement, though her fellow contestants in the hall paid her not the slightest heed. The woman sitting directly across from Edna stared vacantly ahead like a wax figure, streaks of colored ink smeared across her face like a Maori mask. On Edna's left, an elderly black man in a soiled, ripped turtleneck gazed up at the high ceiling while his outstretched hands groped blindly about on the wide table. He swept his ink dauber and stack of playing cards onto the floor and made no effort to retrieve them.

In a remote way, this total disinterest in her good fortune rankled Edna, who was competitive by nature. In the old days, when a player's numbers came in, folks had not just sat there like stones. Most cheered as the caller checked off the winning numbers. Others groaned and everyone applauded like disinterested businessmen at a luncheon. Some even glared at the winner with genuine hatred, muttering under their breath as they discarded their losing sheets. This was no way for a Christian to behave, Edna knew, but she could commiserate; she herself had sat near a big winner on occasion and felt resentment glow in the pit of her stomach like a hot lump of coal.

Tonight, however, Edna felt just fine, thank you. This

was largely due to the fact that she had won every game of the session so far, from the Early Bird up through the Bonus Blackout round. Some of the wins had taken longer than others, but she'd kept at it; hunched over her game sheets, concentrating fiercely while marking off numbers.

A tiny voice inside Edna's head pointed out that though she was undeniably a skilled and seasoned bingo player, the fact that all of her opponents were dead might have something to do with her long string of successes. This nasty little voice, which sounded not unlike her nagging (and thankfully deceased) husband Frank, irritated Edna. Winning was winning and fair was fair. Was it her fault zombies weren't cut out for the fast-paced competitiveness of high-stakes bingo?

The next game got underway. The caller, once a handsome young Creek Indian named Joe, began plucking numbered Ping-Pong balls from the big, Plexiglas hopper on the green-carpeted dais. Joe still wore the tattered remains of his cheap tuxedo outfit, though it was badly discolored and seemed to disappear in and out of his flesh in places. Joe's gray face was beginning to look unsightly, Edna noted—like an ice-cream novelty left unattended in the sun—and he was having difficulty calling the numbers in an intelligible fashion. Some sounded as if he was speaking through a veil of rotted seaweed. To make matters worse, he also ate some of the Ping-Pong balls.

Edna had prepared for this, however, positioning herself at a table close to the calling booth. Numbers garbled beyond recognition could usually be eyeballed before the little white spheres disappeared back into the hopper or Joe's mouth.

In an orderly row before her were the tools of the trade: ink daubers and paper playing sheets. Not long after the Reawakening, Edna had helped herself to several new ink daubers behind the now-deserted concession stand. The daubers were larger, gaily colored, and more expensive than those she had once played with. Her old dauber was squat and plain, and she had refilled it with tap water dyed with food coloring because Frank had strictly limited her playing money. The new daubers, used to mark pink, red, and purple circles on the throwaway paper sheets, were scented to smell like strawberries, cherries, and grapes. Edna didn't mind when, hunched over the table, the sickly-sweet smell of the colored ink filled her nostrils; it almost blocked out the odor of her nearby opponents, who sat in dazed rows and shambled blindly along the aisles.

Edna continued marking her sheets in a businesslike fashion, never missing a single number—the secret of winning (*besides playing against zombies*, the Frank-voice reminded). Towards four o'clock, her stomach began rumbling. How she wished she could hail a uniformed runner and order a burrito with the works and a large Pepsi! In the old days, during a typical eight-hour session, Edna might consume three burritos with hot sauce and sour cream, a cheeseburger, several bags of chips, a small dish of soft ice cream (chocolate and vanilla swirled together), and a legion of soft drinks.

Now, with the food in the snack bar trampled and spoiled, she was forced to bring her own munchies: vacuum packs of beef jerky, vacuum-sealed cans of cheese curls, and scores of candy bars that wouldn't go over—thanks to BTA and TBHQ, whatever they were—until October 2014. There was a sprawling Food King supermarket three blocks from the bingo hall, and until its shattered roof finished falling in, it served as Edna's super-snack bar. Digging through her canvas tote bag, she extracted a Slim Jim and tore into it with her teeth. The taste was salty and greasy and wonderful, though not as satisfying as a deep-fried jumbo burrito with everything crammed inside.

During the next pattern game, in which the winner was required to form a kite pattern, a zombie caromed off the back of Edna's chair causing her marker to smear across the sheet.

There! That had ruined it! And she had been only three numbers away from completing the tail of the kite and winning five thousand dollars. The big tradeoff with zombies, she fumed, was that though they were a cinch to beat at bingo (or any game, for that matter), they possessed the manners of… wild pigs. They might slump in quiet, swaying rows for hours, uttering hardly a moan, or they might knock about like mummies, overturning tables and making a general racket without so much as an apology if they disrupted a game! It was enough to heat the collar of the most patient, God-fearing soul, especially a dyed-in-the-wool bingo fanatic like Edna.

After winning two more games—the "Round Robin" and "Crazy T"—in quick succession, Edna noticed twilight was stealing its way inside the huge hall. She immediately set down her dauber and reached below her chair.

This time the tote bag produced a large silver flashlight, scavenged from the blackened hulk of the bingo security guard's station wagon, a Ford Taurus, which now rested up-side down in the hall parking lot. The long-necked light held six fat D-size batteries in its gut and was heavy enough to use as a club if the need arose. Its beam was strong and steady, like a prison searchlight.

With shadows forming like fathomless pools inside the hall, Edna clicked it on and positioned it so she could read her cards and keep an eye on Joe. With nightfall the interior of the hall would quickly sink into an absolute blackness. Edna would need the light to continue playing and, at midnight, to make her way to an exit. Without its shepherding beam, she knew from experience, one might bump around for an eternity searching for the door.

In the first weeks after the dead had decided to walk again (and feast on live people and play bingo), Edna had found the hall too unsettling to remain in after sundown. Just the zoo-like sounds of zombies shuffling about like blind men had sent icy splinters of terror through her heart. But the light made a considerable difference and didn't attract them.

Nothing seemed to particularly gain their attention, not

even Edna, who might be considered, through the dead orbs of a zombie, to be the biggest deluxe burrito around. Like everyone else Edna had kept her distance from them (and, more importantly, their *teeth*) after they had clawed their way out of the cold ground, but none had ever attacked her. This was, she was now certain, due to years of chemical cancer treatment she had suffered at the hands of young doctors who thought themselves little Gods. The zombies smelled her, yes, but the meat was... no good.

Edna found this situation immensely agreeable. The best part was that zombies wiping out civilization didn't mean she had to quit the only activity that had ever brought her joy. In a way (and He definitely worked in mysterious ones—one look at the hundreds of zombies roaming the interior of the Riverside Avenue Bingo Hall confirmed that!), it was an enormous blessing, a miracle. Edna now enjoyed bingo each and every day, and never paid so much as a penny to play. The coins and bills choking the legion of abandoned cash registers in the city meant nothing. There were none of the worries, setbacks, and anxieties of her previous life. There was no Frank (she definitely had them to thank for that) to complain about bills and starchy meals. The troubles of that dead life had sloughed off as quick and easy as Joe's face. Not even her ponderous weight mattered anymore. None of it mattered. There was only her love of the game.

And now, like never before, Edna was an undeniable winner, the unbeaten empress of all-day, all-night bingo.

Clasping an ink dauber in her plump right hand and hefting the flashlight in her left, she aimed the beam at the silhouetted figure on the dais. Joe, issuing gobbling sounds that might have been numbers, started a new game.

Worm-sacks and Dirt-backs
LEE CLARK ZUMPE

THE SANITARY WORLD around Dr. Kenneth Sprague had rotted away revealing its rancid underbelly.

"Who are we kidding? Reconstituted disinterred entities? The formerly expired? The prematurely lamented?" Sprague had used his last euphemism. Frustration and fatigue finally stripped him of his last ounce of professional prudence as he bickered with the chief of staff at Arnesville Regional Hospital. Surrounding the two men, the dead huddled in a once spotless hallway, many clustered in familial groups, whimpering and trembling. They had spilled into the corridors from an overcrowded and understaffed emergency room. Outside, they shambled through the parking lot, gazed despondently at their reflections in car windows, and picked at their own putrescent flesh. "They're walking corpses. How am I supposed to treat walking corpses?"

"Just do your job, Dr. Sprague." Dr. Zephram Ames responded to Sprague's outburst with a cold stare and an unsympathetic tone. The 50-something physician ran the hospital with an iron fist in the best of times. The current crisis had transformed him into a fascist despot devoid of compassion for his colleagues. "I expect you to treat each one like any other patient: examine their symptoms, manage their pain and monitor their progress. It's all we can do until a treatment or a cure is developed."

"There won't be a treatment or a cure," Sprague said, his tone growing more insubordinate as his discontent and resentment mounted. Those who required and deserved legitimate health care were being turned away from the hospital because of the extraordinary circumstances. Sprague had not worked his way through medical school to spend the rest of his life dealing with an endless parade of moldering patients. "This isn't a disease. It's an aberration of nature."

"We have our orders." Ames referred to strict government directives outlined in a hastily drafted Presidential Executive Order shortly after the onset of the epidemic. "Our hands are tied. The law dictates our actions. I won't risk my career over this."

"And I won't waste mine medicating things that by all rights should be destroyed."

Sprague turned his back and walked down the grim corridor, navigating the ghastly tangle of fetid flesh and moaning cadavers. He longed for fresh air, untainted by the lurid stench of the dead. At the end of the hallway he hesitated in front of a service entrance, wishing he could leave it all behind him, wishing he could ignore his conscience, go home, and wait it out.

He could not help but feel beguiled by the bliss of seclusion, the promise of total tranquility as could only be achieved in complete isolation. At the same time, he feared what might become of the city—of the world—in his absence. What today manifested itself as a plague of the dead could tomorrow become a scourge of the living. He had an obligation to stay alert, to stay focused, to watch for signs of mutation.

After a moment's deliberation he turned toward the stairwell and headed for the roof. Though he had no weather reports to notify him, he could tell a cold front was pushing through the mountains. He hoped the arctic winds would offer a temporary reprieve from the stomach-turning aroma saturating the hospital's lower levels.

Down there, everything smelled like the grave.

He had examined dozens of reconstituted disinterred entities over the last few weeks, poked and prodded them, even gathered specimens to be forwarded to the USAMRIID task force facility located on the outskirts of the city. He continually questioned the military's unprecedented utilization of civilian medical personnel to act as first responders in the outbreak, criticizing army scientists for distancing themselves from the hot zone.

Nothing about the epidemic made sense. The government's initial reaction had been to quarantine the city—a feat made feasible thanks to the area's rugged topography. Set in the Appalachian Mountains in far western North Carolina, Arnesville could be cut off from the rest of the region relatively easily with the closure of four state highways and a 20-mile stretch of the Interstate system. State police simply rerouted traffic through nearby Canton and Waynesville.

A media blackout quickly followed. All television, radio, and newspaper services were terminated with swift and shocking efficiency. The military apparently deployed some form of equipment that jammed external radio signals and made satellite dishes ineffective. All phones, both land-line and cellular, ceased to function. Postal deliveries were halted.

Not a single journalist entered the city after the implementation of the quarantine.

Then, instead of inserting troops to round up the infected corpses, the military positioned itself along the quarantine perimeter and set about patrolling the back country in Black Hawk choppers. No epidemiologists arrived to relieve the overtaxed medical community. No FEMA workers appeared to assess the conditions and provide logistical support. No government representatives visited to address the concerns of local residents, to offer reassurances or provide explanations and chart strategies.

Finally, word came down that the president had extended limited Constitutional rights to those affected—and that the "killing" of any such entity constituted a federal offense punishable by, ironically, death.

Unlike those in Washington D.C., Sprague had no misconceptions about the state of the "corporeal undead," the term employed to describe the entities in the official document. The dead rarely spoke, exhibited no emotion other than chronic depression and appeared to have only limited fine motor skills. He saw no spark of intelligence in their eyes, no flicker of remembrance and no internal motivation to survive. Left to their own devices, they might well waste away into nothingness. They ate nothing, drank nothing, and, aside from wandering aimlessly and groaning unremittingly, they did nothing.

Admittedly, some of Ames' closest associates had achieved some success with experimental therapy. His team worked in secrecy in the upper levels of the hospital, selecting trial candidates through a careful screening process. From the notes he had shared with other staff members, the things could be nourished intravenously, taught to perform simple skills, prompted into speech.

That Ames sanctioned such trials repulsed Sprague. Those responsible for the research argued that their work was a logical extension of their scientific background. They considered themselves medical revolutionaries exploring cutting-edge rehabilitation techniques.

Sprague likened them to grave-robbers bent on harvesting the dead for their own selfish professional purposes.

"Fed up with the working conditions down there, Dr. Sprague?" Arriving on the roof, the physician found a congregation of expatriated interns smoking and sharing a bottle of Jack Daniels beneath the ruddy evening skies. "Or have you come to collect us and usher us back down to our stations?" Randy Donne had apparently been elected as the group's provisional spokesperson. The other greenhorns lacked the courage to voice their antipathy and aversion to dealing with the dead. "If that's the case, I'm afraid that we'll have to decline the invitation."

"No," Sprague said, "I'm here for some fresh air."

"Not much to go around." Donne flicked his cigarette

butt over the side of the building, followed its descent with his gaze. The street in front of the hospital teemed with squirmy corpses. "There's so many of them now you can smell 'em all the way up here."

"Damn worm-sacks and dirt-backs," Freddie Julian said, downing a swig from the bottle. Sprague had heard both expressions in recent days, counted them among the more evocative inventions in an evolving lexicon. *Worm-sacks* referred to corpses over six months old, dug up by optimistic relatives and subsequently abandoned due to their advanced state of decomposition. *Dirt-backs* were the recent dead, in most cases spontaneously reawakened in the midst of their own burial. "Someone should be corralling them, herding them toward a crematorium or something."

"That's not the will of the government," Sprague said with a hint of sarcasm. Black Hawks hovered over the distant horizon, combing the countryside. Occasionally, over the last few days, the firing of artillery had been heard, suggesting that some citizens had attempted escape. "For whatever reason, they want to keep them intact for the time being."

"Probably want to register them for November's general elections." Donne glanced at the stars emerging in the twilight between wispy bands of clouds. To the west, a line of storms crawled along the Appalachian crest. "Why do you think they've all come here, to the hospital? Why not go to their homes, their families?"

"They're suffering physical pain," Sprague answered. "That much we know. Assuming they retain some memories of life, they associate the hospital with feeling better."

"I guess we should be thankful they aren't flesh-eating zombies." Julian—not a particularly squeamish individual—visibly shuddered at the thought of how much worse things could be if the dead had awoken with a ravenous appetite. "I mean, that's what you expect the undead to do, right? Feast on the living?"

"I don't really know what to expect them to do, Freddie."

Sprague looked down upon the crowds, wondering how many had passed through the hospital doors previously on their way to the burial ground. How had the gardens of rest been transformed into the gardens of the restless? Julian's gratitude that they did not more closely resemble their cinematic representation led Sprague down another disquieting avenue of thought: With so many variables at work, so many mysteries as yet unanswered, no one could really be certain that they might not all rise up and start gorging themselves on the living.

"Honestly, I don't think that they know what is expected of them, either."

∞☉∞

The meat-wagons began arriving the following day just after sunrise.

Dr. Sprague had spent the night on the roof with Donne and several other interns, waiting for a squall line that regrettably stalled over the highlands. The first indication the day would be different came with the appearance of dozens of Chinooks sweeping in from the south, flying low over the Pisgah National Forest. Like impatient buzzards they circled the distant Arnesville International Airport, waiting for clearance.

"It's about time," Donne said, his upturned palm eclipsing the morning sun as he followed the helicopters' flight. He imagined the transport copters filled with anxious national guardsmen, ready to take all the dead into custody and convey them out of the city. Simultaneously, a column of black panel trucks maneuvered a maze of side streets and convened along Avery Boulevard. Escorted by local police, the caravan carefully approached the hospital. Some shell-shocked residents stumbled from their homes and along the thoroughfare to watch the grim procession. "Maybe they've come to their senses."

"Maybe," Sprague said, reserving judgment. "I'd better find Ames—see if I'm still employed." Before returning to the stairwell, the doctor peered over the ledge as paramilitary guardsmen escorted the first of the corpses into the backs of the meat-wagons. The dead went willingly without any hint of resistance. They moved like cattle, without deliberation or reflection. "You all should get downstairs, see if you can help. When this mess is finally swept under the carpet people will need our help again. That's why you're here. That's why you'll stay."

∞Θ∞

Sprague found Ames on the 10th floor. He had appropriated an entire wing for his team of researchers, ostensibly to investigate how best to treat the dead. Where uniformed security guards had restricted access yesterday, this morning Sprague found no obstacles.

"Dr. Ames," he called out, catching sight of the doctor down the hall. A tall, gaunt man with greasy hair and an expensive, tailored business suit conversed with Ames in front of a shadowed alcove at the far end of the corridor. From the man's emphatic gesticulations and boisterous tone, Sprague inferred a considerable degree of conceit. As the physician approached, Ames lifted a hand to curtail their tête-à-tête temporarily.

"Dr. Sprague, a pleasure to meet you," the man said, turning to face him. He contrived a disingenuous smile that unfolded across his pallid countenance like a serpent uncoiling itself to strike at some unwitting rodent. "I'm Bernard Chesterton, CEO of Therst Weber Pharmaceuticals." He began to extend his hand to cement the greeting but pulled back reflexively as if concerned about potential contagions. "I was just expressing my gratitude to Dr. Ames for his handling of this situation."

"I'm sorry," Sprague said, looking back and forth between the two men. "This just seems like an odd time to be hawking new drug treatment options, doesn't it Dr. Ames?"

"Actually, Dr. Sprague, Mr. Chesterton is here to take guardianship of our corporeal undead. His company has taken full responsibility for the situation." Everyone knew Ames received kickbacks from the major pharmaceutical companies. His zealous support of their products resulted in endless perks and enabled him to build his palatial 5-bedroom mansion on a ridge overlooking the city while paying alimony to two ex-wives. In addition to pushing unessential prescriptions on patients through hospital staff and local doctors, Ames regularly advocated and approved clinical trials for dubious medications. "Because of its culpability, the company has made arrangements to oversee the re-education process."

"I beg your pardon?" Sprague needed no clarification. As he had suspected from the onset, someone behind the scenes had orchestrated the whole depraved enterprise—and Ames had played a pivotal role. The worm-sacks and dirt-backs had been intentionally revived. "So, you aren't going to destroy them? You're going to treat those things?"

"That's right, Dr. Sprague. It's no fault of theirs' that they've been reanimated. Following a treatment regime developed and tested in part by Dr. Ames here, they will be re-integrated into society. Properly medicated, they'll continue to serve as active members of the community indefinitely."

"As what? Doorstops?"

"Come with us, Dr. Sprague," Ames said, placing a firm grasp on his shoulder, as if to rein him in. "We were about to tour my makeshift recovery ward. I think you'll be surprised at the progress we've made."

Behind the guarded doors, air fresheners masked the stench of decomposing flesh. The revivified dead rested comfortably in hospital beds meant for the living. Unlike their kith and kin downstairs, these pampered examples had regained some semblance of color in their skin. They demonstrated a diverse range of palpable, though imperfect, expressions and displayed rudimentary emotions. Their arms and legs did not quiver and their fingers did not fidget. They exhibited a sense of purpose and identity.

"What have you done to them?" Sprague looked over the dead patients, flinching at their two-dimensional personalities, their deceptively sterilized appearance, their vacant stares. "You can pump them full of chemicals, but they'll never be the same—don't you see that? The spark is gone. Their time is already up. Science can't alter the processes of nature."

"Kenneth... Sprague," a familiar voice called from out across the room. "Kenny, is... that... you?" Sprague went from bed to bed, searching for the speaker. He found him in the far corner, a copy of the Bible lying spread-eagle on his dinner tray. "It's... good... to see... you... Kenny."

"Uncle Howard?" Sprague's uncle had been dead for two years. The cancer that claimed him had resisted every form of treatment available at the time. Dozens of mourners had attended his funeral, watched as he was laid to rest in the mausoleum at Serenity Gardens. "This isn't possible."

"I... can't... explain." he said, his words punctuated by uncomfortably long gaps. Sprague stared at him wordlessly, studied the glowing flesh that should be withered and wasting away. The corners of his mouth twitched as he strained to smile. His fingers remained rigid, his arms fixed at his sides. His eyelids drooped but he never blinked. "How... long?"

"Two years," Sprague answered, realizing instinctively what his uncle wanted to know. "It's been two years."

"Why... am... I... here?" Each word, each movement, had to be meticulously calculated and judiciously executed. Even with the treatment, the body processes lacked the fluid animation of life. They had degraded into clumsy mechanics, driven by an awkward automation mimicking vitality. "Why... was... I... brought... back?"

"I'm sorry, Uncle Howard," Sprague said, trying to repress both his grief and anger. "I don't know why." Sprague swallowed the heartache he had relinquished years earlier, reminding himself that the thing in the hospital bed could only be a shadow of the man he had known. "Those men can tell you why," he said, turning toward Ames and Chesterton. "Those men did this to you—to all of you."

Around the room, Ames' subjects exhibited a collective flash of recognition. Their medically-sustained solemnity deteriorated rapidly as the revelation gripped them. At once, all their misery and anguish and restiveness resurfaced. Something else emerged, too—an emotion thankfully absent until that critical epiphany washed over them. With newfound hatred, the corporeal undead struggled with the restraints confining them to their beds. They fought so violently that the adjacent skin tattered and turned a macabre shade of purple. Their glassy eyes bulged from their sockets.

Sprague recognized in their hostility a thirst for retribution, for justice and, maybe, for blood.

"Damn it, Sprague," Ames said, beckoning his private staff of assistants. Aides swarmed into the room, prepared to sedate the rebellious dead. Chesterton, savvy enough to appreciate a bad situation that might get even worse, quietly slipped out the door. "Get out of my ward, Sprague. Get out of my hospital."

Downstairs, lines of dead had formed in the corridors. They stretched through the emergency room, across the parking lot and down the sidewalk bordering Avery Boulevard. Troops crammed them into the backs of the black panel trucks, which ferried them to the airport. There, more troops loaded them onto Chinooks. When filled to capacity, the helicopters lifted from the tarmac, heading east to some unknown destination.

Sprague, now unemployed, joined in the crowd of spectators watching the dead depart.

∞⊖∞

Later that evening, Sprague rested on his sofa nursing a

bottle of imported Irish stout. Cable service had not yet been re-established, but local television stations had begun broadcasting live reports from Arnesville that afternoon.

Officially, an unnamed pharmaceutical company had been to blame for the epidemic. An allegedly unsanctioned five-year study of a drug said to promote longevity had gone horribly wrong. Ten towns across North America had been affected, including Arnesville. Exposure rates, which should have been limited to 10 percent of the population, had exceeded 80 percent. Though the root cause had been determined, the catalyst that actually triggered the reanimation of the dead had yet to be discovered.

Government troops had begun overseeing an evacuation of all corporeal dead entities from the stricken municipalities. Remote camps had been established to help treat and reintegrate the victims back into society.

At 8 p.m. the president addressed both houses of Congress. Sprague, on the verge of sleep, roused himself to watch the historic broadcast.

"Everything," the president said, "will be... all right." Sprague sat up and perched on the edge of the cushion. He upset the bottle as he hunted for the remote control. "My friends at FEMA... are working with... the military," he continued. His speeches had always suffered from his sluggish tone and staggered delivery. Tonight, though, Sprague paid closer attention to his cadence and inflection. "We welcome... these people... with open arms," he said, his eyes oddly unblinking. His rosy cheeks seemed too red, like someone might have applied blush just before he went on the air. "And I... am willing... to ask my colleagues... in Congress," he stammered. His hands rested on the sides of the podium, completely motionless. "To grant full citizenship... to the victims... in return for... five years of... service to our country... in the United States Armed Forces."

The camera panned across the floor of Congress. Representatives and Senators applauded with mechanical synchronicity, their expressions lacking any emotional subtext. Sprague spilled onto the floor, crawled over to the screen as he scanned the audience. Though some of the older members seemed a bit disheveled, most projected at least the semblance of life. A few, though, had only just begun the treatment. Their ashen faces, their sunken eyes, their leathery flesh betrayed their lingering putrescence. Tonight, the dead governed the living. Tomorrow, the world would know no better.

Regardless of the morning's setback, unflustered by potential impediments, Bernard Chesterton, CEO of Therst Weber Pharmaceuticals, stood among the powerbrokers, contented with his coup.

The Purple Word
ERIK T. JOHNSON

EVERYONE I EVER LOVED owned a cat.

I'd never thought about it until recently, now that I'm the only human left at the "Crumble-Down Farm," as the local children once called it.

My mother, difficult but always there for me, had an orange tabby named Charlie who seemed to be living his first life in a feline incarnation. She had to lift him up onto windowsills because he wasn't sure how to jump, and I once saw him fall off a table and land on his side. How he loved her, too. He was a marmalade shadow always at her side, even, she told me, keeping her lap warm while she sat on the toilet.

And Benjamin was my father's obese, white, deaf cat who shed rugs weekly and kept his tongue sticking out stiff as a little pink depressor. Benny was an affectionate, stupid animal who never used his claws on anything, not even furniture. He liked to play with grapes.

There are so many more I could name, each different than the next, cats belonging to my best childhood friend, my aunt Willa, both my grandmothers. And Joy's cat Winston.

She was a little Tonka truck of a cat with a thick African wildcat tail, and skin missing on her flank where some cruel boy had thrown hot tar. Everything about Winnie was round—marble green eyes, neckless head, paws. When Joy and I would leave her alone too long she'd grow angry and swipe at our feet and shins upon our return. But then she'd curl up with us later in Joy's bed, making our warmth sweeter with purring...

These trivial details are so important to me here in the attic. I roll them round me like a kitten with balls of yarn, trying to lose myself in the unwound threads of lost lives. If I stare at the snow that's fallen through the roof I see the cats so clearly, like pictures projected on a white screen.

Everyone I ever loved is gone.

They were in town at The Egg Festival when the blue sky was overwhelmed by an infinity of stunning purple. An impostor sky.

A stomach virus saved me from this plague. I was home sick at the farm and saw it through my window. It moved like a time-elapsed movie of an approaching storm, abnormally quick and arching itself over the horizon until there was just a glowing purple above the world. It shone bright as sunlight, but the sun was nowhere in sight. It only lasted a few days but was so immense it seemed years from end to end. It brought cold with it too, and that first day was like January in Maine. When it left I heard dogs howling all over the countryside, then the howls got dimmer and dimmer. They left for some other dog place.

But the cats stuck around.

The farm is so quiet. I like that. The old gray wood doesn't creak; it's pliant and spongy beneath my heavy steps. It makes me feel I could lay my head anywhere and sleep, as if the whole place is one great bed. I'm on the highest hill in the county with a view of the land all around. There are plenty of trees around the house, with overgrown grass in the summer to make me feel far from civilization. The nearest town is five miles away. I don't know if anyone lives there any longer. There's a highway close, but it never bothered me. It sounded like the ocean.

Last month was November. After the impostor sky left and the blue returned, the leaves died. I let them fall and pile up all over the yard. Flakes of red, orange, green, and yellow, like the down of an enormous tropical bird. One day at sunset I sat on the back porch in great-grandmother's rocker listening to the zombies complain down in the valley. I watched the leaves shiver, the trees scrape back and forth. And then I saw a small white and black cat I'd spotted around a lot, walking funny along the tree line fifty feet away. As my eyes followed him I realized he hobbled because he was missing one back leg.

It must've come off in a fox trap.

He disappeared behind a log pile without looking over his shoulder.

The next day I did something I'd never done before: I went into town to get cat food. I knew it would be difficult because by then I was sure everyone I knew was walking around dead. When the wind blew strong from the south I could smell them rotting and hear their moans. They seemed to be trying to articulate a particular word their ruined mouths couldn't make clear. It sounded something like:

Ooh ooh ooh ooh ooh...

Somewhere in that hellish sound was Joy's voice. She was at The Egg Festival with the others. Once she got her finger caught in our Chevy's door. The howl she made, I never wanted to hear it again. I strained my ears to find it among the wailing as they shambled below Crumble-Down farm.

Like trying to pick out one raindrop's splash in a thunderstorm.

How did I deal with this? What was I thinking?

A white paw batting black grapes across a pink rug... a marmalade tail... two lidless marble eyes rolling across my mind, the slices of darkness in the middles spinning like the propellers of a plane that can't take off...

The road to the store was deserted as the sun slid down. The Egg Festival signs hung with bright pictures of Chickens from poles along the way. There was a poster for an omelet-eating contest in Gentry's Mercantile's window. I parked and saw the store's front door swing back and forth.

No breeze.

Something had just walked through.

Out or in?

I entered slowly. Vegetables were stacked in display cases, some covered with colorful mold resembling coral reef formations. Cans lined the shelves orderly as barcodes. Rotten eggs were on prominent display in a small refrigerator. A thin layer of sawdust like wooden snow had been recently disturbed by shoe tracks. Each step I took announced itself with a thud. I walked back to the front and looked out at an empty street.

I'd never looked for pet food at Gentry's before, but I figured it must be in the back.

I passed the frozen meats when I heard ice falling.

Mr. Gentry wriggled from a refrigerated display case the size of a child's coffin. His skin peeled off in lasagna strips, tiger-striping his face deep purplish red. One eye was missing. The other gaped unblinking as a cave mouth. I ran to the back and grabbed a case of cat food. When I turned round he was halfway out, massive torso hanging down towards the floor and head just an inch above it. He'd forced his three hundred pound, six-foot-five body into the five-foot long frozen meat case. His legs were smashed and twisted completely around and he'd got his toes caught under something.

"Needed cold," Gentry coughed wetly. He lashed out at the ground and thick bloodstreams dripped from his open mouth.

I stepped back in shock, more at hearing him speak in that state than seeing him that way. The shelf came down. Steel bars cut hot into my back as I hunched over and shielded my head with my hands.

Through the ringing in my ears I could hear footsteps.

I shifted into a push-up position beneath my burden. Sticky blood ran into my eyes and I could feel the lumps growing on my head.

One Mississippi...

Something scratched at the floor before me.

Two Mississippi...

Moaning from above.

Three Mississippi…

I pushed myself up and scrambled out from under the shelf, tripping over scattered cans and standing up right before stumbling over the mess of Gentry's head.

A case or two had landed on it and one eye lolled like a panting tongue. Another loose can had hurled smack into the middle of his over-ripe face and the bottom stuck out of there, where mouth and nostrils had been. Even then a noise percolated in his throat and his bloody scabby hands were like two red crabs having epileptic fits, clawing at the floor with overlong nails.

Don't panic. Think: white whiskers tipped black at the ends… gray ears erect like teepees… soft body warm as cup of tea curled on lap…

Twin headaches burst out from the epicenters of my temples. I picked up another case and walked toward the streetlight shining through the front door.

One foot away from the exit I remembered the footsteps…

I spun around to an empty room.

Something tapped me on the scalp. A blood-drop. A widening dark stain spread across the ceiling. I heard footsteps again. They came from above.

Floorboards hit me seconds before the bodies. Two women with dead meat faces knocked me on my back. They didn't seem to notice me as they faced each other over my legs. They lay on their bellies, each on a pillow of red guts spilling from their open stomachs. Without lifting their skeletal arms they bit at each other's mouths. No tongues. No lips. I'd never seen lesbians before. The stench of their hisses and grunts was unbearable.

I shifted my hands behind me and pulled myself to the door. The movement caught their attention and they tried to bite my legs, but when I saw I couldn't sneak away I jumped up, knocked them down, and ran to the truck. Night had fallen, blue and cool as a freshly washed sheet.

About to turn the key in the ignition, I asked myself what I was doing in *this* nightmare.

I wanted to feed those cats. Small mouths lined with sharp teeth. Rough tongues coated in medicinal saliva.

Looking up I saw lights in the houses, and figures shuffled back and forth past the windows. I heard things crashing to the ground in the apartments. Still bodies must've started stirring at once. I took a crowbar from the truck, determined to get that food.

It seemed hundreds of lost shadows crossed the street, thrown by zombies in the windows. I walked through them to the store and kicked open the door, crowbar in hand.

As other doors creaked open and doorknobs rattled in the street behind me I breathed deep and plunged in.

The two fallen women feasted on Gentry's entrails by the frozen meat display case. They ignored me, and I managed to get a lot of cases to the truck before I could see the rest, coming for me like sleepwalkers from all directions. They were a block away.

Everyone I'd ever known.

I sped off as their strangled calls rose in the cold night where chimney smoke once coiled and broke apart.

Ooh ooh ooh ooh ooh... Were they crying "blue," asking the sky why it had turned on them?

The next day I stored the food in the attic and put a can out near the porch. I found myself in the rocker waiting for Peg Leg to come again. I laughed with a strange sense of amusement, as I realized I'd given him a name. I'd never named anything before, and I used to wonder how the pet owners I knew chose from so many options. Now I saw: names just appeared from nowhere, like purple zombie-making skies.

The pain in my head and my sides shut me up fast.

He did not come that day. November bugs laid their eggs in the food and I had to throw it out.

The next morning I sat with my coffee on the porch. There was a trace of coming rain in the air, so the screen doors gave off a pleasant metallic odor. I watched an old clothesline suspended from the third story to a tall oak tree guarding the border between the yard proper and the woods. A faded red scarf hung by the side of the forest, clothespined to the line. It was put there to dry by my mother. It might've been the last thing I'd seen her do.

A rustling drew me from the cloth. I raised the shotgun I now kept near by at all times. A cat approached the fresh food I'd put out when I woke. The cat sniffed the ground, head moving side to side and rubbing his chin on the earth as he crawled, like a solider advancing under enemy fire.

His coat was confederate gray but it might've once been white. Under his nose was a black mustache smudge. I wondered if he was blind, as he didn't look up at me, but seemed to have found the food by scent alone. He ate rapidly. Then thunder pealed, and he raised his head with taut masticated ears. He had no eyes. A shiny BB gun pellet was lodged in one socket.

The rain fell hard and he zigzagged in a crazy pattern toward the trees, more like a fly without wings than a cat. The sky turned the color of his coat.

But my thoughts ran to friends and family. Perhaps the rain would melt them away like a herd of wicked witches of the west. Or perhaps having forgotten what rain is they would seek its source and come up the hill to look for it, finding me instead of clouds.

Why not? Weirder things have happened.

The days grew colder. It became my daily ritual to sit on the back porch, waiting for cats to get the food I'd put ten feet from my seat. I'd wait with anticipation to see who would arrive, cleaning my shotgun to kill time. I found if I left five or six cans I could get as many as ten cats to come up to the house. Sometimes it was Bandito (as I started to call the mustached cat). Other times he'd not appear for days. I also named Pickle, Jester, Streak, and Crush, orange tabbies like my mother's Charlie; three Calicos called Mike, Jesse, and Bombay; gray tigers (Lee and Max were my favorites), and a striking dark chocolate brown cat I think belonged to a friend of my cousin. I called him Friend Lee. They tended to remain quiet. I didn't see Peg Leg for weeks.

Then one frosty December morning I woke with him sitting on my chest.

His eyes were a pale violet I'd never seen on any feline. Of course, I never looked face to face with a cat before. I pet them now and again. But the cats weren't mine, and you don't look eye-to-eye with what isn't yours. But still, they seemed unusual.

He must've come in through the torn screen door on the back porch, although he would've had to be smart enough to figure out how to lift the loose piece of screen up before slipping in. I couldn't help but think he wanted something from me, and was waiting for me to understand.

"What do you want?" I asked, for the first time talking to an animal, as I'd seen so many people do before.

We locked eyes.

Black slices of darkness in the middles of his eyes like propeller blades on a plane resting between flights...

I wasn't sure what to do. Though I'd been around cats plenty, I'd never picked one up. They even made me a little uncomfortable. Winston slept near me, but only when Joy was there to stroke her and make her happy. My presence in the bed was incidental.

As if sensing my discomfort, Peg Leg jumped off. I heard claws jutting from three feet patter on the wood floor, and the hinges on the back-porch screen door move as he slid out.

I didn't see him again for a long time.

The first week of December the snow started, slow and light. The house gets frigid at this time, as it's in a real shambles. One afternoon a thud drew me to the attic. Part of the roof had fallen in. Squirrels nested in a corner next to a steamer trunk filled with old curtains and doilies. I thought the house might not last the winter once it gets going.

Through a hole in the attic roof I noticed a knot of activity down in the town center where the Queen of the Egg Festival would've been crowned atop a massive hen-shaped float, all yolk-blonde tresses and shell-white skin. On Festival day the sky went purple at two o'clock—an hour before the ceremony—so this would be the first year with no Queen. Now the bodies gathered there, moving more rapidly than I'd seen before, walking in duck-duck-goose circles.

Remember what Gentry said?

Needed cold.

They wanted it to snow.

I moved the cans of cat food to the back-porch, where they would be shielded from the wind and snow. I would then sit behind the screen door in the rocker with my coffee and watch from that warmer vantage point. None of these cats figured out how to get through the screen door like Peg Leg, so I didn't worry about them getting in. Peg Leg seemed smarter than the rest. But I didn't know cats enough to be sure.

To my surprise the number of visitors to my porch increased as snow fell in earnest. I worried there wouldn't be enough cases to last the winter. The cat food was looking pretty good to me now as my own supplies dwindled.

I always liked Crumble-Down Farm in December; the gray wood outhouse, the tool-shed, the caved-in barn, the wet, black trees covered in the same blanket of snow, the yard a picture of quiet stillness. But now intermittent cat-movements invaded the calm. Paw prints Rorschached the snow, and I heard their steps up the porch stairs, and aluminum cans clanging into each other as they ate in a hurry.

It was a strange sight from the third story window. I saw the dark shapes of the cats set in the whiteness below, some still and washing up or scratching, others jumping after squirrels or birds, and most going somewhere unknown to me.

Usually I didn't look toward town, but I'd hear them, like demented backup singers in some dead pop star's insipid love song.

Ooh ooh ooh ooh ooh ooh ooooh…

Near month's end I saw fewer cats as heavy snowstorms swept over this part of Connecticut. The town was nothing but a blank valley and the moans stopped—or else I mistook them for the wind living in the skeleton trees. I imagined the yard was drowned in all the envelopes lying around the post office, great piles of white that hid messages forever undelivered. Congratulations, greetings, apologies, love… The snow drifted five feet high in some places there, which I guessed made cat-travel difficult, if not impossible. And the other night I spied a fox eating cat frozen food that had sat untouched for days. I let him finish it; then I threw out the cans and stopped the attempts at feeding.

Until this morning.

My isolation must've got to me because I spoke out loud to myself for the first time ever (So many firsts lately: First cat fed! First thing named! First lesbian sighting! First cat seen eye-to-eye! First zombie knocked over! First day of the end of my life!). My exact words were:

"Thank God, they need me. God bless those cats. Thank God. Thank God…"

See, now I had cats like everyone I ever loved… and I knew a little of how they must have felt having t*heir* cats, and it meant that in some way I still shared my life with those people, like they weren't really gone.

There was a herd… I counted at least twenty—some reddish, some black, some brown, some white and barely distinguishable from the landscape. They crept up the hill, no doubt risking sinking with each step. I thought I recognized some, but not all. I figured they were starving smaller cats—they had to be light as balsa to tread on such fragile ground. I got the food out in expectation of their arrival.

Not long after I saw Peg Leg.

I'd gone to the cellar for some dwindling firewood. I was about to hit the attic, to use fallen roof for tinder, when the cat stepped out from behind a rusty old wheelbarrow. He didn't say anything, just looked at me with those violet eyes, now dyed a deeper purple.

He had a muzzle of blood.

I put down the logs.

"I bet you've been living down here all this time, haven't you?" I asked.

If he'd stuck around the house it would've been easy for him to get down to the cellar. After all, he knew how to get through the hole in the screen door, and there were mice to eat living in the walls.

Peg Leg hobbled closer and sat down, looking up at my face.

"What do you want?" I asked him, stooping down to his eye level.

He kept staring at me. Then he got up and went over to the trapdoor that led outside.

I followed him and opened it outward. Snowy air blew in and stung my face. The cat climbed up the ladder leading to the eastern side of the house with difficulty, pulling himself up by front paws and swinging one back leg after him. I followed when he'd reached the top.

We stood in a few inches of snow. That side of the house is protected by an awning where there was a porch ages ago. All round the sheltered area were five and six foot high walls of glimmering snow.

And the cats.

Fifteen lay at our feet glazed with frost. Friend Lee was missing, and the cat with no eyes, too. They were huddled together, as if still trying to keep warm in death.

The snow came down—they'd be buried in a few hours.

"Is this what you wanted me to see?" I asked Peg Leg.

He looked at me with a quiet I could feel. It choked my

heart.

Raised his little face to the endless dark air.

I saw the herd of unknown cats I'd expected. They crawled to the awning as though drawn to Peg Leg. But something wasn't right.

Cats have heads and eyes and tails and legs. These were just oval mounds of fur moving over the snow.

The wall before me burst open in a cocaine sneeze explosion as a co-worker of mine staggered out. I'd thought the auburn hair atop his head was a rusty tabby I used to see sometimes. But it was Vitolo the guitar-playing mailman walking through the snow.

Under it.

They got stronger with the cold, and now they had enough energy to make it up the hill...

I lifted my shotgun and fired. The shot went through a gaping hole in his chest and into the snowbank behind him. He stopped as though startled. Purplish-black blood sprayed from the snow as another zombie appeared behind the first. It was a little girl with no head. She kept treading forward, her pale flesh flapping like she was made of tattered surrender flags.

I raised the gun and pumped it. The girl pushed Vitolo forward. He slid onto the gun so the barrel stuck out his back, and threw blue arms around me. If shit could take a shit, he smelled like that. I thought he winked at me but it was a black beetle crawling around in his eye. He tried to speak but had no lower jaw and wretched a spluttering sob, repeated over and over like one stuttered word. I kicked his feet out from under him and he fell spread-eagled, taking the shotgun down with him.

Its barrel pointed up at my mouth.

The headless girl tumbled onto Vitolo's body and the one finger left on her tiny dead hand curled around the trigger and tightened.

I stepped back and threw a hand out to knock the barrel

away.

Wave good-bye, hand.

The shot clanged in my head. My face stung as though a thousand angry bees had been loosed from the barrel. I started down the ladder and tried to use both hands. One was a phantom and the floor came up hard against my cheek.

Above, the zombies broke through the pristine snow. Their putrid shadows fell in first and then their bodies. I heard a broken melon noise as one crashed headfirst.

I ran for the door and up to the attic. Crumble-Down Farm's spongy gray steps shook and groaned. I'd never treated the stairs that way. I felt I was stomping on my mother's face. Noise in Crumble-Down farm! Another first. My, how things had changed...

I shut the attic door as well as I could. Through the holes in the roof the freezing storm blew against me. Snow lay in heaps round the room. I grabbed an old shovel, and piled it against the door. Packing it with one hand was slow painful work.

I couldn't tell how smart they were. Maybe if I'd made it up fast enough, they wouldn't find me.

What about the blood trail from the stump at my wrist?

I sat down, leaned against the snow, and stuck my arm deep into the pile. As a red circle grew round it I felt weary. I put my good hand to my face. It was there, but singed by the blast that maimed me.

The snowflakes in the air faded and bits of cold night blew into my eyes until I couldn't see. I grew numb.

Fell asleep.

I don't know how much time passed. Something soft hit me on the nose and I jerked awake, throwing my left hand out for the gun.

But I had no left hand.

It was Peg Leg. Relief woke me from my daze.

There must be a cat-sized hole somewhere in the shadows.

"What do you want?" I asked him.

He climbed on my chest and put his paws on either side of my face and his nose to my nose. His eyes were so icy, so purple.

Impostor eyes.

I wept. The tears stung my blasted cheeks.

He opened his jaws to speak for the first time and a strange meow came out. It sounded as though he was trying to articulate a human word but had the wrong mouth for it:

Woo woo woo oooh...

He was such an unusual cat. The purple sky must've gotten him the way it got the others. Perhaps it took longer for him to change... I stroked his head and he lay down on my lap. I felt I was being lowered into icy water.

I tried to think, to focus: furry head lapping at toilet water... Mother... purring under a plaid cotton sheet... Father... tiny cries at birds outside a window... Joy... broken wings versus fangs... nobody had a dog... all the dogs got away...

I heard sodden footsteps on the stairs, and bodies tumbling down steps...

∞⊖∞

Now the zombies have reached my door. Their nails and bones scrape the wood. Their fists pound. They want in. They want me to share myself with them. So far the door has opened a half-inch or so as they push it against my body's weight and the packed snow.

And I know what Peg Leg wanted all this time. To draw them to me. And I can hear them answering his call. I was never close enough to hear what they were saying so clearly.

The word is *you*.

That's me.

And here I am.

Sabbatical in the Ohio Methlands
JOE McKINNEY

NOT REALLY ZOMBIES.

Not like in the movies, anyway. To begin with, they're alive. And they don't eat their victims. They'll rape you, rob you, murder you, sure, but not eat you.

The rest of it's the same, though.

They lurch around looking dead. They smell dead. Boils, abscesses, old infected injuries—they all do their part in approximating putrefaction. Sometimes a murmuring haze of flies will surround their eyes and mouths. They look like skeletons in leather sheets. Their knee joints have a bigger circumference than their thighs. Starvation and malnutrition are the norm. But their crippled movements and disoriented moaning can be deceptive. Step into the street with your head elsewhere and they'll swarm you.

Afterwards, your corpse will look like it's been eaten.

But they don't eat you. Just... tear you up.

I've seen it happen too many times. Some family in a station wagon, just passing through, gets lost, doesn't see the roadblocks. College kids looking for a gag. Survivalists, testing their mettle, and failing. I even watched them get an Ohio state trooper once. But usually those guys know better.

This is the sixth year I've been coming to what used to be Gatling, Ohio. Like most of the small towns in America's midsection, Gatling was abandoned after the Meth Rebellion of 2017, given over to the meth zombies who now wander its streets and sleep in the doorways of its uninspired, post-WWII architecture. The buildings are falling apart. Few windows remain unbroken. Insulation hangs from the ceilings. Scrolls of wallpaper curl off the walls. The only life here is that which feeds off meth and wanders the streets, moaning like something out of a Romero film, looking for the high that will take them through the coming night.

Luckily, the little second floor dentist office I've taken over as my observation point has escaped the depravations. During the day, when the meth zombies are most active, I can sit at the window and get film footage or dictate notes, whatever I feel like doing. At night, I sit in the old patient's chair and read Jack Finney novels and drink gin. It's diligent fieldwork—don't get me wrong—but I enjoy my summers here in Gatling just the same.

Gene Northrop, a chemistry professor from Texas A&M, has a similar setup across town in the old New Life Baptist church. I've seen him around some. He's working on a paper on aboriginal techniques for methamphetamine production in the post-industrial ruins of abandoned America. Sometimes, late at night, I'll hear a building explode at the edge of town, and I think to myself, *Ah, one of Gene's grad students just scored himself a paper.* Some night soon I'm going to visit him. Maybe we can compare notes.

In the meantime, I've been working on a paper on the mating habits of the female meth—

Okay, I need to change gears for a second.

There was a noise outside the door just a bit ago and I had to make sure it wasn't a wrecking party. The males can be dangerous when they're scavenging for a high. I had to shoot a few of them earlier this month. I hated doing it, but I have to preserve this observation post.

Luckily, it was only Susan.

She started coming here, to my office, two years ago. She's a white female, early 30s, which means she was in her teens when the Rebellion happened. The meth has charred most of her mind to cinders, but her survival instincts are still strong.

She caught me off guard the first time she came here. It was late at night. I had gone through a lot of gin. I got up from my dentist's chair to jot down some notes on something I'd seen that day, forgetting the front door was still unlocked. I heard a floorboard creak and turned around. She was squatting in the middle of the floor, dressed in rags, her long brown hair a frizzled, shaggy mass around her dirty face, nicks and cuts all over her hands and arms.

Have you ever been watched by a squirrel? Same nervous, unblinking look I got from her.

I tried to speak, but she scrambled toward the door. She didn't make it far, though. She was hungry, dehydrated, her body weak.

I gave her some clean water and let her sleep on my couch. When she woke the next morning she was going through withdrawal. She looked at the clean clothes I'd dressed her in, touched her face that I'd scrubbed clean, and panicked. *Residual feelings of violation?* I wondered. I watched her from my desk. I put a military MRE on the floor. She snatched it up and backed toward the open door. I didn't make a move to stop her, just went on smiling.

I was delighted when she came back the next night.

We developed a routine. I'd leave the door cracked at night, a little food and water on the chair next to my bed. Though she never talked, she could still communicate, with her eyes and her body language.

She seemed grateful. I know I was.

I started calling her Susan, after this girl I used to dream of dating back in my grad school days. I don't think my meth girl minded. It seemed to comfort her, just as she became a comfort to me, a bulwark against the loneliness that used to overwhelm me here at night in the Methlands.

I've been back in Gatling for three days now. That first night, when I was still getting settled, she came to me. She had something to show me, a memento of our night together last August.

Now I'm sitting here at my desk, watching her rub her belly. I wonder if her baby will be born without a soul, or if it will lose it along the way.

Like its father.

A Sense of Duty
GREGORY MILLER

THE FOUR MEN worked hard with handkerchiefs tied around their faces. The September floods had been very bad, the worst in a hundred years, and the graveyard by the woods outside town had paid the price. Now someone needed to clean up the mess.

"Ain't no work for a man," said one, shoveling clear a load of muck from the top of a disintegrating pine box.

"We volunteered, Hugh," said another. "It don't do no good to complain."

"We didn't volunteer for *this*, Carl," Hugh insisted.

"Stop your whining and shovel," Carl said, lifting the handles of a broke-down wheelbarrow full of bad earth and turning away with it. "Whining ain't fitting a man, neither."

"Carl's right," said the third. "Volunteer firemen are in for it, no matter the calamity. You signed up as a volunteer fireman, you volunteered for this. So here you are. It's for the good of the town... 'Course, it sure is nasty," he added, peering into the dank hole before him... mostly empty, but not quite.

"I guess, but it strikes me this here's a bit above and beyond the call of duty, or what have you," said Hugh. "You'll change your tune if you fall in there, Ted," he said.

The fourth man, the groundskeeper, returned from his trip to the storage shed, pulling an empty cart behind him. "That was Mr. Wilbur Collins I just stored. Wiped off the name plate," he said. "The newer boxes all have 'em."

"Never did like Old Man Collins," said Hugh. "Shot me

with rock salt once for cutting across his north pasture."

"How many we got in there now, Mike?" Carl asked.

Mike let go of the cart and wiped his brow with a gloved hand. "So far there's eleven... and some spare... odds and ends. Phew! For late September it sure is hot." He looked sick and pale.

"Eleven," said Ted, turning away from the open grave only to face another. Carefully, he picked his way back to clear ground. "That means," he continued once safe, "there's a good... well..."

"The chart says ninety-two," Mike said, rummaging in his overalls for a battered sheaf of papers. "Yep, ninety-two. But to be honest, this one hain't been updated in some time. The new chart, I'm afraid it was warshed away. Can't say as I can recollect all the names, seeing as I just took the post six months ago, but there's probably a few dozen more than what we see here."

"Jesus wept," groaned Ted.

"With all the stones strewn about, we got our work cut out for us," Mike agreed.

Hugh thumped Mike on the back, grinning. "Ain't you glad you got the job when you did?"

"Pineville's a small town, thank God for that," said Carl. "It could've been worse."

∞ϴ∞

Around three they rested on a log at the far end of the cemetery, carefully checking before they sat to make sure there weren't any surprises lying nearby.

"Looking at it from this vantage point, I think I'm gonna cry," said Ted. "I don't wanna go back there."

From where they sat it became apparent just how little their day's work had achieved. One corner of the yard was mostly clear, tombstones neatly stacked against the low stone wall, nothing else in sight but a long hole every now and again or a bulge in the matted grass signifying a risen coffin the waters hadn't entirely freed.

The rest of the yard, sixteen square acres, was a charnel garden. Tombstones lay strewn about, some face down, some face up, some cracked, some broken, some sticking in the earth by a corner after being tossed end over end by the current. Only a few of the heavier, expensive granite stones remained mounted and upright. In almost all cases the remains they memorialized were no longer where they belonged.

It was an old cemetery, some coffins planted so long ago there was nothing *left* to float, but Pineville had also been gifted with several generations of skilled casket makers who knew how to prolong disintegration and fit boards tight together; thus, many had risen when the waters called, only breaking open when those same waters currented them into trees, tombstones, rocks and each other. Scores of broken wood caskets littered the yard, along with their long-hidden contents that turned the stomach and watered the eyes... some still under lids, others strewn across the muck. Friends, family, and ancestors society had long ago accepted as lost had now returned, but they were not wanted.

"If only everything wasn't so *damp*," said Ted. "A little sun, a little heat—"

"Heat would only make it worse." Carl sniffed.

"But at least it would make everything less... less *dead*. I hate autumn. Cold mists, colder rains, and never enough sun. It's the sun I need more than anything. Besides, we won't be able to rebury any of these folk until the ground dries. We should pray for sun."

"Prayer is good, I won't argue none with that, but we should pray for strength more than sun," Mike said, "and hurry up and get on with our job before what strength we got left gives out." He stood, stretched, and trudged slowly back to his cart.

The others, equally slowly, followed.

"What we *should* pray for is a miracle," muttered Hugh,

bringing up the rear. "Something involving me never having to see anything like this ever again."

∞☉∞

By sundown the shed—formerly used for storing shovels, spades, hoes, rakes, bags of peat and wheelbarrows—stored three-dozen occupied coffins, and the remains of a dozen and a half Pineville citizens without; the latter were securely tied up in burlap sacks. Outside, four stacks of tombstones lay in front of the shed, which were to be sorted through and re-stored to their proper places later.

"Another two days should do it for the gathering," Carl said. "Then we can help Mike here with the sorting and put everybody back proper who can *be* put back."

The night was clear but moonless, the wind gentle but cool. They slept in Mike's cottage on the hill next to the shed, setting up two-hour shifts to guard the cemetery from animals that might worry the exposed remains. Mike lent out his rifle for the purpose, along with an oil lamp so no one would take any bad steps in the dark.

Carl picked the short straw and kept watch first. He walked the grounds carefully, handkerchief tied tight around his face, trying not to think. For two hours his only excitement was chasing a red fox away from what was left of Abigail Wilson. At two he gave Ted a kick in the leg and turned in.

Ted didn't go through the graveyard, just circled around it. He didn't want to stumble over any gaping holes in the dark, didn't even want to *risk* it, so he kept to the perimeter, scaring off rats and raccoons then stumbling over, not a hole, but a wooden coffin that gave way as his boot pressed down.

Forty-five minutes later, still wiping his heel on the grass, he shambled, muttering, back to the house and woke Hugh.

Hugh chose sitting rather than walking, and parked himself on Mike's porch swing for guard duty. It was in pretty poor shape, the weatherworn wooden seat hanging from rusted chains that looked ready to break, but it felt good to sit, and everything held. In fact, it felt so good that after a while, probably not more than a couple of minutes, he drifted off into uneasy sleep.

He dreamt fitfully of mildewed linen, dank holes, and the sighing of fretting winds through dark tree boughs. The sound conjured images of waving doors that shouldn't be open; clattering attic shutters in abandoned mansions; cold, wet-ashed chimney flues... and after a time it grew louder, more distinct and insistent, until with a start and a cry he awoke.

But the sound did not cease.

"What's that?" he hissed, then clapped a hand over his mouth. "What *is* that?" he hissed again through white fingers. He looked back toward the front door and the black inside space beyond. Silence there, save for snores.

"Christ Almighty, that ain't *them*, he said, and fumbled for the dark lantern. "Gonna see," he said. "Gonna see what that goddamned sound *is*."

But he couldn't bring himself to strike a match.

The sound was like a tide, cries washing over voices, voices demanding answers. The sound was faint but resonated with the power of a multitude. Over the voices came the tread of feet on grass and leaves, the knocking of knuckles against wood, the ripping of fabric with fingernails.

"Lord a' mercy." The words could have been Hugh's but were not. They came from *behind* him. He spun like a top, arms raised to fend off or strike.

Carl grabbed him. "Now, now, it's just us." Mike and Ted stood beside him in the dark, holding their breath.

Together they stood on the porch and listened.

"It's coming from the bone yard," Mike whispered.

"Some of the kids from town come back to cause trouble?" Ted whispered.

"Hell no," Carl said. "No one would cause trouble with

that." His shadow nodded toward the cratered lawn.

Mike took a deep breath and said, "Come on now, let's not get panicked. It's my job to see this property's residents are kept safe. I'm turning on a lamp." He fumbled with a match. Yellow flame sprang up, touched an oiled rope. The lantern glowed.

Hugh gasped. Ted shut his eyes tight. Carl grabbed the rifle from Hugh's hand.

Mike raised the lantern.

The noise rose for a moment, then, protesting, faded quickly and completely away.

Nothing moved in the cemetery but rats and leaves.

Even so, no one caught a wink the rest of that long night.

∞☉∞

"Well, I'd say something looks different."

Everyone looked at Mike, who was surveying the cemetery, hands on hips and nodding slowly. "It don't look as messy today."

"That's cause we worked our behinds off yesterday," said Hugh. "Now my first order of business is to get that damned pine tree to give up her goods. It just don't look *right*, that thing all the way up in a tree." Shouldering a coil of rope, he walked over to the spruce planted in the middle of the lot and looked up into its cover, where the glint of a brass handle betrayed the presence of a coffin lodged between two branches some eight feet off the ground.

"I'd better help him," said Carl, following. "If the damn thing drops sudden it'll probably land on his head."

"Bag duty for me," said Ted, holding up a pile of burlap sacks with a grimace. "Gonna go in the woods and search for strays. Feel free to trade whenever you feel inclined."

"Gonna try and start matching pieces together, one stone to one coffin, one coffin to one body," Mike said, and went off to the shed.

The sun was bright and warm, good for drying out the earth but bad for what needed to be re-interred beneath it. They found their cologne-soaked handkerchiefs, tied them in place, and the work went on. There was no talk about the previous night.

Not until noon did something happened to put everything else on hold for a time.

It was Ted, out in the woods, who picked up on it first, and when he did he came running out from among the trees, waving his arms and ringing his hands. Everyone stopped and stared, and when he got close he called out, "There's a child in there! I can hear her crying!"

The search began immediately.

"No way anyone's in here," said Mike, turning to Ted as they picked their way among the trees. "You sure it wasn't a barn owl? They sound kinda like tikes when they're riled."

"Hey now, I know what I heard," Ted replied.

"It don't make no sense. The nearest farm—"

He was cut off by a wail the likes of which none of them had ever heard. It came from farther in the forest, but not too far, and worked its way into their bones until their footsteps slowed and they all grew still. It started high and ended low, but not low enough for an adult, and there could be no doubt it was a person. Ted was right. It sounded like a child, hurt and terrified.

"My God, that was it, that was the sound," Ted whispered, grasping Carl's arm.

"Leggo," Carl hissed. "Someone needs help." But for a long moment all they could do was stand in place looking toward the thickening cluster of pines that stood before them, and Ted held on.

The silence was deathly.

Then the cry went up again, the desolate wail of someone utterly lost and alone. "Mama!" that someone called. "Mama."

It was Hugh, of all people, who was stirred into action by

the sound. He was a father and knew *that* call of duty when he heard it. "Come on now," he said, and trotted off toward the noise. As if waking from a dream, Carl tore free of Ted's grasp and followed Hugh. Mike and Ted kept pace behind him.

Hugh moved rapidly, trying to pinpoint the location of the sound before it died away again. He pushed through the dead lower branches of some pine trees just as the wail was fading away, and arrived at the source of the sound before the last echo died.

There could be no doubt who had made it. The sound had led them to her, and they had found her.

The little girl in the faded pink dress lay in a shallow mud puddle in the shade of the trees, but there was no need to help her up. She had been dead for a long, long time. The skin of her face stretched tightly over her skull, dehydrated and tanned by long years underground. Her long, blond hair rested in dusty, disintegrating braids across her chest. Her hands were clusters of brittle white twigs. Her hollow eye sockets stared vacantly.

Around her lay the shattered remains of a small, white coffin.

Hugh let loose a yell that sent blackbirds flying off in fright. Mike and Ted simultaneously turned and were sick. Carl leaned against a tree, swallowed his risen gorge, and shut his eyes. When he opened them again he looked up, and said, "The waters took her all this way. Guess it would be a good turn to take her back. Guess that's what she wants."

Like a funeral procession they filed slowly through the woods and back to the sun-struck graveyard, a small bundle in burlap carried between Carl and Mike. After depositing the bundle in the shed they went quickly back to Mike's house, trudged inside, and worked no more that day.

Later that night before they fell asleep in front of a cheery, popping hearth fire. Hugh snuck over to the door and latched it tight.

No one asked where he had gone when he came back.

∞☉∞

By morning they had collected themselves enough to return to work, and for the next three days they labored diligently, ignoring flitting shadows and sheltering themselves at night by laughing too hard at jokes and sticking cotton in their ears when they slept. Although they remained on the property out of a sense of duty, they didn't keep watch on the grounds after dusk anymore.

They made fine progress. Soon all the "litter" was gone from the grounds and Mike began making a great many identifications, due in part to his own detective work, but mainly to a somewhat disturbing discovery he made one bright morning: during the night, someone had used a sharp stone, branch, or (here Mike shuddered, thinking of it) fingernail to scratch names onto all the coffins, and mud to write names on all the burlap sacks. Despite the issues this raised, it helped a great deal, and the four men figured that no matter how it had come to happen, the act was a gift.

One afternoon, after the reburials had begun in earnest, Carl was touching up a hole when he saw Mike sitting off by himself on a rock at the edge of the yard.

"Everything dandy?" Carl asked, but was taken aback by Mike's appearance. He looked sicker than any man he had ever seen. There was sweat on his forehead and upper lip, but Carl could tell it wasn't the good sweat of work, but the kind that comes with brain fever. He looked so pale the light seemed almost to shine through him, and his breathing was labored and loud.

"Lord a' mercy," Carl said, and put his hand out to touch Mike's shoulder. Mike shied away, and Carl withdrew with a raised eyebrow and a frown.

"You look sick, Mike. I don't know what to make of it, but I think you'd best get inside and lie down."

"I ain't *sick* sick," said Mike. "To be honest, right now I just want out of here for a bit. I want this over. I need time away."

"Well why don't you go, then?" Carl asked gently. "You've worked damn hard. No one can say different."

"Because if I leave now this job is history, and I need it bad. What with the Depression on and a score's score of people ready to take over if I up and run, I'd be a crazy to walk away."

"Depression?" Carl said. "I don't follow."

Mike gazed at him long and hard, then motioned for him to sit down beside him. This time he didn't shy away.

"I found something 'bout an hour ago," Mike said.

"Yeah?" said Carl.

"I found the updated chart of the cemetery."

"Oh yeah?" said Carl.

"Just sittin' there right as rain, a little stained but still readable, right on top of my desk like it had been there all along." He pulled out a folded sheaf of papers from the front pocket of his overalls. "Here it is."

"Well that's fine, Mike, just fine. Now we can know for certain if we're missing anybody. But I don't see—"

"It'd please me if you took a gander at it. 'Specially the bottom of the second page."

Carl took the list, flipped to the second page, scanned it, and stopped short.

He breathed in and out, long and deep.

"My, oh my," he said.

Mike swayed beside him, mopping his wet brow.

"Oh my," Carl continued. "Oh my, oh my."

∞⊖∞

"What you need, Carl?" Ted asked. Several hours had passed. Carl had taken some time to collect himself, then gathered everyone together on Mike's front porch.

"Ted, Hugh, I got a question for the both of you. Before this job, what's the last thing you remember?"

Hugh snorted. "You drunk, Carl?"

"I just wanna know."

"Well... I..." He trailed off. "It's kind of hazy, now that you mention it."

"Ted?"

"Well hell, Carl, I guess my house and my wife and working in the mines. I got lotsa memories."

"I know you do, but what about *right* before? What do you remember about the flood? Who came and told you we needed to do this job?"

"Oh, now, Carl, that's easy... I mean... that is to say..."

Mike stepped in. "Hugh, what year is it?"

"1912," Hugh said immediately. "What the hell year you *think*?" He stood up. "You've all gone crazy, I —*ouch!*"

"Oh!" Ted grunted, grabbing his hand. "What'd you do that for?"

Carl held up a knitting needle.

"The year," Mike said flatly, "is 1934."

"Look at your fingers, fellas," Carl said.

The two men raised their fingers. Eyes, suddenly wide, suddenly terrified, examined them closely. A thick, clear liquid dribbled down both hands in slow rivulets.

"Embalming fluid," Mike said. "Unless I'm mistaken, I'm the only man here with a pulse."

∞☉∞

There was a great stir on Mike's porch, and after the screaming and the exclaiming and the accusing and the shaking heads and frantic cries had ceased, three men walked the dirt road to Pineville and sought out their homes.

A short time later they returned, glassy-eyed and resigned.

"Now do you believe me an' Carl?" Mike said.

Hugh and Ted nodded their hanging heads. Their houses

were abandoned, their families gone.

"What year you say this is again?" Ted asked quietly.

"1934," Mike said. "Pineville's been dead since the early '20's, when the coal gave out. I'm the only one here. All I do is tend the cemetery, see that no one bothers anything. Come from Pittsburgh, originally. Paid by the county."

They trudged into Mike's living room and slumped down in rocking chairs by the fire. Outside the wind blew cold, sending dried leaves scuttling across the porch boards and stressing the roof beams.

Mike said, "According to this chart, you all... er... passed away on the same date: May 23rd, 1912. You remember anything at all about it?"

They thought for a moment. "Come to think of it," Ted said, slowly, "I do remember something... something about water. But it's distant, like a dream."

"The mines!" Carl exclaimed. "Culver Lake. The flood."

"The roar... the rocks," said Ted.

"By God," said Hugh, "the collapse."

"We all work... or worked... the same midnight shift," Carl explained. "Looks like we didn't make it out of that one with all our faculties intact, as the doctors say."

Mike moaned. "This'll teach me for not taking an interest in other people's lives. If I'd only asked what you all did and where you all lived when you first got here... I just assumed you lived in Still Creek over the hill and were sent down to help. I never thought... that is, I never... I should have known when you was talking about Wilbur Collins. He died in 1893, and you all look so young, I—"

"Enough," said Carl. "Don't worry yourself over it. What we need to worry on now is the best course of action. There's something going on here that ain't natural, we've all guessed that since Day One, but now it seems we're a pretty big part of it ourselves. Well, to be frank I've got to say I don't think we belong up here, walking and talking, anymore than the rest of the folk out there who seem to be a tad restless too."

"Agreed," said Ted and Hugh.

"And I think we'd also agree that this is a fair bit, well, *upsetting* for us, what with us being dead and our families all moved on and away... Upsetting for our friend here too, who ain't done nothing to deserve this kind of stress," Carl continued, nodding to Mike. "So the sooner things get back to normal, the better. Now, we've laid out there quiet for twenty-two years and change. Why we up and walking again now?"

"The flood," Hugh said.

"That's how I see it," Carl agreed. "The flood warshed us all up, something needed done to fix it, so we came back to ourselves. Taking care of this kind of thing is our job as volunteer firemen, after all."

"Agreed."

"But what about the others?" asked Ted. "Why are they up and about too?"

Mike said, "It's like that saying my granddaddy was fond of, the morbid cuss: 'The dead take care of their own.'"

"Sounds about right, given what's happened," said Hugh.

"Everyone out there in that yard and in that shed are doing their part, and we're heading up the project," Carl said.

"So all we got to do..." Hugh began.

"...Is finish what we started, and things'll fall back into line around here." Carl turned to Mike. "After all this, you mind if we stay on at the house a little while longer? That fire feels good, even if we ain't supposed to notice such things in our condition."

"Well hell, boys," Mike said, and they were glad to notice the color had returned to his face, "I'd say you deserve that at the very least."

∞Θ∞

They had the cemetery back in good order at the end of two weeks. Some gravestones needed replaced, including

Carl's and Ted's (Hugh's was found in a rain gully a short distance from the grounds, a little chipped but otherwise fine), but Mike made a trip over to Still Creek and came back with a half dozen new stones. Finally, on October 27th, they lined up in front of Mike's cabin and looked out upon the graveyard, grass neat, stones straight, and declared it finished.

All except one thing.

"Everything trim and tidy again, everyone tucked back in," Carl said. "Guess it's time you saw us off, Mike."

"Boys, it's been my pleasure." Mike shook hands all around. "You ready?"

They were. Three open graves lay side by side. Carl, Hugh, and Ted, dressed in smart, new tailor-made suits, climbed carefully down into the holes, minding the dirt, and lay down in the pine boxes they'd built for themselves the previous day.

"Feeling a bit tired, to be honest," Hugh said, reaching up to close his lid. "Miss my kids. Maybe if I go to sleep I'll see them again. So long, folks. Catch ya again sometime, I guess." He shut the lid, knocked twice, and Mike stepped down and latched it.

"I guess all this was fitting," Ted said, squirming slightly to get comfortable. "There ain't many people left to look after us… It would've been too big a job for you to do alone, Mike."

"You did great, Ted." The lid creaked shut. Mike latched it.

Carl shook Mike's hand again. "I want your honest opinion… You think this place looks good? Really good?"

"Even better that it did before."

"An untended grave is a shameful thing. It was quite a shock, this, but I'm glad we came back to do it." He reached up, grabbed the edge of his lid, and started to pull it closed over himself. "Oh, hey!" he added. "I almost forgot!"

"What's that, Carl?"

"We talked it over, and if you ever need any help keeping

your house in good order—a paint job, new roof, whatever—
don't hesitate, eh? We owe you."

The lid shut. Mike latched it.

Later, he found himself whistling as he shoveled on the
dirt.

The Basement
WILLIAM VANDEMARK

JULIE SCREAMS. She's in the kitchen.

I'm in the basement stacking canned goods next to bottled water. I glance up at a barred window. Outside, misshapen figures shuffle past. I drop a case of Dinty Moore and run to the stairs.

"Get down here," I yell. "Right now, or we're dead!"

Julie opens the door. She stands at the top of the stairs, pale with fear. She is claustrophobic. Yesterday, the idea of seeking refuge in a dank basement terrified her more than televised reports of zombies. This morning, the TV signal died.

Glass breaks—a picture window's timbre.

I take the stairs two at a time and grab Julie.

I pull, but she won't let go of the door jam. Behind her, a wreck of a body appears. From its face, tendrils of skin hangs like a spider's web. The zombie, teeth sharp and broken, lunges at Julie. I yank at her, slam the door, throw the deadbolt.

A voice howls. Fingernails scratch at the door. The scrabble gives way to pounding.

I hit the door back. "Hah, you bastard. No way in."

And no way out. I turn to Julie, who clutches one hand with the other.

"It's okay," I say. "We'll just wait 'till they go."

I take her hands in mine. They're warm and wet—slick, even; the top joint of her index finger has been severed.

I swallow hard, resisting the urge to vomit. "Please tell me I did that with the door."

She rocks back and forth. "I don't know." Tears roll down her cheeks. They spatter on the floor with drops of blood.

∞☉∞

Hair unkempt, Julie sits on the floor, rocking; her jeans dark with stains. Ropes bind her wrists and ankles to bolts lagged in the cinderblock wall.

With an X-acto knife, I slice my thumb and drip blood onto a sponge. I take the sponge to her cracked lips.

The whites of her eyes bulge like boiled eggs. As I paint her lips red, she shies away. Suddenly, I'm greeted with her amazing azure irises, the highlight of my day. For a moment she looks at me. I reach out, but stop. She's trying to draw me in.

I'm under no illusion. If she had the chance, she'd sink her teeth into my Adam's apple.

She licks her lips, her eyes roll upwards; the azure disappears as she looks into the top of her skull. She moans and her head lolls. Blindly, she snatches at air. Ropes tighten.

∞☉∞

Outside, the world has fallen apart. My radio hisses static.

Inside, sinew and bindings still hold.

Time crawls, the world whispers, floorboards creak. All the while, the door thumps like an arrhythmia.

On good days, when Julie moans, I close my eyes and remember the times when such sounds came from other primal desires.

On bad days, I lean forward. Ever closer. Waiting for her hot breath to splash across my throat.

Working Man's Burden
DAVID C. PINNT

HAROLD KNEW THINGS were about to go cock-eyed when Betty 248 stuffed the chicken guts in her mouth.

He sat up on his stool and flicked off the Mossberg's safety. The rest of the Z-crew, Betties and Barneys they called them in the break room, continued to work the eviscerating carousel, shoulders slumped and jumpsuits sagging, hands moving slowly but efficiently as the chicken carcasses rotated on the hooks. Grabbing the breast with the left hand, right plunging into the gut slit and a quick pull and tug, dropping the offal to the stainless steel mesh. Heart, gizzard, and liver, onto the conveyor and the rest down the trough to the waste bins. The regulators implanted in the backs of their skulls, leads burrowing into their shriveling limbic systems, winked green, a slow happy cadence to a shift boss like Harold.

But Betty 248, he'd been watching her close anyway. So new she hardly looked dead, flesh sagging just a bit on her face, deep circles under her eyes. She'd been in the line three, four days? Soon enough her skin would take on a gray, waxy sheen and eventually, despite the hosing down with chlorine each night, it would break open. Dark, dry tissue, the blood long clotted. The sores opened at the knuckles first, then the elbows. Harold knew the repetitive motion—hour after hour gutting the chickens—was just too much for the dead flesh to bear.

Harold swung off the stool and edged around the carousel to see her face. The other crew kept at their jobs, jaws slack, weight tilting from side to side, their various numbers stenciled large across their backs and small over the left breast. The chickens, gleaming white skin still oozing droplets of blood from the defeatherer, swayed on the carousel. Emaciated fingers in rubber gloves grabbed, twisted, pulled, and separated.

On the far side of the carousel Harold stooped, a ratcheting pop sounding off in his left knee. Sure as shit, Betty 248 had a crimson smear across her cheek where she'd crammed the guts into her mouth. The other Z-crew stared straight at the carcasses or worked with eyes closed, but 248's sunken orbs rolled left and right and Harold fancied he could hear a high keening rising from her smeared lips.

He jacked a shell into the Mossberg and thumbed open his radio. "This is Harold in EVR-4... I've got a situation. Send a crew down." Maybe his voice tipped her over or the chewed entrails hitting the desiccated, empty stomach, but Betty 248's regulator failed for certain. She yanked a carcass off its hook, ripped out a mouthful of pearlescent flesh, and turned on the Barney next to her, yellowed teeth gnawing the side of his face, latex-tipped fingers raking his cheap cotton jumpsuit.

Holy shit," Harold flicked the radio open again. "Right now! I need a crew right now!"

The Barney, 109 on his chest, shuffled sideways his regulator working fine, still trying to gut the chicken before him, as Betty 248—shrieks rising in her throat—slavered and chewed at his neck. Harold crab-walked under the carousel, keeping one eye on the Z-crew, not knowing if the fracas would overload their regulators too. His boots squelched on the wet floor, stray clumps of feathers and gobbets of meat in the treads.

Betty 248 ripped off Barney 109's ear, shriveled gray flesh on a zombie so old. The wound lay purple black under the harsh fluorescents.

With one economical step Harold slipped behind the pair, socketed the Mossberg's barrel at the base of the Betty's skull, just below her regulator—now amber—and pulled the trigger. The top of Betty 248's skull vaporized, bone, hair and brain splattering across the carousel, the Z-crew and the chickens. Her body dropped to ground, head gone from the nose up, jumpsuit collar smoldering. Barney 109 turned back to the carousel, left hand twitching for the next chicken.

Levi and two rustlers banged into the evisceration room. The rustlers held lollysticks, steel tubes six feet long, a wire loop at the far end and a shank handle at the other to pull the loop tight. Pistol-gripped Mossbergs hung over their shoulders, barrel down.

Levi took in the scene, Barney 109's gaping head, Betty 248's still lump on the floor, and hooked his thumbs through his belt loops. One of the rustlers slapped the red kill switch by the door, shutting down the assembly line, chickens jerked and swayed on their hooks and the Z-crew stopped, limp.

"Goddamnit Harold, you shot her? Protocol is to wait on the rustlers. We just got her last week. Five thousand dollars! She had a good six months in her. Jesus Christ!"

Harold bit back his first reply. Still cradling the Mossberg he tipped its barrel toward Barney 109's ragged head. "Her regulator failed all the way, Levi. Look at that one. She'd taken him down, the whole bunch might've tripped over." He cocked his head toward the rest of the Z-crew, now complacently shifting from foot to foot, staring at the denuded chickens. "They could have all tripped over, you know? Every one. You want that happening?" Harold felt a thick muscle swell in his neck, veins bulging out along his temples—Christ, he'd been working the evisceration room for a dozen years before this ass-wipe was hired and now here he stood riding him on protocol. "They trip over and you got two dozen rampaging around the plant, who knows what happens. I'd be dead, the rustlers you send down dead, who else? A hell of lot more than five thousand dollars I can tell you that, hell of a lot more."

Levi opened his mouth, red flush creeping into his ears,

and then seemed to think better of it. He pulled the radio from his belt. "I need status check on the regulator for F-248. Variances for the last twenty-four hours."

While Levi waited for answer the rustlers moved closer to Harold. One held his lollystick in a two handed grip.

"Any contact?" the second asked peering at Harold's bare arms, his neck.

"Contact? Christ no. Only contact was with the Barney there." They continued examining him, made him open his hands, show them his knuckles. Harold felt the post-adrenal surge working from his body. He needed to sit down. Even one scratch, Harold knew, and the loop would be over his head, dragging him into a quarantine room, waiting for the infection to surface.

Levi's radio crackled and he held it to his ear, nodded as if the speaker could see him "A bad regulator, dipped 15 minutes ago and went off-line."

Harold had been in the control room before. A technician monitoring all five hundred Z-crew in the plant, watching the output from the regulators, making sure the urge, the overriding urge that moved them, stayed dampened, the creatures docile.

Harold spit between his feet, prodded at Betty 248's flaccid corpse. "Tell you what, Levi. This'll happen again, the company going on the cheap like this. An approved regulator won't drop completely in 15 minutes with no stimuli. Half this crew's up from Nogales, ain't it? Undocumented. What's the cost now to slip in under the CDC?"

Levi's tongue probed at his back teeth, lips parted. His ears stayed red. "You want to watch what you're asking there, Harold. Two, three years to pick up your pension? Wouldn't be right for man your age to be turned out this late in the game."

When Harold didn't reply Levi allowed himself a small, self-satisfied smirk and clipped the radio to his belt. He beckoned the rustlers "Move this crew out and get the room sanitized. Get this mess cleaned up." He prodded Betty 248's corpse. "And the chickens, shit, those four are gone. Run the rest back through the baths." Barking orders now, the flush left his face. A rich pall of cordite and the yeasty smell of the Betty's brains hung in the air, fighting through the ever-present chlorine, through the chicken offal's briny scent.

"Harold, head up to H.R. Fill out your incident report and clock out. Take the afternoon off."

∞⊖∞

Traffic on the drive home was light early in the afternoon, giving Harold time to ponder. At Federal and 12th panhandlers stood four abreast, some made eye contact, others kept their heads lowered, shuffling alongside the cars trapped at the stoplight.

WILL WORK FOR FOOD

HARDWORKING

DISABLED VETERAN, ANYTHING HELPS!

and the last...

ZOMBIES TOOK MY JOB

Harold did his best to ignore them and fight the guilt at the same time... there but for the grace of God and such. He caught the left turn signal at 17th as it flipped to amber. These blocks had taken it hard during the Epidemic, lot after vacant lot, the burned foundations poking through the weeds. There'd been talk of rebuilding, townhouses or something, but there were too many empty houses now. Why build more?

Though fifteen years had passed since the Epidemic began, since the first corpses clawed their way from their black rubberized body bags in Houston, Harold still marveled at the way society slipped back into normalcy.

The first dark days were right there if he closed his eyes—the world in chaos, round-the clock coverage on all channels, the cities burning with soldiers rattling through the streets in their Humvees. He and Val had worked hard and furious when the reports first started, screwing plywood over the windows, double nailing closet doors horizontally over the front and back entrances, listening to the relentless *thump, thump* against the wood.

The tanks and APC's at last roaring into the city to restore some semblance of order, of safety.

And then Stephen had come home.

Harold rubbed at his dry eyes, willing the memory away. He knew the Z's must have some vestigial intelligence down there under their all-consuming hunger. Maybe that's what had brought Stephen north from Colorado Springs, to their doorstep.

All the blood and terror of those first days boiled down to mere seconds on his front porch.

"And look now," he muttered as he made the wide arc around Custer Park. A Z-crew shambled about the grounds, running push mowers back and forth, their overalls spattered green to the knees. Two city foremen and three Rustlers watched them. Another bent over his transponder board, eyeing the regulators' discharge.

One foreman turned his head as Harold's truck rattled by, a shotgun propped on his hip and the sunlight winking from mirrored sunglasses. The city crew looked in bad shape, skin sloughing and lips pulled back in rictus grins. At the plant, after the second shift, all the zombies were herded downstairs and into the safe room, where the day's offal bins were rolled. They were locked up and the control boards shut down, letting them come alive, plunge into the viscera, gobbling it down. Harold had watched a time or two on the security monitors. The technicians waited until the offal was gone, until the first Barney tried to take a bite from his neighbor, and then flipped the regulators back on, leaving them all shuffling aimlessly, stupid, staring at the cement walls.

Such quick and loose use of the regulators was prohibited if a company was using Z-workers. The CDC would shut them down in a blink if they caught wind of it, but Levi and the management thought it worth the risk. The workers lasted longer if they could feed. Still, maybe flipping the regulators on and off weakened them, the way taking too many pain pills eventually stopped helping with the arthritic grinding in his knee.

∞Θ∞

"You're early today."

Harold twisted the bolts on both locks and dropped the counterweighted bar, snugging it against the steel sheathed front door. Val sprawled on the couch, one hand working the remote and other rubbing her bare foot. In the back room the swamp cooler thrummed, pushing damp air through their little rambler. She had unzipped the front of her polyester cleaning blouse, and few strands of hair hung loose at her temples. Sweat beaded on her neck and the bags under her eyes were so dark they seemed purple.

"Had one the Betties flip over today," he rummaged a beer from the refrigerator. Recounting the afternoon's events between swallows, he tried to sound casual, not mentioning how the flesh crept along his scalp as he slid under the carousel, how his guts sloshed as he thought the others were going to flip over, or the dry crumbling of the Betty's brains spraying across the chickens.

"Levi threatened your job? Really said that to you?"

"I tell you Val, they're cutting costs across the board.

Bring in those Z-crews on the cheap. I know they couldn't have been certified. They're setting themselves up for one big mess."

Val thumbed the mute button, sighed, and rubbed the inside of her wrist across her forehead. "Well, it's a hell of a day for us, I'll tell you that." She looked off in the distance as she always had when bringing up bad news. "I lost the Chavez Building account today. They came at me with a bid—well damn—so low I would've had to clean the whole place myself to make any money. It was my biggest account. I had to let Esmeralda go. She's got kids, too, you know—it was hard. Said I'd bring her back if business picked up, but there's not much out there."

"Cheap," Harold ran his finger around the bottle top, moisture rippling up in a tiny wave. "Were they—"

"Yep, some outfit out of Greely. I guess they can make 'em push a mop, empty trash cans. Can't think they'll do a decent job." She was silent for a moment and when she spoke again her voice quavered. "Those... things. Those goddamned fucking things." She tossed the remote on the coffee table. "You know, it seemed the world went to hell overnight and then we pulled it back up, but it's just sinking again, in a different way."

Harold glanced at the mantle, at the picture of Stephen in his cadet uniform, so bright and earnest, the world at his feet. He wished, not for the first time, Val had been the one to look through the peephole that night. Would she have only seen her son? Would she have turned a mother's blind eye to the twigs in his hair, the dirt rimmed lips and nostrils, the dried bloody tendrils snaking from his scalp and ears. Maybe it would have been better than all this, better if she had opened the door wide and let him lurch into the house, better to have had it all end then.

On the television two talking heads shared a screen, below them the words—*A Shifting Economy?*—crawled. Harold turned up the volume. "This has the potential to skyrocket the GDP, vault us over Asia and Europe—"

The blow-dried head's adversary cut him off—"But isn't it just slavery under another name? Aunt Mildred kicks the bucket and her family gets a quick thousand to ship her off for processing, regulator implanted in her skull and the next day she's making widgets, free labor."

"Well certainly there will be some birth pains—they are all but taking over the unskilled job market. Ultimately it will bring us all a higher standard of living. People are going to have to become better educated, more skilled workers." He leaned back and chuckled. "I know no zombie could do my job, though I'm not so sure about Chet here."

Harold clicked the television off before Chet could reply.

He sat the empty bottle on the table. "You know it wouldn't be so bad if the controls were followed. They're supposed to be burning ninety percent of the bodies, strict protocol for the regulators, but—"

"But they're greedy," Val finished his sentence.

Harold nodded. It was an old topic for them "Trucking them up from the border. Who knows how cheap their circuits are. Business, it's greedy, and the government's turning a blind eye to it. I guess you can't blame them down south for selling the bodies off—even if they get five hundred dollars each, it's more than most of those folks see in a year."

Val let her hair loose, rubbing her neck.

Harold felt a small hitch in his chest when he realized her brown eyes were shiny with tears.

"I can blame them. Look what we've become," her mouth softened. "We're sinking into hell and all anyone cares about is 'can I make another dollar on this?'" She slumped, "There was a time when you would just work. You could go to work and care for your family. If you were willing to work hard, it was enough. You could raise your family and have a decent life."

"Well, we did that. We had a decent life before..." He lost steam, fumbling over the right words. "I'm sorry," Harold said and he hoped she knew what he meant.

"I just don't know" her voice hiccupped, "I just don't know how it can keep moving. The world. I don't know how we can keep moving."

"I don't see we have a choice. I know Stephen—"

Her voice rose, cutting him off, "Don't."

∞ϴ∞

Later, in bed, he splayed a hand across the swell of her hip, her nightgown cool beneath his fingers. Her breath caught and he knew she wasn't asleep, but she kept her eyes closed and turned her back to him, burrowing her head into the pillow. Harold's hand dropped.

He knew better than to say their son's name in front of her. She would spiral down for days, breakfasts and dinners with a palpable wall of silence separating them. Her eyes glossy and staring past him, mouth, cheeks and forehead creased with hard shadows.

He was already gone, Harold thought. He knew it. The dried blood, the dirt and twigs, yet still that part of his mind which took such sadistic delight in waking him deep in the night, asked the question again and again. Was he? Was he really? How fast did you bring the shotgun up Harold? Didn't you see a glint, just a flash of awareness in his eyes?

He'd buried Stephen in the soft ground of the garden along the back fence. Zipped his near headless corpse into a day-glow orange mummy bag and shoveled dirt over him, blocking out Val's wailing from the house, letting her anguish blend with the braying sirens, the clattering Strykers and staccato bark of AR-15s filling those first days of the Epidemic.

No man should have to bury his son with his own hands.

Harold turned over. Outside a low warbling siren grew closer. Revolving red and blue light seeped through the cracks of the heavy plantation shutters bolted to their windows.

He rose and levered the shutters open, filling the room with muted moonlight and the oscillating flash of an emergency vehicle. A sheriff's SUV, blue and white, stopped at an angle across his street. The virus, the infection—whatever had caused the dead to walk was still in the air, weaker, but enough to keep the crematoriums busy.

About every third corpse now became infected and sometimes people died alone in their homes, no one to strap them down or phone their death into the CDC.

A Barney shambled along the street, an old man, eighty-five or ninety, sloped shoulders and sunken chest curled with wisps of white hair. His flaccid belly jiggled with his stiff-legged walk, toothless mouth gaping and his pee-soaked pajamas falling off his scrawny backside.

A second sheriff pulled up in front of the Barney. The competing headlights threw perpendicular shadows on the ground. The first SUV's door opened and an officer stepped out, shotgun at port arms. He circled around the Barney, who had stopped as the second set of lights washed over him, circled until the other officer was free from his line of fire. In what could have been a replay of Harold's movement earlier in the day the Sheriff took two quick steps, nestled the shotgun in the back of the old man's head, and pulled the trigger.

Before the echoes rolled off down the street and the Barney's frail body hit the pavement, Harold snapped the shutters down, not sure if he should get back in bed, knowing there'd be no more sleep tonight.

∞⊖∞

The next morning Harold slipped into his usual parking space at the plant. Val hadn't woken when he'd told her goodbye. Or if so, she'd done a good job of hiding it, keeping her breathing slow and regular. He'd snipped a rose from one of the bushes out front and left it in a tumbler of water on the kitchen table with a scrawled "I love you," on the back of an envelope.

Harold tucked his thermos under one arm, lunch box swinging from the same hand, when he saw Bert, one of the QC's, striding across the parking lot. Bert's fingers beat a rapid tattoo against his pant leg and the muscles in his jaw bunched like he was swallowing a pair of marbles.

"Knocking off already?" Harold smiled and squinted into the rising sun.

Bert unlocked the door to his Chrysler, his eyes feverish, burning in their sockets. "Knocking off for the rest of the week, Harold—shit I guess knocking off for good."

"You're quitting?" Bert's time was as short as Harold's.

"Not quitting," Bert's gaze skittered around the parking lot filling up for the morning shift. He nodded his head at the pebbled cement walls of the processing plant. "Listen, I got to get out of here before I do something stupid. Go talk to that sonofabitch yourself if you want the story. Tell Levi he better hope I don't see him on the street. Kick his fucking teeth down his throat if I do," his hands shook as he opened his car door. "Tell him that if you see him."

∞❸∞

"It can do the job, Harold. Don't see why you're so worked up." Harold had button-holed Levi near the end of the wrapping line, packages of 8-piece fryers slipping along. A Barney stood at the line's end, head jerking left to right as the packs rolled before him. "It's not like I didn't offer Bert another job—he's just too proud to take it"

"Back on the gut crew—swilling out eviscerators at the end of the night, half as much money—what'd you think he would do?"

"It can do the job, watch," Levi grabbed one of the shrink-wrapped packages off the rollers. He tore loose an edge of the cellophane, pulled a drumstick half out, and set it back on the conveyor. As the fryer crossed in front of the

Barney his head jerked down and he snatched the damaged pack off the rollers, dropping it in a bin at his feet, his sunken, milky eyes unblinking as more clicked by. "Now why would we pay someone eighteen bucks an hour when we've got him?" He slapped the creature's shoulder. "They're just tools, Harold. If a business is going to make money you can't be afraid of tools."

"Christ, Levi, don't you remember? It hasn't been so long. Don't you remember being boarded up in your own house, watching your friends, your family torn apart? Don't you think about what they are—what they were?"

"It's progress Harold. It's the new order of business. People like you had their way we'd still be living in caves, shitting ourselves during a thunderstorm."

He made a point of glancing at his wristwatch. "You been on the clock now for about half an hour? Maybe you ought to be worrying we aren't training one of these guys to watch for green lights to go blinking off."

Through the rest of his shift Harold fought to stay focused, watching the Z -crew as they gutted the chickens, but his mind hiked out on its own tangents. Had they really forgotten what brought these things forth? He raised the Mossberg and sighted along the backs of their heads. The regulators winked green at him over and over. What if they hadn't found a way to control them in the first place? Would it have been better if they all burned?

Levi's words echoed in his head. Maybe he ought to be worrying about his own job, never mind Bert's. He was a secondary warning system, nothing but another set of eyes, where the technician in the control room leaning over the transponder board had the ability to turn the regulators on and off at will.

Harold straightened his leg from the stool, wincing at his knee. The Mossberg held five shells and he carried another twenty in his utility belt. He could shoot them all right now, walking along, firing and reloading. They wouldn't blink.

Each would keep pulling at its chicken guts until he put the barrel against their skull, squeezed the trigger. What would they do? Fire him, maybe charge him with destruction of property?

They've forgotten what they are, he thought.

The clean-ups come so easy in the middle of the night now, sanitary. Two cops in front of his house. The old Barney falling limp like a string-cut puppet. It's like the entire world had forgotten.

He avoided Levi the rest of the day.

∞ϴ∞

Val's Honda was still in the driveway when Harold came home.

He threw back the deadbolts and stopped, one foot on the rug. The swamp cooler wasn't running. The television wasn't on. His breathing echoed through the still rooms, the heavy air.

"Val?" In the kitchen the water glass stood empty, a flower stem on the table and a small pile of petals on the floor. Beneath his scribbled note Val's spiky, handwriting filled the bottom of the envelope.

—I'm so tired, Harold. Tired and sorry. I know I haven't shown it but I never blamed you for Stephen. I just couldn't say it to you. You did the right thing and you've carried that awful burden alone. I pray you'll do the right thing again if you have to. With all my heart—

Harold read the note a second time, tracing fingertips across the words. "No, Val, you couldn't have," he whispered. "You wouldn't do that to me."

He couldn't leave the kitchen. The rose petals were soft, wilted, curling in on themselves in the heat. The only dishes in the sink were his from this morning, a coffee cup—brown stained porcelain as he'd forgotten to rinse it—and a bowl and spoon with flecks of shredded wheat gluing them together. He filled a glass with lukewarm tap water and drank it down. Rinsing the coffee cup and bowl, he gazed out the window at the vegetable garden.

Stephen was down there, bones wrapped in down-filled nylon.

The second tumbler of water was cooler and he passed its cold curve across his forehead, hearing the faint pops and creaks of the old house as it expanded and eased in the evening warmth.

After what seemed hours, as cool blue shadows crept across the back yard, Harold opened the hall closet and grabbed the Remington pump, the one they'd left loaded by the front door through all these years after the Epidemic.

He walked heavily to the bedroom door, twisted the knob and cracked it open. With shades drawn tight the room was cave-dark, cooler than the rest of the house.

"You didn't do this to me," he whispered again, but the air in the room carried a sour undercurrent, vomit and urine. He took in Val's still form, the comforter pulled to her armpits, the empty brown Valium bottle on the nightstand. She lay turned on her side, back to the door and one hand splayed on her thigh.

Harold eased himself onto the bed, shifting quietly as if he might wake her. He held the Remington awkwardly in his left hand and thumbed the safety off. With his right hand he grasped Val's cold, slack fingers, interlaced them with his own.

He knew the accepted thing was to block the door and call the CDC, the police. They'd be out in minutes, zipping her up and whisking her away to the crematorium, but he also knew the virus had waned over the years. There was a better-than-even chance Val was dead, dead and gone. At some kind of peace now. He couldn't bear the thought of some group of haz-matted strangers clomping through their house, tumbling her body into a rubber-lined bag.

"In the morning, Val. I'll call them in the morning." He

closed his eyes and tried to conjure memories of their first days together, her quick step and the bright sparkle in her eyes.

The bedside clock read 11:45 when her fingers clenched hard on his. Her back arched and her heels drummed into his thigh.

"It's alright," he whispered, and canted the Remington across his chest, barrel pressing into her skull. He pulled the trigger before a sound could escape from her writhing lips.

Harold spent the night lying in the dark, ears ringing.

∞☉∞

"Harold, didn't you call in sick?" Sally at the front desk smiled at him as he stumbled by. "Jonas's been on your shift three hours."

"A bug, but I'm better now," Harold mumbled. He stepped quick down the corridor to the locker rooms. How long before Sally phoned Levi and the little prick came snooping around for him?

In the echoing tile-floored locker room he tugged on his vest and pulled the Mossberg from its brackets, thumbing the red cartridges into the magazine. In his locker door's seam he had tucked a photo of Val and Stephen, taken some twenty years before at Lake Powell. They both wore goofy, sunburned grins, squinting into the camera lens, framed by placid blue water and smooth sandstone cliffs.

"It'll be okay," he slipped the photo into his shirt pocket.

Would this make any real difference? Deep down he had the answer. One man can't shift the world's balance. But people needed to know—to remember what happened. He couldn't be the only one who thought like that.

He pressed the Mossberg along his leg as he left the locker room, turning right toward the control center rather then left to the hydraulic push doors into the plant itself.

Harold didn't know the technician inside the control

room, which was just as well. The man slouched in a rolling desk chair, a slight cowlick sticking up as he sipped from an insulated coffee mug. Video monitors stretched across the wall far wall, tiny black and white images of the plant jerking back and forth. To the left a flat screen monitor displayed a rapid cycling of numbers and digits, each culminating with tiny green dot, F237, M24, M458, F17.

The technician turned his head, catching Harold's reflection in the screens as he stood with door propped open by one foot. "Hey you know the rules, buddy. Nobody but management or control crews in here."

"Yeah, I know the protocol," Harold stepped into the room, keeping the door open with the barrel of the Mossberg. "This door's supposed to be locked down too, isn't it?"

"Hey," the technician's eyes darted to the shotgun, and he leaned to put his coffee cup on the desk. Harold stretched his free hand forward, clamping down on the bird-thin bones of the technician's shoulder, his thumb pressed against the seat back. He jerked and the man rolled backward, past Harold and through the open doorway. The chair bounced hard over the threshold and the technician spilled into the corridor. Harold kicked the chair out after him and slammed the door. On the inside was a thick bolt. The control room was designed as a refuge of last resort. He threw the bolt and turned his back on the technician's pounding and indignant squawking, narrowing the sounds from his consciousness.

The control board was clearly labeled and no great shakes to cipher out. Harold thumbed off the override controlling the plant's electronic doors. Every door would swing free and easy until he turned it back on. A flurry of activity in one of the monitors caught his eye, Levi barking into his radio, rustlers running haphazardly before the camera. Maybe they'd all leave the work rooms, come thundering into the corridor.

Harold removed the photo of Val and Stephen and propped it beside the screens. All he had held dear in one faded scrap of paper.

"I guess this'll about do it," his voice was a cracked whisper. This might shock them back into reality, make them remember what everyone had so easily forgotten.

Something heavy hit the control room door and it shook in its frame but he paid it little mind. The technician's radio squalled over and over. Harold cycled up the regulator controls and began shutting them down, one hundred to a screen. Five screens filled with urgently winking amber pinpoints when he was done.

On the video monitors the Z-crews stopped their methodical movements, heads twisted back and forth, hands jerked, clawing at the air as they looked for something, anything to quell their hunger.

Harold shut the monitors off one after another. This wasn't something he wanted to see. Thin screams seeped through the walls, between static bursts of the radio. On the last monitor Levi and half dozen rustlers were in the corridor outside. They stopped pounding at the control room as, from the far end of the hall, a pack of Barneys and Betties surged through the swinging doors, coveralls stained dark, gloved hands and mouths smeared and clotted.

They'd soon be out of the plant, lumbering into the city.

Harold laid the shotgun up across his knees. When the noise died down he'd throw the bolt open and go out.

He'd go out and see if he couldn't get his family together again.

The Last Supper (The Anatomy Of Addiction)
JOHN CLAUDE SMITH

"...Yes, my friends, there is nothing new to report on this, the 300th day of... of infestation. As if there will ever be anything new to report. No, the turmoil that prevails is quite obviously terminal: the attrition of humanity... Just take a look out your windows... that's if you haven't already boarded them up. Otherwise, take my word, oh yes, yes. The horrors are real... and relentless..."

∞Θ∞

The drug haze swells in his head as Razor tries to wake (WAKE UP!), but the effort is more akin to wading through mud. It feels like a turgid, convoluted descent into someone else's 'no longer private' hell; someone's corrupt imagination. Surely these images of decay and extinction cannot be nourished into fruition by the unconscious reels that project from the back of his brain and onto the white cranial screen he now views. It is a wasteland, a grainy, gray and rust-hued visual documentary cataloging the demise of civilization as we know it. *Holocaust to the nth!* Only it is much worse than an exclamation point, for there is no finality.

The landscape is littered with dead people; walking dead people; feasting dead people. The morbid, leering eye—the prime reaction culled by the masses since the onset of the disease being cathode ray addiction, voyeurs of the visceral—gleans every bit of perversion, presenting in excruciating detail, the aimless gaze. The savage quest for anything meat:

rats, cats, dogs... *people*; the horrendous corrosion and disorder. In one fell swoop the world changes; this is the way it is destined to be, there is nothing to be done about it. It is the blatant intrusion of grade Z cannibal films as Headline News (5, 6 and 11). The eye constantly scours the desolation, peering with clinical (*carnivorous*) curiosity as the final days unravel. It is a painstakingly slow process. Like picking a scab off a dying race, repeatedly prying it off to search underneath for the reasons why, prolonging the moments (*seconds into minutes into hours into days...*) before The End (my friend). Leaving the grave unoccupied...

Razor twitches, realizing the scenes he witnessed are external, not internal. Cathode ray addiction indeed, amongst many other addictions ingested, snorted or shot into eager veins. He slams his eyelids shut, incinerating the light with the precious cool darkness, canceling the TV's brutal exhibition. He immediately nods off. There are no dreams. There is no reason for them anymore.

∞☉∞

When he wakes his eyes feel like they are throbbing, not enough room in the sockets. As he shoved the throb to the back of his head, to the abandoned place where dreams once roamed free, he hones in on Sara. She's still, lying still. Ribbons of blood trickles from her mouth into a pool of saliva, creating patterns that seem vaguely familiar. He remembers nothing (*hitting, pummeling—this is my ride, senorita—Go away!*), remembers something (*sorry, I'm sorry, babe*), and, as usual, denies everything, even his existence; this existence. She is face down on the hardwood floor: flat and smooth, the floor. The baby—*what was her name?*—is her miniature twin. Razor notices a slight rise in Sara's torso, a slight ripple in the ever-expanding pool. He is uncertain if he can notice any discernable indication that the baby is breathing. Then again, his vision is tweaked, seeing doublouble and even tripripiple.

He sits up, gaining focus while viewing the TV screen. The volume is forever mute. The color is faded like the bleached terrain outside, basking in hues of gray and rust. The radio is a whisper screeching in the far corner, settled into a nook next to a pile of filthy clothes. It emits an array of clicks, blips and static, epitomizing the final wheezing breath of this dying planet.

Razor, stricken with pangs of compassion (more likely, flushed with guilt), unsteadily props himself up on his hands and knees. He belches and bile fills his mouth. He coughs, spitting the putrid yellow and red fluid on the hardwood floor; it splats, quickly assuming a Rorschach quality. Mesmerized, he searches for faces, secrets, unlocked doors...

Suddenly Razor peripherally glimpses the hypodermic syringe. The needle—

(*Something sharp.*)

He reaches out and his balance sways, stumbling into the warm fluid, soaking his shirt. But he doesn't realize this. Everything is sucked into oblivion, the comforting vacuum of nothingness...

∞⊖∞

"...why do I persist to report the carnage? Perhaps it is journalistic instinct. Perhaps it abates some of the internal suffering, hoping that I've made a connection with somebody out there, my friends. At least one of you who understands, who is not already grist for the bone mill. [cynical snicker] Perhaps... perhaps it is the knowledge that if I sign-off, well..."

∞⊖∞

There are no dreams, only memories:

Razor bends the spoon, slightly, setting it on the table. It does not wobble. He then rips the end off of a Q-tip, setting the tiny cotton ball next to the spoon. He nervously twists the remains into a question mark. His hands are moist, his heart beginning to race. Anticipation is such a sweet addition to the rush. He taps the dope from its plastic baggy onto the spoon, the specifics of said dope unnecessary, the gist here deals as much with the process as it does with the high; nonetheless, the dope is crank, cocaine's dirty white trash cousin. His anxious fingers are now concrete in precision. He squeezes water from the syringe onto the dope. Flipping it over, Razor uses the plunger end to stir the mixture; it dissolves almost instantly, leaving an oily film over the top. Good. He closes his eyes, his nostrils flare; a hint of ether. Definitely some good shit. Blood sings in his ears. His brain is a beehive—oh, yes, very good shit. His thoughts are focused, streamlined; he is the conductor. He drops the cotton ball into the mixture. It soaks up the liquid like the sponge it is meant to emulate, like the putty of a child's mind. Always wanting more, whether it is knowledge, attention, or satisfaction.

For Razor, it has always been satisfaction. Circumstances have only magnified this desire, altered the means by which his satisfaction is achieved. Now, satisfaction means escape, running away, hopping on the metaphysically mutated freight train raging through his body. He vaguely remembers some ancient classic rock performer's nasal bleat and cackle: *All Aboard!*

Razor uses the needle end to roll the cotton ball around, making sure to get everything. He puts the flat end of the needle on the cotton ball, drawing the plunger back. He raises the syringe to eye level, admiring the yellowish color. He pulls down on the plunger again, taps the syringe with his forefinger, and watches the bubbles rise. Sweat trickles down the sides of his face. Razor firmly presses the plunger back up. He clenches and unclenches his fist, tightens the belt around his upper arm. The veins protrude like mountains on a relief map. The needle pierces flesh. Razor gets the register; he is perfect as always: blood flows into the syringe. He inhales and exhales, emitting an audible sigh of pleasure.

Now: Razor presses the plunger, slowly (*teetering* [patient])—Hold it (*this is better than*), hold it (*any heaven they… who are they?*), hold it (*could promise*), pulling back on the plunger (*in the afterlife: 1. death 2. hunger…*), jacking off (that's what Metal Fred called it, milking the high, lingering before surrender: *teetering…*), so good, so good… pressing in again, fully, the freight train in overdrive (*All Aboard! Hahahahaha…*)—Pounding on the door—*shit, the cops*—yanking the needle from his arm—

SHITSHITSHIT! (pounding—no, wait—*scratching…*)
derailed by paranoia, by…
(scratching?)
cops?

∞☉∞

eyelids
quiver in defense
light streaming in like sandpaper (*abrasive*—WAKE UP!)

SOUND: scratching at the door, muffled pounding—*the cops?* Confusion. Why don't they say something? Why don't they—*(WAKE UP!)*

There are no dreams, only memories… *and Reality!*

The door splints from the pressure. They—*the dead*—slowly shamble through the opening; a throng of arms and legs and gaping maws converge to fill the allotted space. Like excrement forcing its way through an ever-widening sphincter, the bodies fill the doorway with disregard toward everything but the purpose at hand: the acquisition of food. They are scavengers driven by the hunger. That is all that they are.

Rubbing his eyes, Razor back-peddles on his rump to as neutral a corner as possible, gagging on their abhorrent stench. His eyes are watery but clear, lucidly soaking in the true Reality manifesting before him. A Reality he had so tried to avoid… to escape from…

The dead, in all their revivifying glory, tear the baby—*what was her name?*—to pieces, clutching and yanking with selfish fingers more akin to vulture's talons. Eyes glazed like slivers of shattered stained-glass hope, patches of skin gray with putrefaction… if there is any skin at all; they are nothing more than the urge: to feed. This point is made abundantly clear by the constantly flexing jaws, chewing air, in desperate search of meat. And when meat is procured, momentarily sated by a fistful of flesh, stringy entrails, or once vital organs: grist for the bone mill.

Sara's scream cuts through the monotony, a jagged, agonizing wail, much like the rotting teeth that penetrates her flesh and unconsciousness. Razor cringes, impotent to react, eyelids slamming shut, fingers plugging ears, trembling. It is not as if he cares; his body coils inward—closing himself off out of a learned, well-oiled reflex of denial. She squirms, but already too many bony fingers dig into the freshly excavated cavity in her abdomen. They scoop her intestines into their dust dry mouths, sucking as a child would on a plate of spaghetti. Her farewell refrain is a gurgling confirmation of participation in the ultimate physical travesty: to be eaten alive, a violation beyond reciprocation. The gurgling coda is eclipsed by one of the androgynous dead—gender and genitals having been withered by the passage of time—as it chews her tongue right out of her mouth.

When Razor harnesses the courage to open his eyes again, it is to the same bleak scenario that closing his lids had blotted out. With dull, machine-like precision, the dead continues to strip the last of Sara's meat from her bones, slurping the final droplets of blood from the hardwood floor. Some even suckle on her clothing—much as a baby would its mother's bosom—drawing blood from fabric, or possibly even sustenance from the very scents that lingered within.

Razor whimpers. It's all his body can muster as a response to the cruel play before him: an improvisation of insanity. All he wants is to be away from this ramshackle thea-

ter of the macabre. It, too, is a violation beyond reciprocation, a reiteration of the reality in which he is trapped.
Scrunched into the corner, he wishes he were wood, wishes
he were able to blend into the wall. His eyes flicker to and
fro, still looking for a means of escape... when he spots one.

It glimmers, a winking reflection of light, a light at the
end of the tunnel: *the hypodermic syringe.* Equidistant between
the gorging horde and him laid the needle. *Naked and singing,
singing to him!* He instantly becomes transfixed on it, focusing
to a point of blocking out the madness. The bogus barrier his
mind creates gives the impression that it had eradicated the
obscene exhibition, bringing down the curtain, but not in the
purest sense. He can still see them, but now it is as if they are
behind a TV screen—their usual mode of intrusion, cameras
poking out of windows, or on top of buildings, peering down
on the deluge—their heinous acts being transmitted from
some place far beyond the confines of the studio apartment.
They are real—*TV never lies*—but are no longer his immediate
concern.

Razor crawls toward the syringe, oblivious to everything
but the hypnotic lure of the needle. A needle that serenades
him with promises of escape, of attaining the state of sweet
nothingness he so covets. As his fingers pluck the syringe
from its solemn resting place in the middle of the room, his
wrist is roughly accosted by one of the dead. Illusory TV
screens melt into pools of stark reality. A gasp squeaks from
his larynx, a gasp of shock and futility. Worse than the cold,
bony grip on his wrist, though, is the revelation within the
syringe: it was empty. The promises it tendered, all counter-
feit.

So why was it still singing?

Razor breaks free from the skeletal grip, breaking a couple of bony fingers in the process, scampering rat-like to his
corner. But it is too late. His scent is the only enticement they
need as they crawl and stumble toward him. Intoxicated:
caught in the forever feeding frenzy.

He jabs the needle into his arm. Something sharp to set him free—*that is all he ever wanted anyway*—but nothing. Again he jabs, repeatedly puncturing himself, ripping many holes like tiny, lipless mouths, lipless and laughing (*HAHAha*)... They all laugh (*HAHA*), drowning out the spiking pain. (Drowning...) Blood trickles like crimson streamers, decorating his arm with the appropriate attire indicative of the sullen celebration. Disillusionment blossoms on his face; a serrated slash devoid of verbal release blooms from his mouth. He continues to assail his arm with the needle; many more tiny, lipless (*mocking*) mouths join in the chorus of laughter (*HA-HAhaHA-HAHAhaha*) that fills his head. The dead paws him, and swiftly indulge. Razor is impervious to everything but the morbid quest at hand, desperately jamming the needle with vicious intensity into his now mutilated arm, knowing full well that death is near—its imminence assails his nostrils, dulls his brain, his motivation quickly disintegrates into listless, automated repetition—and not wanting to face it. Not realizing that in death he will finally be set free.

(*HAHAhahaHAHAHAha*...)

∞⊝∞

"...as another day comes to a close, my friends, another day like all the rest, accumulating as scratch marks on the wall. I can only hope your day was as uneventful as mine. A tepid plea, I know, my friends. After all, misery loves company, but suffering is integrated into our very souls, woven into the very fabric of each of our lives. A neck within a noose—*waiting*..."

Memory Bones
MICHAEL STONE

THE SICKLY BUTCHER'S SHOP smell got stronger as he ascended the stairs. The carpet stuck to his feet.

"It be the bedroom on the left, Doctor."

Messinger turned to acknowledge the speaker but he had already ducked from view. He muttered his thanks and continued up the stairs, his Gladstone bag bumping against his leg. A dust-dimmed window let in just enough light for him to make out two doors, one on each side of the tiny landing. He pushed open the door to the left.

The room stank of open wounds and wet bandages. Wrinkling his nose, Messinger peered myopically into the darkness, trying to discern edges and corners in the flat grayness.

"You must be the doctor."

Messinger faced the voice and a bed coalesced in the gloom. "Ahh. Mr. Lode, I presume." The attempt at humor didn't bring any response. He asked politely if he could draw back the curtains. "I need to see you if I'm to examine you."

"Aye." The speaker sounded hoarse. "If you must. It's just that my eyes are very sensitive at present."

"I shall take a look at them in a moment, Mr. Lode." He parted the heavy drapes to let in a chink of light.

"That's enough! No more than that."

There was just enough sunlight for Messinger to see a man propped by pillows, his body hidden by a high-collared, ankle-length nightshirt. The doctor smiled wanly. The nightshirt looked to be the source of the bad smell that pervaded the room. The patient's age was difficult to determine—his hair was as thin and colorless as melting snow, but his long face was unlined, the skin around his jaw smooth and tight. Lode's pupils were pinpricks in pools of baby blue.

Messinger sidled to the bed and eased himself down, placing his Gladstone bag between his feet where it clanked on a bedpan. It was then he noticed the scratches in the wall behind the bed: reminiscent of a prison cell, hundreds of short vertical strokes with a diagonal slash denoting groups of five covered an area of wall larger than the bed's headboard.

"So what seems to be the problem, Mr. Lode?"

"It's not me you've come to see, Doctor."

"Oh! I do apologize. I was told the patient was in this room. By your brother, would it be?"

Lode nodded. "Aye, he weren't having you on." Lode reached out and gripped Messinger's wrist. "You've taken over old Dr. Dimmock's practice, yes?"

Messinger nodded.

"Did he mention me?"

"No, but I didn't actually have the pleasure of meeting Dr. Dimmock. I was appointed by a selection committee after he retired."

"Pity. He was a good man, Dimmock. Open-minded. Are you a broad-minded sort of lad?"

"Well, yes, I suppose I am." Messinger tried to smile.

"Good, because I want you to listen to me. Right?"

Messinger nodded, although he felt things were far from right: Lode's grip was surprisingly strong.

The grip lessened and Lode settled back on the pillow, his blue eyes never leaving Messinger's. "How old do you think I am, lad? You won't find the answer in your notes so don't bother looking."

Messinger straightened up. "And why won't I find any mention of it in my notes?"

"Because your predecessor made up a name and date of birth for me, that's why. Like I said, he was a good doctor;

I'm hoping you'll be the same. Now answer the question: how old do you think I am?"

Messinger considered arguing that Dimmock wouldn't have falsified Lode's details because of the minefield of National Insurance, NHS records, vaccination programs and the like, but decided to humor the man. Maybe that was what Dimmock had done; humored him. It was a fact that consultations went smoother once one had gained the patient's confidence.

Messinger's eyes were becoming adjusted to the dim and dusty light now, giving him a better opportunity to observe the patient's features: the unlined face and clear blue eyes that contrasted sharply with the thin hair and liver-spotted hands. "If I had to guess at your age, I'd venture that you're somewhere in your early fifties, perhaps."

Lode laughed. "Way off, lad, way off. Actually, I'm 149!" He laughed again, throwing his head back. Messinger noticed that his teeth were unusually small, very white and even. Lode's laughter snapped off suddenly as he looked squarely at the doctor. "You think I'm mad?"

Messinger gave a non-committal smile. "That's not within my remit," he said smoothly. "However, I'm a busy man with a lot of patients to see this morning, so can we stop playing around?"

"You ought to show some respect for your elders!" barked Lode.

The bed squeaked as Messinger pushed himself to his feet. He heard a corresponding creak on the landing.

Lode shouted. "It's all right, Eustace; the young man is not going anywhere!"

Messinger heard footsteps retreating down the stairs. Disquieted, he sat down.

"I *am* one 149 years old. When I was born, Victoria was on the throne and Britain was at war with Russia. Just accept that. I could verify it by telling you loads of historical details but you would dismiss them as mere fancies learned from books. My bones are as full of memories as yours are of marrow jelly, lad.

"When I was in my mid-forties—I forget exactly how old I was—something strange happened. I fell under a carriage. It ran straight over my arm here," Lode indicated a point below his left elbow, "severing it completely. I picked it up and ran home to my wife. Screamed my bloody head off, I did!" Lode chuckled at something he'd said before fixing Messinger with a searching stare. He shook his head. "Regular little doubting Thomas, aren't we, lad?" He rolled the left sleeve of his nightshirt up to reveal a thick, ropey scar that circumscribed his forearm.

Messinger peered closer. "There's no way they could have stitched your arm back on in the 1890s," he said. "They didn't have the know-how."

"Nobody stitched it on. It grew back!"

"Of course," Messinger sighed. "Silly me. It grew back."

"Don't get sarcastic, lad, I'm warning you."

"And what became of the arm? Did that grow into a pet?"

"I buried it in the compost heap."

"Pity, you could have hand-reared it."

Lode's lips tightened.

Messinger sighed. "You were saying, Mr. Lode."

By way of answer, Lode leaned forward and raised the hem of his nightshirt to reveal his knees.

Messinger recoiled. "Jesus Harry... who did that?"

"Eustace."

"The bastard must have used a lump hammer!"

"A sledgehammer, actually. Every other Thursday. He seems to think I might run away." Lode sucked on his teeth. "There are times when he might have been right."

Messinger jumped to his feet, unclipping a cell phone from his belt. He saw again the scratches on the wall behind the bed, and again he thought of a prisoner counting the interminable days of incarceration. The fives were arranged in columns of ten, and there were fourteen completed columns... making over 700. But 700 what? Days, weeks? Surely not months?

"If that's what I think it is, put it away, lad."

Messinger put the phone to his ear.

"If you don't put it away, I shall call in Eustace." Lode let the threat hang in the air.

Messinger shot a nervous glance at the door as a floorboard creaked, and felt the fight in him drain away. "Ah, sorry. Wrong number. Yeah, my mistake. Bye." He broke the connection.

"Now come and sit down." Lode patted the side of the bed. "Come on, lad."

He sat down. "But why——" he began.

Lode held up a hand. "All in good time, lad."

"But this is crazy."

Lode's face softened. "Aye, lad, I know I'm asking a lot of you." He looked at the doctor from under lowered eyelids and chuckled. "The best is yet to come."

"I can't wait."

"I'll ignore that. Anyway, Bessie and me, we kept the arm incident a secret. I lay low, hardly venturing out while the arm and hand were growing back. We nearly starved to death, with me not being able to go to work. Times were different then. That's when we started the vegetable garden, all the way back then."

Lode's eyes clouded over. "Bess died in 1919 of 'flu. Bloody terrible, that was. You young 'uns don't know you're born, I swear. We weren't any more able to cope with grief then as you are now, you know? Just because folks lost babies to disease and brothers and husbands to war, it don't mean we became immune. I was one of twelve children. Only eight of us reached adulthood. My mother used to keep daisies in four little jam jars. 'One for each of my little mites in Heaven,' she used to say.

"But when Bessie died, I don't know, I just couldn't cope

with it. I was an old man, what did I have to live for? In the end, I went down to the Cotton End Bridge." Lode indicated behind him with a thumb. Messinger realized the man was referring to a bridge over a railway line that had served the local collieries. The track was long gone. He hadn't even known before now that it had a name.

"And?"

"I threw myself under a goods train. When I came to, I couldn't see. I was blind." He looked at Messinger, obviously checking that he was paying attention. "I staggered for a short distance and then gave up and lay down where I was. I could tell by my sense of touch that I was among those tall weeds, the ones with the pink flowers."

"Rosebay willow herbs," supplied Messinger automatically.

"Right. And I could also tell by touch that my head was missing."

Messinger blinked, then slumped and covered his eyes. "Jesus Christ! You had me sucked into your crazy little world then. For a moment, I actually *believed*."

"And so you should," said Lode. "It's all true."

Messinger shook his head. "Oh no. You're not catching me out again. I'm off." He started to rise.

Lode grabbed his wrist.

"You're leaving without examining your patient? What sort of doctor are you, eh?"

"A sane one," he retorted.

"You think I'm insane? I've been crippled and bedridden since 1952; what d'yer expect? My only contact with the outside world is through Eustace." Lode's eyes flicked meaningfully at the bedroom door. He sat back, breathing heavily. "Please, lad. Stay a little longer."

Messinger sagged. He hated himself for it, but he wanted to hear the end of the story. He knew that all he had to do was peel back that high collar and examine Lode's neck, but he wouldn't—it would be an admission of gullibility. And on a deeper, more primitive level, he *couldn't*. "Okay, but it's against my better judgment."

"Good boy." Lode patted the side of the bed again.

Messinger sat down obediently.

"My head grew back," Lode continued, "just as my arm had. I had no idea how long I lay there among them pink weed things."

"Rosebay willow herbs."

Lode took the correction graciously. "I recovered enough to find my way here and recuperated over a period of several months."

"Forgetting for the moment the sheer implausibility of you surviving decapitation and any subsequent regeneration," Messinger allowed himself a smile, "if what you are saying is true, you wouldn't have any memories. You had grown a completely new brain from scratch. You would, mentally, have been like a newborn. Your story has a plot hole I could drive a bus through."

"We pondered long and hard on that one, me and Dr. Dimmock. He suggested that as cerebral fluid surrounds the spinal cord, it could act as a repository of memories." Lode shrugged and spread his gnarled hands as if he really didn't care. "Anyway, while my body was growing a new head, my old head had been busy growing a new body. Eustace turned up. Eustace, like all my brothers, is *me*. A clone. It was Eustace that started to call me Mr. Lode. It's a joke, you see––I *was* Eustace Orr but now he is and I'm the lode. He keeps me crippled and when he wants another brother––"

"He removes your head and grows another. Brilliant! Can I go now please?"

"You are being very rude, Dr. Messinger."

"Frankly Mr. Lode, Orr, whoever you are, I think I'm en-titled to be rude after all the crap I've had to take from you." Messinger grabbed his bag and stood. "I shall be sending for an ambulance as soon as I have left here, thereby discharging my obligations to you."

Lode raised a shoulder and let it fall, a one-shouldered shrug that said it was Messinger's loss if he left now. "Before you go, take a look out of that window, lad. Tell me what you see."

"What's out there, the tooth fairy?"

"Just look, will you?"

Messinger rested his hands on the windowsill and gazed out, blinking at the change of light. "There are a few old guys at the bottom of the garden. Weeding by the looks of it."

"They'll be tending the vegetables. We grow our own as much as we can. Look closer at them. Notice anything unusual?"

Messinger narrowed his eyes. He turned back to the man in the bed. He did a double take out of the window and then back at Lode.

Lode's smile was that of the cat that has found the cream. He indicated the scratches on the wall. "I have spawned 738 of us so far, with another on the way. And some of them have become lodes too, I daresay."

Messinger licked his lips with a dry tongue. "Why?"

"Why what?"

"Why would you want to create so many clones of yourself?" Messinger thought about what he had just said, and added: "That's assuming your story had a single grain of truth in it, which it doesn't, of course."

Lode laughed that bitter short laugh of his. "Haven't you ever dreamed of a world without divides? A world where everyone agreed with one another? One religion, one government, one mind; everyone living in harmony? Eustace has watched the world go to hell in a handcart, watched history repeat its mistakes—correction, he's watched *people* repeat their mistakes. He's taking steps to put things right."

Messinger rubbed his eyes. "My predecessor must have been a gullible old fool if he went along with this lunacy. I'm leaving now, and when I get back to my surgery I shall remove the names Lode and Eustace Orr from my panel. As from this moment, you are no longer my patient."

"I've told you, it's not me you've come to see."

Messinger made a show of scanning the room. "So where's my patient?"

Lode motioned with his chin at a deep chest of drawers. "Top drawer," he said. "He's a slow developer, this one. We're a bit worried about him."

Messinger dropped the bag carelessly and crossed to the drawer in question. Glaring angrily at the heavy-looking brass handles, he gripped them tightly to still the quivering in his hands, his nostrils full of the almost overpowering stench of blood and disinfectant. On the limit of hearing he could hear a gentle sighing, a sound like a damp paper bag being slowly inflated. Was it the soft swish of his own blood pulsing in his ears, or the rhythmic rasp of raw, embryonic lungs pulling air? He whipped his head round and glared at Lode, sitting in the shadows… who grinned right back at him expectantly, his teeth a string of pearls in a peach-fuzzy face.

I have spawned 738 of us so far, with another on the way.

"Bullshit," Messinger growled. Annoyed with himself for even hesitating, he snatched open the drawer…

Going Down
NANCY KILPATRICK

SHORTLY AFTER THE DEADIES got up to stroll the boards on Manitoulin Island, Paddy ran out of meds.

She'd been on largactyl for years—brain mangulations, dry gut ruttings, critical BO. The stuff stripped polish off floors and tasted rat-poison sweet so her insides undoubtedly resembled the arm of a kid she'd seen gnawed by a combine. She could've lived with that, though. But when everybody started coming back from the dead and chomping on everybody else, what was the point of taking drugs, even if she had any, with so much good film noir available?

Still, those asphyxiation-blue tabs had propped up everything crumbling inside her skull. Like the retaining wall that kept water from swallowing the land, her wall had worked pretty good most of the time. But nothing aired on TV anymore. Or radio. The movie theater closed. Her retaining wall was eroding fast.

Paddy opened Daddy's channel changer and twisted the wires so she could corkscrew holes in her wrist. The vein kept jumping out of the way and she ended up with ten round oozing bloodeyes. She sucked and tasted fresh flesh. Shit, she thought, now that the Deadies trudge the pebbles on the lakefront around the clock, nobody's left to ferry to the mainland. She'd seen all the videos and DVDs on the island. The pills from the drugstore might be gone, but residue floating in her blood stream still broadcast too loud and clear. Anyway, the second Marilyn Monroe got back, that signal would dim. Marilyn would like the Deadies, at least Paddy thought she would.

God knows, Paddy liked them. She'd tried to join their club before there was a club and if she'd done it right she'd have been a charter member. ODs. Hemp slung over the beam in Daddy's root cellar, where he used to lower his pants and pull down her... She'd dropped her eyelids once and the screen went blank. *Marilyn's steady hand plunged the bread knife into her heart.* She missed the projector and Paddy'd been pissed. Her lung felt like badly spliced videotape and that's all. *Marilyn refused to visit Paddy the whole time she was in General Hospital.* Paddy'd thrown a fit until they gave her more drugs and a new flat-screen TV.

Life had been tabula rasa with no chalk. But then the Deadies started. Right away Paddy saw they were luckier than her. They never worried about getting aced in the butt by stray emissions and they didn't have to memorize lines. Anyway, did they care why they were chained to this rocky poor-reception island, or wonder who would rip out their liver this week in 3-D, or make them sit in a hair seat and suck in a teen comedy then fuck them doggie style with blurry trailers, or any of the other stuff Paddy worried about all the time? All they thought about was grabbing somebody with their slimy green hands to snack on. She could handle that. She could be a Deadie.

But the Deadies didn't want Paddy. She stank wrong.

"It's an insult," Marilyn assured her when she finally deigned to visit. She waved a spotless silk hanky in front of her perfect transparent nose. Paddy was hurt until Marilyn said she had an idea.

"Shove your fingers past their cold black lips, into a living porridge mouth and let things crawl over your skin. Action!" Marilyn giggled.

Paddy tried it. No cracked molars clamped. No spoiled tongue licked. The switched-off eyes didn't flicker. "I'm not good enough for them," she whined. *Marilyn slapped her silly and shrieked, "I told you before, diamonds are a girl's best friend."*

Paddy felt iced as the black waters rose. The volume increased. Dense moisture plugged every orifice of her body like giant chilled-wax suppositories and the world slipped away on basic hypodermic steel.

Everybody she knew got to be a Deadie.

Everybody but her.

Meryl Streep, Tom Cruise, those anonymous B-zombie brats with mouse-turded hair and kiss-my-deceased-ass grins. Everybody on the island she hated, and that was everybody but Daddy. *Even Marilyn got to chat with the Deadies at the Bus Stop and they listened like she emitted extra-terrestrial short waves, but she said it was because she was an Icon and closer to them than Paddy could ever be. That made Paddy real mad, especially when Marilyn signaled Daddy.*

Nobody sent signals to her Daddy but her!

Paddy tore Marilyn's white arms, legs, and ears off, and pulled the blonde hairs out of her pube until she stopped broadcasting.

∞Θ∞

Paddy squatted on a boulder eating a double box of Twinkies and drinking warm Upper Canada Lager from the big tins. Two Deadies lumbered after Rewind, one of the last living dogs left. The collie belonged to the Woods, who used to run the video shop. As the three got closer, Paddy saw it was the formerly living Mr. and Mrs. Woods lunging at their golden-haired pooch. Rewind bounded like he was having fun. So did the Deadie Woods. To Paddy's camera eye, they made a nice nuclear family.

Man, she thought, life is incompletely unfair. All the two-dimensionals get everything and people like me who are the truly brilliant and can satellite dish every movie channel are relegated to minor sitcoms. How'd *they* like to be inside out for a living? Life always tunes you out. It's depressing as hell. She swallowed a couple of Tylenol to the third power she'd found in Mrs. Soles' medicine cabinet. At least they had co-deine in them and that was better than nothing, almost.

She chucked a pill-shaped stone at the stinky mould-grey

water and it skipped across the surface. One. Two. Three. Three was the right button. She clicked on a Dolly Parton song, turning up the volume on the old tape player so she could masturbate in peace. The Deadies didn't notice. Mr. Woods had caught Rewind and they were biting each other, which was fun to watch, until Mrs. Woods joined in and blocked Paddy's view.

As Rewind howled, Dolly wailed about never gettin' what you need when you need it. Yeah, don't I know it, Paddy thought. Her body spasmed. Like killing yourself's easy. She wiped sticky fingers on her filthy shirttail and shoved another Twinkie all the way into her mouth. Everybody thinks it is but that just shows you what they know. If it was easy, everybody would have been dead before she was born and Paddy'd have managed it by now too.

Shit! She kicked dirt at Fat Eddie the Deadie as he passed. He ignored her, just like he always had. She wanted to be part of the Deadies more than she'd ever wanted anything. Maybe, when Marilyn came for her next visit, *she* could figure some way for Paddy to get in with them, to make them see Paddy's dead potential. Dolly sang about possibilities. If only Paddy could be a Deadie, she just knew she'd be happy forever like Miss Dolly Parton. She closed her eyes.

"Take three hundred and twelve: Norma Jean to the Rescue!" Marilyn appeared half naked and boxed Paddy's ears good until she was bored. Finally the sex goddess grabbed the last Twinkie and admitted, "I've been working on a plan."

"It's about time," Paddy said, wiping blood from her ear lobe.

Marilyn tilted backwards and hiked up her full white skirt until her pink lips grinned at the camera. She shoved the Twinkie up inside herself and crooned, "Happy Birthday to You."

Paddy opened her eyes. Rewind, or what was left of him, lay in the background of the shot, a golden prop, much of Mr. Woods' forearm sticking out of his mouth. Suddenly this movie came into sharp focus.

∞Θ∞

Paddy's Daddy wandered home every night by instinct, just the way he used to before he became a Deadie. Not that he needed rest. He never had; he was no different now.

Paddy boarded up the windows. *Marilyn nailed a two by four tornado warning across the door.*

Daddy stared, eyes hungry, same as always. Finally Paddy picked up his mottled hand and hauled him down to the root cellar, the way he'd done with her all her life.

She lit the hurricane lamp. Bushel baskets of rotting potatoes and carrots and cabbage lined the shelves and the floor was littered with broken jars with pickled foods she'd put away she didn't know when. The place stank, but no worse than Daddy.

She positioned him on a Peaches and Cream Corn crate. His glazed, half-rotted eyeballs wandered the room aimlessly, like he didn't recognize anything. Paddy was used to that. All the Deadies resided in Bliss, a drive-in theater she hoped to visit real soon.

Marilyn stood in a corner, legs spread, hands on knees, cleavage scrumptious, waiting for the wind to whistle up her skirt on cue. Paddy nodded. Daddy's head kept bobbing like an antenna in a storm because his neck had snapped so she held it steady and made him look in her direction, but she couldn't get his eyes to stay put. Black mixed media belched from his lips; his digestive juices were working; he must be watching the screen.

Marilyn hiked her skirt and turned. Paddy, skirt lifted, waved her backside at Daddy's oscillating face, the way he always liked. Nothing.

Marilyn peeked over her shoulder and pouted her lips into an 'O'. Paddy planted a movie smooch on Daddy's crisp lips. His rotted nose mashed against her cheek and a chunk with crusty stuff inside broke off. *A blowfly with eyes like Daddy's emerged. "Thanks ever so!" the fly said. Paddy yelled at Marilyn, "Cut!" MM tossed back her platinum hair, thrust out her tits and giggled.*

Paddy glanced down at her nearly flat chest and felt lousy. Daddy had always hungered for her before and now he didn't and now she was truly alone on the set. She plunked down onto the dirt floor and cried, something she hadn't done since way before she started taking the meds she'd run out of. The leak created micro mud puddles between her legs. *The fly dived into one and bathed. He smiled up at her with Technicolor eyes in all his clear iridescent holiness and winked.* Paddy found enlightenment. She saw the solution to all her troubles.

"It's a wrap," she said, *but MM refused to vacate the studio. Instead, she straddled a Mason jar of pickled banana peppers and mumbled on and on about misfits and how some of them like it hot.* Paddy fast-forwarded.

She crawled to Daddy and peeled rotting fabric from his groin. His penis, always so big and full, dangled like a thick black connecting cable with green eyes. The eyes leaked puss-yellow tears that white life forms swam in. *Those baby bugs are joining heads to tails! Paddy realized, astonished. The word LOVE flashed onto the screen and a ball bounced along the letters. Wasn't this what Dolly Parton always sang about, and what Marilyn always got?* Now Paddy knew exactly what everybody meant.

She closed her eyes and opened her mouth.

And bit.

Daddy didn't complain. He didn't seem to miss his cock.

Paddy sat back on her haunches and munched.

Marilyn skipped over with a rotting banana pepper dangling from her wet lips. "When it's hot like this, I store my undies in the ice box."

Made sense to Paddy. She swallowed the last bits of her Daddy, the bits that meant anything to her. He tasted like all the buttered popcorn they ever ate watching movies together.

As his head bobbed her way, he grinned like he used to, and Paddy felt proud. At last she'd landed a part in The Deadie Movie. She would play Daddy's Little Deadie Girl and the movie would run forever, or at least until the reel ran out of film.

Sweetbread
TONIA BROWN

MARY MOONEY stood in the doorway of her kitchen with a shotgun aimed at her icebox. Or rather, she aimed at the black clad rump of some stranger poking out of her icebox. The rump wiggled about as its owner's front half rooted through her leftovers. Now, it wasn't unusual for someone to stop by for a glass of iced tea or an hour's gossip, but never unannounced and certainly not at five in the morning. Mary caught the flash of a blueberry pie with the middle scooped away. The whole, freshly baked pie was spoiled.

"My icebox aint no trough," she said.

The rummaging stopped as the rump stilled.

Mary reached beside her and flicked on the light.

"Get your hands up and step away from the pie," she demanded.

She cocked the gun, to show the rump she meant business, which she most certainly did. A pair of big hands, caked with filth and every nail black with grunge, lifted as the stranger stood. He was as tall as the fridge, almost as broad, and looked like he hadn't seen the inside of a washtub in a good year. His black hair was greasy and short on his grubby neck. His black jacket was sore-fully tattered, too short for his long arms and covered in grime. He looked like he had spent the last hour rolling around in the pig pen. Smelled like it too.

"Now turn round, real slow like," Mary said. "One wrong move and I'll empty this here buckshot inta your butt."

When he turned to face her, Mary regretted having asked him to. He was a horrible site. The skin of his face not cov-

295

ered in blueberries had a sick green tint to it, like a moldy hide stretched taunt across his skull. His lips were thin, black lines pulling in a tight grimace from his blueberry stained teeth in an eerie half grin. His eyes were milky, dark marbles floating free in their sockets. In short, he was a monstrosity. A big, filthy, blueberry pie stealing monstrosity.

"Hey honey," it said through a mouthful of pie.

It was then that Mary recognized him as her big, filthy, blueberry pie stealing monstrosity.

"Rufus?" She dropped the shotgun and covered her mouth as her eyes flew wide with terror.

"Careful Mare Bear," Rufus said as he pointed to the clattering gun.

"But Rufus," Mary said through her fingers. "You're d-d-d-dead!"

"Well that's a fine 'how'd ya do.' Come down for a snack and you wanna kill me fur it?" Rufus frowned as he wiped the pie from his face. He stopped as he spied the berries on his muddy sleeve. Understanding came upon him and he felt duly guilty. "That pie was for church. Weren't it? I'm sorry, sugar. 'Aint no need to shoot me over it."

He stretched his black lips back, baring his teeth. Mary's stomach lurched at the gruesome sight. What should have been a sweet smile ended up a slavering snarl. Her knees wobbled and she grabbed a kitchen chair to steady herself.

"Roo, it 'aint about the pie," she said. "You was dead, honey. Stone dead."

"You been at my still?" Rufus asked, raising a half brow and cocking his head at her with a loud crack.

Mary sat at the opposite end of the table, far from her dead husband. "You been dead 'bout near two weeks."

"You sure you 'aint been at the shine?" His head was pounding, his guts were growling and she stared at him so hard it made his skin crawl. Or rather she made him feel like something under his skin was crawling. He jerked his chair from the head of the table, and the sound of twisting leather rose from his knees as he sat.

"Roo, we put you in the ground and everything."

Rufus looked down at his dirt caked hands and soiled suit. He realized he looked like he just crawled free from a hole in the ground. But that was to be expected because he had, indeed, just crawled free from a hole in the ground. "Well, that would explain a lot. I thought I fell asleep in the field and got all plowed over by Charlie."

"No Roo, you was dead. I swear it. Here…" she paused and slid a pie pan down the table. "Look at yourself."

Rufus lifted both brows to her as he lifted the pan to his face. In the dull metal he saw a monster staring back at him. "That 'aint me," he said. The monster mouthed his words and Rufus groaned. "Aww Mare Bear. What happened to me?" He patted his rotting face with a decaying hand.

"You don't remember? Charlie kicked you in the chest. Broke your chest bone and crushed your heart is what the Doc said."

"Dammed mule 'aint never been nothing but trouble." He ran his hand over the breast of his muddy suit, and felt it give where his heart should have been. He didn't dare open his shirt to look inside, for fear he might see inside his insides, and that would be too much insides for one man to bear. He looked back to his reflection and frowned. "Am I really dead?"

"Didn't you see your stone when you came up?"

"It was dark. Plus I weren't really looking for it, was I? You don't wake up in a hole and just assume you're in the grave, do ya?"

"I wouldn't rightly know."

"Speaking from experience, ya don't. And it wasn't like there was a whole lot of graveyard giving me a hint."

"Well, ya said ya wanted to lay to rest on the farm. Weren't no help that I had to rush the funeral."

"Why rush it? I wasn't going nowhere."

"In this summer heat you set to stinking right away."

Rufus lowered his gaze in a sudden bout of shyness. "How was it?"

Mary squinted at his odd question. "Well, it was kind a like... boiled fish heads, mixed with wet manure and week old eggs. 'Course you smell a lot less now, but I reckon—"

"I don't mean my scent, woman, I mean my funeral!"

Mary glared at him and pursed her lips. "I see dying 'aint done nothing to your temper."

Rufus hung his head.

"Besides," she added in a tender yet devious voice. "I don't rightly remember a whole lot about it. I were knee deep in grief over ya, Roo."

But Rufus would not be moved. "Ya don't remember nuthin?"

"If I'd a known you'd be back for a play by play, I'd 'ave took notes." Mary crossed her arms and returned her lips to their previous purse.

The couple fell quiet and stared at one another. Thirty years of marriage had seen them through a lot, but nothing prepared them for this.

"Sorry about the pie," Rufus said. "But I couldn't help myself. I got this powerful hunger, Mare Bear." As if on cue, a rumble rolled across the quiet kitchen and Rufus covered his belly with his big hands. "Why ya lookin' at me like that?" he asked. She was looking at him the same way she did when she thought she had caught him doing something wrong. Which was to say, she was looking at him the way she always did.

Mary clicked her tongue.

"What?" Rufus asked.

"Nuthin'," she lied.

"Ya clucking like a mother hen. That means ya got an idear."

Mary frowned. She didn't want to think of this dead thing as her Roo, but he sure acted like it. "Maybe you're one of those things they make them movies about. A zomblie."

Rufus scowled even harder as his stomach rolled again.

"You aint never seen a zomblie movie, have you Roo?" she asked.

Rufus shook his head and his neck creaked like a dry wind blowing across an old tombstone.

Mary had only seen one zomblie film, when she was much younger, but she was sure they all pretty much had the same plot. "Zomblies eat… people… the brains mostly…" her words trailed off. Rufus was lifting his nose, sniffing at the kitchen air like an old hound dog.

"Brains you say?" Rufus asked as he breathed deeper, enjoying a sudden delectable scent. He nosed around, wondering if Mary had something on a slow boil, until he realized it was coming from her. Rufus Mooney, despite his best effort to the contrary, began to drool.

Mary stared as the dead man raked his black tongue back and forth across his putrid lips. He was looking at her the same way he looked at her whenever he wanted that certain special something. Which was to say, he looked at her with hunger. She went white in terror.

Her look of horror snapped Rufus back to his senses. This was his wife, not some early morning buffet! "I don't think I could rightly eat people," he said to ease her mind. He lied, because he was sure he might just be able to choke down a chunk or two. "Besides, if all I eat were brains I'd starve in this town inside a week!" He laughed, forced and hoarse.

Mary shuddered at the horror of it, but part of her laughed with him. Part of her knew he was an abomination, yet part of her wanted him to stay. But want as she might, she knew in her heart that her Rufus was long gone, kicked to death by his own ass.

She stood and went to the fridge. "Maybe we can find something to satisfy your hunger."

"That's more like a wife." Rufus gleamed with pride.

"Ya know, I'm not really your wife. Not no more."

"Whatcha mean? I still got my ring!" Rufus held up his

decrepit left hand. A golden band glowed against his ghastly flesh.

Mary shook her head. "Don't you remember our wedding vows?"

"Yeah. Love. Honor. And obey. Now obey and make me some flapjacks!"

Mary looked down at Rufus. "I mean the bit at the end."

His milky eyes lit with unholy desire. Mary smelled delicious. "He said I could kiss the bride."

She shook her head again. "Till death do we part."

"So."

"Honey… you died."

Mary waited as the bitter truth sank into Rufus's soft skull.

"I can't stay, can I?" he whispered.

"I love you, Roo, but you know you can't stay. Not… like this." She ran a trembling hand across his rotting face.

Rufus could feel her quiver with fear. His heart ached to bursting, but he knew what he had to do. He pushed her away, stood and stalked towards the door.

"Rufus!" Mary shouted, but she didn't give chase. She heard the door slam as the first tears came. It was as painful as the day they brought his broken body home.

Maybe worse.

Just as quick as it closed, she heard a knock at the door. She stood and went to it. The knock came again before she could get there. Mary pulled open the door and on her porch stood Rufus, propped against the frame, still dead.

"Widow Mooney," he said with a nod.

Mary narrowed her eyes.

"Mamm, I'm sorry about your recent loss but I must confess that I've had my eye on ya for some time. Unfortunately, I have to go away for a while. I don't know how long I'll be, or if I'll ever come back."

"I'm sorry to hear that. You seem… like a fine man."

Rufus turned his milky eyes to the horizon and nodded

again. "I thought maybe we could break some bread and watch the sunrise. One more time, before I go."

Mary wiped away her bitter tears. "As long as it 'aint my sweetbread."

Rufus grinned.

It should have been goofy, instead it was gruesome and Mary didn't mind at all.

"Come on in. I was just making flapjacks," she said.

And Rufus Mooney came home, one last time.

About The
AUTHORS

JAMES ROY DALEY ~ is the brains behind BOOKS OF THE DEAD, the author of The Dead Parade, Terror Town, 13 Drops of Blood, and Into Hell. He is the editor of Best New Zombie Tales Volume 1, 2 & 3, and Best New Vampire Tales Volume 1. Upcoming work includes Zombie Kong, Best New Werewolf Tales Volume 1, and Best New Zombie Tales Volume 4.

ROBERT ELROD ~ Award-winning illustrator and graphic designer, Robert Elrod, strives to embrace a variety of styles and genres. He works in acrylics, watercolors, inks, colored-pencils, pencils, and digitally. He's active in local and national art shows and conventions, focusing primarily on images that depict horror, fantasy, and science fiction. His portfolio includes book covers, CD covers, comic books and pinup artwork. Robert's work can be found in *Vincent Price Presents* (Bluewater Comics), *New Horizons* (the British Fantasy Society), and in galleries across America.

PAUL KANE has been writing professionally for almost fourteen years. He currently lives in Derbyshire, UK, with his wife – the author Marie O'Regan – his family, and a black cat called Mina.

NATE SOUTHARD ~ is the author of Just Like Hell, Broken Skin, He Stepped Through, and the graphic novels Drive and A Trip to Rundberg. His short stories have appeared in such venues as Cemetery Dance, Thuglit, and numerous anthologies. Red Sky, his debut novel, will be available later this year. Nate lives in Austin. You can learn more at natesouthard.com.

JEREMY C. SHIPP ~ Jeremy C. Shipp is the Bram Stoker nominated author of Cursed, Vacation, and Sheep and Wolves. His shorter tales have appeared or are forthcoming in over 50 publications, the likes of Cemetery Dance, ChiZine, Apex Magazine, Pseudopod, and Rosebud. While preparing for the forthcoming collapse of civilization, Jeremy enjoys living in Southern California in a moderately haunted Victorian farmhouse with his wife, Lisa, and their legion of yard gnomes. Thankfully, only one mime was killed during the making of his first short film, Egg.

MURRAY J.D. LEEDER ~ is the author of the novels Son of Thunder and Plague of Ice for Wizards of the Coast, as well as almost twenty-five published short stories. In addition, his academic writings have appeared in such journals as the Canadian Journal of Film Studies, the Journal of Popular Culture and the Journal of Popular Film and Television. He is a currently pursuing a Ph.D. at Carleton University in Ottawa.

SIMON WOOD ~ is the Anthony Award winning author of six books as well as over 150 published stories and articles. He writes thrillers, mysteries, and horror fiction. His previous books include Working Stiffs, Accidents Waiting to Happen, Paying the Piper, Terminated and We All Fall Down as well as The Scrubs and Road Rash under the pen name Simon Janus. His upcoming titles include a first in a new mystery series set in the world of motor racing, Did Not Finish, and the crime-caper, The Fall Guy. You can find him on Red Room, Crime Space, Good Reads, Facebook, Twitter and MySpace, which is home to his blog.

JG FAHERTY is an Active Member in the Horror Writers Association. His credits include Cemetery Dance, Wrong World, Shroud Magazine, Doorways Magazine, and several major anthologies. A freelance writer with over 15 years of experience, he has a varied background that includes working as a laboratory manager, accident scene photographer, zoo keeper, research scientist, and resume writer. He also contributes regular columns, interviews, and book reviews to the HWA newsletter, FearZone, Dark Scribe Magazine, and Horror World.

AARON POLSON ~ When Aaron Polson isn't arguing about the definition of irony with his high school English students, he can be found chipping away at a twisted tale in his basement dungeon. Many of his stories take place in the fictional town of Springdale, Kansas, a strange place modeled after his own hometown. He currently lives in Lawrence, Kansas with his wife, two sons, and a tattooed rabbit. Aaron's stories have appeared in various publications, including Reflection's Edge, Nectrotic Tissue, Big Pulp, and several anthologies.

TIM LEBBON ~ has been published for more than ten years now, and you can find out loads about him at his website www.timlebbon.net. He is the author of over thirty books, including the Noreela series of fantasy books (Dusk, Dawn, Fallen and The Island), the NY Times Bestselling novelization of the movie 30 Days of Night, and several books with Christopher Golden, including The Map of Moments and the forthcoming Secret Journeys of Jack London for Harper. He has also written several screenplays and some TV proposals. Tim has won several prestigious awards, and some of his work has been optioned for the big screen.

JOHN L. FRENCH ~ is a crime scene supervisor with the Baltimore Police Department Crime Laboratory. In 1992 he began writing crime fiction, basing his stories on his experiences on the streets of what some have called one of the most dangerous cities in the country. His books include THE DEVIL OF HARBOR CITY, SOULS ON FIRE, PAST SINS and the upcoming HERE THERE BE MONSTERS. He is the editor of BAD COP, NO DONUT, which features tales of police behaving badly.

SIMON MCCAFFERY ~ is former magazine editor who sold his soul to high-tech corporate America, living with my wife, Angela, and three amazing children in the Tulsa, Okla., area. He has been writing and selling fiction since 1990, and owes his love of zombies, science fiction, and things that go bump in the day and night to his father, James McCaffery, who taught him to read at an early age and gave him a box of paperback books when he was eleven, *Something Wicked This Way Comes* among them.

LEE CLARK ZUMPE ~ discovered long ago that using the written word to spin yarns and evoke emotions is both a challenging and a rewarding enterprise. The author's zeal for writing led him to college after several misspent years where he recently earned a Bachelor's Degree in Professional and Technical Writing. In his spare time, Lee is an avid reader of speculative fiction, and a confessed bibliomaniac with an ever-expanding private library. Since his first sale to *Nocturnal Lyric* in 1992, more than 200 of Lee's short stories and poems have been published in magazines and anthologies in North America, England, and Australia. Most recently, his work appeared in the pages of *Wicked Hollow*, *Lunatic Chameleon*, and *Voicings from the High Country*. Look for Lee in upcoming issues of *Star*Line*, *Weird Tales*, and *Mythic Delirium*. In January 2003, *Anxiety Publications* published Lee's first chapbook of poetry titled *An Invisible Shimmer*. Lee lives on the west coast of Florida with his wife, artist Tracey Potter Zumpe, and four feline muses purportedly descended from the cats of Ulthar. Visit Lee's website at: blindside.net/leeclarkzumpe

ERIK T. JOHNSON ~ Erik T. Johnson lives in New York with his wife, son, and a little dog too. His stories have appeared in *Underworlds Magazine*, *New York Stories*, *Trunk Stories*, *Sein und Werden*, *Saucytooth's Webthology*, and the Midnighters Club anthology, among other places. More of his writing is forthcoming in *Electric Velocipede*, *New Horizons*, *Morpheus Tales*, *Black Ink Horror*, *Golden Visions*, *Dead But Dreaming 2*, *The Zombie Chronicles Volume One*, and *Best New Zombie Tales Volume Three*. His website is eriktjohnson.net.

JOE MCKINNEY ~ Joe McKinney is the San Antonio-based author of numerous horror, crime and science fiction novels. His longer works include the four part Dead World series, made up of Dead City, Apocalypse of the Dead, Flesh Eaters and The Zombie King; the science fiction disaster tale, Quarantined, which was nominated for the Horror Writers Association's Bram Stoker Award for superior achievement in a novel, 2009; and the crime novel, Dodging Bullets. His upcoming releases include the horror novels Lost Girl of the Lake, The Red Empire, The Charge and St. Rage. Joe has also worked as an editor, along with Michelle McCrary, on the zombie-themed anthology Dead Set, and with Mark Onspaugh on the abandoned building-themed anthology The Forsaken. His short stories and novellas have been published in more than thirty publications and anthologies. In his day job, Joe McKinney is a sergeant with the San Antonio Police Department, where he helps to run the city's 911 Dispatch Center. Before promoting to sergeant, Joe worked as a homicide detective and as a disaster mitigation specialist. Many of his stories, regardless of genre, feature a strong police procedural element based on his fifteen years of law enforcement experience. A regular guest at regional writing conventions, Joe currently lives and works in a small town north of San Antonio with his wife and children.

GREGORY MILLER ~ Gregory Miller was born in State College, Pennsylvania in 1978. His short fiction and poetry have appeared in a number of national publications. His first novel, Big Cicadas, was published in 2003 and his first collection of poetry, Four Autumns, in 2005. In October 2009, a collection of short stories, Scaring the Crows: 21 Tales for Noon or Midnight, was published by Stone-Garden.net Publishing, and received positive reviews from authors such as Piers Anthony and Brad Strickland. Ray Bradbury recently wrote, "Gregory Miller is a fresh new talent with a great future." He recently edited the Static Movement anthology, Don't Tread On Me: Tales of Revenge and Retribution. A high school English teacher, he currently lives in Pittsburgh with his wife and two young sons.

WILLIAM T. VANDEMARK ~ William T. Vandemark writes speculative fiction. He can be found wandering the back roads of America in a pickup truck. He chases storms, photographs weathervanes, and prospects for fulgurites. When wanderlust ebbs, he resides in San Antonio or Seattle, depending on weather and inclination. Currently, he serves as editor of the Science Fiction Writers of America blog.

DAVID C. PINNT ~ lives near Denver, Colorado with his lovely wife and myriad children and animals. His work has appeared in a number of anthologies and periodicals including *Andromeda Spaceways Inflight Magazine*, Permuted Press' *The World is Dead*, and the upcoming Modernist Press anthology *Art From Art*. He keeps a sporadically updated blog at: dcpinnt.livejournal.com.

JOHN CLAUDE SMITH ~ has had 40+ short stories, 3 poems, and 1,100 pieces of music journalism (everything from reviews to profiles, interviews, ad copy) published. He's currently working with an agent getting his first two novels in shape while writing number three. He lives in San Leandro, CA. with his sights set on Rome, Italy, soon. He has no fear of zombies; he's ready for the battle!

MICHAEL STONE ~ was born in 1966 in Stoke-on-Trent, England. Since losing most of his eyesight he has retreated from your world to travel the dark corners of inner space—or to put it more prosaically he thinks "What if?" a lot. The signs are clear to those that know him well, for his one not-so-bad eye glazes over and he is rendered deaf to all English except for "Would you like a cup of tea, Mike?" He will then engage with reality long enough to ask if there are any biscuits before drifting off again. While agreeing that this can be very trying for those around him, he remains unrepentant. He is the author of over fifty published short stories as well as the novella collection, *Fourtold. In 2010 he co-edited a crime anthology called Requiems for the Departed (Morrigan Books), 2011 will see the publication of his novella, Lemon Man (Morrigan Books) and a short story collection from Graveside Tales, called Memory Bones.* His vanity has a name: www.mylefteye.net

NANCY KILPATRICK ~ Award-winning author Nancy Kilpatrick has published 18 novels, 200 short stories and 1 non-fiction book. Her genres are mainly horror and dark fantasy. Currently she is editing her twelfth anthology Danse Macabre—Close Encounters with the Reaper, and her next completed anthology Evolve Two: Vampire Stories of the Future Undead will be released August 2011 (both for Edge SF&F Publishing). She's published several zombie stories and is working on a zombie novel. www.nancykilpatrick.com

TONIA BROWN ~ is the author of Lucky Stiff and lives in NC with her husband of many years. She shares her home with a brood of moody cats, and her likeness with an identical twin sister. She likes coffee and fudgesicles, though not always together.